STA
MAGE

AGENTS OF
MARS

BOOK THREE
OF THE RED FALCON TRILOGY

This edition published in 2018 by:
Faolan's Pen Publishing Inc.
22 King St. S, Suite 300
Waterloo, Ontario
N2J 1N8 Canada

ISBN-13: 978-1-988035-38-3 (print)
A record of this book is available from Library and Archives Canada.
Printed in the United States of America
1 2 3 4 5 6 7 8 9 10

First edition
First printing: September 2018

Illustration © 2018 Jeff Brown Graphics

Faolan's Pen Publishing logo is a trademark of Faolan's Pen Publishing Inc.

Read more books from Glynn Stewart at faolanspen.com

STARSHIP'S
MAGE

AGENTS OF
MARS

BOOK THREE
OF THE RED FALCON TRILOGY

GLYNN STEWART

**FAOLAN'S PEN
PUBLISHING**

faolanspen.com

CHAPTER 1

"YOU'D THINK that they'd *learn*, sooner or later," Alexander Jeeves noted drily as the red icon of a pirate missile drifted lazily across the bow of their ship and detonated. The warning shot didn't slow the wiry little gunnery officer in the process of allocating targets and setting up *Red Falcon's* weaponry as he spoke, though.

David Rice, Captain of the independent merchant freighter *Red Falcon*—which just *happened* to share a hull with the Martian Interstellar Security Service's covert operations ship KEX-12—chuckled and shook his head as he studied the incoming flotilla.

"Give them credit, Jeeves," the stocky merchant officer turned covert ops commander replied. "Most of the folks who discovered what we're actually armed with died in the process. All anyone really knows is that pirates who go after us cease to exist."

"And they brought five whole ships!"

Red Falcon was a Martian Navy–built Armed Auxiliary Fast Heavy Freighter, carrying antimatter engines alongside a civilian jump matrix. Equipped with four Mages, like David's crew, she could outrun almost anything in space.

Her sister ships in civilian service had had most of their weaponry removed. David, however, had done the Mage-King of Mars some large favors three years before. *Red Falcon* had come into his hands intact, to the regret of everyone who'd been on her wrong side since.

"I'd dearly love to talk to Mr. Newberry," his XO observed. Kelly LaMonte was a lithe woman who currently had dark turquoise hair. She was a terrifyingly capable programmer and engineer, and had become his executive officer just over eighteen months earlier.

Isaac Newberry was the man their current cargo—a shipment of unregistered military-grade weapons falling at about three out of five on the illegal scale—belonged to. He was also the only person who'd been supposed to know their actual course, which raised the question of just how the pirates had known they were going to be here.

"Do we reply to their message?" LaMonte continued. "Assuming relatively standard missiles, we're *in* their missile range for real shots."

Which, as his XO had carefully not pointed out, meant that the pirate ships had been in *Red Falcon*'s range since they'd emerged from their own jump flares twenty minutes before.

"We *are* hauling an illegal cargo, Officer LaMonte," David pointed out. "There was always the chance these people might be someone legitimate we were going to have to talk down."

It had happened before, after all. *Red Falcon* had very different reputations depending on who you talked to—though, as Jeeves had pointed out, most pirates were *terrified* of the ship now.

Which meant his new friends probably weren't going to settle for less than him dumping his magazines and flushing his fuel tanks before they got much nearer. That wasn't going to happen.

"But since they have sent messages of several types now"—including the warning shot—"I think we can respond in kind. Mr. Jeeves," he barked, and his gunnery officer sat up straight, hands poised over the console.

"Two lasers for each of our friends, if you please, then follow up with missiles," he said conversationally. "If we can leave one or two intact-ish, I'm sure Leonhart would *love* to talk to them about how they found our course."

Rhianna Leonhart was their security chief, also a Marine Forward Combat Intelligence Captain and the CO of the Marine platoon aboard *Red Falcon*. Any pirate that ended up in her hands would survive to the custody of appropriate authorities.

They just wouldn't *enjoy* said survival.

The fight should have been over before it even started. Lasers were lightspeed weapons, leaving no time to react or to even see the incoming fire, and the pirate commander was still posturing on David's video screen—giving them thirty seconds to surrender "or else"—when Jeeves hit the button.

Red Falcon's beam armament rivaled that of a destroyer of the Royal Martian Navy that served the Mage-King of Mars and his Protectorate. Ten five-gigawatt beams lashed out into space, and the five ships that they'd targeted didn't even dodge.

That should have been the first clue that everything wasn't as it seemed. The five pirate ships vaporized...into bursts of steam?

"Jeeves?" David asked. "That doesn't look right!"

"No, no it's not," the ex-Navy officer replied. "Please tell me we're—"

Return laser fire lit up the screens, cutting through the space where *Red Falcon* would have been if Kelly LaMonte hadn't fired up the big ship's engines the moment Jeeves had fired. There was nothing visible on David's screens, and he growled at his gunnery officer.

"Jeeves? Where the hell are they?"

"Ice shells," Jeeves replied, which wasn't really an answer to his Captain's question. "They strapped engines onto ice shells and used those to replace their own signatures. They gave us easy targets."

"Okay, so that's how they hid from us. Where are they?" David demanded again, watching as missiles appeared on the screens to follow up on the laser fire.

"*There.*"

There were only four icons now, not five, and their engines were more muted and shielded than the cheap fusion rockets they'd strapped to their decoys. Heat signatures at this range weren't precise things, but none of the icons were as large as the drones had been, either. They'd been radiating their heat into chunks of frozen water—and their now-visible power levels gave the lie to their apparent size.

"Neither I nor our MISS files know what the hell these guys are," LaMonte told David sharply as she danced the armed freighter out of the way of another salvo of laser fire. *Falcon*'s Rapid-Fire Laser Anti-Missile turrets were opening up on the incoming fire, but the math wasn't looking good.

"They're small for jump-ships, maybe two hundred thousand tons each, but each is packing a five-gigawatt laser and at least a dozen fusion missile launchers."

"Destroyer-killers," Jeeves said grimly. "The Navy tries to suppress the designs, but the concept keeps emerging—pirates with access to shipyards build them. They're supposed to operate with other pirates that actually carry cargo and boarding troops.

"Their job is to catch up with a Navy destroyer in groups and fuck it up from outside amplifier range."

"And I am suddenly wishing we actually had an amplifier," David muttered. "Again."

His ship, despite her military heritage, was still a freighter. The runes woven through her hull were a civilian jump matrix, designed to allow a Mage to teleport her a full light-year. A *warship*'s equivalent runes would amplify any spell—and any ship that entered the vaguely defined range of an amplified Mage would simply die.

"Keep us maneuvering," he ordered, watching the last missiles die in a glittering flash of blue fire as *his* Mages ignited their fuel stores. "Mage Soprano, we appreciate the assist, but I'd *love* some new ideas."

Maria Soprano's image appeared in one of the small screens on his command chair, the tanned-looking dark-haired Mage looking unusually grouchy.

"Don't get shot?" she suggested. "They might be slow, but that's a *lot* of missiles out there."

A lot more than *Falcon* could launch. David watched grimly as the ten missiles Jeeves had launched disappeared in the teeth of the pirate ships' own RFLAM turrets.

"Jeeves?" he said, as calmly as he could manage.

"Skipper?"

"Full-court press. Clear my damn skies!"

"Full-court press" meant that *Red Falcon's* crew stopped pretending they weren't a fully-equipped warship. Electronic countermeasure systems no civilian ship would ever be permitted to own came to life, trolling the second wave of missiles with siren songs of false targets and jamming their sensors as they came close to *Falcon* herself.

It didn't stop all of the missiles—but it stopped enough. The RFLAM turrets tore into the rest, and the handful that made it through that vanished in blasts of magic as Soprano and her people played backup.

Their own missiles weren't getting through either. The incoming pirate ships were continuing their deadly pattern of laser fire. LaMonte had learned her trade well, but no one could keep dodging a twenty-million-ton starship around that.

The first salvos of antimatter missiles took the pirates by surprise. Even working for the Martian Interstellar Security Service, David only carried a handful of those aboard his ship and used them sparingly.

To his knowledge, no one who'd seen *Red Falcon* fire antimatter missiles had survived—and these pirates were going to be no exception. With over six times the acceleration of the pirate missiles, the first salvo of ten blasted through the pirates' defenses and blotted the closest ship out of space.

Three more pirates closed, but the jammers weren't just confusing the pirates' missiles. The deadly dance between the ships and lasers continued—but Jeeves's jammers were lying to the pirates about where *Red Falcon* was. A second ship dodged *into* one of the freighter's lasers, disintegrating under the crushing power of the five-gigawatt beam.

Their careful planning clearly hadn't extended so far as to provide them an escape plan, as both surviving ships charged at *Red Falcon* as fast as they could. Missiles continued to flash through space both ways, and the massive lasers all three ships carried cut invisible lines of death.

David held his breath. His XO was doing better than he'd feared, but this dance could only end in one way—and his ship *lurched* under him as a pirate laser struck home.

"Damage report," he barked.

Even as he spoke, a third pirate disintegrated as another salvo of anti-matter missiles struck home. The fourth tried to dodge and bring her laser to bear again—only to be bracketed by *Red Falcon*'s entire laser armament.

David wasn't even sure how many beams hit the pirate, but the ship disappeared in a blast of vapor.

He sighed.

"It could have been worse," LaMonte said quietly. "Beam hit the cargo and burned clean through. We'll need to check containers and see what we've lost, but..." She shrugged. "We'll also need to get in touch with Kellers and see how much work the spine is going to need.

"According to our systems, the spine was breached sixty meters to the rear of the simulacrum chamber and has been sealed off by the automatic safeties. We lost about a third of the power lines and atmosphere conduits, but we can maintain atmosphere and power in both halves of the ship."

She shook her head.

"No casualties, but we're in rough shape, skipper."

CHAPTER 2

"WELL, WELCOME to Madrigal, everyone," Jeeves said loudly as the jump flare faded from their scanner screens. "Home to the ungoverned, the ungovernable, and the assholes who sell guns to both sides."

"That last includes us today," David pointed out gently, keeping an eye on his ship's course as LaMonte brought the engines online. The Madrigal System was a wealth of resources with multiple asteroid belts, two gas giants, and a large, if metal-poor, habitable planet.

About the only thing the various factions arguing over the system could agree on was that they didn't want anyone *else* exploiting those resources. One of the asteroid belts was inhabited, though most of the Madrigal Belters' industry was focused on simply surviving. A Martian fueling station orbited the inner gas giant, well separate from the locals but playing host to a trio of destroyers.

The Protectorate Charter was...fuzzy on whether the Royal Martian Navy was supposed to get involved in the civil wars of the member systems, which kept the destroyers mostly out of the line of fire—while remaining a pointed reminder that Madrigal *was* a Protectorate system and there were lines the factions couldn't cross.

"It's included *me* for years," the tactical officer reminded him. Jeeves was still technically a prisoner of the Martian government, seconded to David Rice's custody. Among his crimes were gunrunning and "being left holding the bag because you're an idiot."

"There's few more-reliable markets for guns in the Protectorates," he continued. "Let's see: the Belters will take anything that can operate in space; the orbital stations mostly want defensive gear to make sure everyone else leaves them the hell alone; the highland clans want planes, walkers, and anti-tank weapons—and they want anti-tank weapons because both of the lowland 'governments' want every tank they can get their hands on."

"And everyone wants artillery, small arms, and ammunition," David agreed. "That's why we're here. Kelly—can you send our bona fides to Truce Station? See if you can raise our delivery contact."

"What do I tell him about the lost cargo?" his XO asked. "We're indemnified for pirate attack, but they may still get difficult."

"Tell him whatever you want," David replied. He trusted his young executive officer's judgment at this point. "Just don't lie to him."

"Perish the thought," LaMonte murmured. Most of her attention appeared to be on the screen linking the bridge to the simulacrum chamber that allowed the ship's Mages to teleport *Red Falcon* across the stars.

That probably had something to do with the gooey look Xi Wu, one of said Ship's Mages and also LaMonte's lover, was sending her through said screen. David managed not to visibly shake his head.

He'd been young once, he was sure, and his first marriage had worked out *far* worse than any of Kelly's relationships that he'd seen.

"Remember, we're here to ID the distributors and pass that data along to MISS," he reminded his people. "We *aren't* here to hack their files ourselves or anything similarly productive-feeling. We're worth more to the Protectorate as a 'known player' in the smuggling business than as flagged agents."

He and MISS had spent a lot of effort to make it look like *Red Falcon's* last series of conflicts had been a private vendetta against the legacy of a crime lord they'd killed. He'd hate to lose that cover already.

Truce Station was one of four standard ring stations orbiting Madrigal III. The planet had other names, but since using the wrong one to the wrong people tended to start fights, most outsiders just used the technical name.

Those four anchored the orbital network above Madrigal III, whose population did their best to stay utterly neutral in the continuing seesawing five-way civil war taking up their system.

Even as *Red Falcon* drifted in toward Truce Station, the freighter's sensors picked up a launch from the highlands of the largest continent. Three armed shuttlecraft shot into space on carefully designed fusion rockets. Their course would take them clear of the neutral orbitals, heading toward the closer asteroid belt, presumably to reinforce some position held out there by the highland clans.

"Docking in ninety seconds," LaMonte announced. "Our contact has *finally* responded to our message," she noted as well.

"Anything actually useful?" David asked.

She shook her head.

"Not even an attempt to open a channel," she told him. "Just a boilerplate notice that they'll be in contact after we dock."

The Captain sighed.

"Too paranoid to put anything in electronic form, I assume," he admitted. "There isn't anyone in Madrigal with enough authority to declare the shipment illegal."

"The Orbit Council could," his XO pointed out. "Those shuttles that just launched? They were being tracked by a weapons platform from the moment they broke atmo. They may say they're neutral, but they could cut the Belters out of the fight in a minute if they chose to."

"And if they stopped people like us transshipping weapons in orbit, they could cut off the supply of off-world arms, too," David agreed. "But the Sienar and Kovian governments have enough resources to destroy the ring stations. MAD at its finest."

LaMonte shook her head.

"It's bloody stupid."

"Most conflicts that involve people shaking nuclear-tipped missiles on planets are," he agreed. "But the Sienar, the Kovians, the highland clans, the Belters and the Orbit Council each have their own very contradictory goals. From the MISS brief, the Protectorate *wants* the Council to step in as a neutral arbiter and force a peace, but the Council's leaders are too scared of the surfacers' surface-to-space missiles."

"And here we are, throwing more fuel on the fire," she said.

"Yes," he agreed. "But the trick, my dear XO, is that the fuel *we're* throwing on the fire has frequency-hopping remote-activated trackers in it. Which means the firemen who come after us will know whose hands it passed through."

He smiled grimly.

"We can't cut the channels off quickly, not without showing our hand, but once we know the players in the distribution chain, MISS can start squeezing those channels shut."

David wasn't a fan of shipping guns, but he understood why MISS needed him to. Sometimes, they were even delivering them to people with real needs and real causes.

He couldn't really say that about anyone in Madrigal, but it *did* happen.

David left LaMonte and Kellers to deal with organizing repairs for the damage to the ship's spine and boarded Truce Station, heading to the observation deck above their docking port. The central spindle of the ring station had no gravity, allowing him to move quickly and easily to the open space looking out over the docks.

Some stations would have Mages put in runes for magical gravity, but that was expensive. Truce Station apparently didn't bother with the expense, leaving the docks area in zero gee.

As he'd anticipated, there was only one individual in the observation deck. A tall and heavyset woman in a carefully tailored pantsuit floated, watching his ship through the tall glass panes.

"Captain Rice," she greeted him. "Newberry may have understated your ship...and it appears you needed all of it. Just what happened?"

"Pirates," he said calmly. "They also underestimated us, but they knew our exact course. That always leaves... entertaining questions to be asked."

The floating woman sighed and nodded, pulling herself to the window.

"You may call me Amandine," she told him. Neither of them was going to pretend that was her name—and he wasn't going to tell her he'd know her real name by the time he got back to his ship.

"My contract calls for the delivery of eighteen hundred cargo containers," she continued. "I notice there seem to be some missing."

"We took damage to twenty-seven cargo containers when the pirates attacked us," David agreed. "Ten had to be ejected and destroyed for the safety of the ship. Our scans suggest approximately seventy percent of the cargo in the remaining seventeen damaged containers is intact."

"That's a lot of lost gear, Captain," Amandine told him. "Enough to wipe out your entire payment for this transport job."

"That's your problem, Ms. Amandine," he pointed out. "The contract specifically indemnifies us against loss due to pirate attacks so long as we don't voluntarily surrender our cargo."

"Do you really think you can go to a contract lawyer over this, Captain?" she purred.

"I have all the paperwork to say I have no idea what I was carrying," David told her brightly. "So, I'd happily go to a lawyer and even a Navy dispute resolution panel. Would you?

"Besides." He shrugged. "Right now, I have your cargo. If you don't pay me, I keep your cargo. And we're back at, well, 'you really think you can go to a contract lawyer over this?'" he echoed her own words back at her with a small grin.

She wasn't *quite* bluffing. Fortunately, neither was he. They could play some very ugly games here.

"I don't think that would end quite as well for you as you think," she said coldly.

"Ms. Amandine, my ship demonstrably has the firepower to engage anything you could possibly round up to field against me," he replied, his voice equally frigid. "Don't try to threaten me. We both know what the deal between me, you, and Newberry was. Honor it, and we'll have no problems."

The observation deck was chill and silent for several long seconds, and then Amandine laughed.

"Newberry told me you were a hardass," she said. "He was right. Any idea who sold you out?"

"Unless you and your people knew more about our trip than I would expect, it had to be someone in Newberry's staff," David replied carefully. "I don't think he would risk his cargo himself, but one of his people might have got greedy."

"Then they'll regret it," Amandine said flatly. A black transfer chip appeared in her hand, seemingly from nowhere. "Payment in full, Captain Rice. We'll begin offloading immediately, if that's acceptable to you?"

David paused, taking a moment to scan the chip with his wrist-comp, and then nodded as it confirmed the numbers.

"We want those containers off our hull so we can patch up the spine," he agreed. "Sooner you move them, the happier we all are."

David sent word on ahead to *Red Falcon* of the agreement with Amandine, which turned out to be a good thing, as his wrist-comp chimed at him less than a minute after he'd left the observation deck.

The message was innocuous enough: a request for a meeting from a local import/export broker. Less innocent, though, was the time frame. For him to make the meeting, he'd have to head directly to the broker's office without even returning to his ship.

Normally, that kind of message would be ignored or sent back with a polite—or not-so-polite, depending on mood—request to reschedule.

Despite the boilerplate text of the message it included several specific series of words and numbers that his wrist-comp happily flagged for him when he ran his MISS decryption codes.

The broker was their MISS contact, and they were flagging as a priority well above urgent. The codes were a "drop everything and run" order. Given that most MISS local operators knew better than to risk the cover of mobile agents...

David sighed and sent an acceptance message back.

He trusted MISS's people not to push the limits without reason, but if this *wasn't* good enough, someone was going to hear it. At length.

CHAPTER 3

SHIP'S MAGE Maria Isabella Soprano had just stepped out of a long, hot shower when her wrist-comp buzzed at her, alerting her to an urgent message. Drying her hair briskly with one hand, she dripped onto the mat in her tiny shipboard bathroom as she prodded the waterproof piece of electronics to disgorge the message.

Unlike her Captain, Maria had been an MISS agent since she'd first been hired aboard *Red Falcon* over two years earlier. She'd had months of keeping her MISS affiliations concealed aboard ship as well as off, which meant she recognized the codeword sequence embedded in the message even before she activated her decryption codes.

Reading over both the cover and real message, she shook her head. Wrapping the towel around her head, she crossed to the closet and pulled out a shipsuit. Urgency was *never* a good sign when dealing with spies—and given the timeframes involved in any interstellar communication, it was an even worse sign.

It would be over a day before *Red Falcon* was even unloaded. Another day to finish the repairs, and at least a day beyond that to load the big ship with the cargo they couldn't justify leaving Madrigal without.

And yet the local MISS team thought whatever news they had was urgent enough to justify this level of priority. The dark-haired native of Earth's Brazil was still shaking her head when she finished dressing and went to leave her quarters—only to find Kelly LaMonte standing outside, about to knock. The XO was wearing "civilian" clothes, slacks and shirt, instead of the one-piece-with-concealed-vacuum-helmet shipsuit they normally wore aboard the ship. She was clearly planning on leaving the ship.

"You got the same meeting request," Maria said briskly. It wasn't really a question, but LaMonte nodded anyway.

"If we both got it, then they almost certainly pinged the Captain," LaMonte said. "Any idea what this is?"

"No more than you do, XO," Maria admitted. "Only that if it's this urgent, it can't be good news."

"Offloading doesn't even start for ten minutes. Whatever it is, it could probably have waited."

The Ship's Mage chuckled. From the acerbity in LaMonte's tone, the message had interrupted something.

"I would agree, Kelly," she said quietly. "Except that I *do* trust most MISS system agents to not use that priority lightly. So..."

LaMonte sighed and nodded.

"So, we go find out what the hell is going on," she agreed. "I booked a transit pod to meet us at the airlock in ten minutes. That enough time for you?"

"I'm already ready. Let's go."

Despite a surprising degree of traffic, Maria and LaMonte's transit pod carried them through the zero-gee center of the station and out to the rotating rim in perfect time, the pair of them arriving just as a second transit pod disgorged their broad-shouldered captain.

Rice was clearly unsurprised to see them, waiting for the second transit pod to slow to a stop and let them out. Maria tapped a command on her wrist-comp to transfer payment to the automated taxi vehicle, and stepped over to her Captain.

"I'm glad you got pinged as well," he told the two women. "Not sure why we weren't all sent the same message. Not the best communication."

"Someone rushed," Maria concluded. "Things never work out the way people want when things are rushed. But..." She shook her head once again. "That level of rush makes no sense. It'll be days before we're able to move—and they had to know whatever they want to tell us already. It's not like Madrigal has an RTA."

The Runic Transceiver Arrays were the only method of instant communication available to the Protectorate. Massive complexes of black stone and silver runes, they projected the voice of a speaking Mage to another RTA in another star system. An RTA was an immense undertaking to build and only about half of the MidWorlds had one.

Madrigal's internal difficulties meant it would probably be the last of the MidWorlds—the more densely populated, self-sufficient colonies that made up the bulk of the Protectorate—to get one. Maria suspected that many of the newer, currently poorer, Fringe colonies would end up with the complexes first.

"Well, we're not going to get answers guessing out here," her captain groused. "Let's go."

The broker's office had a plain lobby, just a handful of chairs and a desk with a frazzled-looking young man behind it.

"Good...morning," he greeted them after a careful check of the time. "How may I assist you?"

"We were all requested to attend a meeting with a Ms. Handell," Rice told him. "Given the timeline, I'm guessing—"

"Yes, of course, Captain Rice," the receptionist cut him off. "Come with me, please. Ms. Handell is waiting for you."

Maria raised an eyebrow at her boss, but they fell in behind the young man as he led them back to a conference room tucked away deeper in the office.

"The room is fully secured," the young man told them. "Once I close the door behind you, you won't have signal for your wrist-comps. Faraday cage; fully sealed to prevent bugs. We sweep the room twice a day as well."

"Thank you," Maria replied. "Who are we meeting?"

Rice hadn't asked that. The whole situation was weird, and Maria didn't trust that the name they'd been given was correct. She did, mostly, trust that the frazzled young MISS agent acting as a secretary would tell them the truth.

"Ms. Elizabeth Handell, System Chief," the youth said after a quick glance down the corridor toward the entrance. "And one other. I'm not authorized to disclose their identity."

Maria sighed and exchanged another look with her boss.

"You lay down with spies, you wake up with cloak and dagger," he said gruffly. "Let's go find out what this is about."

Maria entered behind David and Kelly. The other two were probably armed, but if someone was planning on trying anything out of line, the best defense they had was an irritated Mage. She wasn't a Royal Martian Marine Corps Combat Mage or anything similar, but she had been an officer in the Royal Martian Navy.

She could handle herself magically in a fight, which meant that it would take entire companies of regular soldiers to stop her. Only a fool would pick a fight with a starship captain whose Ship's Mage was standing at their shoulder.

It didn't seem like picking a fight was on anyone's agenda. There were exactly two other people in the room, exactly as the young man outside had told them, and the heavyset blonde woman at the center of the conference table waved them to seats with a tired expression.

"Captain Rice, Mage Soprano, Officer LaMonte," she greeted them. "I am Elizabeth Handell, MISS System Chief for Madrigal. This"—she gestured to the near-skeletal man next to her—"is Alan Delacroix, also of MISS.

"Mage Delacroix is one of our couriers."

Maria nodded as she took in the pale-skinned man, who wore a similar golden medallion at his throat to her, and seated herself. *Courier* was a misleading title in MISS. The man commanded a small starship of his own with a six-Mage crew, including himself.

An MISS courier was responsible for keeping as many as six star systems fully informed, and they were given a *lot* of discretion as to what courses they picked and what messages they carried. There was a sector chief in the area—based out of the Nia Kriti System, with a Navy Fleet Base to hand—but the couriers were that woman's right hands.

Like the Hands of the Mage-King of Mars, the couriers spoke with their bosses' voices. The limitations of the RTA communication network required it.

"Mage Delacroix," Rice greeted the pale Mage. Hopefully, he remembered the nature of the MISS's couriers as well. "I'm guessing the urgency of this meeting was due to your presence?"

"Yes," he said in a raspy voice. "I arrived shortly before you did, and I will need to leave within the next couple of hours at most. I came here directly from Nia Kriti and the RTA there, carrying orders from Mars for you.

"Your mission has changed."

Maria leaned back in her chair, studying Delacroix. She wasn't surprised. There was no other reason for them to be yanked into a high-priority meeting like this, though she wondered what her captain was making of it.

"Our current mission is mostly exploratory," Rice told Delacroix slowly. "Once our delivery here is off-loaded, most of the immediate follow-up sits with Ms. Handell. We are tied up here for several days at a minimum and need to find a cargo."

"Cargo will be easy," the courier replied. "Officially, I was here to organize a humanitarian relief expedition to Ardennes. The civil unrest there spiked into a short and bloody revolution, and the Protectorate is mobilizing resources to make sure everyone is fed and medicine is provided."

Despite Madrigal's problems, the lowland governments produced massive food surpluses, and the highland clans produced extraordinarily useful natural pharmaceuticals. There was a reason all of the system's factions could afford to import weaponry, after all.

"Ms. Handell's firm will contract with you to transport those supplies to Ardennes," he concluded. "It won't be a full load, but we'll pay a premium for rush delivery to justify the use of your ship—and the rush delivery is needed."

"What *happened*?" LaMonte asked, her voice suddenly very careful.

Maria realized she wasn't entirely sure which planet her XO was from—beyond "a MidWorld with a significant French-speaking population." A description that covered far more than just Ardennes...but also included Ardennes.

"Hand Alaura Stealey was investigating a terrorist incident where a small town was destroyed," the courier explained. "It was supposedly carried out by the local revolutionary front, but..."

"I'm guessing it wasn't that simple?" Maria asked. It was *never* that simple, not if a Hand was involved.

"No." Delacroix's voice was flat and he glanced over at Handell. "This doesn't leave this room, people, but you three need to know and Handell is cleared for it. The town was destroyed by orbital bombardment—from a *Navy* cruiser."

If Maria hadn't been sitting down, the ground would have fallen out from beneath her. The Navy was supposed to protect people. The concept of a Navy ship turning its weapons on a civilian town...it was beyond atrocity. For the Navy officer she'd been, it was closer to *blasphemy*.

"Commodore Cor had made some kind of deal with the Governor," the courier continued. "Things had gone a lot worse than anyone expected, and the worst happened."

The worst. Maria didn't even dare guess what *more* the pale man meant by that. She let David meet the courier's gaze as she tried to process the sheer scale of the betrayal Cor's actions entailed.

"We believe the Hand had evidence of the Governor's corruption," Delacroix said quietly. "We're not sure what happened, but Mage-Governor Vaughn killed Hand Alaura Stealey."

The room was very quiet for a surprisingly long time.

David finally shook himself out of his shock, glancing over at Soprano to check in on his ex-Navy Mage. She seemed even more shaken than he was—but then, he'd been a Navy Chief. *She'd* been the executive officer on an RMN destroyer.

"How?" he finally asked, trying to take control of the meeting while he processed just what had to have happened.

"We're not sure," Delacroix admitted. "We know she died and we know that Hand Montgomery was shot down. The details of the events leading to Hand Stealey's death are unclear."

"Wait." David couldn't possibly have heard the courier right. "*Hand Montgomery? Damien* Montgomery?"

"Yes," he confirmed. "Mage Damien Montgomery was attending the mission as an observer, bearing his Majesty's Warrant and Voice. They say when one Hand falls, another rises—and that's what happened on Ardennes.

"If Mage-Governor Vaughn believed murdering Hand Stealey would end his problems, he was very, *very* wrong. Hand Montgomery took over her mission and completed it."

"You said he was shot down?" LaMonte said quietly. Damien Montgomery had been her boyfriend once. For all that David was quite sure she was happy with her current relationship, the young Mage had certainly made an impression on them all.

"How did he go from being shot down to stopping the Governor?" *Red Falcon*'s XO asked, her voice impressively level.

"That's why he's a Hand and I'm merely a courier," Delacroix said with a chuckle. "He coopted the resistance and turned a bunch of rebels and the icon of Stealey's rank into a force that toppled the planetary government."

David shivered. Somehow, he couldn't put that beyond the intense young man he'd once hired.

"So, we're going to meet Damien?" he asked carefully.

"No. As of my leaving Nia Kriti, Montgomery was on his way back to Mars with Hand Stealey's body," Delacroix told them. "One of the things he *did* discover, though, was that Legatus had been arming the rebels through a number of intermediaries.

"MISS and Protectorate Secret Service agents on Ardennes are investigating further and should have collated more information by the time you arrive. Your orders are to proceed to Ardennes and touch base with

Mars via the RTA there. Most likely, I expect that you'll be called upon to use your connections and cover in the arms smuggling business to follow the chain back to Legatus."

The courier shook his head.

"We need proof, Captain Rice. Proof we can lay before a court and the Council of the Protectorate," he noted. "Suspicions and hearsay and coincidence may convince *us*, but we're spies and our job is to find the pattern.

"The Council needs the hardest of proof if they're going to sanction a Core World government."

"I know the deal," David replied. He shook his head slowly. Alaura Stealey had recruited Damien off his ship. She'd saved his life and the lives of every member of his old crew at the same time—and she'd been the one to recruit David himself into the Martian Interstellar Security Service.

"If Legatus helped killed Hand Stealey, we'll find out," he promised.

Delacroix sighed.

"That's the problem with this particular situation, isn't it?" he asked. "They may have illegally armed a rebellion—but that rebellion just ended up *helping* us bring a rogue Governor to justice. It makes it easier to track them down, but..."

"Still feels odd to use the time they helped us against them," David agreed. "But that's our job, isn't it?"

He didn't *like* being a spy. He just didn't have it in him to stand aside.

CHAPTER 4

ALAURA STEALEY WAS DEAD.

Despite all of the shocks in his meeting with the MISS courier, that one stuck out in David's head as he and his officers made their way back to *Red Falcon*.

A Hand of the Mage-King was dead. That happened, he supposed—Damien Montgomery had come into possession of the rune that had saved their ship on a piece of skin flayed from the skin of one—but it wasn't common.

The saying "a Hand falls, another rises" wasn't normally quite so literal as it had apparently been on Ardennes. Normally, it simply meant that killing a Hand inevitably brought another Hand, and the replacement tended to show up with squadrons of the Royal Martian Navy and battalions of the Royal Martian Marine Corps.

Alaura Stealey had saved David's life and crew as much as Damien Montgomery had. Montgomery had killed the crime lord chasing them, but that man's last act had been to initiate a missile launch that their ship couldn't survive.

Stealey had arrived in time to intercept those missiles. She'd then drafted Montgomery to the service of the Mage-King, destroyed David's old ship with its insanely dangerous upgrades, and gifted David a new ship: *Red Falcon*.

Later on, she'd recruited him for the Martian Interstellar Security Service. He wouldn't say he knew her well, but he'd known her. She was a rock in his interactions with the Protectorate government, someone he trusted completely.

And she was dead.

His brain was going in circles and he knew it. He glanced over at Soprano and LaMonte. The Mage seemed as calm as ever, and he suspected LaMonte was more thrown by the reveal about Montgomery.

It wasn't every day you learned your ex-boyfriend was now a Hand of the Mage-King of Mars.

David forced himself to exhale and then firmly met his officers' gazes in the transit pod.

"We'll talk back at the ship," he told them quietly. "The walls have ears here in Madrigal and I want to pull in everyone."

The walls had ears everywhere, for that matter. Madrigal's continuing civil conflict just meant there were even more reasons to listen in.

"But...we have a contract," he concluded. "It's better than shipping empty."

His words were those of a merchant captain. His *meaning*, though, was different—and the two women knew what he meant.

Red Falcon's crew had a mission now. A more immediate one than the general slow infiltration of the arms-smuggling world they'd been engaged in for the last year.

They had a job to do.

Red Falcon's cargo spars were sufficiently separated from her rotating gravity ring that there was no vibration or noise to let the officers gathered in the briefing room know the ship was being off-loaded. One wall of the briefing room was set to a video feed from an exterior camera, showing the swarming shuttles and EVA-suited workers off-loading the big ship's cargo.

David had gathered all of his officers in the room. Alexander Jeeves sat next to the video screen, poking at a tablet in front of him. James

Kellers, the black-skinned chief engineer, was next to the gunner, with his own tablet.

The Captain was close enough to see that Kellers was going over a schematic of the damage to the spine.

Next to them was his First Pilot, LaMonte's boyfriend, Mike Kelzin. The First Pilot had been promoted about six months before, leaving LaMonte and her lovers running half of David's ship. If the three of them weren't so good at their jobs, he'd be worried.

Rhianna Leonhart sat between Maria Soprano and Kelly LaMonte on the other side of the table, the broad-shouldered blonde woman studying the rest of the officers.

"So, I'm guessing we've news?" the Marine said grimly.

"Yeah, and little of it good," David replied. "Hand Alaura Stealey was killed in action three weeks ago on the planet Ardennes. *Hand* Damien Montgomery has resolved the situation, but we're being called in for two purposes.

"Firstly, we have been officially contracted by the Royal Martian Navy to carry a humanitarian relief shipment of food and medicine to Ardennes. It sounds like the conflict was relatively localized, but the Protectorate wants to make sure no one slips through the cracks. We'll report to the interim Governor on arrival and provide whatever assistance we can under that contract."

He paused, letting the shock of the news of Hand Stealey's death sink in.

"Ardennes is currently in a state of flux," he continued. "Hand Montgomery"—a combination of words that still made him shake his head in wonder—"removed Mage-Governor Vaughn for treason and Hand Stealey's murder. He used local *rebel* forces to enact said removal, and there are apparently concerns about reprisals and similar issues.

"The planet is currently under the direct rulership of Mars," he told them. That was even rarer than the death of a Hand. The Protectorate Charter allowed the Mage-King to take direct control when things went truly sideways, but it was a messy process and one that had only been executed twice before.

"There's a second purpose to our visit?" Leonhart asked. "Because just helping out in the aftermath of that kind of chaos seems like *plenty* to keep us busy."

"That problem, Rhianna, rests with the Martian government and the Martian Navy," David pointed out. "*Our* job is to deal with longer-term threats to the Protectorate than the immediate unrest on one world—not to mention that we're supposed to deal with subtler threats."

"What kind of threat are we looking into, then?" Jeeves asked. He paused in thought, then shook his head. "Wait. I can guess. Unless Montgomery had an army in his pocket, those rebels had to be *far* better equipped than they had any right to be."

"I don't have full details," David admitted, "but it appears that Montgomery gave the galaxy a *very* thorough demonstration of what happens when a Hand goes to war. But you're right."

What information he had suggested that David's old Ship's Mage had *single-handedly* stormed the fortified planetary command bunker. That didn't line up with the quiet but intense young man he'd known, and yet...

"I've seen Hands fight," Leonhart said quietly. "I don't know Montgomery, though I know some of you do...but if he's a Hand, the Governor didn't know what hit him."

"Basically," David agreed. "But he didn't do it alone, and the people he worked with had access to quite the arsenal of weaponry—from Legatan battle lasers to Legatan stealth gunships."

"Legatan," Jeeves echoed. "Were they dealing with Legatus?"

"That's the interesting part," David continued. "So far as the intel I have says, no. There was a lot going on, and only the most basic information made it to Nia Kriti before Mage Delacroix had to leave. We'll get an update when we arrive, but that is where we come in."

"We're tracking the source of their guns," Soprano explained to everyone. "We'll need to play our cover by ear, taking contracts as we can find them to follow the trail, but since the rebels on Ardennes are willing to talk to us..."

"That's one hell of a thread to yank on," Jeeves agreed. "A gunrunner's worst nightmare is a client that decides to talk to authorities. If we can follow the trail back to the source of the guns..."

"Then we may actually be able to dig up the evidence MISS wants on the Legatans causing trouble," David finished. "I don't think we're going to be able to directly talk to the rebels, this 'Freedom Wing,' but there are agents on the ground interviewing everyone as we speak. By the time we get to Ardennes, we should know enough to start looking."

"Isn't that going to be suspicious?" LaMonte asked. "If we visit Ardennes and then start following the chain back from there?"

"We'll have to be careful," he agreed. "We'll cover our trail as best as we can, but we'll also be looking to deal. Our smuggling bona fides should hold up to anyone we make contact with, and we'll see how deep into the onion we can go.

"We may not peel back everything this time around, but even knowing who the middlemen two or three layers back are will make the next round of investigations easier."

Red Falcon's crew would almost certainly not be the ones to get the proof needed for Mars to move against the first and most powerful UnArcana World. But every piece of groundwork they laid was one step closer to ending whatever game Legatus was playing.

Hopefully, *before* it turned into outright civil war.

CHAPTER 5

KELLY LAMONTE dodged a transport cart carrying replacement parts for *Red Falcon*'s damaged core with practiced ease despite her distraction. The repair needed to be complete before they could start loading their cargo for Ardennes, and the reports she had been reading said they needed to be at her homeworld sooner rather than later.

It was odd to think that she'd be going home. Of course, that was assuming she had any time to step off the ship when they were in the star system. Work came first, and it wasn't like she had anyone left on Ardennes.

She'd had a grandfather left. He hadn't quite understood his not-Quebec Reformation Christian, not-straight granddaughter, but he'd *cared*. Anthony Hellet had cared about everything and everyone, from his work, to his friends, to his town.

That had dragged him into politics and, apparently, eventually into rebellion. And when Mage-Governor Vaughn had decided that Karlsberg was going to be an example, Kelly LaMonte's grandfather had been at ground zero of a kinetic strike launched by a warship of the Royal Martian Navy.

Going home was going to *suck*.

"Hey!" she barked as raised voices echoed through the loading dock, launching herself purposefully across the zero-gee space with almost-grateful determination. "What are you lot going on about?"

Three new men had materialized out of nowhere and started hassling the team trying to offload the load of hull plating. They turned to face her with a precision difficult in zero-gee, and she fixed them with her coldest glare.

"Not sure how it's your business, missy," the center figure told her.

"That cargo of plating is heading into my ship," Kelly told him firmly. "It's fixing damage we took fighting pirates so that we can deliver a cargo of humanitarian suppliers to my *homeworld*. Any delay in that repair puts the lives and health of people at risk, so if you want to cause trouble, you need to talk to me."

"Ain't your business, still," the man replied. "This lot haven't paid their dock access fee; it's local business."

Translation: they hadn't paid their protection money, and the leg-breakers were here to demand it. From the stubborn set of the workers' faces, it wasn't going to go well for anyone.

Kelly's cold gaze didn't waver.

"The Madrigal System is astonishingly lacking in a central government," she said calmly. "Do you *really* think anyone would manage to sort out the paperwork to arrest me before we left with our cargo if I shot you dead right here and now?"

In the back of her mind, she was calculating every reason that was a *horrible* idea, but she was just a *little* pissed off right now.

"You dare threaten me!" the thug spluttered.

"I don't care in the slightest about your 'local business,'" she told him. "You can discuss that with these gentlemen at any time and any place...except here. Except now. Because if you get in the way of my repairs, I will *end* you."

There were four "security guards" positioned around the space with zero-gee carbines. They were Forward Combat Intelligence Marines, elite soldiers trained to deadly perfection—and then trained again to hide it. They might be slouching in zero-gee and looking as distracted as she'd felt a moment before, but she knew they were watching this confrontation.

She might not be able to outdraw the thug—but she knew the Marines *could*.

"And there's a lot of fun legal questions about what the executive officer of a starship is allowed to do in the loading bays, aren't there?" she asked. "I suggest you get the *fuck* out of our way and have your discussion another time.

"Clear?"

Kelly held the thug's gaze for several seconds, and then he unexpectedly barked a loud laugh.

"We're clear, little tiger," he told her, then glanced at the workers hauling the plating. "I suggest you boys do good work for the tiger here," he continued. "It appears we don't want to get on her bad side!"

A half-mocking, half-serious salute later, and the thugs were gone.

Somehow, Kelly doubted that was going to be the last *Red Falcon* heard from them.

"So, what's this I hear about death threats on the loading dock?" the Captain asked over the senior officers' working dinner several hours later.

"Some local leg-breakers were trying to collect protection money from the team loading our cargo plating," Kelly replied with forced cheer. "I convinced them to see the error of their ways, at least in regard to causing trouble on our loading dock."

Rice snorted.

"And what would you have done if they decided to push it, my dear XO?" he asked drily.

"I don't know about the security team, but *I* was carrying a SmartDart gun," she replied with an innocent smile.

SmartDarts were self-contained tasers that came along with a small suite of expensive medical sensors. They assessed the weight and health of their target and then delivered a carefully calibrated charge. They were all but guaranteed to both take down the target and do so nonlethally.

Each individual SmartDart was also roughly the price of an entire magazine of, say, merely explosive munitions.

"So, you *would* have shot him," Rice said with a chuckle.

"Yep. He'd have *lived*, too, though I suspect the Orbit Council's security people would love to have had a few words with him."

Her Captain shook his head, glancing around the table. Following his glance, Kelly realized everyone else was distracted and the pair of them were isolated at the end of the meal.

"Ardennes is your homeworld, isn't it?" he said quietly. "You have family."

She sighed and stared at her hands.

"Folks died while I was at school. Industrial accident of the kind that doesn't happen on most planets," she admitted. "Granddad was left...but he ran a union in Karlsberg. You read the report."

Rice winced.

"Knowing him, I probably have a message waiting for me when I get there," Kelly said quietly, "but I'm pretty sure he was right in the middle of whatever went down there. He was a Freedom Party MP for a long time."

He'd been elected just before she'd left to attend a prestigious engineering school in Tau Ceti. She remembered him full of hope for change and advancement.

Nothing she'd seen from her homeworld had suggested any of *that* had materialized in the last decade. The Freedom Party's MPs had become the leaders of the Freedom Wing's armed rebellion and, well, her granddad had died when Karlsberg was attacked from orbit.

"You going to be okay?" Rice asked.

"So far as I can tell, Damien already killed every single son of a bitch involved in my granddad's death," Kelly said fiercely. She loved Xi Wu and Mike Kelzin, but Damien Montgomery had been something more. She never expected to see him again—not if he was a *Hand* now—but it was somehow *right* that her ex-boyfriend had avenged her family.

David Rice shook his head.

"The details I have are terrifying," he admitted. "Hard to think of Damien as a walking weapon of mass destruction...but he *is* a Hand now."

"And we get to see the aftermath of that," Kelly agreed. "Repairs will be done by noon Olympus Mons Time tomorrow; loading will be finished sixteen hours after that. Less than two days before we can be on our way."

"And the moment we're loaded, we're gone," her Captain confirmed. "We'll help finish the fix Damien started, Kelly, even if putting everything back together is a job for other hands than ours."

"We never stay long enough anywhere for that," she said quietly. They homeported in Tau Ceti along with *Peregrine*, the other ship David owned, but they were there maybe once or twice a year. Only the ship was home.

"That's the job," he agreed. "As merchants or as spies...that's just the nature of the job. You know you can..."

She laughed.

"Retire?" she asked. "At the grand old age of 'not quite thirty'? Nah, boss. Just wishing I'd had one last chance to see my granddad. I wouldn't give up this job for anything short of a ship of my own."

Rice saluted her with a wineglass. They both knew her XO's share of their jobs was rapidly amounting to enough to retire on most worlds but was still far short of enough to buy a starship.

But "a ship of their own" was the ambition of every executive officer in the galaxy, and *Captains*, especially Captains who owned more than one ship, were known for making sure their XOs made that happen in the end.

CHAPTER 6

MARIA WASN'T EVEN remotely sad to see Truce Station in their rear cameras. Madrigal was a continuing failure of both her old service and her new one. The Protectorate should have been able to put a stop to the constant five-way civil war, but it had never happened.

Both the covert spy she'd become and the naval officer she'd been could understand why. Resolving Madrigal's problems would have required the Protectorate to either pick a side in the war, and none of the local factions' hands were clean, or move in and occupy the entire system.

Neither of those options would be bloodless or cheap. So, the Mage-King had left Madrigal to sort their own problems out, like so many other systems.

Maria wasn't under any illusions that the Protectorate's system was perfect, but it was still jarring to run into a failure of this scale—an entire star system left to feuding clans and low-intensity bloodshed.

"Simulacrum chamber, this is Rice," a voice echoed into the enchanted space at the heart of *Red Falcon*'s hull that allowed her to jump between the stars. "I make it six hours to jump space. What are you seeing?"

Every sensor that *Falcon* possessed routed to the simulacrum chamber. Every wall in the room was layered with screens that showed the exterior camera feeds and could be overlaid with a thousand more esoteric scans.

Looping through those screens and covering every inch of the roughly oval chamber were the silver runes of the starship's jump matrix. To have both the screens and runes visible and useful to the Mages required very careful design, and every simulacrum chamber Maria had ever used had been functionally identical.

She tapped commands on the console next to her. A small platform suspended her in the air against the ship's acceleration, positioning her next to the simulacrum itself, a semi-liquid silver model of *Red Falcon*. The "model" was, in a strange sense, the ship—and its existence was the only reason the ship could move between the stars.

"We could jump in three," she told the Captain. "I know I won't enjoy the headache, but I get the impression that cutting even half a dozen hours off our trip might be worth it."

"It might," Rice said. "You know I don't like to push your people, though."

Civilian rules said a Mage couldn't jump more than once every eight hours and couldn't cast the spell in any significant gravitational field.

Navy rules cut that minimum wait to six and allowed a maximum gravity over an order of magnitude higher. The Navy sustained that by having much higher minimum standards than most merchant starships. Maria had hired two ex-Navy Mages and, well, Xi Wu. Xi Wu might not have all of the defensive and combat training of the Navy Mages, but she certainly had the capacity to jump like them.

"We'll make this run at Navy standard," she decided. It was her call, after all. "If any of them complain, I'll have Xi Wu make puppy eyes at them. She's worried about LaMonte, and that woman has *weapons-grade* sad eyes."

Rice chuckled, but there was an edge to it.

"*I'm* worried about Kelly," he admitted. "It looks like whatever family she had left died before the Governor was overthrown. The whole mess is ugly, and I'm going to be keeping a careful eye on her."

"She's your executive officer," Maria pointed out. There was only so much "keeping a careful eye on" LaMonte that Rice could do without undermining her authority as the ship's Second Officer.

"I know, and I don't plan on babysitting her," the Captain agreed. "But she's still young and most of us didn't have to come back to a homeworld that just saw a revolution."

"We won't be there for long," she replied. "Drop off the cargo, pick up the information, find a contract to move on, right?"

"Depends on where we need to move on *to*," Rice said. "I don't even know what will be shipping out from Ardennes right now. Our contract covers costs to travel away from Ardennes if we can't find a cargo—pretty standard for humanitarian relief contracts," he explained, which Maria appreciated. She hadn't been involved in a humanitarian mission except from the Navy side before.

"But we can't justify going anywhere particularly far," she guessed.

"Exactly. A cargo will help; otherwise, we're basically heading to the next system over and finding work. It's hard to justify running *Falcon* empty."

Maria helped LaMonte and Rice review the books every month. *Red Falcon* was much bigger and faster than most merchant ships in the Protectorate. So long as she was carrying cargo, she was making money hand over fist.

If she was running empty or sitting still she was burning money almost as fast as she made it while working. MISS underwrote their operations to a degree, but she still couldn't burn cash for long without questions.

"We'll see what we find in Ardennes," Maria said. "Every step afterward comes from there."

Maria gathered her three subordinates in the "Mages' Sanctum," the mixed office and working space next to the simulacrum chamber in every starship. On many ships, the Sanctum was the only space in the ship with working gravity runes.

Falcon had those throughout her key working areas, but the Sanctum remained the primary working space of her Mages and the best place to nail them all down for a conversation.

She made sure to be seated before they arrived. They all knew she'd just jumped them out of the Madrigal System, but there was no point in being visibly weakened and exhausted in front of her people.

Alessandra Barrow and Karl Nguyen were an almost-matched pair. Both were of merely average height and bore the distinctively mixed ethnic features of the families produced by the Eugenicists' Project Olympus. They had skin the tone of faded parchment and eyes with noticeable epicanthic folds.

Like the majority of the Protectorate's Mages—and Maria herself—they traced their ancestry to the forced-breeding program carried out in Olympus Mons to recreate the gift of magic in humanity. That program had eventually backfired on the Eugenicists when the older "subjects" revolted, led by the man who would become the first Mage-King of Mars.

Both sat ramrod-straight, the legacy of a decade of service in the Royal Martian Navy. Xi Wu, the attractive Chinese Mage who was Maria's second-in-command, lacked that discipline.

She was also more powerful than any of the Navy Mages, if less well trained. Rice had hired her before Maria had come aboard as Ship's Mage, on Kelly LaMonte's recommendation before the pair had been lovers.

Maria had chosen not to object then—and continued to rank that as one of her smarter choices.

"All right," she greeted them. "If you have somehow managed to miss it, we're carrying a humanitarian cargo to the Ardennes System. There's some more layers to the mission after that," she noted with an airy wave of her hand, "but that's the immediately important bit."

She met Xi Wu's gaze levelly.

"What you *may* not know, if you're not Xi, anyway, is that Ardennes is Officer LaMonte's homeworld. She's understandably concerned about the conflict even if she seems enthusiastic enough about the Governor's overthrow to make me wonder just what the asshole was *doing*."

"So, we're Navy-jumping it," Barrow said brightly. She checked the schedule on her wrist-comp. "That puts me up in about seventy minutes, right?"

"Exactly," Maria confirmed. "Usual rotation, but we're running on six-hour jumps. Xi—can you double-check the schedule and make whatever adjustment is needed to make sure I make the jump into the system? I figure I can shave another two or three hours off at that end, too."

"We can do it," Nguyen said firmly. "Hell, boss, I was half-expecting it just on the 'humanitarian aid cargo,' even *without* knowing that it was LaMonte's homeworld." He coughed. "Which, I admit, I didn't."

"We don't exactly publish everyone's homeworld on the door to their quarters or anything, Mage," Maria pointed out. "I appreciate everyone's willingness."

"Hey, I didn't agree yet," Xi Wu pointed out with a chuckle.

"And what are the odds you *aren't* going to go out of your way for your girlfriend?" Maria asked.

"Zero, but you should at least *ask!*"

CHAPTER 7

ARDENNES WAS an oddly colored planet. The pale purple native trees were extremely hardy and had managed to spread across easily seventy percent of the planet's surface. Massive deposits of heavy metals and rare earths, combined with those trees, had made the planet an attractive target for colonization. A massive fault line, clearly visible from orbit, rendered one of the three continents not quite uninhabitable, but the other two were temperate and resource-rich.

Kelly remembered some of what was hidden behind that gorgeous purple color. The harsh, almost vicious pressure applied to grow the local industry. The cavalier disregard for safety regulations. The industrial accidents that killed at almost four times the average rate of a MidWorld.

She'd been too young to really understand what Mage-Governor Vaughn and his Prosperity Party had been doing, until her parents' deaths had driven home three terrifying facts to a fifteen-year-old top student.

Firstly, the industrial accident that had killed them both shouldn't have happened. Basic safety precautions in the construction of the factory that had fallen on them would have prevented their deaths.

Secondly, that they hadn't needed to die. Both had survived the initial chaos when the factory had collapsed across the road they'd been driving along. Prompt medical attention would have saved their lives...but triage on the planet Ardennes went by political importance before it went by need, and a Prosperity Party MP's son had also been in the blast zone.

Lastly had been why she'd fought her way into the scholarship that got her off-world: nothing on Ardennes was going to change. There'd been an inquiry—the involvement of the MP's son had guaranteed that!—but it had scapegoated the shift supervisor, dead in the explosion, and whitewashed the owners and managers of the factory who had cheaped out on the proper containment vessels.

She'd thrown herself into getting even *better* grades, earning one of the one thousand scholarships available for MidWorld students to attend the Tau Ceti Institute of Technology, and getting off-world.

Her grandfather had gone into politics...and a recorded message had been waiting for her when *Red Falcon* arrived in the system. Kelly didn't want to listen to it, not really. Once she did, she'd know for sure he was gone.

But she owed it to him, too, and she sighed and tapped the command on her wrist-comp.

She recognized him instantly. The years she'd been away hadn't been kind to Anthony Hellet, but she'd know him anywhere. His hair had gone white and patchy, and he'd acquired a new scar across his face, but it was him.

"My dear Kelly," he began. "This message has been left with people I trust, who know what I'm up to and can make sure it doesn't get used against me. That's the only way someone can be honest on Ardennes today.

"Sadly, if you're receiving it, I am dead. Our efforts to reform our world politically ended as you always warned me they would," he admitted. "We failed. Vaughn had us locked down every way we could turn.

"So, some of us are going one step further. We're going to try and fight. You know I can't stand by, not after what happened to your mother. We'll take the fight to Vaughn and we will fix this, I swear it.

"I can only hope that if you are seeing this, I died liberating our world and not for nothing," Hellet said quietly. "Either way, know that I died doing what I believed in. I will *not* leave our world in the hands of a monster for one day longer than I have to.

"I'm sorry it has come to this and one sad recorded message," he told her, "but that's life, I suppose. I hope you're well. I hope you're happy. Know that I always loved you."

The message ended, and Kelly turned her head back to the main screen in her office with its view of the planet below.

All she could see through her tears was a purple haze.

"I'm guessing the battleship is new?" Captain Rice asked Kelly when she joined him on the bridge a few minutes later, gesturing to the sensor screens.

Several of the Royal Martian Navy's battleships were based out of Tau Ceti, so the merchant officer had at least seen one before. She was even relatively sure she'd seen this particular battleship before—it wasn't like the RMN had very many of the things.

"There were cruisers posted at the logistics base when I left home," she told her boss. "Never a battleship."

There were still cruisers. Four were active, positioned equally around Ardennes's equator in orbits that allowed them to watch the entire star system. Active sensors washed out from them on a regular basis.

A trio of wrecked cruisers hung in a lower orbit as shuttles swarmed over them, probably from the Navy logistics ship nearby, as they assessed whether the cruisers were reparable. Three intact cruisers and eight intact destroyers, the smaller ships probably Kelly's homeworld's fleet, shared the logistics ship's orbit in silence—directly under the battleship's guns.

"There's *still* a detectable radiation storm where the battle took place," Rice said grimly. "I'm guessing the Navy cleaned up loose munitions, but the battlespace looks as ugly as some chunks of Sol."

Sol was still, almost two hundred years later, paying for the century-long Eugenics Wars between the madmen who'd conquered Mars—and created the Mages—and Earth. All of those old missiles and railgun rounds were long dead, but vacuum was a powerful preservative.

There were still sections of space, continually updated by trained professionals, where ships couldn't safely fly. It would be *another* hundred years before it was all cleaned up, at least.

The Martian Navy was far more careful about cleaning up after themselves.

"I'm heading down to Nouveau Versailles," the Captain continued. "I'll want you to come with me as a native guide. I get the impression the city is physically intact but in...moral shock, I suppose."

Kelly snorted.

"The people here were always good at professing morals and looking blankly the other way," she said bitterly. "It's good to know they woke up eventually."

"Are you okay to come down?" Rice asked.

She exhaled slowly, then nodded.

"Yeah. There's nothing for me here, but we'll do what we can. Any of our people can oversee the offloading. With only half a cargo, I'd be all right leaving it to Ardennes Orbital to take care of."

"Let's leave it with Mike," the Captain suggested. "No offense to your homeworld, but I prefer *my* people in charge of my ship."

She forced a half-chuckle.

"Fair enough, skipper."

It felt like Nouveau Versailles should have changed more. Kelly had only ever visited the capital in passing, but it felt like nothing much had changed. It was the same sprawl of suburbs and crappy government-built tenements wrapped around corporate towers.

The Governor's house was a wreck and there were signs of combat in the downtown core visible even from the air, yet the city seemed unchanged. Given everything that had happened, that almost felt more obscene than if the city had been in flames.

"We're being directed to an operations center north of the city," their pilot informed them. "The interim Governor is waiting for the skipper there."

"What do we know about the Governor?" Rice asked Kelly.

Glad for the distraction, she brought up the MISS file.

"Josephine Red Fox," she read off as she refreshed her memory. "Earth native, from Canada. Spent ten years as a crisis counselor in the North America region, followed by another ten years as mobile conflict arbitrator for planetary issues. Entered the Martian Diplomatic Corps"— which was basically just Red Fox's conflict arbitrator job on a new scale—"seven years ago.

"The Mage-King sent her out directly from Mars with a staff of about five thousand," she noted. "About half of those are cops; the rest are counselors and bureaucrats."

"She's supposed to put an entire planet back together," Rice murmured. "I don't envy her the task."

"Doesn't look like it's the first time she's been called in to put things back together after a Hand removed the obstacles," Kelly told her captain.

"Yeah." Her boss studied her for a long few seconds. "Does 'Hand Damien Montgomery' sound as weird to you as it does to me?"

She snorted.

"I loved him, the fool I was," she admitted. "But...no, not really."

When he'd left, he'd *told* her that he felt he had to go, to take on a burden others couldn't carry. Kelly LaMonte hadn't been *happy* to see him leave, but she'd understood. And because she'd understood, learning what he'd become didn't really surprise her.

"He was always going to find himself in bigger and bigger trouble, trying to help people," she told her boss. "If he's strong enough to be a Hand? He's just going to keep trying to help people."

She shook her head.

"It'll probably kill him," Kelly admitted. "It nearly killed all of us, but...he doesn't have it in him to stand aside."

Rice coughed as if she'd touched a nerve, but he nodded as the shuttle swooped toward the ground.

"Fair enough, I suppose. Let's go talk to the Governor."

CHAPTER 8

GOVERNOR RED FOX was a tall woman with heavyset, dark-skinned features and night-black hair pulled back into a severe bun. As a Marine led David and LaMonte into the prefabricated office she was operating out of, three men in what appeared to be the uniform of the Ardennes planetary military stumbled out.

Two looked to be in shock, where the third looked almost smug. David suspected their meeting with the interim Governor hadn't gone the way they were expecting.

"The Honorable Josephine Red Fox," the Marine introduced the woman. "Captain David Rice and Officer Kelly LaMonte, of the merchant ship *Red Falcon*."

"Come in, come in," Red Fox ordered briskly. "You're the medical shipment from Madrigal, correct?"

"Yes, ma'am," David confirmed as he and LaMonte took the indicated seats. "It seemed a fair ways to reach out for humanitarian aid," he said carefully, unsure if she was aware of their double life.

"Madrigal is near to an RTA and relatively close on a direct flight taking that into account," she told him. "We've been reaching out for supplies and personnel from everywhere we can reach. Mage-Governor Vaughn left a legacy of chaos and disruption that it's going to take a lot of effort to put right."

David wasn't sure just what the late Governor had been up to, but from LaMonte's stiff expression next to him, Red Fox could easily be understating it.

"That's outside my purview, ma'am," he admitted.

"I know," she agreed. "I insisted on meeting with all of the ship captains who arrived, Captain Rice, to get a feel for the people carrying our supplies. I won't be here on Ardennes for more than a few years even in the worst case, and it is useful to know who can be relied on for safe shipment."

"We hope our reputation precedes us," David demurred.

"Oh, it does," she told him. "Meeting with all of the captains also covers those in need of more...subtle meetings as well, doesn't it?"

She winked, and David nodded as he realized that she *did* know who he worked for—and didn't necessarily trust this single-room prefabricated structure in the middle of a barely secured operations camp to be entirely secure.

"I wouldn't know, ma'am," he told her. "How can I and *Red Falcon* be of assistance?"

"I presume your contract included travel to another system for work afterwards?" she asked. "That shouldn't be necessary. For all of the issues we're addressing, the Ardennes economy continues to operate and produce their traditional exports...and I may have abrogated a large number of pre-existing shipping contracts while we investigate irregularities.

"You should be able to find a cargo here, Captain Rice. I suggest you talk to my staff before you return to your ship. Especially Johannes Van Der Merwe. I believe they may have some useful information with regards to local shipping movements that may be of use to you."

Translation: *Van Der Merwe is your MISS contact and has the data on the arms shipments.* Also, *You're dismissed, Captain.*

"Thank you, Governor," he told her, rising as another knock came on the door. "You appear busy."

"You have *no* idea," a new voice told him as a bland-looking, almost mousy man in a plain suit stepped through. "Ma'am, we just got the latest reports from the Versailles Bastille. There's been—"

"Another riot, I'm guessing, Mikael?" she said.

"Yes, ma'am," the stranger confirmed. "Captain, if you can give us privacy, please?"

"We were on our way out," David told him.

Johannes Van Der Merwe's office was at almost the exact opposite side of the encampment. David recognized the style of the structures of the encampment from his time in the Navy—the Martian military used much the same prefabs everywhere.

Unlike the Governor, Van Der Merwe's office was inside another structure. This one was a three-story barracks unit, normally intended to hold a company of Marines and their administrative offices.

The troops on the ground floor were definitely Marines, and they stopped David and LaMonte at the door with brisk efficiency.

"Sir, can I help you?" the Corporal in charge of the guard detail asked crisply.

"We're here to meet with Johannes Van Der Merwe," David replied.

"May I see your ID?" the Marine asked.

David considered the situation carefully for several seconds and then tapped a command on his wrist-comp that transmitted a different ID from his usual to the Marine's own wrist-comp.

From the way the guard relaxed when she saw the details of the MISS identification codes, he'd made the right call.

"Of course. Van Der Merwe is upstairs, on the top floor," she told him. "Remember, Captain, Officer—whatever you see in here, this is just another security barracks. Understand?"

David chuckled.

"We understand completely," he assured her as they were waved in. The main floor looked exactly as he'd expected, the quarters and secured armory for two platoons of Marines. The *second* floor, however, was fascinating.

The designers of the prefabricated structure had designed it to be defensible, not easily traversed. The stairs from the second story to the third were on the opposite side of the building from the stairs to the second story. Walking along the hallway, David glanced at the spaces around him and noted two distinct details.

Firstly, one of the platoon living areas was gone, replaced with a data center even more secured than the armories downstairs.

Secondly, none of the people on the second floor were wearing uniforms. They were all in civilian clothing—but here, at least, they moved like soldiers.

"FCI?" LaMonte murmured to him as they passed the undercover agents.

"Maybe," David said. "Possibly...PSS, actually."

The Protectorate Secret Service wasn't part of MISS or the Marine Corps. They reported directly to the Hands and the Mage-King, serving as both bodyguards and covert agents for the Mage-King's troubleshooters.

His guess would be that the building was a mix of MISS, Marine Forward Combat Intelligence and PSS people. Agents, analysts...the "security barracks" was the beating heart of Martian intelligence ops on Ardennes right now.

Any doubt he had on that disappeared when they reached the top floor and were met by a pair of young men with the gold medallions of Mages in unmarked black fatigues. Their medallions marked them as Combat Mages and they carried themselves like Marines.

"Captain Rice," the taller Mage greeted him with a nod. "Director Van Der Merwe is waiting for you. You're expected. Please wait one moment."

The other Mage produced a scanner and ran it over them while the first Mage studied them with magic.

"Director?" he murmured to the guards.

"Van Der Merwe is the Regional Director for MISS operations in this area of the MidWorlds," the bodyguard Mage told him. "They'll brief you more once you're inside."

It seemed that Ardennes was being treated with the utmost importance. The Martian Interstellar Security Service only *had* ten Regional Directors!

The Director was not...quite what David had been expecting. He hadn't had enough experience with the senior members of the MISS to really have formed an opinion of what they were like, but he realized he'd been unconsciously expecting someone along the lines of Alaura Stealey: a gray-haired middle-aged woman with a spine of iron.

Johannes Van Der Merwe was none of these things. The Director had short-cropped black hair, night-black skin, and an androgynous body type that defied any attempt to gender them. They wore a tight-fitting bodysuit in a deep purple tone David suspected would sparkle when hit with light.

The Director's eyes warned David that anyone who underestimated them wouldn't last long. They sprang up as David and LaMonte entered the room, shaking both of their hands in silence and directing them to chairs as the Director poured coffee.

David was unsurprised when Van Der Merwe made both his and LaMonte's drinks exactly as they preferred before returning, still silent, to the seat behind the desk and smiling at them.

"Captain Rice," the Director finally said. "It's a pleasure. Your reputation precedes you, of course. I've followed your career with us with some interest. It's not often Hands directly recruit people for us."

"The Hands do what they wish, and the rest of us mere mortals simply follow along and try to keep up," David agreed. "Hand Stealey was an intimidating woman, but there was never any question about her goals."

"There generally isn't, with the Hands," Van Der Merwe agreed. "I haven't had the pleasure of meeting Hand Montgomery, though I understand you have?"

"He worked with us before Hand Stealey recruited him."

"It almost feels as if I've met him, I have to say," the Director continued with a nod. "Much of the aftermath here shows his hand. He made quite the impression on the Freedom Wing—and it's made *my* job much easier."

"How so?" David asked carefully.

"Most of the Wing's leadership has taken what appears to have been his advice to heart and vanished from the public eye," Van Der Merwe said. "There's a few exceptions, to the good and the bad, but they seem to understand that we can't just let the rebels take over.

"Mikael Riordan, for example, has stepped up as Governor Red Fox's main local advisor. He's proven reliable and gets where we're all coming from, which makes him worth his weight in gold. Some others have been less...helpful in their visibility, but that is life, I suppose."

They shrugged.

"Since, thankfully, the ex-Wing members regard the Protectorate as an ally instead of an enemy now, they've been extraordinarily willing to fill us in on where their weapons and supplies came from," Van Der Merwe concluded. "At least some of them realize that Legatus was setting them up—others were apparently present when the original unofficial offer of assistance was made and rejected."

"Wait, *what*?" David asked.

"Yes." The Director nodded calmly. "At some point, around when the Freedom Party was still in the Planetary Parliament but the structure of the Wing was already taking shape, Ms. Armstrong was approached covertly by agents of the Legatus Military Intelligence Directorate.

"They offered to fund and arm her rebellion in exchange for holding a referendum on making Ardennes an UnArcana World once they were in power. Armstrong refused."

Lori Armstrong had been the politician who'd created the Freedom Party, managed to get six seats in the Planetary Parliament, and then later given up and formed the Freedom Wing for more direct action.

"She refused?" LaMonte asked. "I would have expected her to take any help."

"So did Legatus," Van Der Merwe guessed. "When she refused their direct help, they decided to make sure she still had the ability to cause trouble. They clearly funneled large quantities of arms and high-quality aircraft and gear to her rebellion through other channels."

"Those channels are what we're supposed to follow back," David said grimly. "Whatever data we can get will help."

"We're crunching data still," the Director confessed. "My on-planet resources are still quite limited versus the scale of what we face, and frankly, making sure we've cleaned up Vaughn's secret police is a higher immediate priority.

"We'll hand over all of the data we got from the Wing and that we've identified out of the shipping logs. I've got the levers in place to arrange a shipping contract to...well, anywhere you're likely to be going."

"I'm guessing you have at least an idea?" David asked.

Van Der Merwe shrugged.

"The usual suspects," he admitted. "The guns came from all over, but...the aircraft came through Amber."

"Of course they did," David said with a sigh. Amber was a perennial headache for the Protectorate, a world founded by libertarians from the old United States on Earth. They had a legal system best described as "loose," which made the system a useful stopover point for transshipping illegal cargo.

It also happened to be the star system where David's girlfriend lived and, among other things, ran an underground syndicate dedicated to supplying arms to the resistance movements that met relatively strict criteria around goals and morals.

They'd need to go through MISS's data...but he wasn't going to be surprised if he found Keiko Alabaster's lovely long fingers tucked into this mess.

And wasn't *that* going to be an awkward date conversation?

CHAPTER 9

"IT WASN'T EASY."

The softly attractive blonde woman in the video looked tired. That was fair, David reflected, since the date in the video was only a handful of days after Lori Armstrong had helped Damien Montgomery overthrow a planetary government.

She shook her head in response to the question of where their weapons had come from.

"It wasn't easy," she repeated. "Even then, I was kind of relieved by that. Even when *I* wanted to buy enough weapons to equip an army, I didn't really want it to be easy.

"We started by sending six people we trusted *completely* to six different systems with a hundred million in untraceable credit chips apiece," she explained. "Reputation and rumor gave us at least a few places to start, but we knew *nothing* about dealing with smugglers and the underworld."

She chuckled.

"I regretted turning the Legatans down more than once. Never enough to try and reach out to the agents who'd contacted me, but there were days..."

"Where did you send those agents?" the unseen interviewer asked.

"Where do you *think*?" Armstrong snorted. "Amber. Corinthian. Chrysanthemum. Others as well, though we weren't successful at most of them. Chrysanthemum exports arms and vehicles, but I wasn't sure how successful we'd be buying from them without an official license.

"Amber we knew we could buy from. Transport would be hell, but Amber's laws meant we could at least pick up small arms and ammunition. But we needed aircraft and ground vehicles...and we couldn't get them at home.

"Vaughn had Ardennes's military manufacturing tied up close." She sighed. "Corinthian was a bust. A bad one. Our agent is in a Corinthian medium-security prison, along with the folks she tried to buy from. That system's underworld was in a mess when we tried to get involved. Bad timing on our part."

David grimaced. That was, well, almost entirely his fault. Montgomery had ended up in a Corinthian jail and he'd broken his Mage out. Along the way, he'd pointed Hand Stealey at a significant chunk of the local underworld.

"Chrysanthemum went better than expected. We should probably have been suspicious when the gear started showing up and it was all Legatan-made instead of Chrysanthemum, but there were so many layers and cutouts that the man who made the purchase was in a different *star system* when the gunships arrived.

"That was really only the gunships, though. They made a hell of a difference in the end, but that was all that came through that funnel. Everything else...everything else was at least purchased through Amber.

"We were told it was being bought from third parties to help cover our Amberite contacts' trail," she noted. "Helped salve our suspicions when the top-line stuff was Legatan. A lot of it was from Amber, too, but the coms gear and the lasers and so forth...all Legatan."

"And that didn't make you suspicious?"

"I had other concerns at the time," Armstrong said drily. "Like the fact that my planetary Governor was arranging for fatal 'accidents' for the handful of elected MPs we still had in the Parliament. Or the latest round of government-'assisted' buyouts of corporations that weren't owned by Vaughn's cronies."

The interviewer didn't say anything.

"Honestly? I wasn't involved enough in that side of things to put the pieces together," Armstrong admitted. "Other people were taking care of getting the guns into our people's hands. I'd arranged the funding and helped out with covers for the shipments, but...actually receiving and handling the weapons was on others."

"And did those others know about the LMID offer?"

Armstrong snorted again.

"I didn't exactly bandy that about," she noted. "Only the people who'd been top members of the Freedom *Party* knew about that. Almost no one who played a major role in the Freedom Wing knew."

"Can you tell us who you dealt with in Amber?" the interviewer asked.

"We weren't really on a names basis," she replied. "Code phrases and identifiers. I'll hand over the files we have. I don't know how much use it will be.... I'm not entirely comfortable betraying the people who helped us, either."

"Honestly, Ms. Armstrong, we don't *care* about most of the people running guns," the interviewer told her. "In a perfect world, we'd intervene in any possible revolution before it got that far. We *do* care about the Legatan connection."

She nodded.

"The only name I know is the Captain who delivered most of the cargo. Seule. His name was Nathan Seule."

"I'm guessing that name means something to you?" Soprano asked him once they'd ended the recording and David had leaned back thoughtfully, studying the now-dark screen.

"Captain Nathan Seule of *Luciole*," David replied. "*Luciole* is one of the few civilian ships I've ever seen with antimatter engines—and the only ship I've ever seen with *both* antimatter and fusion engines. She was built in Sol for the Navy, an experimental blockade runner they decided they had no real use for."

He sighed.

"I owe Seule my life and the lives of my crew," he continued. "When bounty hunters came after us while we were working with him, he intervened. Drove off the hunter, saved *Blue Jay*. But...he's an arms smuggler, all right.

"Works with Keiko, delivering her 'revolutions in a box' to the groups that meet her strict moral standards. I presume he worked with others, but..." David studied the screen and smothered a curse.

"It's entirely possible he was working with Keiko when he delivered to Ardennes," he noted. "Either way, she's our best chance for finding him and he's our best chance for following the chain."

"So, Amber, then?" Soprano asked.

"God, I wish I saw another answer," he admitted. "I'm relatively sure that Keiko at least *guesses* my side job, but the last thing I want is to sit down with my lover—the woman who runs a multisystem trade syndicate and arms revolutions as a hobby—and go 'so, hey, I'm actually a cop and I need to know about your gunrunning.'"

His Mage chuckled.

"What, you don't think that will go over well?"

"You've *met* Alabaster," LaMonte noted from the other side of the table. David's XO was being uncharacteristically silent. "It's going to go over like a ton of bricks and you're going to have to dig upwards fast, boss.

"But...she's also always been in the gunrunning business to make a *difference*, not to make a buck," the XO noted. "There's a difference between arming the people you see acting as the Protectorate's conscience and helping Legatus foment outright civil war."

"We don't *know* that's what's happening," David pointed out. "We can guess, we can postulate, but we have no real data to support that Legatus is trying to destabilize the Protectorate."

He could guess and postulate with a high degree of certainty, and it felt strange to him to say they *didn't* know, but...they really didn't. The stack of circumstantial evidence and questionable actions and deceptions and guns and bodies was a mile high...but none of it was *proof*.

Even if he could point at that stack of possible and say that Legatus had been acting in bad faith...he wasn't sure *why*.

"We need that data," he said quietly. "We need that proof. MISS as a whole is *convinced* Legatus is preparing for a civil war, but we have nothing that could justify Mars acting. That conviction can fuel preparation, can fuel security measures...but without proof, we can't do anything until they move."

"So, we go talk to your girlfriend?" LaMonte replied. "I don't envy you that chat, boss."

"No. But it's our only option. I'll talk to Van Der Merwe, see if they can get us a cargo to Amber."

He sighed again and shook his head.

"And I suppose I'll tell Kellers we're visiting his homeworld. He'll want to stock up on hard liquor before we leave."

The chief engineer was *from* Amber. To David's knowledge, James Kellers went back only when David dragged him. And he usually managed to get *very* drunk on his way in.

CHAPTER 10

TO DAVID'S SURPRISE, the response to his requesting a meeting with Director Van Der Merwe was silence for several hours...and then the Director showing up at the docking tube for *Red Falcon*, politely asking that the security officer let them aboard.

The jumpsuit-clad head spy seemed to enjoy the degree to which they'd discomfited David's crew. Today's jumpsuit was a deep maroon—but, in the lights of the space station and *Red Falcon* herself, unquestionably glittered.

"There are two paths to anonymity, Captain Rice," they told David as they took a seat in his office. "One is to blend in. The other is to present an easily classified image, one that is filed and forgotten...and never investigated in depth."

Van Der Merwe grinned at him. "Plus, well, I like this style."

David chuckled, shaking his head as he poured coffee for the Director.

"I didn't expect you to come all this way yourself," he noted.

"I was already on my way up for other reasons," Van Der Merwe admitted. "Since I was up here already, simply showing up seemed the most convenient method."

"If not necessarily covert," David pointed out. His ship's cover as a civilian ship with its fingers in the underworld was worth a lot to the MISS. He didn't *think* the Regional Director had just blown his cover, but it still seemed odd.

"This outfit is the height of fashion in a set of younger spacers," the spy told him. "There are at least two or three hundred glitter-suits on the station, and believe me, *no one* is looking past the jumpsuit to see the faces."

They shrugged.

"Plus, well, there's a worm in the station's network that replaces my face in any video or pictures taken with a randomly selected other person. If I was being physically followed, they might have been able to identify me boarding your ship...but between myself and several bodyguards that *your* security officer didn't notice, I don't think they'd have had as much luck as that."

David made a *touché* gesture.

"Never question a spy's tradecraft, I suppose," he admitted.

"No. *Always* question the tradecraft when your cover is on the line," Van Der Merwe replied instantly. "Your cover is worth a lot to MISS," they noted, echoing David's thoughts from a moment before. "I have no intention of blowing it.

"Now, what did you need?"

"I need a contract to Amber of sufficient mass or urgency to justify sending *Red Falcon*," David told him instantly. "We've identified one of the Captains who delivered the arms to the Freedom Wing, and while I may not find him on Amber, I know people there who *can* find him."

The Director nodded.

"Amber is quite some distance away," they noted. "Ardennes does some business with them, but not much. In normal times, you wouldn't have much luck getting a cargo heading in that direction."

"And right now?"

"Right now, I figured the odds were about sixty-forty we were going to be sending you to Amber, so I made special arrangements," Van Der Merwe told him with a grin. "There are a number of businesses that do ship there, and I arranged for all of their regular shipping plans to fall through.

"So, they're looking for a carrier," David concluded. He concealed a sigh at the fact that MISS's needs were, once again, damaging businesses.

"Indeed. They'll also all come into some contracts from the interim government to cover the losses and freight premiums they're going to have to pay," the Director noted, replying to David's unspoken concern. "I need them to ship with you. I don't need them to be out of pocket for the extra cost."

"So, I can post for secondary cargos, but I'm guessing none of them are big enough to justify being the primary?"

"No," Van Der Merwe admitted. "That one took more arranging, but there's several multi-million-ton cargos of processed metals that the interim government is sitting on. There are a *lot* of contracts the government shipping broker is going to have to default on, so they've been waffling over whose contracts to fill.

"Since we need a cargo to Amber, that helps make the decision. There's a five-million-ton order outstanding from Amber for supplies for the Amber Defense Cooperative. Given the Protectorate's general opinion of Amber, it would normally be one of the last contracts we'd fill, but in the circumstances..."

"I get to haul metal to the cooperatives," David concluded. "Put them in touch with me, Director, and we'll make it happen.

"And then once in Amber, I'll start poking in dark corners. Let's hope I find Seule and not poisonous snakes."

David spent the evening officially "looking for cargo," trawling the usual sites and contacts even while making sure not to accept any actual work. Given *Red Falcon*'s size and armament, he could justify charging rates that would price out most of the market—he didn't usually, since her speed meant he could do twice as many contracts in the same time as most ships.

It made it easy to look like he was holding out for a good job until the next morning, when the Governor's office contacted him. He recognized the mousy, plain-looking man who appeared on his screen as the aide that had entered Governor Red Fox's office at the end of their meeting.

"Greetings, Captain Rice. I am Mikael Riordan, one of the Governor's aides," he introduced himself.

"Greetings, Mr. Riordan." David considered. "I'm correct in remembering that you were part of the Freedom Wing?"

Riordan laughed carefully.

"That's one way of putting it," he agreed. "I was a rabble-rouser, really, not all that close to the center of things until Hand Montgomery came along. That young man changed my life."

"You're not the only one," David murmured. "How's Damien doing? He used to be my Ship's Mage."

The aide paused, clearly considering his words carefully.

"Hand Stealey's death shook him, I think, though I can't pretend I know him well," Riordan finally answered. "I know I never want to get on his wrong side. I was in the background when he stormed Vaughn's command center. There's a vast gap, Captain Rice, between understanding that our antimatter supplies come from Transmuter-certified Mages—and watching a Hand use matter-antimatter transmutation as a *weapon*."

David shivered.

"I didn't think that was *possible*," he noted.

"My impression is that the Hands don't subscribe to anyone else's ideal of 'possible'...and Lord Montgomery is no exception. He was injured while he was here, but he recovered. I don't know if his...heart, I suppose, healed so well.

"But I trust the Mage-King to have the best counselors and to understand what is needed after the death of a mentor."

"So do I," David agreed. "What did you need from me, Mr. Riordan?"

"The Ardennes government was the major broker for a massive trade syndicate running on Ardennes," Riordan told him. "We're still going through the books related to this—and it seems like a *lot* of money went astray—but...the fact is that we find ourselves responsible for completing a vast number of shipments of materials and goods.

"At the same time as we are sanctioning, dismantling, or otherwise penalizing most of the companies that made up that syndicate," he concluded. "Fulfilling all of those contracts will simply not be possible, but we will be able to fill *some* of them.

"One of those orders is for the Amber Defense Cooperative, who have now made it clear that they will proceed with legal action if the cargo doesn't arrive within the next seven days."

Riordan smiled mirthlessly.

"Forty-two light-years, Captain. Six-million-ton cargo. Can you load and deliver in seven days?"

"I have four Mages aboard, Mr. Riordan. We can move twelve light-years a day without even asking them to pretend they're still in the Navy. A day on each side for sublight travel. That's five and a half days, give or take. How quickly can you get your cargo to me?"

Six million tons was six hundred cargo containers. Even *Red Falcon*'s heavy-lift shuttles could only move four at a time.

"Two-thirds are in orbit, but our surface-to-orbit transshipment capability is...limited," Riordan admitted. "And, frankly, we have higher-priority uses for it. The station has the gear to load that portion of the cargo in twenty-four hours. The other two hundred containers are near Nouveau Versailles."

Red Falcon had ten heavy-lift shuttles...and ten shuttles that could lift a single container each. Fifty containers at a shot would call for four lifts.

"An orbit-surface-orbit flight for my people is a four-hour process," David noted. "Loading onto our cargo spars is another two hours. That's twenty-four hours, *if* you want to hire my shuttles and crews."

Kelzin would complain. That would be a brutal schedule, even with his pilots able to catnap throughout most of the flight down and up.

Riordan sighed.

"You've got me over a barrel, Captain, and anything you care to charge is going to be cheaper than the ADC's lawyers are going to hand us. Name your price."

David grinned. He wasn't going to be *too* mean, but despite the MISS's involvement, he still preferred to make a profit.

He'd want to retire someday, after all.

Kelly LaMonte sat on the hill above the shuttle pad and watched the sun go down on her homeworld for what she suspected would be the last time. Beneath her, the immense ten-thousand-ton cargo containers were being tracked into position for the next pickup.

That would be her pickup as well. She'd asked Mike to drop her off down here when they'd come down for the first flight, but she wasn't going to add any additional trips for her own benefit. She'd even been working from her wrist-comp.

Sort of, at least.

She hadn't been sure why she'd come down when she'd asked her boyfriend for the ride, but she knew now.

She'd come down to Ardennes to say goodbye and to watch the sun set over purple forests one last time. There hadn't been much drawing her back home before her grandfather's death—and there was nothing now.

"Ma'am?" one of the security guards said quietly behind her. She turned to look at the young man. He was one of the Marines seconded to the interim government, the replacements for a local police and military no one was sure they could trust yet.

"Yes, Corporal?"

"The call just came in. The shuttles are on approach and have entered the upper atmosphere. Thirty minutes or so."

"Thank you," she told him, mentally judging. Loading would be another half-hour, but she was easily ten minutes' walk from where she needed to board the shuttles.

With a sigh, Kelly LaMonte turned her gaze back to the purple hillside and gave her homeworld one last sad smile.

"Then let's get going," she told the Marine. "As the old sailors used to say, the tide waits for no man—and as every merchant shipper ever understands, we have a cargo to deliver."

CHAPTER 11

WITH THE Azure Legacy and the attached bounty on his head long gone now, David didn't find his ship getting jumped on *every* flight. It was still a relief to make a journey between star systems without even a blip, and he spent most of the trip to Amber watching his sensors like a mother hen.

They arrived in the star system exactly on schedule, and David took in the now-familiar shape of the system. They'd come in closer than usual, emerging inside the asteroid belt outside the fifth planet and barely a day's flight from Amber itself.

The shipyard complexes in orbit around the planet were expanding again, he noted. They were far rougher frameworks than you would see in other Protectorate systems. Amber's Prime Cooperatives, the closest thing the system had to a government, enforced the bare minimum of Protectorate rules and regulations to prevent the Mage-King coming down on them with the full force of the Charter.

The system served as something of a safety valve for the Protectorate. The people who were convinced that all government was bad and that the old libertarians had things right moved there...and the people who decided that they preferred not having to pay road tolls to private corporations to leave their houses moved away.

"Is that a new destroyer?" Jeeves asked quietly as the scan data came in. "That's quite the investment for the ADC."

The Amber Defense Cooperative ran the security forces that protected Amber. Paying for a membership reduced a number of fees charged for traveling around the system and helped support the mutual defense. Membership in the three Prime Cooperatives—Defense, Medical, and Judicial—was the criterion Amber used for Citizenship.

David was there often enough that he now had those memberships. He saved enough on docking fees for it to be worth it.

And, apparently, his membership fees had allowed the ADC to double their jump-capable ship strength. *Osiris*, the flagship of the ADC, was an old ex-Navy ship with its amplifier matrix downgraded. Orbiting next to her now, though, was a brand-new Tau Ceti–built "export" destroyer.

"Something's got to be making them nervous," David murmured to his gunnery officer. "If they just bought a destroyer, though... Bets my ADC fees are going up?"

"No bet," Jeeves replied. "The Amber Cooperative fees only go in one direction, boss."

David chuckled and fired off a message to Heinlein Station, the main orbital platform, identifying his ship and his Cooperative membership statuses.

"That's fair enough," he agreed. "In this case, though, some of those fees are coming back to me to pay for this trip. Can't complain too loudly."

"I never do, boss," the other man replied. "Keep your eyes open, though," he continued. "Looks like they've increased the orbit patrol."

David looked at what Jeeves was indicating and nodded slowly. *Red Falcon* had much better passive sensors than most civilian ships, which meant she could pick out the boxy corvettes making their ballistic orbits around the star.

Normally, the ships were positioned so at least one would orbit past anyone flying in from outside the belt, but today...there were at least twice as many ships as usual, with a cluster of a dozen ships orbiting just outside Amber's own orbit.

Anyone who focused on the destroyers was going to get a nasty surprise when those ships, each packing a laser equivalent to *Falcon*'s own five-gigawatt beams, brought up their drives at the closest approach on their unpowered orbits.

The ADC was feeling twitchy. Those deployments cost money, and if there was one thing David had learned about Amber's Prime Cooperatives, it was that they did *not* spend money they didn't think they needed to.

Citizenship and being a recurring visitor made the docking and accounting process smoother than it had any right to be. It was still an expensive endeavor—things that were considered "public service" and performed by government employees elsewhere were fee-operated enterprises here—but David had all of the accounts set up and knew what he was going to be paying.

His first visit there had been a confusing mess, but that had been years before. He knew the drill. His Citizenship allowed for his crew to get visitor passes with ease, and it wasn't like Heinlein Station was dangerous.

It was safe in different ways and for different reasons than most places, but it wasn't dangerous. It was just an unusual experience for anyone used to the regular Protectorate setup.

For one thing, even aboard the space station, *everyone* was armed. David had visited frontier worlds with actively dangerous wildlife where a smaller portion of the population went armed than Amber. Culture shock was inevitable.

Now, of course, he and his people simply strapped on their guns and set about their business. He, LaMonte and Soprano converged in his briefing room after they docked, all three of them wearing obvious holsters—a contrast to their normal concealed armament.

"Kelly, I need you to deal with the cargo," he told his XO. "Most of this is for the ADC, but we're carrying something like fifty secondary cargos. Handle them."

She had admin staff for that as well, and he trusted her skills.

"Can do. If they decide they need to talk to a Citizen for any of this, will you be available?" she asked.

That wasn't unheard-of, though it usually meant someone was intentionally being a prick.

"I can't say for sure," he admitted. "However this conversation with Keiko goes, I doubt it will be over quickly."

Or at least, if it was over quickly, he was going to be in both professional *and* personal trouble.

"Right. I'll ping Kellers, make sure he's available then," LaMonte told him. The chief engineer kept up his memberships to avoid problems when he came home.

"I'll coordinate with Leonhart," Soprano promised. "We'll make sure the locks are guarded and we've got at least one Mage on the security detail at all times."

"We shouldn't need that here," David replied.

"*Something* has the Defense Coop spooked," she pointed out. "And while I trust Keiko, I don't trust her countrymen. You've been shot here before, after all."

"That was when Azure had a bounty on us," he protested. "With both the Blue Star and the Legacy gone, no one has any prices on our head that I know of."

LaMonte snorted.

"Well, wandering around Heinlein Station incautiously is a good way to find out if there are any," his XO told him. "Let's keep an eye on the ship, boss. If nothing else, I don't want any inquisitive locals poking around and realizing how well armed we are."

A lot of people had probably figured that out by now, but it was still mostly a secret. David hoped.

"You're not wrong," he conceded. "I'm going to see Keiko alone, though. No escort for that."

"And if someone does jump you?" Soprano asked sweetly.

"Have you *met* the Amazon brigade that runs this ship for me?" David asked. "I'll just surrender and leave it to you lot to rescue me!"

"Again," LaMonte noted with a sigh. "When did our Captain become a professional damsel in distress?"

Heinlein Station's Quadrant Gamma had a large gallery at its core, a multistory open space with balconies ringing it filled with offices and market stalls. It was one of the largest shopping spaces on the ring station and had the crowds to prove it.

The ubiquity of firearms still disconcerted David, even with his experience with the system's culture. It threw his finely tuned professional paranoia completely off, but thankfully he made it to the discreet office door on the "bottom" floor of the gallery without interruption.

Inside the discreet door was a quiet reception area lined with plants. A small number of comfortable-looking chairs were tucked in one corner for people waiting, and a petite, dark-skinned young woman with short-cropped hair sat behind a desk.

She looked up at his arrival and gave him a brilliant smile.

"Captain Rice! We didn't know you were in-system," she told him.

"I'm sure Keiko does, Jenna," he pointed out with a chuckle. "We just docked with a cargo for the ADC. I need to talk to your boss."

"Of course you do," Jenna agreed with a chuckle of her own. Jenna Alabaster was Keiko's niece—and also the niece of David's chief engineer. "I don't think she's on-station at the moment, but I can check."

"I'd appreciate that," David said. "It's more urgent than I'd like, too, so…"

Jenna nodded and was already tapping away at a concealed console in the desk with one hand while she gestured him airily to the chairs with the other. She might *look* like a receptionist still, but David knew that the young woman now ran most of Keiko's Heinlein Station operations— and her brother was now the second engineer on one of the ships their aunt owned.

She continued typing for at least a minute, then produced a headset.

"Yes," she said into it immediately. "I can keep him here or get *Falcon*'s dock number. Which do you—" She paused, waiting for a moment. "He said it was urgent."

Jenna shifted the headset on her ears and looked at David thoughtfully.

"Yeah," she finally agreed, and gestured him over. She took the headset off and passed it to him.

"Hello, lover," Keiko's warm voice echoed in his ear. "What's going on?"

"It's complicated," he told her. "I'd rather discuss it in person, for more reasons than one, but it's urgent."

She sighed.

"I am all but literally tied up in a major Prime Cooperatives convention," she told him grimly. Unless David missed his bet, that was the next best thing to a meeting of Parliament for Amber. "Jenna flashed me a priority signal to get me out of a meeting, but if I don't get back in there, these idiots either *aren't* going to buy a cruiser or are going to spend way too much on it."

A cruiser?

"I would hate to impose," he demurred, "but..."

"You don't use the word *urgent* lightly, David," she finished for him. "Tell Jenna to give you the hotel. She's not supposed to know where the convention is, but if she *doesn't*, she isn't doing her job.

"Can you get to the surface by, say, twenty hundred OMT?"

He checked the time. That gave him six hours to either find a shuttle or get clearance for one of Kelzin's. Plenty of time.

"I can manage that," he promised.

"Then meet me at the hotel," she told him. "That's as fast as I can manage an in-person meeting; sorry."

"It's as fast as I could hope," he replied. "See you then."

The channel went silent and he passed the headset back to Jenna.

"She says you're not supposed to know where she is," David told the office manager. "But that you do and can tell me what hotel to meet her at."

Jenna chuckled.

"Yeah, the Prime Coop meetings are pretty locked down," she confirmed. "Officially, if you aren't in the top five hundred unit-holders of one of them, you aren't cleared to know where they're meeting."

That meant, given the overlap between the major unit-holders, that there were probably less than a thousand people on the planet who were supposed to know where the convention was. That said...

"And?" he asked.

"Nine Seasons Hotel, downtown Garnet," Jenna confirmed instantly. "Keiko is in room 55–260. If you let me know your course, I'll have one of our people meet you with the papers you'll need to enter the hotel right now."

CHAPTER 12

RIDING AN AUTO-TAXI in Amber's capital city was both similar to and quite different from riding one in any other city in the Protectorate. Every city would have the "tolls" section of the fee, much like the cab carrying David through Garnet.

In Garnet, however, that section was ticking up even faster than the regular fare. Streets had been built by private interests, and a complex system of RFID tags and area coding in vehicle computers made sure those private interests were compensated for their construction and continued maintenance.

No single toll was particularly significant, but it added up to slightly more than the cost of the cab ride itself by the time he reached the Nine Seasons Hotel and authorized the machine to debit his account.

Whether, over the course of a year, the tolls would add up to less than the portion of taxes another world would have assigned to building those streets was for others to work out. David just paid whatever he was asked to pay wherever he was.

That was always the lot of those who traveled. They didn't get much say in what went on in the places they traveled between.

The Nine Seasons Hotel, at least, didn't look any different from its counterparts on other worlds. A massive edifice of artificial granite and tempered glass, the luxury hotel occupied an entire city block in Garnet's downtown core, towering a hundred stories into the air and shadowing the streets around it.

There was no sign outside the hotel that anything unusual was going on inside, but as soon as he stepped in it began to be obvious. There were none of the crowds of people checking in and out that you would normally see at a hotel of this size. The Nine Seasons had over *twenty thousand* rooms and suites. Even with automated systems handling ninety-nine percent of the process, there were enough people with problems requiring a human touch that the lobbies would normally be full.

Today, they were empty. Discreet signs announced that the restaurants were closed, and the uniformed hotel staff hovering attentively around the main floor were being attentive for different reasons from usual.

"Excuse me, sir," one of them said, descending on him with near-instant teleportation. "The hotel is being rented for a private event. We are full."

"I have an access pass," he told the woman, tapping a command on his wrist-comp to bring up the document.

A wave of her PC over his transferred the file, and she examined it meticulously.

"I see, Captain Rice," she allowed, waving at someone.

The slightly older man who arrived at her gesture was wearing a hotel uniform...but it clearly wasn't his *usual* uniform. His black hair was cropped close enough to his skull that it was hard to see where his similarly shaded skin ended and the stubble began, and he moved with the athletic purpose of a lifelong soldier.

"Mr. Mbeki here will take you up to the fifty-fifth floor," the staffer told David. "The Nine Seasons Hotel appreciates your respect for our guests' confidentiality, of course."

His pass had come along with a seven-page nondisclosure agreement. So far as he could tell, he couldn't even admit to having seen anything here to himself, let alone to his crew.

The soldier gestured for David to follow, and he fell in obediently. As they passed through the lobby, it rapidly become clear to the merchant captain that at least half of the "hotel" staff were either ADC troops or private security.

Some of them were probably hired by the hotel, but the type of people who became top-five-hundred unit-holders in the Prime Cooperatives had their own security. It might be a "mere" hotel, but the Nine Seasons was probably currently the most defended location on the planet.

To no one's surprise, David was sure, Keiko Alabaster's "room" was an extensive suite done in tasteful dark granite and blue fabric. Despite his being exactly on time, the suite was empty.

That, too, wasn't really a surprise. His understanding was that the kind of convention he was crashing only happened twice a year or so and was where a lot of what would be the "business of government" on other worlds was decided.

The suite had a kitchenette with a full complimentary bar so he busied himself making two of Keiko's favorite cocktails with the plan of waiting for her.

He'd barely finished mixing the drinks before the tall redheaded woman swept into the hotel suite with a final "pull together a briefing and send it to my PC" instruction out the door to whatever staff she was leaving behind.

With a smile, David offered the cocktail across the bar, and Keiko laughed.

"All right, Captain, that buys you a few minutes of my time," she told him as she took the drink. "It's been a *hell* of a few days."

"Everyone is busy sorting out how to keep a planet with no government running for six months until the next time you all meet?" he inquired.

She snorted.

"That part is normal. ADC's new wish list, though...that caused a meltdown on the part of some of our unit-holders."

"A cruiser?" he echoed her earlier comment.

She shook her head.

"You're flying around in one of the most over-gunned excuses for a jump freighter in the galaxy," she pointed out. "How many times have you been attacked by pirates in the last year?"

David paused thoughtfully.

"We do deal in high-value cargos," he said slowly. "But...four? Maybe five?"

"And you have the guns and the speed to make going for your cargo a bad idea," Keiko said. "Piracy rates are up across the board. Ships are getting lost, people are dying...the Navy is moving heaven and earth to do their job, but it seems like every bug they squash, three more crawl out of the woodwork."

He winced. That was worse than he'd thought—but Keiko would know.

Of course, the usual source for those pirate ships was right there.

"I know what you're thinking," she confirmed. "It's bad enough that the Judicial Coop just asked for—and got—authorization to start inspecting shipyards and enforcing a restriction list on the sales of armed warships."

David blinked. That was counter to everything Amber tried to stand for. They must be worried.

"So, new jump-ships?" he asked.

"The only real argument is whether we buy Tau Ceti's or build our own," she told him. "Hence potentially paying way too damn much for the *one* cruiser the DC wants. There's no point in us building the infrastructure for manufacturing large-scale warships, plus..."

"Plus, the Protectorate would *never* trust a major military-grade shipyard in Amber," David finished for her. He sighed.

"None of that was what you wanted to talk to me about, though," she realized. "Sorry, I think I just vented three days' worth of frustration and a pile of classified information on your head." She finished the cocktail.

"I know I can trust your discretion. Can you make me another one of these as well?"

He laughed and pulled out the booze.

"What did you need to talk to me about?" she asked.

"Trouble," he admitted as he considered how to phrase it. "I need to find Nathan Seule, Keiko."

She was silent as she took the drink, considering her answer.

"That's not what I expected," she admitted. "Neither of you subcontracts shipping, and if you wanted to get involved in *my* gunrunning, you already would be. What's going on, David?"

He stared at his own drink for several seconds, then downed it in one gulp and looked Keiko Alabaster directly in the eyes.

"You know damn well Stealey recruited me for Martian security," he said quietly. "Well, now she's dead and we're staring a potential interstellar civil war in the face. Nathan Seule ran guns into Ardennes, guns we're pretty sure Legatus paid for and supplied.

"We need to know where they came from."

"'We,'" she echoed. "MISS, I presume?"

"You don't presume; you know," David objected. "We've never talked about it, because this isn't part of my life I wanted to involve you in, but I *know* what your intelligence network is like."

"My intelligence network, to be honest, thinks you got tied up in a one-man war against the Legacy and grabbed whatever allies you could," she pointed out. "None of them thought you'd actually been recruited." Keiko sighed. "I knew better, but I didn't expect you to try and use *me* as a source."

Her tone left no question of her opinion of this.

"That was never my intention," he told her. "We both have parts of our lives that don't enter the room when the other is there. We always have. Unless one of us decides to completely *change* their life, we always will. I'm not going to move to Amber and become a kept man, and you sure as hell aren't going to move aboard *Falcon*."

"No, probably not," she agreed. Her tone softened...slightly.

"You just told me you *know* everything is going to shit," he reminded her. "Something is *wrong* in the Protectorate, Keiko. Someone is stirring the pot. It could be the Families—God knows Julian Falcone didn't stay in jail very long!—or it could be some unknown factor or another crime syndicate.

"What we know right now is that Legatus offered the rebellion on Ardennes military hardware if they agreed to a vote on UnArcana World status after they took over," David explained. "We also know that even though they declined, most of the heavy gear that ended up in their hands was Legatan. We need to track it back, Keiko. We need to know if Legatus is trying to break up the Protectorate."

She was silent for a long time.

"Stealey's dead, huh?" she finally asked.

"Mage-Governor Vaughn poisoned her, apparently," he confirmed. "I can't lay that one on Legatus, but it does give a certain urgency to the matter."

"Even when the Legacy was after you with fleets, you never came to me for more than safe harbor," Keiko said quietly. "Why this? Why now?"

"Because I know Nathan Seule wouldn't want to be involved in somebody's scheme to tear apart humanity," he told her. "I *know* he'll help me if I ask him...but I can't find him. And I know no one other than you who can."

Keiko grabbed the next cocktail almost before David had finished making it, and stalked over to the hotel room window, looking out over Garnet's streets.

"You were never an easy one," she said quietly. "You're right. Seule wouldn't want to be used like that—I know *I* wouldn't. I wasn't involved in this particular chain, though, if you were wondering."

"I didn't think you were," David told her. "If nothing else, I'm pretty sure you don't have channels to acquire barely last-gen Legatan gear."

"No," she confirmed. "My heavy hardware is usually Tau Cetan...or, hell, Martian. Almost never Legatan, and it isn't new when it is." She shook her head. "That *stinks*, David."

"A lot. But we need more than a bad smell to allow us to move against a *Core World*," he told her. "So, I need to follow the chain back, and the first link I have is Nathan Seule."

"I don't know where he is," she admitted. "I have ways to get ahold of him, but I don't know where he is right now."

She was still looking away from him, studying the city beneath her.

"If Legatus is behind this, you realize what that means, right?" she asked.

"War."

The word hung in the air like a crashing anvil. Civil war, rebellion... secession was the *best* case, but if Legatus was already stirring the pot this much, they were expecting it to get violent. With the amount of blood David suspected they were responsible for, they were all but guaranteeing it would get violent.

"Do you want to be responsible for that?"

"I want to *know*," David said grimly. "That's the job I took, Keiko. To make sure that the guilty get caught and the innocent go free. If it *isn't* Legatus, someone is playing us all for fools—and if it is, I need hard proof to back up our stack of circumstances."

She turned away from the window and crossed to him so swiftly, he barely registered her moving before she'd wrapped her arms around him and buried her face in his shoulder.

"I don't have it in me to stand aside," he told her. "Neither do you."

"No," she agreed. She lifted her head to kiss him.

"I don't know where he is, but I can make arrangements for him to *be* somewhere," Keiko Alabaster concluded. "I'll make you haul a cargo for me to meet him, but you can call that fair trade for the information."

"More than," he confirmed. "I'm sorry to drag you into this, but I had nowhere else to turn."

"I know," she agreed. "And it needs to be done. But I'm not happy. That said, if you"—she touched his face gently—"think I'm mad enough to let you get out of this star system *without* sleeping with me, you have another think coming!"

CHAPTER 13

"OFFICER LAMONTE!"

The person shouting Kelly's name was a stranger to her, a tall, heavyset woman with shoulder-length blond hair and a black uniform.

"That would be me," she told her, ducking past a zero-gee cargo hauler with practiced ease and grabbing on to a handhold. "What can I help you with, Ms...."

"*Major* Angelika Turati," the officer introduced herself as she pulled herself to a halt next to Kelly. "I'm with the ADC, supervising the cargo off-load."

The bay Kelly was currently working in was on Heinlein Station but had been taken over by *Red Falcon*'s crew. Many of their secondary cargos were too small to fill even a single ten-thousand-ton container, so bays like this were designed to take two or three containers from a cargo ship and allow crews to open them up and divide their cargo.

They were on the third round of breaking out containers, and Kelly had rented enough bays to handle ten containers at a time. Another twenty units remained for them to get clear, but this was the most time-intensive part of off-loading.

"Last I checked, the last of your units came off our spars forty-six minutes ago," Kelly told Turati. "The tugs flashed the correct ID, which means you've got your cargo."

"That we do," Turati confirmed. "We've completed our initial scans and everything is in place." She offered a thin tablet over to Kelly. "If you can thumbprint here, we'll send over your payment."

Kelly felt some of the tension in her shoulders release. There'd been enough money in the penalty the ADC had tried to level on Ardennes that she'd worried that they'd try to play games.

"I have to admit, we didn't actually expect the cargo to arrive," Turati confessed as she reclaimed the tablet. "Yet here you are, a full day inside the deadline."

"Your people did threaten Ardennes with quite the penalty," Kelly pointed out.

The ADC officer chuckled.

"And we weren't really bluffing," she agreed. "We *were*, admittedly, expecting the Protectorate to intervene. Probably to negotiate a lesser penalty and then pay it on Ardennes's behalf. We didn't even know if they had a ship that could make the delivery."

"Lucky for everyone we happened to be there, then," *Falcon*'s XO told her. There wasn't much luck involved, not when MISS was moving the pieces. "Why does the ADC even need this much refined metal? Unless that's classified?"

Turati shrugged.

"We don't really *do* classified around here, Officer LaMonte," she admitted. "The ADC is expanding, and there's been a lot of arguments over whether we're going to build the ships here or buy them elsewhere. If nothing else, we're going to be upgrading our orbital defenses and building more in-system corvettes. It won't go to waste."

"Who do you expect to attack you here?" Kelly asked. It wasn't really an idle question. There were worse-defended systems than Amber in the Protectorate, though most MidWorlds were better secured. Part of Amber's defense was always the knowledge that it headquartered most of the Protectorate's legal and semi-legal mercenary forces.

"That's well over my head," the ADC Major admitted with a smile. "I know there's a lot of talk about anti-pirate convoys and patrols. I doubt anyone's worrying about *Amber*, per se, but it never hurts to be safe."

"That's true enough," Kelly agreed, turning to watch the massive crate containing a portable fusion power generator get carefully maneuvered out of the shipping container. Amber was more lightly defended than most systems with their wealth. She could see the temptation to a powerful pirate.

"You'd think the destruction of Darkport and the Blue Star would *reduce* piracy," she sighed.

Turati snorted.

"Who understands the criminal mind?" the Amberite asked. "I barely understand the rest of the Protectorate, let alone the kind of sick crew that decides to take up piracy."

Kelly had just completed her sweep of the four cargo bays handling the breakdown of *Red Falcon*'s cargo when her wrist-comp chimed with an incoming call. She hadn't heard from Captain Rice since he'd gone down to the planet the previous evening—she hadn't expected to, to be honest—but she wasn't surprised to see his name come up.

"LaMonte," she answered the call, drifting into a quiet corner of the zero-gee gravity bay. "How was your evening, boss?"

"Better than I was afraid of," he told her. "How are we on offloading?"

"All of the main cargo is done, and ADC has signed and paid for delivery," she replied. "We're two or three hours from being done with the breakouts, and we'll have the rest of the secondaries off the spars by then too.

"Refueling will be getting started once I'm back aboard. We had no problems sourcing antimatter, even if the price made me wince."

"It always does," her Captain replied. "So, we'll be able to start loading a new cargo in, say, six hours?"

"We could start in three," she suggested. "I'd rather have at least a few hours to cycle teams and let the crews rest, especially if we have any secondaries we need to assemble."

"Nothing like that," Rice told her. "One ten-million-ton cargo, proper containers. It'll be shifted over to us by tugs from one of the orbital depots. No secondaries, and we're not filing a flight plan with anyone."

Kelly winced. Amber was the only system in the Core or MidWorlds where they could even do that. They filed false flight plans a *lot,* and no one really checked up on them outside the Core unless someone came looking, but still. There was a reason for the requirement, after all.

"Do I want to know what we're hauling?" she asked carefully.

"One of Keiko's specials. Manifest will come by encrypted relay through her people," he told her. "Standard containers, thousand units. There's a time premium on this, but not enough of one to rush the loading.

"Six hours will be fine."

The manifest was eye-opening.

Kelly had heard the cargo they'd hauled for Keiko Alabaster before referred to as "a revolution in a box." She'd only been a junior engineer then, though, and hadn't seen the details.

This was ten times the size of that shipment and was more than a revolution in a box. It was an entire *state* in a box. A million rifles and suits of body armor. Twenty thousand tanks and an equal number of aircraft. Prefabricated maintenance depots for all of the gear. Communications arrays, satellites, mobile headquarters...

And that was just the blatantly military component. Two full ten-thousand-ton containers were just earthmoving equipment. Several more just...buildings. A grade of prefabricated structure Kelly hadn't encountered before. Everything from small offices to police stations to what looked like a government house, packed flat with "easy" assembly instructions.

"Impressive, isn't it?" Rice asked from the door of her office, and she looked up in surprise.

"When did you get back aboard?"

He made a show of checking the time on his wrist-comp. "Four minutes ago? I came straight here from the airlock. I figured you'd need the same explanation Keiko gave me."

"This isn't just guns, boss," she pointed out. "This is...the entire infrastructure of a government. Where are we even *going* with this?"

"Darius," Rice replied instantly. "It's an UnArcana Fringe World; *I* hadn't heard of it before Keiko and I started going over this cargo."

"The name's crossed my path, but I don't know much," Kelly admitted. She only really knew anything about the UnArcana worlds she'd actually visited. The Protectorate had just over a hundred star systems and she couldn't keep track of them all, let alone the class of worlds jump-ships often avoided.

"Nobody does, which is why they're having the problems they're having," her Captain said grimly. "They're under blockade by a private corporate fleet out of Legatus. They *had* a Legatan-provided defense force, but..." He sighed.

"Darius had an election a year ago, and a coalition of parties determined to end their UnArcana status took control of the government," he explained, clearly echoing and summarizing what he'd been told. "Portions of the prior government refused to recognize the transfer of power, and most of the defense force backed them.

"From what Keiko knows, it got ugly and their entire original space defense is just...gone," he concluded. "The attempted coup didn't die with the space fleet, unfortunately, and they got Stellarite Development Corps involved. SDC sent a fleet of jump-ships to blockade the system."

"So, the elected government is losing," Kelly said grimly.

"Most of the military forces on the planet wiped each other out in the first six months," he noted. "There's no one on the surface with the equipment for the mass manufacture of modern arms, and the government controls the only spaceport. The SDC can't land significant supplies for the rebels, but the government can't get anything past the blockade.

"Both sides have food, bullets, and bodies...but neither side has heavy weapons or combat vehicles sufficient to push the other out of their fortified positions."

"So, your girlfriend is actually backing the legitimate government for once," Kelly said.

"Darius is a mess, and the whole UnArcana versus open system layer to the conflict makes Protectorate interference...even messier," he admitted. "We're running this cargo to a rendezvous with Seule. His ship can dance circles around the corporate mercs in the system—especially if we provide a distraction."

Her Captain shook his head.

"It'd be a favor for a favor, in exchange for the help tracking back the cargo at Ardennes, and well...it sounds like the folks on Darius need a break."

Kelly nodded slowly.

"I'll pull what data we have on SDC," she promised. "We may be able to pull some tricks with their systems, depending on how good their gear is."

"We can't use MISS tricks for this," Rice warned. "Mars *cannot* be seen to be involved here."

She grinned at him.

"If they're corporate mercs, Captain, I won't *need* MISS's tricks."

CHAPTER 14

MARIA RAN through the numbers for the course one last time and leaned back in her office with a sigh. The AE-237 system was an empty hunk of space no one had ever bothered to name, without enough objects visible from the nearby systems to warrant anyone even sending a scout ship.

That meant there were no charts for where it was safe to jump into the system. She wasn't quite guessing on her last two jumps toward the lonely star, but the lightspeed delay meant that the data she was working with was years old.

She'd revise as they got closer and *Red Falcon* was able to get data that was, at least, only a year old. As trouble went, though, she'd take it. Especially compared to, say, having an ex-boyfriend aboard the ship who would turn out to be a traitor working for the people hunting Captain Rice.

Maria was alone in the office sanctum of the ship's Mages for the moment, having sent her subordinates off to enjoy Heinlein Station's amenities while she worked on the course to the system no one knew they were heading to.

There was a time she'd have joined them. Right now, she mostly just felt tired. The covert nature of their work now added to the already-mountainous difficulties of maintaining a relationship with someone off ship.

Her last non-disastrous relationship had been before she'd even left the Navy. Since then, they either hadn't qualified as relationships, had fallen apart quickly under the pressure of *Falcon*'s semi-random schedule or, well, been traitors who tried to kill everyone.

"Are you moping around again?" James Kellers's familiar voice echoed into her office, and she looked up in surprise.

"Chief," she greeted him. "My moping is supposed to be a private activity. What's up?"

"I'm hiding from my homeworld and waiting for a cargo of guns to be loaded up for an arguably illegal shipment," Kellers agreed cheerfully, his teeth flashing bright white against his dark skin. "You?"

"Plotting a course to a system that has no records whatsoever," she told him. "If anyone has been to this hole in space, they didn't *tell* anyone."

"And neither will we, as I understand it," the engineer agreed. "How's the moping?"

She snorted.

"Six months since I had a lover without batteries," Maria told him. "I don't think I'd *ever* gone that long without at least swinging through a dockside bar."

"Why haven't you?" Kellers asked softly. "It's not like Heinlein doesn't have a collection of those. Or even paid escorts with nondisclosure agreements, if you're feeling paranoid."

Maria laughed.

"I have no idea, honestly," she admitted. "Just hasn't been appealing. I must be getting old."

Kellers arched an eyebrow at her, the shaven-headed engineer eyeing her questioningly.

"You're a long way from old, Mage Soprano," he told her. "I've got what, six years on you?"

"Service ages us all," she replied. "First the Navy, now MISS. Who knows how much longer we can keep going?"

"I don't know," he admitted. "We do what we can, Mage Soprano."

She laughed at him.

"James, we've served on this ship together for two damn years," she told him. "You can call me Maria."

"Fair enough," Kellers allowed. "Now, I don't know much about brood-ing and moping, but my understanding is that you do speak Spanish?"

"Brazo-Portuguese, technically," she pointed out. "I can muddle through Spanish; why?"

"I *do* speak Spanish, and I happen to have come into possession of a copy of the original version of *Estrellas del Destino*," he told her. Maria blinked. That was a famous, almost century-old now, galactic love story movie about war-torn lovers and family on Earth and Mars during the Eugenicist Wars.

It was beyond a classic. It was a *legend*—and she'd only ever seen it in English, and critics claimed it lost something in the translation.

"Since you're the only other person on the ship who'd understand it...I wondered if you wanted to join me?"

Maria woke up with a start, realizing she'd fallen asleep at most half-way through the movie. She'd been enjoying it, but she'd apparently been much more tired than she thought. There was a warm weight on her lap, and she looked down to see the ship's big black cat curled up in her lap, on top of a blanket she didn't remember pulling over herself.

The movie was still on the wallscreen of the officer's lounge, but it was paused. She wasn't sure how long after she'd fallen asleep it had been paused, but...

"You're awake," Kellers said gently as he stepped around the couch. "I figured Joey was doing his furry best to keep you sleeping. How are you feeling?"

"Like I passed out in the middle of a damn good movie," she replied. "Didn't think I was that tired."

"I wasn't entirely surprised," the engineer admitted. "Thankfully, there were a couple of blankets in the closet when I realized you'd fallen asleep." He smiled down at the cat. "Joey showed up all on his own. I'm pretty sure he's supposed to be hunting mice somewhere, but I guess he smelled an available lap."

"So I see," she murmured, stretching carefully so she didn't disturb the cat. "And you, Mr. Kellers?"

He chuckled.

"I figured I'd keep an eye on you," he told her. "The ship's not busy and neither am I, but I figured it didn't cost me anything to have a quiet bite to eat while making sure you slept."

Maria snorted. She'd known more than a few men who would have taken at least some advantage of the situation, even if they had been watching the movie together as friends. That wasn't a trick that tended to end well, but that didn't seem to get through to the male brain sometimes.

"Want to finish watching the movie?" she asked. "I don't think Joey is going to let me move, but there's room under this blanket for one more."

The blanket wasn't *that* large. Two people could fit under it, but only by getting very friendly.

Maria gave Kellers a warm smile just in case he didn't get what she was suggesting...and was rewarded with what was most definitely a blush.

"My dear James, I'm not entirely familiar with your coloring, but are you *blushing?*" she teased him.

"You, Maria, are trouble," he pointed out.

"I'm not threatening you," Maria replied. "Just offering to cuddle and watch a movie. Think you can manage that?"

The engineer shook his head but slipped under the blanket. His leg was warm against hers as he scratched Joey's ears—and Maria leant against his shoulder with a soft exhalation.

It might not lead to more, but it was nice to just cuddle and watch a movie.

CHAPTER 15

"TWELVE HOURS TO JUMP," Maria told Rice as she studied the screens in the simulacrum chamber. "Are we expecting any trouble on the way to the back end of nowhere?"

He chuckled.

"I have learned to *always* expect trouble, Maria," the Captain replied. "We seem to be a magnet for it, even if things have been quieter of late."

"Don't jinx us, David," she said with a shake of her head. "Everything at least *looks* quiet. I can hold down the watch while you go sleep."

Rice yawned, then flushed.

"I didn't get much sleep while we were on Amber," he admitted ruefully. "Wake me up if anything happens."

"Can do," she promised. "I have the watch."

Rice closed down his system, transferring command authority to the simulacrum chamber. Maria took a moment to skim over the sensors, flagging the larger ships in the system. The ADC's pair of destroyers hung in their orbits, the pyramid-shaped starships seemingly quiet as they kept an eye on the entire star system.

Three more ships flagged her interest as she went over the data and she pinged Jeeves.

"Alex, when did the Navy show up?" she asked. "I don't remember them being in-system."

"They made orbit as we were leaving, on the opposite side of Amber," the gunnery officer told her. "Regional patrol. They're probably checking in on the Amber shipyards to see if anyone is building pirate ships."

From what Rice had said, that was unlikely. It took a lot to get the Cooperatives to crack down on something, but the number of pirate ships that had come from Amber had finally crossed that difficult-to-assess line.

"Let's keep an eye on them," she ordered. "We're all on the same side...but we're currently hauling a *lot* of guns, and while the customer is a planetary government..."

"Somehow, I'm sure Ms. Alabaster didn't worry about getting the paperwork fully filed," Jeeves agreed. "I can buy access to the ADC's sensors for a closer watch on them. Should I?"

Maria hesitated. That access was available here but still wasn't cheap—not least because the ADC sold it in weeklong chunks and they were only going to be in-system for half a day.

"No," she decided. "Our sensors are damn good. We'll keep our own eye on them and try not to cause trouble."

"Wilco," he said. "Keep an eye on our big brothers and make a nice, quiet run for the outer system."

They were already burning at three gravities, the maximum for most merchant ships. *Red Falcon* could go up to ten, the same safe acceleration as the destroyers, thanks to the artificial gravity runes Maria and her people maintained.

She *could* go faster, but it would almost certainly draw attention.

"Nice and quiet," she agreed. "With a *very* sharp eye on the Navy."

After about an hour, Maria was starting to think that she was being excessively paranoid...and then the sensors flashed to life with a nearby jump flare.

"Jeeves, what have we got?" she demanded as she started to collate numbers.

"Looks like...trouble," he said grimly. "There was apparently a fourth destroyer in the outer system, and she just jumped in front of us. Her engines are live...yep, that's an intercept course. She'll match velocities and rendezvous with us in just over two hours."

Nine hours before she'd been planning on jumping.

"Let the skipper sleep," she ordered. "They're still two hours away. Let me know the instant they make contact—I can't see them shooting at us, but..."

"Understood," Jeeves replied. "Do we accelerate?"

"Not yet," Maria told him. With both LaMonte and Rice asleep during what was supposed to be a quiet trip out-system, she wasn't even sure who was at the navigation console. There should be *someone* there, even with them flying a preprogrammed course, but they'd be pretty far down the list of people qualified to fly the multi-megaton freighter.

"Linking transmission to your screen," a coms tech of a similar grade reported.

A tanned-looking young man in the black uniform of a Martian Mage-Commander appeared on Maria's screen, looking levelly at the camera.

"*Red Falcon*, this is Mage-Commander Sans Abel of *Fierce Tide of Glory*," he introduced himself politely. "There doesn't appear to be a course plot on file for you. You are a rather large and heavily armed vessel; I'm afraid I must ask you to confirm your destination, please."

Maria muttered a series of curses under her breath in Portuguese. Amber didn't require a course filing, but the Navy had the authority to ask for it. Especially if they had any grounds for suspicion.

"Regardless of your course, however, I am also asking you to heave to and prepare for cargo inspection under Section 36 of the Protectorate Charter," he continued. "I have grounds to believe that you are carrying a shipment of unregistered arms, and while *Amber*'s rules may be lax, if you are shipping between systems you fall under the authority of Section 36."

Mage-Commander Abel smiled sadly.

"The nature and presence of your ship tell me that you are well thought-of by the Protectorate, so this is an unfortunate accusation to be leveled against you. Since I am sure it is in error, the easiest way to make sure everyone gets through this with the minimum delay, I suggest you cease acceleration and allow my vessel to match course.

"A simple survey by my Marines should establish the truth of the matter. I look forward to your response."

The recording stopped and Maria swore again.

"Mage Soprano?" Jeeves asked.

"Wake up the Captain."

By the time Rice had returned to the bridge, *Falcon*'s continued progress toward the destroyer was clearly beginning to make the Navy nervous.

"They've begun adding small evasive maneuvers," Jeeves reported. "They're subtle, but they're layering in some low-key ECM. Enough that we probably wouldn't be able to hit them with lasers if we decided to be stupid."

"Well, that's not happening," the Captain said. "Maria, what are you thinking?"

The Mage shrugged.

"A Section 36 interception like this is usually pretty sharp," she told him. "Abel is playing softball so far because he figures anyone flying an ex-Navy ship like this is unlikely to be carrying illegal arms—but he's following procedure perfectly. He has us boxed in."

"Can we jump before he intercepts?" Rice asked.

"With our current courses? No," Maria replied. "With our full acceleration, we should be able to break for the outer system on a course he can't intercept before we jump, but evading a Section 36 intercept...well, it'll get us flagged in every Navy database."

"I'm relatively sure our MISS friends can stop that happening," the Captain said. He was studying the screen with discontent eyes. "He's *in* frigging missile range. What happens when he stops playing softball?"

"If we continue to ignore him, we'll get one more summons to surrender with him *not* being nice," the ex-Navy officer laid out. "Then he'll launch boarding shuttles as he closes. If we do anything remotely threatening or change course, he'll fire a warning shot."

"And if we actually attempt to engage..."

"He'll throw the kitchen sink at us," Maria said flatly. "He'll attempt to disable us with missiles and lasers as he closes to amplifier range. If we manage to make him feel *threatened*, he will blow us to hell instead of disabling.

"Section 36 interceptions go bad a lot."

"What about our MISS identification codes?" Rice asked.

"Do you want to flash them to the entire star system?" she said. "We'd need to be closer to tag them with a tightbeam, and once they're that close..."

"Them breaking off will flag to everyone in the system that something isn't right," Rice agreed.

"New incoming message," the tech interrupted them again.

Abel appeared on the screen once more, and his sad smile had been replaced by a far grimmer countenance.

"*Red Falcon*, this is Mage-Commander Sans Abel of *Fierce Tide of Glory*," he repeated. "We have been advised that you are carrying illegal armaments in violation of Section 36 of the Protectorate Charter. Under the authority granted to the Royal Martian Navy under that Section, I am ordering you to cease acceleration and prepared to be boarded.

"Any attempt to evade or target *Fierce Tide of Glory* will be regarded as a hostile act and responded to with all due force at my command. You are ordered to stand down."

The recording stopped and David Rice smiled wryly.

"Maria?"

"We could always let them board and *then* give them the MISS codes?" she suggested.

"Except it seems half the system knows we're carrying guns. What's plan B?"

A thought hit Maria and she smiled wickedly.

"Well, now that you mention it..."

Red Falcon ran. They flipped in space and burned for a zone they could jump in at ten gravities.

A careful eye could run the math and realize they hadn't picked the best course. That their new course wouldn't fully evade the Navy destroyer—but there were no courses where they really could.

If the course they were on wasn't quite intended to do that, well, that was between Maria Soprano and David Rice. And, shortly, Mage-Commander Sans Abel, whose response to their attempt to flee was exactly what Maria had predicted.

He hadn't fired yet. Hadn't launched missiles or assault shuttles—but *Fierce Tide of Glory* was now pushing twelve gravities and closing with *Red Falcon* at a blistering pace. That was enough on its own to make a statement.

"Time to five million kilometers?" Maria asked quietly.

"Just over ten minutes," Jeeves replied instantly. "If I'm reading this data right, we won't be able to jump for at least two hours after that."

"Everybody knows that," she agreed. Five million kilometers was generally regarded as the effective range of combat lasers. It was also, unfortunately, roughly the range at which laser or tightbeam communication could be carried out without anyone else knowing.

"What happens if he opens fire once he's in laser range?" Rice asked.

"He won't," Maria assured him. "So long as we just try and run and he *can* bring us to amplifier range, he will hold off on engaging until he can use magic to hold us in place."

Unspoken was that Mage-Commander Abel was overloading his ship's engines. Presumably if he was comfortable running *Fierce Tide* at twenty percent over her designed maximum, he had faith in his engineers—but that kind of faith had a bad habit of being misplaced at the wrong time.

Minutes ticked away and Maria watched the targeting system for the laser coms.

"See if you can link us in," she ordered. This was actually risky. They couldn't risk transmitting their MISS authentication codes until they were certain no one else could receive the message—but the test pulse to confirm that could easily be read as a *weapon* targeting system.

"No joy," Jeeves replied. "At least I don't think we pinged her... Never mind."

An array of red warning lights flickered across the screens as *Fierce Tide of Glory* locked *Red Falcon* up in her sensors. They'd clearly pinged the destroyer's threat-detection systems—and Abel was returning the favor.

"Try again," Maria said urgently, sharing a strained glance with Rice. *Falcon* could defeat a salvo of missiles from the destroyer at range, but she couldn't survive a laser fusillade or the Mage-Commander unleashing his amplified magic.

"Hold on...hold on. Positive pulse!" Jeeves reported. "We have communications lock and... Huh?"

"Guns?" Rice demanded.

"Someone over there realized we were being clever buggers," the gunnery officer replied. "I have a com system interrogation pulse from *their* laser system."

"All right, put Maria on," Rice ordered.

Maria swallowed hard and faced the camera.

"Mage-Commander Abel, I apologize for our maneuvers and deception," she said quickly. "*Red Falcon* is an MISS covert operations ship, designation KEX-12. We *are* carrying illegal arms as part of a deep-cover operation and we need you to help maintain our cover.

"I am Ship's Mage Maria Soprano, former Navy Mage-Commander, current MISS Agent level six. Authentication codes are attached."

She paused, tapping a command to load a file onto the transmission, then hit Send.

"Captain, keep us at five million kilometers," she asked. "Let's see if we can make this look good."

It took almost twenty seconds for their message to reach *Fierce Tide of Glory*. Maria's experience suggested it would take under thirty for the

Navy crew to validate their codes, and another ten for their response to be decided.

Every second after about the first minute and a half was torture. Rice was playing the angles to keep the range open, twisting his vector in space to buy them seconds more as the destroyer continued to close.

There was no response...but the destroyer also hadn't opened fire or launched shuttles. They were now close enough that Maria would have been doing one of those in such an odd intercept.

"Incoming transmission!"

"Agent Soprano," Abel greeted her from the recording. He looked... unimpressed. "Your codes check out, but I must protest. Any violation of Section 36, even under the auspices of MISS operations, risks the security and stability of the Protectorate. I don't know what game you are playing, but it puts lives and systems at risk."

He inhaled sharply.

"Your authentication codes give me no option but to cooperate," Abel admitted. "I won't blow your cover, Agent, which means we're already in an interesting position if we are to avoid suspicion. We should have been advised of your mission in advance."

Maria snorted. She'd *been* Navy and she couldn't agree with that idea. Everyone would have been better off if someone—probably one of Alabaster's rivals, she figured—hadn't tipped the Navy off to their cargo.

"I had to check with my engineer to confirm we could do this safely, but *Fierce Tide* is about to suffer a critical engine failure." He raised a hand. "Do me a favor, Agent Soprano. For the service you shared with me...don't screw this up, okay?"

The transmission ended.

"Captain?" she asked.

"Honestly? If he hadn't told me they were faking it, we'd turn back at the first sign of a major engineering casualty," Rice replied, his voice gentle. "We have the codes to get ourselves clear, and I'd take *those* problems over letting them drift in space."

"I appreciate that," Maria replied. "When their engines go down, flip to line up with the nearest jump-clear zone and burn hard."

"Will it be that obvious?" Jeeves asked.

Both Maria and Rice looked at him for several seconds.

"He's about to fake a critical engine failure on an antimatter rocket," Rice pointed out. "Even if they do everything right, that's going to be—"

A brilliant flash of white light blazed across their sensors like a newborn sun.

"Please tell me they're still here," the Captain said grimly, his hands already flying across his console.

"They're still here," Maria confirmed instantly, her own access to the sensors sufficient for that. "Mmm. Mage-Commander Abel may dislike spies, but it looks like his engineer would make a good one. They rotated the ship so no one except us could see what they did, and then ejected an entire engine assembly.

"It'll look bad even when they limp into Amber orbit for repairs, but they should be fine."

"And us?" Jeeves asked.

"Jump in two hours, fifteen minutes," Maria confirmed. "We're flashing our ass to the entire star system...so everyone knows we ran from the law."

"Hopefully, it was worth it," Rice agreed. "Because while that rep is going to help, I'm more than a bit concerned about how the Navy is going to feel about it."

CHAPTER 16

IN DAVID'S OPINION, Maria Soprano was solidly the second-best Jump Mage he'd ever commanded. Given that his best had transformed a jump matrix into a combat amplifier and turned out to be some strange kind of super-Mage, that was a pretty high recommendation.

She jumped them into the AE-237 System with precision and calm, even though David knew that they didn't have anything resembling detailed charts of the system.

"We're in," she announced. "No problems."

"Well done," David told her. "Guns? Sweep the system, every sensor we've got. Let's see if we can dial in enough of the junk while we're here to make our next trip safer."

"We can hope there's never another trip, right?" LaMonte asked from the navigation console. "This place is going to be a nightmare to navigate, and there's *nothing* here worth making the attempt."

AE-237 was a brown dwarf about ten million years post the supernova of its distant binary partner. Any planets or significant asteroids had been consumed in the supernova, leaving behind radiation fields that made sensors unreliable and debris patterns that made flying in a straight line hazardous.

There was nothing big enough to make a decent anchor for a mining operation—and any such operation would have looked more like a giant vacuum than a drill. There was little in the debris that was left to be worth visiting the star system, too. Mostly ice and other material that had vaporized and been flung outward by the supernova, only to be caught by AE-237's gravity field and coalesce into new debris as the nova dispersed.

David's understanding suggested that there should be *some* exotic materials and such in the debris fields, but no one was willing to go through ten million tons of ice and carbon to find fifty grams of uranium. Not when they had to travel to a different star system to do it.

"Well, somewhere out there is our rendezvous and our mission," he reminded his staff. "Keep an eye out for other ships, Jeeves. *Luciole* is supposed to be here somewhere, but that doesn't mean there isn't anyone else."

"Why the *hell* would there be anyone else here?" LaMonte asked.

"Well, not least because we are," David told her. "And someone already sold us out to the Navy. Plus, anyone here saw our jump flare."

"Right," she conceded. "I'll set up some first-pass analysis on the sensor data, see if I can at least try and narrow down where ships aren't."

"I'd like to pick up *Luciole* before we start spamming the recognition signal," he continued. "I know Seule is a sneaky bugger, so we may have to start transmitting blindly, but I'd rather avoid it if we can."

Half an hour later, David was beginning to sympathize with whoever had decided that AE-237 wasn't worth visiting. Where they could manage to penetrate the radiation fog, all they could see was debris. The entire system was just...soup.

"Well, the good news is that I can point out a whole half of the system where there *aren't* starships," LaMonte said drily. "The bad news is that only leaves, oh, a five-AU-radius sphere in which someone could have hidden a fleet. Or six."

"I don't suppose anyone is transmitting 'hello, world' out of that storm?" he asked.

"Nothing," his XO replied. "We can pulse the entire segment, though it will be hours until we get a response if *Luciole* is on the other side of the system."

David sighed.

"We were given slightly more detail than 'the AE-237 System,'" he pointed out. "He should be somewhere in this quadrant. Send the recognition code."

A radio transmission powerful enough to reach ten astronomical units—eighty-three light-minutes, give or take—would melt the paint on anything close to *Red Falcon*. The ex-Navy ship had the transmitters to send it, but they were going to be a beacon for the entire star system.

"Then take us to battle stations," David ordered after a moment's thought. "Get the full defensive suite up and load the launchers. This system makes me itch."

Alerts began to ring through the freighter's hull, and sections began to light up in different colors on the repeater screens on David's command chair. The Rapid-Fire Laser Anti-Missile turrets were almost entirely automated and came online first. Then the capacitors for the battle lasers started flashing yellow as the crews arrived and began charging their weapons.

Red Falcon wasn't a warship—there were emergency options built into her to dump her cargo and turn her *into* a pocket warship, but those weren't reversable. Nonetheless, she was a covert ops ship, and her crew drilled on her weapons and defenses regularly.

The three and a half minutes it took to get the ship to battle stations wouldn't have pleased the captains of the Navy ships David had served on—but it wouldn't have embarrassed them, either.

"Any response yet?" he asked LaMonte.

"Not yet."

"Jeeves?" David continued.

"We've gone fully active on the sensors," the other ex-Navy man replied. "There is nothing within three million kilometers of us. Ninety-five percent certain we're clear to six million kilometers. Eighty percent certain to twelve."

Jeeves paused.

"All launchers are loaded; all lasers are fully charged. Anyone who decides our message is an invitation to jump us is going to have an ugly surprise waiting."

"Response code!" LaMonte interrupted. "And I have a fix. We have *Luciole*'s recognition signal at four light-minutes." She shook her head. "Jeeves, I'm not getting a clear read on her. What do you see?"

"Looks like he's hiding in one of the denser debris clouds. We can maneuver to intercept, but—"

"Four light-minutes is a *long* way," Soprano interrupted. "Xi Wu is up and Nguyen is fully rested. We can jump to *Luciole*, or at least jump much closer to her, and still be ready to jump clear of the system if something overwhelming happens."

"XO?" David asked.

LaMonte shrugged.

"Fifteen hours if we fly it. Ten and a half if *Luciole* comes to meet us and also pulls ten gees. If we can jump it, it'll save us all a lot of headache."

"I agree," David said. "Maintain battle stations. Ship's Mage—you may jump us whenever you're ready."

There was the always indescribable moment of discomfort as reality tore and *Red Falcon* was suddenly there instead of here. The screens updated around David, sensors and computers rapidly collating data to confirm where the armed freighter was now.

"Confirmed, *Luciole* is now two million kilometers away," Jeeves reported. "Establishing direct tightbeam link."

Two million kilometers was still a thirteen-second two-way communication delay, but you could only get so much accuracy out of an in-system jump. David's people had just moved his ship seventy-plus million kilometers in the blink of an eye.

He wasn't complaining.

"*Luciole*, this is Captain David Rice aboard *Red Falcon*. We have a few crates full of presents for you and your client."

David waited. A video link opened thirteen seconds later, and the familiar dark-haired, grinning visage of Nathan Seule appeared on his screen. The last few years had aged the smuggler, but his hair was still black and his skin was still tanned.

"Captain Rice, it's been a long time! Last time we met, I was the only one rich enough to burn antimatter. I see the years have been kinder to you than we would have guessed back then."

David returned the grin and inclined his head.

"It's good to see that you escaped the consequences of helping us, Captain Seule," he told the smuggler. "Is this channel secure?"

Seconds ticked away, but David could tell when Seule received his question, as the other man checked his own consoles.

Both of them were running camera feeds focused specifically on them. Seule couldn't see *Red Falcon*'s bridge and David couldn't see *Luciole*'s. It was a minor security measure, probably pointless at this juncture, but the habit served them well.

"Looks like we've both got each other locked up with nice, tight beams," Seule finally confirmed. "I'm not seeing any leakage, which means we can be pretty frank. I've got an update on the blockade at Darius and it doesn't look pretty. I'm wondering if I can impose on you for a favor."

"I've a favor I need to ask you as well," David admitted. "But there's limits on what I can do, Captain. *Red Falcon* may be better armed than most corporate merc ships, but I'm not picking a fight for the Darian government."

Thirteen seconds later, Seule laughed.

"I wouldn't expect you to. We'll discuss once we've made rendezvous. May I invite you and your new Ship's Mage to join me for dinner aboard *Luciole*? Our fixtures and meals may not be up to Navy standards anymore, but I think you'll be pleasantly surprised."

Like *Red Falcon*, *Luciole* had been born as a Navy auxiliary. She'd been a smaller version of the AAFHF program, a Rapid Deployment Collier. Several of her sisters still served in the Navy, unlike *Falcon*'s, but the RDCs had also proven extremely effective as blockade runners.

Luciole had been in Seule's hands for far longer than *Falcon* had been in David's. He doubted much of the ship's interior still resembled her Navy days.

Nonetheless, his curiosity was piqued—and he needed to ask some questions of Seule that it was better no one else knew about.

"Mage Soprano and I would be delighted, Captain Seule."

CHAPTER 17

KELLY COULDN'T HELP but feel ambivalent as the shuttle carrying her boyfriend and her bosses took off for the much-smaller ship drifting a few dozen kilometers from *Red Falcon*'s bow. On the one hand, AE-237 was as dead and abandoned as anywhere in space. On the other, it was also one of the messiest places she'd ever had the misfortune of trying to find anything in—and with Rice and Soprano aboard *Luciole*, Kelly LaMonte was in command of *Red Falcon*.

"Let's take the ship down to Alert Bravo," she told Jeeves after the shuttle was clear. "Battle stations doesn't seem necessary, but I don't want to stand everyone down just yet."

Alert Bravo held a minimum crew on the weapon mounts and kept the capacitors and launchers loaded. It would cycle one-third of the crew through rest breaks at a time, while keeping the rest ready to get into a fight.

Even a Navy crew couldn't sustain Alert Bravo forever, and for all of their secrets and tricks, most of *Red Falcon*'s crew remained fundamentally civilian.

"Got that itch between your shoulder blades too, huh?" the gunnery officer asked as he tapped commands to change the alert codes on the system. "Captain's running off for tea, and we're drifting out here with our ass bare naked to the stellar breeze."

"I think the Captain is feeling it too," Kelly told him. "Otherwise, we'd already be transferring cargo."

Luciole could only handle a tenth of *Red Falcon*'s current cargo, a twentieth of the big ship's full capacity. With the two vessels' combined shuttle fleets, they could load her in a few hours. They'd have to decide what to do with the *other* nine million tons of cargo.

Kelly's assumption was that they were dropping it in a stable orbit somewhere for *Luciole* to finish the job, but that was up to the Captain. She'd recommend against leaving it *here*, but they could make a couple of jumps towards Darius and leave the cargo a light-year or two away from its final destination.

"Do you see that chunk of fog?" she asked Jeeves as she studied her screens. A chunk of even denser radioactive debris was about seven million kilometers away but drifting directly toward them.

"Yeah," he confirmed. "Can I say, XO, that I fucking *hate* this star system?"

She chuckled.

"I agree completely. That cloud is moving fast. Can we pulse it directly?" she asked.

"Too far away to get anything really useful from it," Jeeves admitted. "Strange that *Luciole*'s crew didn't mention it; you'd think it was a local hazard."

"Not really," Kelly said. "Eight million kilometers is a *long* way. It's moving fast for a rad cloud, but it's still hours away. We'll be done before it's a problem. Assuming it isn't hiding something."

"I could drop a missile into it from here," the older man offered. "Straight kinetic shouldn't do much to the cloud, but we've got some nukes. Even some of the Navy's big anti-missile MIV swarms."

The Multiple Independent Vehicle system was a countermeasure the Royal Martian Navy had developed for its ships that didn't carry heavy RFLAM armaments—ships like *Luciole*. It launched in a standard missile but had *far* less fuel.

Instead, it blew apart relatively quickly after launch, spreading out a wall of nuclear submunitions that detonated on proximity. They were designed to wipe out entire missile salvos.

"We have, what, six of those?" she asked. "Let's not waste them on an itch. It's not like they'd get there in less than an hour, either."

Kelly studied the approaching radioactive cloud and then looked at the rest of the system. It wasn't unusual, but it was the closest to them and moving directly their way. It was natural enough, she was sure...but it was still suspicious.

"Pulse it with our full sensor suite," she ordered. "We may not get anything...but if someone is using it as a screen, we can spook 'em."

"And if we do?" Jeeves asked quietly.

"This is the back end of nowhere, Guns. If they don't back off when we tell them to, we do whatever it takes to defend ourselves and our business partner."

They'd worked together before, but David had never set foot aboard Seule's ship. Even his pilots hadn't, as they'd simply hauled cargo containers over to the blockade runner.

He wasn't expecting it to be a horror show, but he was still somewhat surprised to exit his shuttle into an operating flight bay with artificial gravity. Silver runes glittered over the floor and the air smelled fresh and clean, despite the fact that a shuttle just landed.

Nathan Seule was shorter in person than he'd expected, but the smuggler was right there, offering his hand as David and Soprano left their shuttle.

"Welcome aboard *Luciole*, Captain Rice, Mage Soprano. May I introduce Les Camber, my senior Ship's Mage?"

Les Camber was a gauntly pale man who towered over everyone in the room, his golden medallion a sign of his authority even as he bestowed a faint smile on everyone.

"Technically, Captain Seule is the senior Ship's Mage himself," Camber noted in a hoarse voice. "I simply administer our juniors while he runs the ship."

David turned his attention back to Seule. The smuggler wasn't wearing the medallion that marked a Mage, but that didn't mean much.

Tradition and habit were one thing; survival in a world where some systems banned Mages was another.

"Mage Camber gives himself too little credit," Seule said promptly. "Yes, I am a Mage, but I've never been an overly *good* one. I can jump a ship, that's all. No point advertising that fact, eh, Captain Rice?"

And yet somehow Rice was very sure that Camber wouldn't have dropped that tidbit without his Captain's permission. Seule was playing a dangerous game here, testing to see just how far he could trust David and his crew.

"You have multiple Mages aboard?" he asked instead. "I find most merchant ships underestimate the advantages of that."

"I don't think it's so much they underestimate the advantages as they balk at the cost," Camber replied. "I have two junior Ship's Mages who report to me, which allows us to move between systems as swiftly as we can move within them."

"An advantage I'm sure you've realized yourself," Seule concluded. "Come with me. We can save conversation for while we're eating, in privacy."

David nodded to himself and shared a knowing glance with Soprano.

He doubted his Mage was any more sure of what game Seule was playing than he was...but they were both *very* sure he was playing a longer game than he was admitting.

As Seule led them deeper into the ship, David noted just how much the interior of the ship had been redone since *Luciole* had left Martian service. The gravity runes were standard in the RMN—but the thickly padded carpet *Luciole*'s runes were embedded in was not.

The faint whirring of a cleaning robot following them down the hallway explained how Seule and his people kept the ship clean.

The other thing David noticed was the complete lack of crew other than Seule and Camber.

"Your crew seems notably absent," he murmured to the other Captain.

"I'm trusting you a lot," Seule pointed out. "We both have reasons to be having this conversation, Captain Rice, but I'm not going to put my crew at risk. *Vous comprenez, je l'espère?*"

David was reasonably sure he followed the smuggler's comment and nodded his understanding. He was wondering how much Seule knew of his own activities.

Their journey ended quickly enough, with the Captain leading them into a small private dining room. The walls had been covered in a hand-painted mural and a couple of quality sideboards had been added, but the table was an original installation, classic Navy light-and-solid plastic.

"Have a seat, Captain Rice," Seule said with a wave of his hand. As they obeyed, he opened up one of the sideboards and revealed a series of covered plates inside a concealed warmer. He and Camber served them quickly.

The plates uncovered to reveal a simple stir-fried dish of rice, vat protein, and vegetables. It smelled surprisingly good, and David inhaled as he studied Seule.

"Okay, so just *what* are you trying to bribe me for, Captain?" he asked bluntly.

Seule laughed.

"If I was trying to *bribe* you, Captain, I'd have come with something better than teriyaki vat protein! Consider this...relationship-building."

"Last time we met, you saved my ship and crew from a Hunter," David reminded Seule. "You can consider the relationship built. I owe you, Nathan Seule, even if there's only so far that can stretch."

"Fair enough," Seule conceded with a wave of his hand. "Have you ever been to Darius, Captain Rice?"

"I've only been to four UnArcana Worlds in my entire life," David replied. "Darius wasn't one of them."

"I've been through a few times, on legitimate and less-legitimate business," the smuggler told him. "They're good people. Their Fringe and UnArcana World status makes people underestimate them, but their universities and research campuses could rival most MidWorlds, let alone the Fringe. They're self-sufficient in general, and their plan for the last century has been to leverage home-built technology to get ahead."

David listened carefully as he began to eat. The food was good, despite Seule's dismissiveness.

"That process has led them to be a bunch more individualistic than a lot of places," he continued. "Not quite to, say, Amber's scale, but they're pretty damn live-and-let-live—and that attitude collided head-on with the Mage ban.

"They've been quietly arguing over it in their various political forums for years, but then, well, I'm guessing you were briefed on the current situation?"

"The new government is trying to lift the ban?" Soprano asked.

"Exactly. Unfortunately, the old government tried to deny the election results. Half of the military went with them, half joined the new government." Seule shook his head. "It's a mess, and Stellarite Development Corps has shoved their spoon in deep."

"Where's Mars in all of this?" David said. He knew the answer, but he wondered what Seule thought it was. The man made his living dealing with the problems Mars missed, after all.

"My guess is that they know, roughly, what's going on," the smuggler replied. "But the whole factor of Darius's UnArcana World status being in question means they can't get too involved." He shrugged. "I wouldn't be surprised to find out that the bankers that lent the Darian government the funds to buy our cargos were quietly underwritten by Mars."

David wasn't so sure, though it wouldn't have surprised him. There were a lot of secret ships moving in the night in the Martian apparatus, and they didn't always cross each others' paths even when they should.

"So, everyone's involvement is at arm's length, huh?" David asked.

"Well, SDC is pretty up in the middle of it. The old government has to have promised them some pretty significant incentives for them to have involved themselves this deeply," Seule replied.

"Or someone else did," Soprano suggested. "Like the other UnArcana Worlds?"

"SDC is Legatus-headquartered," their host said. "I wouldn't care to assume the Legatan government *isn't* involved, but you're not going to find any evidence anywhere off of Legatus."

"No, you won't," David agreed. "So, you like the locals and they're worth the effort, I get that...but where does that bring us into this?"

Seule nodded and studied his drink for several seconds.

"We scouted Darius before coming here," he said quietly. "We dramatically underestimated just what SDC was prepared to commit to this operation. I was expecting a blockade of maybe half a dozen jump-corvettes, nothing we couldn't handle.

"Instead, the Stellarites showed up with ten half-megaton ships of a class I've never seen before, and over *two* dozen jump-corvettes," Seule explained. "With a pair of *Venice*-class ships like your old *Blue Jay* for logistics."

David leaned back, swallowing his surprise. That was a lot of firepower for a development corporation to even own, let alone deploy on a single op. He could see Seule's problem.

"You can't outmaneuver that many ships," he said aloud.

"Not a chance. I can dodge and out-dance any individual ship in that flotilla—and *merde*, *Luciole* probably outguns half the corvettes combined, but I can't run a blockade of over thirty ships. Not without a distraction."

"You want us to be your distraction," Soprano said. "That's a big ask. David?"

"I'm not sure that it's worth it for us," David agreed.

"You're not here for money, Captain Rice," Seule said quietly. "I don't know why you took this contract, but you sliding back into smuggling makes no sense to me. Not without an ulterior motive."

"You fly an antimatter-drive ship," David argued carefully. "You know what my operating costs look like, at least in terms of magnitude."

"Yes," the smuggler agreed. "But I can't haul twenty million tons of cargo in half of the time anyone else can. There's only so much demand for a fast packet hauling a million tons when there's three megaton ships that will haul it for cheaper if not as quickly. But you can run half-empty and still make a profit because you turn your cargos so quickly.

"So, I have to think there's something else at play, especially seeing you end up here. I'm guessing you need data, Captain Rice, and I won't ask why or for whom...but I won't sell out my contacts without a reason. Without a price that no one else is in a position to pay."

Nathan Seule, David reflected, was too damned smart for anybody's good. He was still considering his response when an alert signal klaxoned through the room, and Seule grabbed for his wrist-comp.

"Nathan," he answered briskly. "What's happening?"

"SDC is here," an unfamiliar female voice barked. "And they brought a friend I don't recognize."

"Oh, fuck us."

Jeeves's epithet echoed around the bridge as Kelly swallowed her own curse.

Their radar pulse hadn't picked up anything, and for several minutes all had seemed quiet. Then Jeeves had sent a second pulse, "just in case."

Apparently, whoever was in command had decided that meant *Red Falcon* had detected her—or at least was going to detect her if she stayed in hiding. Now the radioactive fog cloud was disgorging a small squadron of ships accelerating toward *Falcon* and *Luciole* at five gravities.

"I take it you also recognize the big one?" Kelly asked the gunnery officer.

"Yeah."

Five ships had emerged from the fog, four of much the same size and a fifth, bigger one, hanging back behind the others.

"Big one is a Golden Bear monitor," Jeeves confirmed. "Seven hundred thousand tons, eight missile launchers, one giant laser gun—unless they've upgraded since the *last* time we tangled with them and handed them their asses."

"And the smaller ones?" Kelly asked.

"Corporate security ships, heavy jump-corvettes," he said. "That's just a guess, though at five hundred k-tons, they're bigger than most CorpSec goes for." Jeeves shook his head. "The Bears had antimatter birds last time we fought them, though given the trick you pulled, they might hesitate to fire them at us."

The Golden Bears mercenary company had come after *Red Falcon* for the Azure Legacy before that organization had ceased to exist. Their survivors were among the few people who'd fought *Falcon* and lived, not least because their fleet had outgunned the covert ops ship badly.

Kelly had used a secret MISS override code to turn their missiles against them. She doubted it would work on the Bears again, but it still might make them blink before firing the more-advanced missiles at the armed freighter.

"What are the odds that the CorpSec ships have AM birds?" she asked quietly.

"Zero, give or take," Jeeves replied. "Almost certainly good fusion birds, though, and at their velocity...they're almost in range for those."

"And so are we," Kelly said grimly. *Falcon* carried antimatter-drive missiles, but Kelly wasn't going to use those without Captain Rice's orders. Their Rapier IV fusion-drive missiles had seven minutes of four thousand gravities of acceleration, much the same as she assumed the corporate security ships were carrying.

"What do we do, XO?" the gunnery officer asked, and Kelly inhaled sharply.

Rice was aboard *Luciole*. Unless he got orders to her—even *if* he got orders to her—Kelly LaMonte was still in command of *Red Falcon*.

"We're not here to start a fight," she finally said. "Get me coms...but Jeeves?"

"Yes, ma'am?"

"If they start shooting, you are authorized to return fire immediately."

CHAPTER 18

"UNIDENTIFIED VESSELS, this is the armed merchant freighter *Red Falcon*," Kelly said as levelly as she could. "We weren't expecting to see anybody in this system, and your approach pattern is extremely aggressive.

"Please clarify your intentions. If you do not break off your approach, I will be forced to regard you as pirates and respond appropriately."

She hit Transmit and checked the status panels on the repeaters surrounding her. *Falcon*'s crew was returning to battle stations. Alert Bravo had kept most of them on hand, but also meant that the third who were being recalled had almost certainly been asleep.

"Minimum one-minute turnaround time," Jeeves noted. "Coms at this range always suck."

"I know." Kelly tapped a sequence of commands, linking over to *Luciole*.

"*Luciole*, this is XO LaMonte. Can you connect me to my Captain?"

"Give me two seconds," a female voice replied. "All right, linking to his wrist-comp."

"Rice here," Kelly's Captain's voice answered swiftly. "Kelly, that's you? What's the situation?"

"We have some new friends and some old friends in the system," she told him. "Four of what appear to be SDC heavy corvettes backed up by one of the Golden Bears' monitors—I'm guessing with their Tracker aboard, allowing them to follow Seule from somewhere."

"From Darius," Rice said grimly. "He scouted the system and I guess he got spotted."

"Where the hell did they get a Tracker?" Kelly heard Seule exclaim in the background.

"They rented them from the Bears," Kelly replied, hoping the other captain could hear her. "Hence the monitor. I doubt she's planning on getting involved, not without extorting a hell of a payday. The Bears are a little...nervous about us."

"They may also be holding a grudge," Rice warned. "Look, Kelly, I can't command *Falcon* by remote. Maria and I will help out Seule from here if we can, but you're in command of *Red Falcon*. Fight our ship, Kelly. I trust your judgment."

No pressure.

"All right," she replied aloud. "I've given them a warning to back off. We'll see what they do. Eventually, I'm going to have to set a line where we will shoot at them."

"Oh, I *guarantee* you that they will at least shoot at *Luciole* before then," Seule interjected. "What happens if they ignore your ship, Captain Rice?"

"My *Captain* is aboard your ship, Captain Seule," Kelly said before Rice could reply. "I don't give a shit *which* of us they shoot at; if they open fire, I will engage."

The channel was silent.

"Fight our ship," Rice repeated. "Good luck."

The channel cut and Kelly looked around the bridge. Usually, she held down navigation while everything went to hell, and Rice sat in the command chair.

Now one of her subordinates held down that console. Her girlfriend was holding down the simulacrum chamber with the exhausted expression of a Mage who had just jumped but was In Charge, Dammit. Her boyfriend was on the likely target of the incoming warships, along with the two officers ahead of her in *Red Falcon*'s chain of command.

"Right," she said aloud. "Let's do this. Any word from the bastards?"

"Nothing so far," her com tech responded.

"They are now *in* our Rapier range," Jeeves reported. "Dialing them in with passive sensors. I'm not detecting active radar from them, but they could be targeting the same way." He paused. "*Luciole* has engaged evasive maneuvers. As have the SDC ships."

Kelly hit a command that brought up an automated program before he'd finished speaking.

"Sarah-Beth, maintain the program I just triggered," she told the subordinate holding down her normal slot. "Throw in whatever random vector changes you feel like, but keep us moving."

She grimaced and opened up her communications control again.

"Unidentified starships," she said flatly. "We have you flagged as a Golden Bear mercenary warship and security vessels of the Stellarite Development Corps. We have grounds to believe you hostile, and bluntly, you're flying like pirates.

"If you approach within seven million kilometers of my vessel without communicating and adjusting your course to maneuver away from us, we will open fire."

She heard Jeeves exhale a long sigh as she hit Transmit.

"Guns?" she asked.

"Right call, XO," he half-whispered. "Right call, but damn if you didn't just throw the dice."

"It's only a gamble if I don't already know they're going to shoot at me."

The mercenaries were already within five minutes' flight time of Kelly's "line in the sand" when the response finally arrived, and it was roughly as cooperative as she expected it to be.

A sharp-featured woman with close-cropped black curls looked down a long nose at the camera. Instead of a uniform, she wore a primly cut navy blue suit—though it looked like she wore it over an emergency vacuum suit.

The only remotely military-looking thing about her was the discreet silver star pinned to the lapel of her blazer.

"I am Flotilla Manager Patience Ferro," she said crisply. "Our presence in this system is of no concern of yours, *Red Falcon*. We are in pursuit of the known criminal Nathan Seule commanding the smuggler ship *Luciole*.

"If you attempt to intervene in our detainment of Seule, you will be treated as an accomplice and we will engage your vessel. We have the jurisdiction here."

That was the extent of the message, and Kelly smiled wryly.

"Do you think she'd back down if I told her she was wrong and that *we* have the legal jurisdiction?" she asked her bridge crew.

"I doubt it, ma'am," Jeeves replied. "'Manager' Ferro looks like she's out for blood. We *might* be able to get her to back down if we completely blew our cover and played all of our cards. Maybe."

"If I thought she would, I might even try it," Kelly admitted as she did the mental math. The Gold Bears monitor had a crew of two hundred or so. Each of the SDC heavy corvettes probably had a crew of about a hundred to a hundred and twenty.

Seven hundred people, give or take.

"Sarah-Beth, maneuver us between the SDC flotilla and *Luciole*," she ordered. "Let's give our Flotilla Manager one more chance."

"Your call, ma'am," her gunner said quietly as the big freighter's engines flared.

"I'm not changing the line, Jeeves," Kelly told him. "Seven million kilometers, you open fire."

"That doesn't leave her much time to respond," he pointed out.

"I know." Kelly brought up the coms one last time and leaned into the camera, forcing herself to keep up the same wry smile that the original jurisdiction crack had awoken.

"Flotilla Manager, we both know *nobody* has jurisdiction this far out in the ass end of beyond," she said brightly. "By my math, you have less than one hundred and forty seconds from your receipt of this message to begin a good-faith effort to break off.

"If you fire on my ship or on *Luciole*, we will take you down like the pirate scum your pretty suit pretends you're not."

Ferro's response was exactly what Kelly expected it to be. Roughly fifteen seconds after the earliest Kelly would have received a radio response, they instead got the lightspeed data of Ferro's flotilla opening fire.

"The monitor has not fired," Jeeves noted. "The SDC ships have. Six missile launchers apiece, twenty-four. Readings make it...Rapier IIIs. Older missiles but still packing a punch."

Kelly pulled up the data on the IIIs in her system and nodded. The III actually had a slightly longer powered range than its newer sister, with five hundred gravities less acceleration but forty seconds more flight time.

There was also a note on the file that made her blood run cold.

"Can you validate which model?" she asked.

A few seconds passed as Jeeves went over his data and then he shook his head.

"What did Seule *do* to these people? You're right—they're Rapier III-Bs. Three-hundred-megaton fusion warhead, as if a sixteen-thousand-KPS impact from rest wasn't enough."

It was "merely" a fifty percent increase in impact energy with the closing velocities in play, but it also meant that they didn't need direct hits.

"Mr. Jeeves?" Kelly said softly.

"Firing," he confirmed. "How hard are we pushing this, ma'am?"

"Stick with Rapiers but go to maximum cycle," she ordered. "Keep the RFLAMs online and include *Luciole* in our coverage. This 'Manager' may look down her nose at me, but she doesn't get to shoot my friends!"

Red Falcon trembled as her missile launchers spoke. Ten Rapier IV fusion-drive missiles, purely kinetic weapons in this case, blasted free and began to close.

"Any action from the monitor?" Kelly asked.

"She's cut acceleration and is letting the SDC ships get ahead of her," Jeeves reported. "I don't think the Bears are being paid enough for this fight."

That was something.

"*Luciole* is launching," Jeeves continued a moment later. "Apparently, Seule is feeling spendy. Those are antimatter missiles: Phoenix VIs. He's going to hit them a good minute and a half before any of our missiles get into play—a full minute before the SDC salvo reaches us."

"Going to be an interesting moment of truth," Kelly murmured as her ship shivered again. "Did I piss Manager Ferro off enough that she's shooting at us...or is she shooting past us and try to hit *Luciole*?"

"Your guess is as good as mine," Jeeves allowed.

The minimum flight for the missiles was almost five minutes. By the time even *Luciole*'s missiles had reached the enemy's defensive perimeter, *Red Falcon* had launched eight full salvos of missiles.

Control at over twenty light-seconds was...limited. The missiles were only so smart, and the defensive plans *Red Falcon* had in place relied on that. Kelly hadn't met many programmers as good as her, and she'd repeatedly reworked the armed freighter's electronic defenses.

"*Luciole* is sequencing her later salvos to arrive with ours," Jeeves told her. "They'll be higher-velocity, but the SDC will have to deal with both salvos."

Kelly could see part of why Seule was only playing with antimatter birds. His blockade runner only had four missile launchers, which made her the smallest contributor to the massed tsunamis starting to lunge between the fragile-seeming ships.

"SDC ships engaging. Oof." Jeeves shook his head. "Well, this is going to be short."

"Jeeves?" Kelly demanded.

"I don't know what they're packing for offensive beams, but they're only got four RFLAM turrets apiece," he replied. "They are *fucked*."

Luciole's first four missiles drove home the gunnery officer's point. They should never have stood a chance, but one got close enough to explode directly in the face of the nearest ship. The radiation hash washed over the corporate ships, making a mess of their sensors in a way no non-antimatter warhead ever could.

"All we need to do is handle six times as many missiles with only twice as many turrets," Kelly pointed out. "Let's not start cheering just yet."

Even as she spoke, she was triggering several of the programs she'd previously coded into *Falcon*'s systems, turning her massive sensor array to purposes for which it had never been designed.

The big freighter *had* an electronic-warfare suite, but it had never fully lived up to Kelly's needs. Now the sensors and communications arrays awoke as well, slaved to the new code. She didn't need long-range sensors to fight missiles—they'd be *useful*, sure, but they'd be more useful in her current setting.

An overwhelming wave of jamming swept out from *Falcon*, blinding the missiles' sensors with garbage as they tried to seek out their targets. The momentary confusion as the computers tried to adapt manifested in seconds of straight-line flight.

And seconds were all Jeeves's team running the anti-missile turrets needed. Half of the missiles vanished in a handful of moments, but the rest adjusted for the jamming and charged forward. Several of the remainder died to the laser fire even with their maneuvers, but Kelly wasn't done with them yet.

She picked the closest missile and hit it with every transmitter *Red Falcon* had. It wasn't, *quite*, powerful enough to be called a maser, but it was strong enough to completely burn out the lead missile's scanners. Blind and deaf, safety protocols hard-coded into the weapon triggered a self-destruct.

It was far less efficient a defense than the RFLAM turrets, but it was one extra missile they didn't have to kill. The others didn't get off unscathed from the massive blast wave of radiation, either. Their sensors confused, their poor computers completely overwhelmed by stimuli the teams sending them into space hadn't predicted, they never stood a chance.

"All right," Kelly breathed aloud as the last missile died. "That is *not* going to work a second time. I've got several more rounds of tricks, but the next time is going to be harder."

Jeeves grunted, his own attention focused on his screen as their first salvo went in. Ten missiles against four ships was a losing proposition, even if the CorpSec corvettes were under-equipped with defenses, but they could still...

"Got one!" he announced. "All right, so the designers weren't *complete* idiots," he continued. "One solid hit on Bogey Three, but she's still with us. That's damn effective armor."

"Once we start stacking salvos, our birds will cover *Luciole*'s," Kelly said. "I don't care *what* they hung on them—they don't have the armor to stop antimatter missiles packed into a five-hundred-k-ton ship."

Ferro didn't appear to be enjoying the discovery of how vulnerable her ships were. Kelly suspected that the concept of someone shooting *back* hadn't shown up in their corporate planning meetings.

Unfortunately, neither had the concept of surrender. Her ships were adjusting their formation, spreading out and rotating to clear their firing lines and provide harder targets for the incoming salvos.

It wasn't enough. The second combined salvo from *Luciole* and *Red Falcon* arrived before the second SDC salvo reached *Red Falcon*. If Kelly had been in Ferro's place, she'd have been planning some blistering conversations with their suppliers and designers.

Of course, if Kelly had been in Ferro's place, she'd have been running for the hills. Ferro clearly had different plans, and *Falcon*'s XO suspected she knew what they were.

"Let me know if that monitor even *twitches*," she ordered as she watched the missiles charge home. The SDC ships had learned a *lot* from the first salvo—and someone clever had been watching what she did as well. Pulses of jamming strobed across the incoming weapons, and several of the Rapier IVs disappeared in moments of confusion.

The Phoenixes, however, were *far* smarter—and Kelly had had her fingers in the code of *Falcon*'s missiles. So, for that matter, had James Keller. While even he would admit Kelly had surpassed him as a programmer, he'd taught her most of what she'd started with.

Two fusion missiles made it through, sending the lead corvette reeling out of the rough formation as her engines flickered and atmosphere vented from gaping holes in her hull.

She was the lucky one. Seule had targeted *his* missiles with a practiced forethought. The farthest ship in the formation was not *quite* hiding behind the others, but she was definitely the most defended.

Seule had clearly figured that was Ferro's command ship and sent his entire salvo after it. The extra distance meant only two missiles made it through, even with the cover from *Falcon*'s salvo.

Two antimatter missiles, closing at almost ten percent of lightspeed and carrying gigaton-range warheads, were more than any privately-built paramilitary ship in the galaxy could survive. The fourth heavy corvette disappeared as the paired explosions vaporized perfect spheres of hull and systems.

"Um. So, the monitor twitched," Jeeves reported in the quiet. "She twitched right the hell out of here—she just jumped."

The damaged SDC corvette had clearly reached the same conclusion as the mercenary ship, and suddenly there were only two vessels facing them.

"Focus on the incoming," Kelly snapped. "Let's get out of this alive."

Two ships could still control all of the missiles in play, and over two hundred missiles were still heading their way.

"Watch it!" Jeeves suddenly barked at Sarah-Beth Vong, but the pilot had already seen it. *Red Falcon* dove sideways as *Luciole* shifted her course, slipping "above" the big freighter and launching a single pair of missiles.

Kelly had seen Seule do this before and swallowed a chuckle.

"Let me guess," she said to Jeeves. "Anti-missile MIVs?"

"Got it," he confirmed in surprise, moments before the two weapons broke apart. Submunitions sprayed across space in front of the incoming salvo, and missiles began to die.

Lasers flared in space and nuclear warheads detonated and the incoming fire withered like ice in the sun.

"How did you know?" the gunner asked.

"He did the same thing once before, and that time, we weren't even expecting him to get involved," Kelly replied. "Handy trick."

She studied the screens.

"There they go," she noted as both remaining ships disappeared. "Smart move, once they realized how badly outclassed they were."

"There's still two hundred missiles out there," Jeeves pointed out.

"Without someone to override them in flight? Those aren't a problem. Give me a minute."

They had MISS override codes for the Rapier III, but Kelly didn't think she trusted Nathan Seule and his people that far.

Not when the Rapier III-B was at best a third-tier weapon with second-class hardware and obsolete software. She had enough data to break the access codes in under thirty seconds.

It wouldn't have worked with newer weapons and it wouldn't have worked with any of the launching ships still in the system, but as it was...

Every remaining missile detonated its nuclear warhead simultaneously, lighting up the star system in a glorious display of horrendously expensive fireworks.

CHAPTER 19

DAVID AND SOPRANO weren't much help during the fight, he had to admit. *Luciole* had the same style of bridge as most true warships, with the bridge consoles and command seating installed in mixed layers throughout the simulacrum chamber.

Seule sat in the center of the bridge, his hands on the floating silver simulacrum of *Luciole* as he barked orders and the three-person bridge crew around him leapt to obey. David and Soprano simply waited out of the way while the smuggler crew went to work.

It allowed him to watch his own ship in action, and he was impressed. He knew Kelly LaMonte and Alexander Jeeves were good, but watching them in action without him made him feel more than a little redundant.

When the dust settled, he found himself at least mildly humbled. His subordinates had handled the fight better than he might have been able to. He needed to seriously give some thought around the idea of working to get LaMonte her own command.

Potentially, all things considered, through MISS rather than private ownership. Her skills would be wasted running a merchant ship, but a covert ops ship like *Red Falcon*—or perhaps something even more quiet and black—would serve her well.

"Your new ship is a significant upgrade over your old one," Seule said calmly as the missiles erupted in their fireworks display. "But I'm *still* pretty sure that's not standard."

"That would be my XO," David replied. "She has a way with computers that I'm not entirely sure is moral or correct in any way."

The smuggler snorted.

"I know the type," he admitted. "Does she want a job?"

"I doubt it," David said with a grin, despite his own thoughts with regards to LaMonte's necessary advancement. "If nothing else, you seem to already have a competent XO."

The black woman at the tactical console glared at him in silence, which he took as at least some measure of agreement.

"That is fair. I appreciate your assistance," Seule said finally. "This Ferro definitely knew what I had; those four corvettes would have made hash of just *Luciole*."

David had been watching the data during the fight, and he shook his head.

"They're warships designed by civilian committee," he pointed out. "Over-gunned, over-engined, over-armored, but under-protected, and I'd bet money they're short on redundancy, too."

"And they still had twenty-four launchers to my four," the smuggler replied. "My people are good, but that's a hell of a weight differential. Thanks to you, it seems we have settled the immediate threat."

"So, shall we talk about those favors we want from each other?" David asked with a grin.

Seule laughed.

"In my office, Captain Rice. I'll go dig up the *nice* booze after this."

Seule's office was as much of a contrast to the rest of the ship as the ship had been a contrast to her original interior. Where whoever had redesigned the rest of the ship had been very clearly intended to make her a home, this room had been rebuilt into a tactician's dream working space.

In the original design, the captain's office had a single wall screen, a desk, and a console. The desk and console were gone now, the metal floor covered in some strange wood-like material that was soft and giving under David's feet.

All four walls had been converted to screens. Part of one slid aside to disgorge two extra chairs at a wave of Seule's hand, immediately closing again to return to an image that resembled nothing so much as a miniature version of the simulacrum chamber.

The smuggler captain took his seat and opened a wooden cabinet to produce three small glasses. He poured a generous dollop of amber liquid into each tumbler and passed them over.

"To old friends coming through unexpectedly," he told them. "I didn't expect the SDC to be able to follow me. The Hunter going after you was the last Tracker I'd met."

"We knew the Golden Bears had one, and they *are* for hire," David admitted. "I would have expected SDC to pick up Aristos's entire little fleet though."

Jason Aristos commanded the Golden Bears and remained one of the most well-known mercenaries in the Protectorate. He seemed to have *mostly* learned his lesson about taking black bounties, too, since David had handed the man's fleet back to him in pieces when they'd clashed.

"I don't know if they could fit him in their project budget," Seule said. "Renting fleets shows up as an expense, after all. Paramilitary corporate security fleets are an *asset* on the balance sheet."

He snorted, and slugged back half of the liquor. David sipped more cautiously himself, the smoothly fierce flavor justifying that.

"I didn't think Amber fire liqueur was supposed to leave the system," he observed as he let the peppery heat run down his throat. The liquor was banned in a good chunk of the Protectorate, due to being significantly higher-proof than generally regarded as safe...and not tasting like it at all.

"I stop in Amber enough to keep a stock," Seule told him. "Look, Captain, Mage. You're already deep in this now. SDC is *not* going to let the fact you blew one of their ships away slide."

"We didn't," Soprano pointed out. "*You* did. We rang a few bells, but it was your missiles that destroyed Ferro's flagship."

"Yeah." The smuggler drained his glass. "I'm going to pay for that, but *merde,* was it nice to put an explosive fist into one of those arrogant assholes' faces. 'Flotilla Manager,' *mon cul.*"

"So, how do you plan on dealing with their fleet?" David asked. "For that matter, how *were* you planning on dealing with them? We have ten full cargos for *Luciole* aboard *Falcon.*"

"Yeah, and one of them is a stash of surface-to-orbit weapons sufficient to at least make the SDC mercs blink," Seule explained. "The *plan,* originally, was to have you bring the cargo to a jump or so away from Darius, and I'd make my first run with those.

"Once we'd landed the STO missiles, they'd be able to open a large-enough window above the spaceport for me to dance my way into."

"How were you going to manage *that?*" Soprano asked, her voice sounding surprised to David.

"*Luciole* was designed by a bloody committee to do a lot of different things," the smuggler replied. "One of those was to be the biggest damn headache the Royal Martian Marine Corps ever gave anybody. The reason the Navy still has any of them in service is because the Corps doesn't want to give them up until they get a *lot* more assault transports in commission."

He grinned.

"*Luciole* can land and lift off again," he told them. "We can't lift off with a *cargo,* but I can land with one and lift off empty. So, we drop onto the spaceport, deliver the missiles, and pop back up."

"And now there's far too many ships for that to be an option," David guessed.

"Even if I deliver all of the missiles, I'm not sure they can open a wide-enough hole for me to sneak *Luciole* into," Seule confirmed. "When we were expecting half a dozen ships, it was one thing. A frigging fleet, though..."

"Isn't that just a lost cause, then?" David asked.

"With just *Luciole,* yes."

"And with us?"

Seule grinned wickedly.

"Two ships and a whole lot of far-too-clever people? They're never going to know what hit them."

David shook his head once the smuggler finished describing his plan.

"Audacious, and asking a lot of our Mages," he said. "Maria? Can we do it?"

The dark-skinned Mage looked thoughtful.

"It won't be easy," she told them. "I wouldn't risk it with any other crew of Mages, but I think my people can do it."

"I know mine can do it with *Luciole*," Seule replied. "But she's a much smaller ship."

"We'll consider it," David said, carefully not making any promises. "Though that brings us to: what do *we* get out of this? I owe you for saving our lives, but taking my crew up against an entire fleet seems a bit much in payment for that."

The other man tapped his fingers on the arm of his chair.

"You sought me out for a reason, Captain Rice," he said, echoing his earlier comments before the SDC had shown up. "I don't know what that reason is, but it was enough for a man the Martian Navy feels indebted to to break the law again. This office is secure, even against my own people, trust them as I do.

"What is it you want?"

"Ardennes," David said flatly. "You delivered attack helicopters, among other things, to the Freedom Wing. I need to know who paid for them and where they came from."

Seule didn't even seem surprised.

"That one was always a touch odd," he admitted. "Middlemen are one thing, but the whole situation smelled off."

"So, explain it to me," David said.

"Uh-uh." Seule wagged a finger at him. "You help me make this delivery to the poor bastards trying to hold Darius together, and I will tell you everything I know."

"And if it isn't actually what I want or need to know?" David asked.

"That's the risk you take," the smuggler replied. "You're buying what I know, Captain Rice, I make no guarantees as to its value. I can't. I don't know what you're after. I don't know—nor do I *want* to know—who you work for."

"Maybe not," the stocky freighter captain turned spy retorted. "But you do know that Alaura Stealey is dead, right?"

Seule froze in the middle of beginning to respond.

"The Hand?" he finally asked.

"Yes. I understand that you met her," David said.

"I sent her after you," the smuggler admitted. "Saved your life a second time, as I understand. The only Hand I ever met, left me with a better impression of the group than I expected. Dead?" He paused. "Did the Freedom Wing kill her?"

"Rather the opposite. Vaughn killed her. The Freedom Wing got coopted by another Hand to take him down. But there are too many cooks in these damn kitchens, Captain Seule, and I think what you know will lead to one of the ones with a damn long spoon."

Seule laughed.

"That is one *tortured* metaphor, Captain Rice, but I get your meaning," he agreed. "I think what I know will help you, but here's a piece for free that will make you think:

"The Freedom Wing thought they were buying the gear from me at a discount, but what they paid me was barely half of what I was paid for the run. The Wing thought it was a charity cargo...but I was specifically hired to deliver that cargo.

"And those helicopters were paid for in full before they ever reached *me*, let alone Ardennes."

CHAPTER 20

"I HAVE to admit, I think I enjoy being a passenger during a battle even *less* when it's aboard a strange ship," Mike Kelzin griped as *Red Falcon's* officers gathered in a small meeting room.

"You get used to it," Kellers pointed out. "But at least aboard your own ship, you can trust the crew and you have at least *something* to do."

The First Pilot grunted, trading a look with LaMonte that said part of his concern had been for his girlfriends. David swallowed a laugh at the—relatively tame, all things considered—antics of the youngest two of his senior officers.

"We survived," David reminded his people. "And with no real losses or damage. We got damn lucky."

"Their ships suck," Jeeves said. "All flash and bang, but no staying power."

"The monitor was a different story," LaMonte objected. "We've fought the Bears' ships before. If her captain had decided to get involved, we would have had a much worse day."

"Fortunately, either she was under orders from Aristos not to engage or Ferro couldn't meet her price," Soprano noted. "Either way, Aristos doesn't currently have more reasons to come after us for blood—but the Stellarites now have us marked."

"Fuck 'em," Leonhart said harshly, the Marine security chief looking entirely unsympathetic for the corporate security force they'd faced. "They mess with the viper, they get the fangs."

"We met four of their heavies today," David said quietly. "They have more of those. And two dozen smaller ships. Their blockade has enough of a legal fig leaf to keep the Protectorate from getting officially involved, or a single destroyer squadron would have already ended it.

"Which means that I'm not flashing a shiny badge around and ordering people to go home—but we can't fight their little fleet, either, which leaves us with Seule's plan."

The room was silent.

"Do you trust him?" Leonhart finally demanded. "I know most of this crew's been on both sides of the law, and *we* certainly have been gun smugglers for a while now, but he's been doing this for years. How can we trust him?"

"We can't," David admitted. "I believe in his convictions and that he is honestly trying to help people, but his is a toxic path. You can't walk it without getting poisoned—it's something we all need to watch in ourselves.

"That said, his plan is...audacious and unexpected. I don't think SDC will see it coming. Almost as important, in my book, is that it will let us pull off our mission without having to kill anyone. We can *hope* that once the Darian government is in possession of enough weaponry to end their damn war, the rebels will concede."

"You know it's never that simple," Soprano warned him.

"I said I can hope," David admitted. "I don't expect that to be the case, but SDC's legal fig leaf depends on the pretense that the government that the election kicked out is still somehow legitimate. Once they've surrendered or been captured, that legal fig leaf dissolves. Then they either get the hell out of dodge, or the Navy breaks the blockade.

"Our cargo will end their damn war, so long as we can get it through the blockade." He shook his head. "I won't pretend that's valueless, but it also gets us what we need."

"What if Seule doesn't talk after we've fought his war for him?" Leonhart asked. "He's a crook. A liar. He could be playing us."

"He could be," David conceded. "I don't think so, but he could be. The thing to remember, though, is that the Protectorate is quite aware of

Nathan Seule and his activities and has, in the main, classified him as a low threat. There are other, much less principled gunrunners out there.

"If he screws us over, that classification shifts. I don't think Captain Seule would enjoy suddenly finding himself higher on everyone's priority lists...and I *do* think he realizes what the consequences of screwing us over would be."

After the rest of the officers had left, David leaned on his hands and studied Kelly LaMonte. His young XO looked exhausted.

"So, your first battle in full command," he said gently. "How are you holding up?"

"I did...okay," she concluded after a moment. "I didn't freeze. Didn't panic. It's weird, though... things I've done, programs I've written...I've killed people before. Feels different this time."

"The orders were yours," David reminded her. "The responsibility was yours. It *is* different."

LaMonte shook her head. "I guess. Wasn't what I expected, I suppose."

"You were expecting to end up in command in many battles, I take it?" he asked with forced humor.

Her chuckle was equally forced, but she was trying.

"Not really, though we seem to end up in enough of them, for all that we're not a warship."

"We put ourselves in harm's way a lot," David agreed. "That was the job we took on, the deal we agreed to with Stealey and MISS. We're out here to make a difference, to try and protect other people. We aren't necessarily doing it in a traditional fashion, with banners blazing as we ride out like knights in shining armor...but what we do is just as necessary to keep the Protectorate safe."

"This whole thing in Darius is nerve-wracking," she admitted. "We know so little about the factions in play, but here we are, providing one of them with enough firepower to force the rest of their planet into line.

"Who are we to judge which side is right?"

"I don't know," David confessed. "I tend to err on the side of the people who didn't start the violence, as a rule, and against the people working for Legatus. That's my own biases speaking, but...in the end, we're agents of Mars. The Mage-King wants us to consider the general good as well, but we exist to serve his interests at least on an equal level."

"So, we fight for the Mages regardless of whether they're in the right this time?" LaMonte asked.

He shook his head.

"We fight for the Mage-King and the Protectorate," he argued. "I've never met him, but my impression from Stealey is that he'd often rather have the right thing done, not the thing that serves him.

"In this case, I think that's the same thing. One group got elected to change things, and others have used everything from violence to this orbital blockade to force things to stay the same." He shrugged. "Their goals align with Mars's goals, so we intervene. The truth is that we're not here for Darius. We're getting involved because we need Seule's information and this is his price."

"So, we'd do nothing otherwise?" she demanded.

"I suspect there are already wheels in motion in MISS to see this situation resolved," David told her. "Certainly, I reported everything Keiko told me up the chain. Regardless of how our visit goes, I don't think SDC is going to enjoy the consequences of getting involved."

Kelly LaMonte nodded slowly, studying the wallscreen showing the projected positions of the corporate fleet blocking all shipments to or from Darius.

"I have my concerns," she said, "but somehow, *that* thought doesn't bother me at all."

With the meeting over, Kelly slowly made her way back to the set of double-sized quarters she shared with the ship's second-most senior Mage and the First Pilot. Rank hath its privileges...and one of those privileges was using the XO's salary to pay for modifications to the officers' quarters.

Like removing the entire wall between the XO and First Pilot's quarters, among other changes.

The lights in her shared quarters were turned down as she came in, and the wallscreen in the living room was lit up with a movie of some kind. Kelly wasn't paying that much attention, presuming to leave Xi and Mike alone as she went to bed.

She didn't even make it three steps into the room before the movie paused and the lights brightened. Xi pulled herself up over the couch and leveled a dark-eyed gaze on the tired executive officer.

"Hey, lover," the Mage told her. "You look as shattered as the rest of us feel. Get over here."

"I didn't want to interrupt your movie," Kelly said quietly.

There was a shifting noise as Mike adjusted to be visible over the couch as well. It was pretty clear that Xi was still sitting in his lap as they both looked at Kelly like owls contemplating a particularly silly mouse.

"We just started it; we can start again," Mike said firmly.

Kelly looked at the screen. Paused, it actually gave the percentage completion of the movie—which gave the complete lie to what her boyfriend was saying.

Xi followed Kelly's gaze and giggled.

"Well, we can start again, anyway," she said. "We're not letting you go to sleep on your own; that's for sure. Get over here," she repeated.

Kelly obeyed, dropping onto the couch next to Mike and promptly finding Xi Wu draped across both of their laps. At that close proximity, she realized that her Mage girlfriend was mostly naked.

The movie reset and Kelly exhaled slowly, leaning against the warmth of her lovers as much of the day's tension left her.

"Hell of a day."

"I hear you," Mike agreed, his arm snaking around her waist and pulling her close to him. "You did good. Now relax."

She rested her head on his shoulder and closed her eyes. They might have restarted the movie for her, but she never saw more than the first few minutes.

CHAPTER 21

RED FALCON arrived in the Darius System to almost exactly what Maria and the rest of her crew had expected. Sitting in the simulacrum chamber at the heart of the big freighter, Maria studied the screens around her as the sensors drank deep of the light around them and the information it carried.

"Alessandra, go sleep," she ordered bluntly.

Barrow was still hanging onto the simulacrum, barely standing as the effort of the jump spell left her. She wavered for a moment but then nodded and began to shuffle out.

The rest of *Falcon*'s Mages were still there, but Wu and Nguyen watched as Maria reclaimed the semiliquid silver model. Datafeeds around them told her the story of the system, years of practice with the iconography of the Martian Navy turning icons and text abbreviations into easily read data.

Darius had no asteroid belts. Only one gas giant, orbiting at the outer edge of the star system. Fourteen rocky worlds of various sizes hung between the yellow dwarf star and its massive outer companion.

Only Darius itself, the fourth planet, was habitable. A gorgeously perfect world, with two large continents on its equator and four smaller ones scattered north and south. It was the kind of planet that easily made the leap from Fringe to MidWorld as millions of people flocked to its forests and beaches.

A continent-wide desert on one of the smaller continents had become the home to most of Darius's industry, with more in orbit.

The orbital platforms told the story of the civil war more than anything else Maria could see. Eighteen space stations, ranging from a standard ring station–style orbital dock to what looked like the embryo of a shipyard, orbited Darius.

All were dark. Even the hab modules had been placed in standby and evacuated. An SDC corvette hung above each of the six largest platforms, playing mothership to a small squadron of shuttles presumably making sure that the power plants were sufficiently maintained to prevent disaster.

In a higher orbit, positioned equidistantly around the equator, were another twenty jump-corvettes. There was no way any ship could get to the planet without crossing the interception path of at least one of the ships and more likely half of them.

Last, but far from least, a high polar orbit held the Stellarite Development Corps main striking force. Eight half-megaton heavy corvettes backed by a pair of the Golden Bears' seven-hundred-thousand-ton monitors.

"I thought Seule said there were ten SDC heavies?" Wu asked.

"I'm guessing the squadron that came after us came from here," Maria replied. "He blew one to pieces and we bashed the crap out of another. I'm guessing that one went home...but he didn't see the Golden Bears' ships, so that makes up the difference."

She considered the relative weight of the poorly-designed SDC ships versus the monitors they'd fought before. Even on a mass basis, the monitors were bigger ships, but they were also far better designed.

"More than makes up the difference," she concluded aloud. "Those two monitors are probably worth as much as the eight heavy corvettes combined."

"So...we're not fighting these guys, right?" Nguyen asked slowly. "I mean...we could take the monitors *or* the heavy corvettes *or* the little guys...probably. But all of them together?"

"That's what the plan is for," Maria told her subordinates as *Red Falcon*'s engines lit up. "Let's see what the SDC has to say for themselves."

Maria didn't have high expectations of the SDC's corporate security fleet's professionalism, but it still took far longer than she'd been expecting for them to respond to *Red Falcon*'s presence. Even ignoring the fact that *Falcon* had been involved in a battle with ships from the blockade only a few days before, they were still a merchant ship heading toward a blockade.

It took just over an hour for the first message to arrive. They were only two light-minutes away, which meant the blockaders had taken their time getting around to it.

The background of the video message looked like the flag deck of any warship in the Martian Navy. The SDC's designer had clearly decided to crib at least *some* features from the only real professional Navy around.

The Navy, of course, would have had software that automatically blurred out the tactical display behind the pudgy suited man standing in front of the camera with a baleful look. Since SDC didn't have that, Maria realized that they now had complete details on the readiness of the blockade fleet.

Assuming those details were accurate. Her faith in them was...low.

"This is Security Vice-President Wayne Charleston of the Stellarite Development Corps," the suited man said in what was presumably intended to be an intimidating tone. He managed to sound more bored than anything else.

"The Darius System has been closed to outside shipping per the orders of Governor Nina Yesim Ellis," he continued. "The SDC has agreed to maintain a blockade of the planet on the government's behalf to prevent outsiders from arming the rebel factions.

"If you approach the planet, you will be boarded and your ship confiscated. We are authorized by Governor Ellis to use all necessary force to achieve this. You are hereby ordered to exit the Darius System in an orderly fashion."

The message ended and Maria shook her head. She glanced at the link to the bridge.

"Was that live, skipper?" she asked.

"It was," LaMonte confirmed before Rice could respond. "I'm processing that tactical display, but did they even look at our transponder code?"

"We're not exactly hiding who we are," the Captain said. "So, I'm guessing no. I'm curious to see what they say as we keep coming."

"Huh," Jeeves interjected in a somewhat-pleased tone. "Those monitors? They clearly *are* reading our transponder beacon. They both just lit up their engines and broke orbit—*away* from us."

There was an evil chuckle across both the bridge and the simulacrum chamber.

"I wonder if mister Security Vice-President over there is willing to listen when his mercenaries run?" Maria asked. "That can't be good for the Bears' reputation."

"I suspect Aristos had given strict orders not to fuck with us unless he has overwhelming firepower," Rice said grimly. "He's not going to let what happened go, but he's also well aware *Red Falcon* can probably take two of his monitors."

The Captain snorted.

"And they probably have an even worse opinion of the SDC flotilla than we do. Kelly, what do we have from their failure of security?"

The XO chuckled.

"Those corvettes playing sheepdog over the orbital platforms?" she said first. "They're not corvettes. If I'm reading the iconography right, they're just shuttle tenders pretending to be warships. No launchers, no beams, just docking ports.

"The rest?" She shrugged. "Hard to say if their readiness states are exaggerated, but the munitions numbers, et cetera, line up with what I'd expect for second-rate two-hundred-k-ton corvettes. None of them are at full readiness, and if they *are* pumping their numbers to look good to the VP, some of the regular ships could be in real trouble."

"What about the heavies?" Maria asked.

"Their status reports look great, but they're all the same class and we already met those guys," LaMonte noted. "Let's not go poke eight of them in the nose or anything, but they're not worth their weight."

"Well, let's see what happens," Rice said calmly. "We're still on a zero-zero course for the planet. Let's see how long it takes them to actually *do* something."

The answer turned out to be "about four hours." That was how long *Red Falcon* continued to accelerate toward Darius without even responding to the blockading fleet's hails before they did anything.

From Charleston's expression in the second video, someone had finally briefed him on Flotilla Manager Ferro's fate and *Red Falcon*'s involvement.

"*Red Falcon*, you have a lot of gall," he said without preamble. "You murder one of my subordinates and then you waltz into this system like the blockade isn't even here? You will surrender and prepare to face justice for the deaths of Patience Ferro and her crew or I will blow you to hell.

"Please don't surrender," Charleston noted with what he probably intended as a cruel or evil smile. "I'm going to enjoy blasting your ship to tiny pieces."

That was the extent of the transmission—but the rest of the Security Vice-President's message was clear. All eight heavy corvettes were now accelerating out to meet *Red Falcon*, and ten of the regular corvettes were joining them.

That left only ten corvettes and five shuttle tenders orbiting Darius itself. The first phase of the plan was going off without a hitch.

"Time to intercept?" Rice asked.

"Looks like another six or seven hours," LaMonte replied. "Missile range well short of that, of course."

"Let's start decelerating, make them think we want to extend our time in missile range," the Captain ordered, exchanging a glance with Maria. "We need to slow down, after all."

"That will push it out to twelve hours, maybe a bit more," the XO told them. "They're only pulling three gees each. Probably only have gravity runes in key locations."

Maria nodded as she studied the fleet coming out to meet them.

"I can't imagine a Legatus-headquartered interstellar has *that* much luck recruiting Jump Mages," she pointed out. "That they managed to find thirty-odd for this blockade fleet is impressive. I can't imagine they have enough on hand to put two or three on every ship."

Every ship they were facing had at least one Mage aboard to use their jump matrix, but Maria wouldn't expect them to have more than one. Mages were expensive to hire, and a Legatan corp would end up paying more as a matter of course.

"How long till phase two?" Maria asked and Rice checked his wrist-comp.

"I figured our timeline on that was way too long. Guess I was wrong," he admitted. "Phase two in five hours."

"We'll be ready," Maria promised, looking around at her Mages.

"I know you will," the Captain confirmed. "So will we."

"I don't think SDC is going to be," LaMonte noted with a chuckle. "But then, I'm not sure I trust them to know which end of the fusion rocket to stand in front of."

The next few hours passed with the usual patient waiting of space combat. It would always take less time to actually fight the battle than it would take to close with the enemy. Few space battles lasted for more than an hour of actual combat, but it would take hours, possibly days, for the ships to close.

If Maria thought she could have managed it, she'd have sent her subordinates to sleep. As it was, Barrow rejoined them eight hours after they'd arrived in the system, and all four Mages waited, quietly, as *Red Falcon* decelerated at the steady five gravities she'd maintained the entire time in Darius.

Her base velocity carried her toward the enemy, but she'd reach roughly zero velocity relative to the planet Darius ten hours after she'd arrived in the system, still a full light-minute from the planet.

The SDC ships tested the waters with a missile salvo and a fusillade of laser fire three hours after they came out after *Red Falcon*. The range was still far beyond any effective capability of either weapon. Against *some* enemies, that might have worked, but *Red Falcon*'s crew was as well trained as any Navy ship now.

Jeeves didn't even bring up the RFLAM turrets. LaMonte maneuvered the ship well out of the way of the SDC salvo, and they continued to drift toward the planet.

"Phase two in ten minutes," LaMonte eventually announced. "SDC flotilla is now approximately five hours from Darius. I make it five million kilometers with a velocity of over five hundred KPS."

"Getting *back* to orbit will take them over twelve hours," Jeeves noted. "I don't think Mr. Charleston was expecting real trouble."

Maria nodded. Charleston was clearly no soldier, despite his current role, and had left half of his lighter corvettes behind out of some concept of redundancy. On the other hand, only one of those corvettes was needed to head off any regular merchant ship.

"Do we taunt him?" Maria asked.

"No," Rice replied with a regretful tone. "No, we want him thinking pretty clearly, all things considered."

"Phase two in ninety seconds," LaMonte reported. "This should be interesting."

"More so for some than others," David agreed. "Keep an eye on everything. I want to know the moment phase two executes, and I want to know how both of their forces react.

"For that matter, I want to know how the *Bears* respond."

The two Golden Bears monitors were on the opposite side of Darius and calmly decelerating toward jump now. There didn't seem to be any unusual hurry to their movement...but they also were clearly not sticking around to see what happened next.

"Charleston probably has the money to get them involved," Maria warned.

"He almost certainly does," the Captain agreed. "And it shouldn't matter. Not today."

"Jump flare!" Jeeves snapped. "*Luciole* is...about fifteen seconds early. But she is exactly on target."

"Not shabby," Rice said as they all studied the jump flare on the screen. "Perfect location, exactly on course."

Luciole had arrived ninety degrees around the ecliptic plane from *Red Falcon* and from an angle of seventy degrees above the plane. There was no way the formation that had charged after *Red Falcon* could intercept her.

And unlike any regular merchant ship, there was no way a single corvette could head off the armed blockade runner.

"And so phase two begins," Maria murmured. "Your call on phase three, skipper."

"Not yet," Rice replied. "Let's see what the SDC does first."

CHAPTER 22

THERE WAS no better way, in the opinion of the Royal Martian Navy and her officer corps—and hence, of one Maria Soprano—to judge the quality of a military or paramilitary force than by watching their reaction to one of their commanders making the wrong call.

The SDC fleet had sent far too much of its available strength after *Red Falcon*. There were ways to deal with that, and the corvette flotilla left behind was capable of at least standing *Luciole* off, given that the blockade runner needed to deliver her cargo intact.

In Charleston's place, Maria wasn't entirely sure what she would have done...but ordering the entire mobile fleet still in Darius orbit out after *Luciole* and splitting his current force wasn't it.

"Yup, that's two of the heavies and six regular corvettes breaking off," Jeeves confirmed. "They're...well, they're out of this fight. And that fight."

As thoroughly as if Charleston had shot them in the head himself. Eight ships were now on a vector where they'd engage neither *Red Falcon* or *Luciole*.

"Keep our acceleration constant," Rice ordered. "If our Stellarite friend wants to keep making mistakes, let him."

"We're in antimatter missile range of the SDC force," Jeeves noted. "Fusion missile range in an hour. Assuming they're carrying the same birds as the ambushers, they'll be in range a few minutes after that."

"We'll hit zero velocity relative to Darius shortly before missile range," LaMonte reported. "We can kick them in the nuts before we go to phase three."

Maria was tempted. The Stellarite paramilitaries were the worst kind of corporate bullies in her experience.

"No," Rice said calmly. "No, I want Charleston to have to explain to either his masters or a Hand—or, better yet, both—just what he did here. I don't want to fight a war here today. We'll execute phase three on schedule."

Luciole was burning hard for Darius, and the ten corvettes were coming out to meet her. If they hadn't realized the remaining ships were shuttle tenders, they'd have thought Darius still had some defenders.

Those five ships had clustered together in a polar orbit, leaving the main spaceport uncovered. If a third ship arrived to make the final delivery, that would have ended up being hard for their commanders to explain—and that kind of concentration was exactly what *Luciole* was designed to take advantage of.

"Are we going to talk to them at all?" Maria asked.

"No," Rice replied. "Let Charleston sweat. He signed on with this kind of bullshit; I have no intention of throwing him even the tiniest rope. Keep your eyes open and stand by for my order. It's almost time to demonstrate why amateurs shouldn't play with starships."

Ten ships hurtled toward *Red Falcon*, riding pillars of fusion flame as they charged the massive freighter. Maria wouldn't have put the odds in the corporate ships' favor now that they'd sent a third of their number after *Luciole*, but their mission there wasn't to break the blockade.

It was simply to evade it and deliver their cargo. The original plan had been for *Luciole* to repeatedly run the gauntlet, delivering the cargo in ten loads. The sheer scale of the SDC blockade had ended that plan and left them with the one that relied on Maria and her people.

The ex-Navy Ship's Mage kept her hands on the simulacrum, feeling the ship's velocity relative to the local gravity wells rather than watching the numbers on the screens around her.

"Missile range estimated in five minutes," Jeeves reported.

"It's your call, Maria," Captain Rice said calmly. "This isn't an easy jump, so...jump us when ready, Ship's Mage."

Maria's subordinates were gathered and she'd have work for them in a moment, but right now was up to her.

Every SDC ship was now at least an hour's acceleration away from Darius. They were between the two smuggler ships and the planet, so that wouldn't have been a problem—except that Maria Soprano had once been a Mage-Commander in the Royal Martian Navy.

And the Royal Martian Navy trained for in-system jumps.

She slid the runes on her hands into place on the simulacrum, exhaled a long breath...and *jumped*.

It was a shorter jump than she'd made in years, and she was jumping into planetary orbit. With a destroyer's amplifier, it was doable but difficult. With a regular jump matrix, it was supposed to be possible.

In theory.

The ship fought her. The *spell* fought her, magic backlashing through the runes into her flesh as she struggled, forcing the magic to complete and exert her calculated force. Energy rippled and her skin *burned*.

And then the screens around flashed brilliantly and *Red Falcon* was above Darius.

Maria inhaled sharply, touching her face as she felt blood begin to drip from her nostrils. She wasn't tired...not really. This wasn't the type of spell that drained all of her energy like a usual jump. This one had just hurt.

"Jump complete," she reported. "LaMonte, please get us into an orbit before we hit the planet. Somebody get us coms...unless we want to *land* this behemoth, my people's job isn't done yet."

"On it," Rice replied. Maria could feel the engines flare to life even without LaMonte saying anything, the big antimatter rockets thundering as they pushed *Red Falcon* into a stable orbit above the capital city.

"Well done, Ship's Mage," the Captain continued. "Well done, indeed. Now go sit the fuck down. We'll take care of this."

Maria, of course, did no such thing. She did move back from the simulacrum and let Xi Wu take over, but she cleaned the blood off her face and grabbed one of the secondary consoles as the communications link was established to the surface.

"This is Governor Jasmina Wasyl Mitchell's office," a well-dressed young man greeted them. "How may I assist you?"

"My name is Captain David Rice," Rice told the aide. "I am in orbit of Darius with a cargo of ten million tons of equipment and weaponry for your government. We have approximately one hour to deliver that cargo before we will need to leave orbit to evade the SDC blockade ships.

"So, young man, *can* you help me, or should I be talking to someone else?"

The aide grinned shakily but widely. "I'll make you a deal, Captain Rice. I'm going to put you through to the Governor while *I* call the spaceport and see if we have a damn clue how to pull that off."

"Connect your spaceport to my Ship's Mages," Rice ordered. "We have a plan. I'll talk to the Governor while you get them on the line, though."

The youth's grin was just as wide but calmer now as he nodded. A few moments later, a tall, dark-haired woman appeared on the screen, looking levelly at her camera.

"Captain Rice, Alexus tells me I need to talk to you," she said calmly. "I am Jasmina Wasyl Mitchell, the elected Governor of this planet, despite what our friends in orbit might have said. If you're in orbit, something very strange has happened."

"Not strange so much as clever," Rice replied. "The SDC blockade fleet is currently in disarray across half the star system. They came after me...but are now over a dozen hours away. None of their ships can even threaten me for at least an hour."

"You're the cargo from Amber?" Mitchell asked.

"Exactly."

"We don't have any intact transshipment capabilities anymore, Captain," she admitted. "Unless you have enough shuttles to transport that cargo in an hour, we may have a problem."

"We don't have enough shuttles," he agreed. "We do have a problem...but we also have a solution."

A flashing icon on Maria's screen told her that a direct channel was being opened to her.

"Ship's Mage Soprano," she introduced herself as she opened the channel. "And you are?"

"I am Soth Jada Weigand," a heavyset man with skin barely a shade lighter than James Kellers's near–pitch black told her. "I run logistics and supply for the Darius Spaceport. I just spoke to our Governor's aide, and he says you have a plan for somehow moving your cargo to us?"

"You have the handling facilities for our cargo?" she asked.

"We do," he confirmed. "This isn't the first ten-million-ton cargo we've had come through, though it's been a while. We have both storage and transport capability if you can get them down to the surface."

"My tests suggest we can teleport about a spar's worth of cargo at a time," Maria told him. "That's fifty containers. I *think* we can get them down to you in a stack of fifty, two rows of two with a fifth on top. But that's half a kilometer of cargo in one shot, Mr. Weigand. And we need to do it twenty times."

He barked a shocked laugh as he considered.

"So, you'll need *very* exacting coordinates for all four corners at the very least," he agreed. "We have the space for it; I think we'll worry about breaking it down and moving it once it's down here."

"That's our problem, not yours. I can get you those coordinates in five minutes."

"We've got an hour, Mr. Weigand. Let's make it happen!"

Xi Wu went first, under Maria's watchful and concerned eye. In pure raw strength, Wu was actually the most powerful Mage aboard *Red Falcon* by a notable margin. Unlike the other three Mages, the XO's girlfriend had never been part of the Royal Martian Navy and wasn't as well trained.

This wasn't a trick that sheer power could handle. Teleporting only *part* of the ship using the matrix was a question of finesse and precision, not pure raw magic.

The big freighter was in a geostationary orbit above the spaceport, her gunners carefully watching the space around them. The shuttle tenders were honoring the threat, the five remaining ships hiding on the opposite side of the planet from *Red Falcon* and declining to engage.

Video feed from the surface showed the spaceport parking lot the Darius government had cleared. Presumably, the spaceport's current all but abandoned state had made that easier than normal, but the massive open spaces allowed for vehicles and buses and aircraft gave the spaceport dozens of square kilometers of cleared and flat space for this effort.

Mages couldn't really sense or feel magic in use. There was a degree of it, a faint buzzing, but the Mages who could detect other Mages working with any reliability were rare. There was some technology that could do so, but even it was unreliable.

Maria was less sensitive than most...and even *she* felt the pulse of power as Xi Wu unleashed her magic, bending the very specific magic of the jump matrix to something *very close* to its designed purpose.

It lasted longer than a usual jump. Longer, even, than the struggle to get *Red Falcon* directly into Darius orbit. Tension filled the air of the simulacrum chamber, and magical static sparked when anything moved.

And then it released like an elastic snapping and one of the cameras was no longer showing an empty parking lot. Fifty ten-by-ten-by-hundred-meter containers now filled the space, and one of *Falcon*'s twenty cargo spars was empty.

"All right, people, Nguyen, you're up," Maria barked as she laid a hand on Wu's shoulder, gently pulling the younger Mage away. They were about to find out how much rest each of them was going to need after this stunt, and *that* would define whether or not this whole stunt had been fully worth it.

Like the original plan, though, the first cargos going down were the surface-to-orbit missiles. The Stellarites might control the rest of the system still, but given twelve hours to deploy the first wave of self-mobile launchers, the government would control the space above their port.

"I'm fine," Wu insisted, breathing heavily. "That's...hard, but not exhausting, if that makes sense?"

That was roughly where Maria ranked in-system jumps into planetary orbit, though at least her subordinates didn't appear to be having nosebleeds. Power flared through the simulacrum chamber again as Karl Nguyen repeated Xi Wu's spell.

It took a noticeable few seconds more with Nguyen casting, but it worked just as well. A second row of fifty containers appeared on the surface, and a full tenth of the cargo was "delivered."

"Barrow," Maria barked, checking the time. Ten minutes for the locals to clear the delivery space and five for them to deliver the first two waves of cargo.

If they kept this up, they had enough time. *Just.* The corvettes that had moved out after *Luciole* were already accelerating back. They'd hit zero-velocity one hour after *Red Falcon* arrived, and then they'd be coming back toward Darius.

They had chosen not to fire missiles with a velocity disadvantage— even the SDC could guess what would happen to forty or so fusion drive missiles crawling toward *Falcon*—but once they were accelerating back, that calculation changed again.

If the next round of teleports went more slowly, they might have a problem...

Again and again power flared through the simulacrum chamber as Maria and her subordinates worked their way methodically through the thousand containers arranged on twenty of *Falcon's* cargo spars.

The second round was faster, the Mages having a better idea of what they were doing. The third slowed down, as did the fourth. Their "safe" hour finished as Nguyen completed his fifth teleport...and collapsed against the simulacrum.

"The corvettes are launching," Rice said grimly, but his words were quiet and his eyes were focused on Nguyen as Maria and Barrow lifted him away from the simulacrum. "We have forty missiles inbound. They aren't *great* missiles, but that's a lot of firepower.

"Is he going to be okay?"

"Barrow, you're up," Maria ordered as she checked Nguyen's pulse and sighed in relief. "He's fine. Unconscious and a hell of a nosebleed, but it looks worse than it is."

Wu stepped up next to her and offered a damp cloth to help clean the ex-Navy Mage's face. Asleep, he looked a lot younger and more vulnerable, and Wu took him from Maria, her magic helping her lift the larger man.

The youngest and most powerful Mage aboard the ship, senior to the older two junior Mages by virtue of date of hire and a natural gift for both magic and organizing a department, didn't look much better than Nguyen. She was just upright and carefully moving the other Mage as she met Maria's gaze.

"We can't run in real space," Wu pointed out carefully. "We've got more acceleration than those corvettes...but not enough. Someone has to jump us."

Power began to coil around Alessandra Barrow as she began to work the spell.

"It'll have to be me," Maria said grimly. "Barrow and Nguyen don't have enough left to jump from orbit, and you don't have the trai—"

"*Fàng pì,*" Wu spat. Maria didn't understand the words, but the junior Mage's meaning was clear. "You're in no better shape than they are. Worse, even. If you teleport the cargo down and jump from orbit, it'll kill you."

She was...*probably* wrong. Maybe. Maria shivered at the thought. She hadn't seen anyone burn out in person, though she'd seen a few get as bad as Nguyen currently was.

"You've never jumped this deep in a gravity well," Maria said. It wasn't an argument, not really.

Energy flared through the chamber and Barrow slumped against the simulacrum.

"I'm okay," she gasped out, slowly lifting herself off and dabbing at the blood oozing slowly from her nose. "I've had better days."

"Missiles inbound," Jeeves reported. "ETA three minutes. We can *probably* handle this lot, but..."

"I can do this," Wu insisted. "And nobody else can. Move those last crates, boss. We've *got* to get out of here."

Maria obeyed her subordinate, sliding past Barrow to slam her hands onto the simulacrum. She was exhausted, but she'd done this four times before. One last spar of cargo containers, one last slot on the surface.

Power flared through her into the semiliquid silver model in front of her, focusing onto a specific section of it. Even on the simulacrum, the spar of cargo *glowed*...and then vanished.

She wavered, stumbling away from the model as her nosebleed started up again. She'd worked her people too hard. *Way* too hard. This could kill them all.

"Engaging incoming fire," she heard Jeeves report. She couldn't see the screens...that was when she realizing her *eyes* were bleeding and everything was a blurry shade of red.

Wu was right. If Maria tried to jump *Red Falcon*, she would die.

But the other Mage was right there, pressing a damp cloth into Maria's hand as she stepped past and dropped her hands onto the simulacrum.

The world *tore*.

For an eternal moment, Maria felt reality break around her. This wasn't a jump. This was half of a step into hell, and her flesh *burned* as the world fell apart around her.

And then Xi Wu's magic wove around them all and rebuilt the universe...and *Red Falcon* was no longer in the Darius System.

CHAPTER 23

"THAT WAS possibly the most excruciating jump I have *ever* been through," David noted aloud as he and the rest of his bridge crew slowly caught their breath. "Simulacrum chamber, report. Is everyone okay?"

There was silence for several seconds.

"Ship's Mage, report," David repeated, starting to be seriously worried.

"We're all here," Alessandra Barrow finally answered in an exhausted tone. "'Okay' would be stretching it. Maria is bleeding from her eyes, Karl is unconscious, and Xi is...well, she's just unconscious, but there's enough raw magic sparking around her that no one is going to get near her for a couple of minutes.

"We'll all be fine," she concluded. "But I think the entire Mage contingent needs to go straight to sick bay and talk to Dr. Gupta. I hope it was worth it."

"I'll have Gupta send people to help you," David promised. Dr. Jaidev Gupta was the senior physician aboard *Red Falcon*, the man who'd installed David's own cybernetic leg and lung. He'd be able to put the Mages back together.

"Thank you."

"We'll find out if it was worth it," he told Barrow. "But I won't forget how far above and beyond you went. Go rest."

He cut the channel to the simulacrum chamber and studied his bridge crew.

"What's *Falcon*'s status, Kelly?" he asked.

"We're fine," his XO replied. "Didn't use any ammunition and we're still at about sixty percent fuel supply. I'd prefer our next trip be to somewhere where we *can* refuel, but...we didn't even get scratched and we completed the delivery."

"Let's hope Seule comes through on his side," David agreed. "Go check in on Xi, Kelly. We'll be fine."

His XO flashed him a grateful smile and rose as he turned to Jeeves.

"Alexander, did we learn anything?" he asked quietly.

"The regular corvettes are a pretty standard design," the gunner replied. "Could have been built in a dozen systems. The heavies were definitely built in Legatus." Jeeves shook his head. "The Bears' monitors jumped out while we were in Darius orbit. Whatever they were being paid for, fighting us wasn't part of it."

"They were probably hired for the Tracker and those ships were just there to keep them safe," David guessed. "Hopefully, the Darius government will make proper use of their new toys. Once the rebels are dealt with, SDC doesn't even have a fig leaf anymore—and then they can talk to the Navy."

So long as the conflict was between pro-UnArcana World and pro-Protectorate factions, the Navy could *not* intervene without setting off a political nightmare.

"How long until Seule arrives?" Jeeves asked. "I don't get the impression we're jumping anywhere soon."

"We're not jumping for at *least* twenty-four hours," David confirmed. "And I'll check with Maria once she's in a fit state, to talk about if we should wait longer. Seule should be here in about eighteen hours. He's going to jump to a random intermediate point, just in case the Golden Bears and their Tracker come back."

"The Tracker will still be able to follow him," Jeeves pointed out.

"I know. But it's all about buying time. We didn't come here to fight a war, after all."

Seule was roughly two hours late, and by the time he arrived, David had sent most of his people to bed. He was going to pay for staying awake as long as he had, but he needed to be the one there when *Luciole* finally arrived.

The smuggler's navigation was once again impressive, the blockade runner appearing less than a million kilometers from *Red Falcon*. David had the battle lasers online in remote control mode and was targeting the ship when the transponder code arrived.

He breathed a sigh of relief. A ship that close would be a nightmare if they were hostile.

A moment later, a blinking icon noted that *Luciole* was opening a channel.

"Rice here," he greeted the smuggler ship.

"Your people did well, Captain," Seule told him as the younger man's face appeared in the screen. "Governor Mitchell asked me to pass on her regards—and a data packet we are attaching to this transmission."

Seule grinned widely.

"If it's anything like the one she sent me, it's the codes to several numbered accounts on Amber as a payment for a job well done. I think we really made a difference, Captain Rice, and you more than honored my request."

"I'll admit that the SDC definitely did their best to make me feel better about screwing them," David said lightly. "I look forward to hearing about Security Vice-President Charleston's reports to his superiors."

"You'll be waiting a long time, sadly," the smuggler replied. "Charleston apparently rushed his flagship back to try and intimidate the Governor into handing over the cargo we'd dropped off. He claimed that his ship *did* have bombardment munitions."

David's own grin tightened uncomfortably. While the Navy made a point of restricting the manufacture and possession of orbital-bombardment weaponry as best as they could, it wasn't out of the question for SDC to have assembled some cruder systems.

"Did he?" David asked.

"I don't know," Seule said. "Mitchell decided not to find out—they'd already deployed the first squadrons of the surface-to-orbit missile trucks. Turns out that those heavy corvettes aren't any better at shooting down missiles coming up from the surface. His flagship is gone."

David couldn't regret Charleston's death, though he supposed the hundreds of others aboard that ship hadn't deserved to die with him.

"That's...unfortunate for him," he allowed. "And the rest of the SDC flotilla?"

"They were falling back from the planet when we jumped," Seule reported. "The blockade may not be over, but they won't be in close orbit anymore. I don't think the Darian civil war is going to last much longer."

"Good. I don't like arming either side in that kind of war," David admitted.

"I choose who I arm carefully," the gunrunner told him. "So does Alabaster. But...I promised you information in exchange for helping me, and you more than kept up your side. We'll make our way in to rendezvous, but may I invite yourself and the lovely Mage Soprano back aboard for supper?

"I think we have a lot to talk about."

Once again, David and Soprano found themselves in a small, intimate dining room as Nathan Seule served them with his own hands. This time, the meal was plainer in many ways, a simple protein and vitamin powder-laced pasta dish that any spacefarer would have recognized.

"I trust my crew," Seule said quietly as they started to eat, "but this room is now sealed and secured. No one aboard *Luciole* knows what we're talking about or what I promised you in exchange for your help in Darius."

"How you keep your secrets is your business," David allowed. "I need to know who sent you to Ardennes, though."

Seule nodded and took a bite of his pasta as he considered.

"You think Legatus was involved." It wasn't really a question.

"Given the gear that showed up in the Freedom Wing's hands and some of what they had to say when it was all over, yes," David agreed.

Seule clearly figured he knew who David worked for. It wasn't hard, for that matter. The smuggler might not know the exact agency, but "these are agents of Mars" was enough for most purposes.

"*Quel merdier.*" Seule shook his head. "A clusterfuck," he clarified in English. "I didn't put those pieces together, to be honest. Legatus is one of the top three weapons manufacturers in the Protectorate. I didn't think much of the cargo being all Legatan, more than I would have thought of it being all from Mars, Earth or Tau Ceti."

"But when you look at the entire equipment set that the Wing deployed..." David shrugged. "The pattern is clear, but we need more than a pattern."

"You want proof."

"Exactly."

"I can't give you proof," Seule warned. "If I don't know that Legatus is involved, I can't give you *anything* to tie directly back to them."

"I didn't expect you to," David agreed. "What *can* you give me? Who hired you for the delivery?"

"Man named Mahometus Kovac in the Condor System," Seule said simply. "He's not a big player in the gunrunning business, but he's a known quantity. Doesn't care too much about who buys the guns, but I wouldn't have fingered him as a Legatan agent."

"Probably isn't one," Soprano interjected. "If he takes people's money without asking questions, he'd probably happily take someone's money to *pretend* to sell guns to someone else. Just a bonus in his mind."

"He's crooked as they come, but he isn't particularly twisty," Seule agreed. "I could see him buying in to that. He operates out of a hotel on one of Condor's secondary transshipment facilities, McMurdo Station. We're pretty damn far from there right now, but I'm sure you can figure it out."

David snorted. Condor was a MidWorld on nearly the opposite side of the Protectorate, easily a hundred light-years away. That was going to be a headache, but...

"We have resources," he agreed. "Thank you, Captain Seule. You have done us all a service and I think we can call all debts paid."

"Debts don't quite work like that, in my experience," the smuggler replied. "But good enough for me for now. I'll wish you good luck once we're done, but now, we may as well eat!"

CHAPTER 24

"A HUNDRED LIGHT-YEARS is a long way, even for us," Soprano noted in the meeting the next morning, once *Luciole* had headed on her way to wherever gunrunners went when they weren't working with spies. "If we jump it Navy-style, it's still almost seven days to Condor. If we give our people a break—and after our stunt in Darius, I am *entirely* for taking it easy—it's almost nine."

"I don't think we're in enough of a hurry to push our people this time," David replied. "Darius was above and beyond, and I refuse to ask *more* of your people until we need to."

LaMonte was already pulling up an astrographic chart and marking their location.

"We're here," the XO noted, highlighting a green dot in deep space near Darius. "The Condor System—properly the Principality of Condor—is here." A green three-dimensional X appeared on the chart.

"The Principality is a solid MidWorld operating under a constitutional monarchy," she continued. "Prince Gadhavi is theoretically only the Governor as far as the Protectorate Charter is concerned, but everyone uses his official title. Our files say the system is rich but somewhat insular, with two habitable planets and more real estate than they know what to do with.

"Gadhavi would probably prefer *not* to have interstellar gunrunning going through his system, but so long as they keep it to orbit, he doesn't seem to actually care. Certainly, his government doesn't care. Bringing something to the planets? It's screened six ways to Sunday. Transshipping or storing in orbit? There's a simple fee per cargo container—and apparently, the inspections aren't really audited and are easy to buy off."

"That's got to make them popular with a lot of people," David noted, pulling the data up on his wrist-comp.

"There's an MISS local station but no RTA," his XO said. "Because... yeah, the system is popular with several streams of the underworld. Most notable from our interest is that la Cosa Nostra seems to be operating a major shipping hub there."

"Is the Prince a Mage?" Soprano asked. "Are we looking at a Mage aristocracy or something...else?"

"Something else," LaMonte replied. "There isn't an official aristocracy outside the Prince's family, though Mages have the usual Compact privileges and value. The Prince is specifically barred from being a Mage, and his family is discouraged from marrying Mages, too. Balance of power, I'd guess."

That was a more reasonable compromise than many David had heard of. Mages were powerful, valued members of society, and the Compact between Mage and mundane had been written by men and women who had been slaves. It erred on the side of protecting Mages rather than protecting equality.

Imposing a major power nexus that was specifically barred from being Mages made sense to him.

"So, we go to Condor," Leonhart said. "I'll have my people brush up on bodyguarding and so forth. What else do we need to worry about?"

"Condor should be safe enough," David told his security chief. "Given what we're going to Condor for, though, we may need your people to brush up on kidnapping instead."

"We call that 'involuntary asset extraction,'" Leonhart said primly.

The Captain snorted. "Whatever we're calling it, we need to be prepared to get our hands on this Kovac fellow. I don't think he's going to want to tell us everything just because we showed up and asked nicely."

David studied the astrography chart LaMonte had up and linked into it with his wrist-comp. With a dash of his fingers, he slowly rotated the three-dimensional image to confirm what he was checking for.

"Tau Ceti is on the way, pretty much exactly at the halfway point," he pointed out to his people. "I suggest we stop in there for fuel and supplies—and to check in with MISS. I'm relatively sure we can get a cargo from Tau Ceti to justify our showing up in Condor, too. Thankfully, no one is going to question us showing up in our home port empty.

"Well, not much."

"Sounds good," Kellers noted, the engineer speaking up for the first time. "We've been lucky so far, but I wouldn't mind a day or three in a decent slip to poke at a few of the shakier parts of the ship."

"Then we'll make it happen," David promised. "Twelve to thirteen days to Condor versus nine to ten doesn't sound like that big a deal to me. Kovac sent this shipment over a year ago. I doubt he's expecting questions now!"

Laying out the course for their journey fell to Maria, of course. She wouldn't have it any other way, though she was more and more getting Xi Wu to help her with the task. Young as she was, the powerful Mage would likely soon move on to another ship.

If nothing else, Maria expected LaMonte to find herself a new command sooner rather than later, and Xi Wu and Mike Kelzin would inevitably go with her. The pair had followed her to *Red Falcon,* and wherever any of them went from here, the others would go.

Maria envied them that. She envied them the bright smile Wu flashed her as she disappeared from the sanctum, returning to her quarters. None of her relationships had ever had the calm warmth and certainty the unlikely trio seemed to muster with ease.

The movie night with Kellers had ended up just being a one-off snuggle. They hadn't even slept together, which she found herself regretting now. The engineer wasn't her usual type. He was older than her, for one thing, and calmer than many of her lovers.

Smarter too, she had to admit. Her taste had not run to...intellectual men. *Capable* men, yes, though that hadn't always ended well. *Red*

Falcon's first tactical officer had been a capable man—and had proven as capable at betraying them as anything else.

Kellers was also either uninterested or...shy. The latter possibility didn't quite fit in Maria's head, but neither did the first. Perhaps she was egotistical enough to assume that no man was completely uninterested in her, but she also didn't think that he'd have suggested the movie night idea without at least *some* deeper intent.

Maria chuckled to herself. She'd spent much of her life pursuing men of one stripe or another. Not usually for more than a single night's fling, but...well, at least some of the skills had to transfer over.

And if nothing else, she knew that Tau Ceti hosted a significant Spanish-speaking population. There had to be *something* she could use the same excuse he'd used to drag him out to.

And from there, well, they'd see what happened, wouldn't they?

CHAPTER 25

DAVID WAS completely unsurprised by the message he received within ten minutes of *Red Falcon* docking at her home station. On the surface, it was a dinner invitation from a cargo broker they hadn't worked with before.

Reading between the lines, it was an instruction to report for debrief and bring Soprano and LaMonte with him. He'd been expecting the message and sent back his response immediately before studying the situation he was in.

Through a simple holding company, David owned two docking slips there in Tau Ceti along with a small office complex. His second ship, *Peregrine*, was home about as often as *Red Falcon* was but was exactly what she appeared to be on the surface. He'd moved his people who didn't want to be spies over to *Peregrine* and made them all keel-plate owners in a new ship.

It seemed to have worked out, and every time *Peregrine*'s financial reports—and attached funds—caught up with him, they'd been a pleasant surprise. She was a relatively standard ship with a small suite of defensive guns added due to David's history.

Amber was as much home as Tau Ceti these days, thanks to Keiko Alabaster, and both were *far* more home than Mars, where, he was reasonably sure, his never-to-be-sufficiently cursed father still lived.

Twelve light-years was about as close as David Rice cared to get to Samuel Rice. The elder Rice had been in jail for the death of David's mother when David had joined the Navy, and David had never told him where he was going.

With thirty more years between them, David could accept that his mother's death in a boating accident had truly been an accident, negligence rather than malice, like the courts had decided. There was still a long gap between that acceptance and *forgiving* his father.

Tau Ceti and *Red Falcon* were better homes, and he had a better family there. Speaking of... he opened a channel to his two senior officers' wrist-comps.

"Our lords and masters have checked in," he told them. If internal coms aboard *Red Falcon* weren't secure enough for that snark, he had far bigger problems. "Debrief is at dinner at the Purple Legate, twenty hundred hours OMT."

"Should I wear a dress?" LaMonte asked lightly. The Purple Legate Italian restaurant was known for its discretion and privacy—and also for being one of the two or three nicest restaurants in the orbitals of Tau Ceti's inhabited worlds.

"Does either of you even *own* a dress?" he said.

"I do," Soprano replied. "I think I have bikinis with more cloth involved than that outfit, but I do own *a* dress."

"I hadn't even considered that as an option," LaMonte said. "I'm sure I can find a halter-top and a miniskirt; we'd be close to matching."

The Ship's Mage laughed.

"No, you'd *still* be more dressed than me," she admitted. "By a lot."

David sighed.

"Ship's uniforms, if you please," he said with false plaintiveness. "Given my experience with our MISS contacts, you two showing up like that might outright kill our poor debriefer with a heart attack!"

"Yes, sir," his officers chorused with unfailing innocence.

"Are we likely to be rushed out?" LaMonte asked after a moment. "I can ask Kellers to hold off on starting his repair work."

"No," David replied. "The type of work Kellers wants to do is easily put back together if they need us to turn around overnight, but I can't see it. They wanted us following these leads and I'm following them to Condor. I can't see us being pulled off of that."

"Good," Maria said crisply. She hadn't been the one talking about delays and David wondered why *she* was happy they were staying.

He then decided there were probably things he didn't want to know.

The Purple Legate was on the top floor of one of the station's main galleries, surrounded and interlaced with small trees while allowing an awe-inspiring view of a thirty-story drop ringed with businesses.

The faint buzz of white-noise generators assaulted the senses as they entered the restaurant. It soon faded into the background, but it was a comforting noise to the three spies. Privacy was important.

"Party of three under David Rice," David told the hostess. "We should be meeting a second party?"

"Of course; Mr. Kieshi is waiting for you," the older woman said instantly. "Follow me, please?"

The white noise generators might cover the sound of conversation, leaving only the burbling of the false brook that watered the trees, but they didn't cover the smell from the kitchen of rich tomato sauce and spices.

Kieshi wasn't a familiar name to David, and he had a moment of concern when they were led into the secluded dining area. He didn't recognize the elderly Asian man sitting at the end of the table. He did, as he realized with relief after a moment, recognize the other man in the room.

Brent Alois was an old standby in the Tau Ceti MISS office, the agent responsible for recruiting many new personnel—including Maria Soprano—while also running, as David understood it, the main counter-intelligence operation for the Navy Base in Tau Ceti. The balding old man tossed the new guests a weak salute and gestured them to the table.

"Captain Rice, Mage Soprano, Officer LaMonte," Alois greeted them. "Be known to Kieshi Deng, System Director for Tau Ceti."

"Normally, your high-level contacts were with Hand Stealey," Kieshi said politely in a soft Earth Asian accent. "I saw no need to interfere with what appeared to be a highly functional relationship. With Hand Stealey's regrettable passing, however, it behooves me to make contact, Captain, Mage, Officer."

"A pleasure," David said, extending his hand and taking Kieshi's surprisingly firm grip. "I didn't know who ran the Tau Ceti Station for Mars."

"We try to keep your kind of independent operative out of that sort of loop," Kieshi said frankly. "You go into harm's way more than most of my people, and that means information you possess is at a certain degree of risk.

"You also need a top-level contact for your kind of operation," he continued. "So, here we are. I understand you just left Darius? Our reports on the situation there are incomplete and...unpleasant."

"I presume there are actions in place to deal with the situation?" David asked.

"I can't say much, due to security, but yes," Kieshi confirmed. "Knowing your rather cataclysmic effect on the enemies of Mars as you pass through, I wonder if those actions will still be necessary."

"You may need to adjust your plans, I'll admit," David said as Maria choked next to him. "How much detail do you need?"

Kieshi held up a hand as a buzzer sounded. "A high level will suffice for now, though I presume you have a report. But let us order. The food here lives up to its reputation."

A few minutes of perusing the menu and ordering drinks and wine, then the waiter slipped away again.

"As part of our pursuit of the supply chain for the weapons on Ardennes, we ended up taking on a contract to deliver weaponry to the Darius government," David explained quickly. "The system was under a tight blockade by the security forces of the Stellarite Development Corps, so the original plan for delivery by Captain Seule and his blockade runner seemed unworkable."

"We were aware of that cargo," Kieshi confirmed, adding weight to Seule's suggestion that Mars had helped Darius pay for it. "It was delivered nonetheless?"

"Despite the best efforts of the SDC ships, yes," David confirmed. "While we attempted to avoid engaging any SDC ships, my understanding is that several of their heavy corvettes were either destroyed or crippled and forced to return to Legatus.

"With the cargo in place, the Darius government appears to have regained control of their immediate orbital space. I have no idea how the civil war has progressed, but with the cargo we delivered, I am hopeful."

Kieshi smiled.

"That is good news," he told David. "I'll want your full report, as I said, to go over in detail and assess how we'll change our measures. If the Darius government is fully in control of their world, we shall need to arrange for them to properly request Navy assistance against the SDC, if Stellarite hasn't learned their lesson already."

"There will be consequences for SDC for their involvement," Alois added. "That part of the file has already been passed on to Hand Lomond."

David winced. He hadn't liked any of the SDC people he'd met, but few deserved to have the man the media called the Sword of Mars unleashed on them.

"And your main mission?" Kieshi asked.

"Captain Seule provided us with the name of his contact, a Mahometus Kovac in the Condor System," David reported. "We're en route to make contact ourselves. In the absence of cooperation or the ability to steal it from his files, we may be forced to, well, kidnap the man for interrogation."

"Kovac is known to us," the System Director confirmed. "I'll make sure you have a warrant for that before you leave Tau Ceti. We know enough to put him behind bars as it is, but it's useful to leave some of those middlemen in place."

"If we're lucky, he can lead us to Legatus—or at least one more step along the chain," David agreed.

"Regional Director Van der Merwe is still working on digging out more information from Ardennes," Alois noted. "They passed on more information for us to give you. It sounds like we've got a hard link to

Kovac, which puts him ahead of the other two names Van der Merwe has pulled up."

"More middlemen, I presume?" David asked.

"Exactly," Kieshi confirmed. "Mitre Borghi, at Amber, and Mehrab Gorman at Sherwood. Neither are major players, we know Borghi is a smaller source than Kovac, and if Gorman *is* a gunrunner, he's evaded our attention so far."

"Sherwood isn't exactly known as a gunrunning hub," LaMonte pointed out.

"And that's probably why he's evaded our attention," Kieshi agreed. "I leave your exact courses of action up to you, Captain Rice; you know this situation as well as anyone now. The less general havoc, the better, but I understand the requirements of our job."

Further immediate "work conversation" was cut short by the arrival of the food.

Once they'd finished eating, Kieshi leaned back from the table and studied David and his officers with a calm expression.

"You know what you need to do," he told them. "Better than I do, I'm sure. My policy has never been to micromanage if I can avoid it, just to make sure my people have the resources they need. So, what *do* you need?"

David considered thoughtfully as he took the last swallow of his single glass of wine.

"It's hard to anticipate," he admitted. "We'll need a cargo contract to justify us going to Condor, but that's not unusual for us. In terms of re-sources...more antimatter missiles won't go amiss if we can sneak them aboard. Any stealth gear that might make infiltration easier on Leonhart's people, though I don't know what they're trained with."

Alois chuckled.

"They're Forward Combat Intelligence," the ex-Marine officer turned spy pointed out. "I *do* know what they're trained with, and there's a few toys you wouldn't have to hand that might be useful."

"We should be able to sneak a cargo container of Phoenix VIIIs in with your main cargo," Kieshi said thoughtfully. "I might be able to break free a trained interrogator or two, but..."

"I believe Major Leonhart is fully qualified in that field," Alois argued.

"I believe so as well," David agreed. "We have a lot of the resources we need already. KEX-12 was set up that way intentionally, to allow us to operate completely independently as much as possible."

"You're not the only covert ops ship, but you might be the one with the most complete setup," Kieshi agreed. "It's a concept we're going to try and duplicate, I think, though probably with less ostentatious ships. More concealed weapons and, well, less-notorious captains."

"My reputation has been both a help and a curse for our operations," David admitted. "I think—I hope—the good has outweighed the bad."

Kieshi chuckled.

"By a long shot, Captain Rice. Hand Stealey chose well when she recruited you," he said. "This mission might be one of the more critical we've ever sent you on. Or at least the most potentially fruitful."

"There has to be more proof out there of Legatan misbehavior than this one chain," Maria argued. "If they're dabbling as widely as we think they are..."

"We have a lot of circumstance and guesses," Kieshi said quietly. "A *mountain* of said circumstance and guesses. Enough that projects to raise funds from loyal systems to build new secret fleets are being negotiated, but we need time and we need proof. Enough to drag before the Council of the Protectorate and have those notoriously stubborn representatives sign off on sanctioning the Legatan government."

"They're preparing for civil war," Maria objected. "We know this."

"We, as in MISS, *believe* we know this," the System Director agreed. "Without proof, though, all we have is circumstance. Without evidence that we can intern an entire planetary government with, all we can do is begin our own quiet preparations for civil war."

David shivered.

"Is it going to come to that?" he asked softly.

"Not for years, if ever," Kieshi guessed. "But if we find proof now, before they're ready, the Navy and the Marines can prevent it ever getting that bad."

"And if we don't?" Maria asked softly.

"Then all we can do is fight them in every shadow we find them in and buy time for those new fleets to be built, for the Protectorate to be ready to defend itself," the senior spy said grimly. "It's a shadow war right now, and while we believe we know our enemy, we're not certain of his targets or his objectives.

"It falls to you to find proof of what Legatus is up to. Others will seek to learn their objectives. When the dust settles, though, it's all about buying time. If they're ready and we're not...it doesn't matter if we have proof."

CHAPTER 26

THE MEETING with Kieshi left Maria feeling more than a little overwhelmed. She still managed to take the time to confirm the research she'd done on her way in, so when they returned aboard *Red Falcon,* she made her way down to Engineering to check in on James Kellers.

He was exactly where she expected to find him: in his office, working far too late as he put together the plans for how to complete the work his team had started earlier that day.

"Hey, stranger," she said cheerfully as she stepped into the room without knocking. "How's your baby?"

Kellers snorted and leaned back in his chair to look at her.

"Despite several people's best efforts, she's fine," he admitted. "A little squeak here, a little rattling there. Nothing a couple of days of going through with wrenches and oil while she isn't flying won't fix."

"Nobody has shot at us in, what, four whole days?" Maria asked. "Just *think* of how far out of our way we're going to keep *Falcon* safe."

He chuckled.

"Yes, avoiding people who want to shoot us does seem to be a strain on this ship's command cadre," he agreed, but he was smiling as he said it. "I'm sure you're not overly interested in the minutiae of which sections of the ship I'm sending people at with said wrenches and lubricating oil. What's up?"

"Probably more interested in that than you'd think," Maria told him. "This ship is my home, James. If I can help keep her flying, that's in my interests too."

"This is preventative maintenance," he admitted. "We could do a lot of it while in motion and survive without the rest for a long while, but I'd rather take the opportunity whenever we're in a safe port to make sure it happens."

Maria grinned wickedly at him.

"Careful, Chief Engineer; I think you just said you didn't need to watch over this process," she told him.

"I could be spared for some of it," Kellers said carefully. "What were you thinking?"

"Well, you were kind enough to grab that copy of *Estrellas del Destino*, so I went looking around here to see what I could find," she said. "Did you know that the station hosts a Spanish-language community theater?"

"No, I have to admit I didn't," he replied, his smile threatening to turn into a grin of his own. "Did you happen to find out what they're putting on right now?"

"A dinner-theater version of an old musical about Argentina. *Evita*, I think it was called?"

"I don't believe I've ever seen that one live," Kellers allowed. "And dinner as well?"

Maria glanced around his office and the scattering of coffee cups—and lack of plates.

"They have a midnight showing, starting in about two hours," she told him. "If, you know, you haven't eaten yet."

That got an outright laugh out of him as he studied the same collection of dishes she'd been eyeing.

"I think you've got me in more ways than one," he admitted. "All right, Maria, let's go see this musical."

"I'm going to go change," she told him. "I'll see you in an hour?"

"It's a date," he promised—and from the look in his eyes, he knew *exactly* what he was saying.

The show was, frankly, terrible.

At least three of the actors, including the woman playing the lead, weren't native Spanish speakers and it showed. The performances ranged from actually impressive to downright atrocious, and the inconsistency almost made it worse than it would have been if all the performers were bad.

The food was better than Maria had expected, and the company turned out to be even more pleasant than she'd hoped. They spent the evening conversing in Spanish, struggling where her Brazo-Portuguese and his Amber-post-secondary Spanish didn't line up, but the struggles were merely excuses to laugh and clarify in English.

By the time they left the show, Maria was feeling confident enough to grab James's hand. He said nothing, only squeezing her hand in return as they made their way through the station's corridors.

Finally, still short of their ship, he stopped. He didn't let go of her hand, though, and Maria smiled as she turned to face him.

"Well, James?" she asked.

"This is nice," he admitted, squeezing her hand again, "but I'm not sure where this is going. I don't exactly think I'm your type, Maria."

"You're not," she agreed with a smile. "Which, given my history with 'my type,' is probably closer to a recommendation than anything else. I think it's safe to hope that, at this point, you're not planning on betraying the ship."

James chuckled, still holding her hand and smiling at her.

"You have picked some winners, haven't you?" he said cheerfully. "What does that make me?"

"What do you want it to make you?" Maria asked, stepping in closer to him. He opened his arms and was suddenly holding her as she rested her head against his shoulder. "I'm...more than willing to give it a shot. Maybe something more solid. I can't predict the future, though."

"No one can," he agreed. "I've just watched the past, and we know each other pretty well by now, don't we?"

"I think so," she hazarded, suddenly uncertain for the first time in a while. God, what was she *doing*?

Then he was looking into her eyes and it didn't matter as they kissed for the first time.

CHAPTER 27

KELLY HAD been an engineer before she'd been an executive officer, and her "soft skills" still sometimes lagged behind where she thought they should be. Her captain didn't complain, but she was aware of the shortfall herself and working on it.

Realizing that *something* had happened between James Kellers and Maria Soprano was well within her ability. All of *Red Falcon*'s senior crew were like family, and she knew them all. The pair had always been friends, like everyone else, but now they were sitting together around the conference table—much like she and Mike Kelzin were.

Soprano's flush when Kelly arched an eyebrow at her, barely noticeable against her skin as it was, confirmed Kelly's suspicions. That, for now, was as much as Kelly needed to get involved. XO or not, this wasn't a warship, and both merchant ships and covert ops ships trusted their people to be adults.

If problems arose, well, there was a reason Kelly LaMonte had spent at least some of her time in Tau Ceti taking counseling courses.

Rice was the last to arrive to the meeting, and he'd pushed the regular morning get-together back two hours already.

"Sorry, people," he said briskly as he took his seat. "Our MISS friends managed to pin down a cargo for us, but we had to leap on it immediately. We now *have* said cargo, but it took up more of my morning than I expected."

"When do we start loading?" Kelly asked instantly. If things were running on that tight a timeline, it might cause problems for Kellers's repairs.

"Tomorrow evening," Rice replied. "The urgency was to make sure we were the ones to step up when the original shipper fell through. The first shipper was a big interstellar, so if we wanted to get the cargo as an independent, I had to hustle."

Most ships with *Red Falcon*'s cargo capacity belonged to the big interstellar shipping organizations. Few of those would be going as far out as Condor which made it rare for them to find a full cargo.

"As it stands, we now have a full twenty-megaton cargo heading to the Condor system, where it'll go into storage and be broken up into smaller shipments for the Fringe Worlds," Rice explained. "Tau Ceti produces most of the satellites and space shuttles and similar high-tech gear for a lot of places, but partial cargos are a pain in the ass for the big industrial cartels.

"So, this kind of shipment goes out. They contract with one of the big hauling lines and move ten, twenty, or thirty million tons of high-tech systems out to a MidWorld with good transshipping facilities, then break it down onto smaller ships like our old *Blue Jay* from there."

He shrugged.

"We're getting paid shit, almost ten percent under the market rate per container, so we have every reason to make this delivery quickly and find out what we can haul out of Condor. Jeeves's main concern, however," he continued with a smile at the covert ops ship's gunner, "is that one of the cargo containers we're getting *won't* be from the client.

"It's coming from the Navy and it contains exactly one thousand Phoenix VIII antimatter drive missiles," the Captain concluded.

Kelly heard Jeeves inhale sharply. As she understood it, that was more missiles than *Red Falcon*'s internal magazines could actually carry—and the VIII was a noticeably superior weapon to the VIIs they'd been given before.

"Obviously, we'll still want to keep our magazines mostly loaded with the Rapiers," Rice told them all. "But having several reloads of the best missiles in the Protectorate isn't going to hurt.

"We'll also be getting a set of upgrade kits for Kelzin's assault shuttles," he continued with a nod to Kelly's boyfriend. "I'll leave getting them applied up to you and James, Mike, but they're supposed to boost your stealth, ECM, and acceleration."

"I look forward to testing them out," Kelly's boyfriend said cheerfully. "Anything spectacular in them?"

"Yeah. Have you heard of a crush compensator?" Rice asked.

Kelzin looked confused, but everyone heard Leonhart inhale sharply.

"Those are *not* supposed to be in civilian hands," she hissed.

"And it's a good thing we're not civilians," the Captain replied. "For the rest of you, a crush compensator is a precharged runic artifact capable of neutralizing about six hundred KPS's worth of kinetic energy at impact.

"Once."

"They're designed for assault boarding," Leonhart noted carefully. "The shuttle itself ends up needing a million or two in repairs after you use the crush compensator, but the boarding team is fine."

Kelly understood her surprise. From what Xi Wu told her, there weren't many precharged runic artifacts in the galaxy—most "magical items" required recharging by a Mage quite often—and the details of how they were built were a closely kept secret. It seemed Deng Kieshi had meant it when he said he'd make sure they had whatever resources they needed.

"We have about forty-eight hours to complete the repairs, assuming you can work while we're being loaded?" Rice turned to Kellers.

"We can," he confirmed.

"That's one hell of a load cycle if they're not starting until tomorrow evening," Kelly noted. "I presume we're getting help?"

"We're going to be making a quick hop over to Prime Consortium's loading facility tomorrow," the Captain replied. "Their systems can load an entire spar's worth of containers at a time. Each load isn't necessarily fast, but when they're loading fifty containers at a shot, it doesn't *need* to be!"

The loading facility was an entirely separate space station from the main orbitals of Tau Ceti *e*. It consisted of a large cylinder, with a small section at one end spun to provide gravity for the working crews of Prime Consortium, and the majority of its length a working space filled with massive robotic arms.

"*Red Falcon*, adjust course by point five meters per second along vector fifty-two by one hundred," a voice echoed in Kelly's headset. A momentary burst of thrust from the forward thrusters provided the requested change.

"That's good, *Falcon*. Hold this course for another thirty-two seconds from...mark. Then slow to a full stop relative to the station."

She tapped the commands into the navigation console and watched the metal maw of the loading station consume her ship. They'd lined her up at a very specific angle and a very specific speed, and she could make out the docking cradle *Falcon* was heading toward.

"And mark," the voice said, at the same instant as her programmed deceleration kicked in. Their velocity was low enough, it took only two seconds to bring the ship to a complete halt, even at the relatively gentle acceleration they could risk inside the station.

"That's good," the control station continued. "Hold position; we are initiating the docking cradle."

The spiderweb of gantries lifted away from the station "floor," locking around *Red Falcon* to hold her in place. Kelly had a momentary feeling of being trapped, but a quick glance at her repeater from Jeeves's tactical station was reassuring...for her.

The charge status of the ship's defensive turrets would have been *terrifying* for Prime Consortium's traffic control staff even before they realized that Jeeves was drawing up a targeting sequence that would cut *Falcon* free from the docking cradle—and then use her battle lasers to cut a megafreighter-sized hole through the exterior of the space station.

It was almost certainly unnecessary, but...she understood the paranoia.

"*Red Falcon*, we are passing you over to cargo control," the controller told her. "We'll talk to you again in the morning. Welcome to Prime Consortium's Allonsi Station."

"Thank you, control; holding for the transfer," she replied. As she waited, she muted her mike and looked over Jeeves's plans.

"Efficient, if horrendously expensive for Prime," she told him. "A little bit paranoid, though, don't you think?"

"This is the most locked-down we've ever been except for actual major repairs, and we get those done in Navy yards," her ex-Navy and ex-gunrunner subordinate replied. "I trust the MISS verification on these guys, I do, but even paranoids have real enemies."

Kelly snorted, then a chime on her headset informed her that she had cargo control on the line.

"This is Officer LaMonte, XO of *Red Falcon*," she confirmed in response to a half-heard question. "Our spars are clear and we should be ready to begin loading."

"Understood," a woman's voice told her. "We have a single-container special package to deliver first; where do you want it?"

That, presumably, was the missiles.

"If we drop it at the core of spar A-1, will that cause problems in your loading?" Kelly asked. The spars were traversable, allowing access to the containers if needed, but the less distance they had to haul ten-ton missiles, the better.

"If we hadn't anticipated it, maybe," the woman on the radio replied with a chuckle. "Don't know what's in it, didn't ask, but figured you'd want it close to home. That'll take us about twenty minutes to get set up, then we'll start loading stacks onto your spars." There was a pause. "I...recommend either *really* good earplugs or sleeping off-ship tonight, Officer LaMonte. This is *not* a quiet process for anyone, even with most of it in vacuum."

"We'll find a way," Kelly said with a chuckle. "We've been through worse."

It couldn't, after all, be worse than actually having missiles hit the ship.

Kelly was wrong. Missiles hitting the ship, for all of the terrifying implications and resounding tones of the impact, lasted only a few seconds.

Cargo being loaded onto the spars was normally almost unnoticeable, with only a single container being added to a given spar at a time. There were a few seconds of a minor vibration that rang through the ship, but that was all.

Allonsi Station's loading equipment was something entirely new in her experience. The machinery moved ten-thousand-ton cargo containers like they were takeout boxes, sliding them around in batches of ten that were attached as one.

It wasn't a fast process, with the ten containers almost grinding into place on the hundred-and-twenty-meter-long spar. Every moment they were in contact, vibrations rang along the support structure into the ship, creating an awful noise in every compartment.

Then it would stop as that set of ten containers was locked into place. But *Falcon*'s cargo spars each held *fifty* containers, and the next set would start mere seconds later.

It took fifteen minutes to load the first spar. Five minutes to realign the equipment and bring up the next cargo load, then fifteen more minutes. A process that would normally take well over a day was scheduled to take roughly seven hours.

Kelly grimly remained on the bridge to coordinate as it continued. She presumed, probably with more hope than reason, that the rotating gravity ring underneath *Falcon*'s forward protective dome was quieter, so she sent everyone else on the bridge to go rest.

Someone had to be in touch with Allonsi Station's logistics people throughout. Kellers's engineers would be working too, so it wasn't like her old job would have required less dealing with this.

"How're your ears?" Rice asked, the Captain suddenly right at her shoulder. Her surprised start clearly answered his question, and he chuckled.

"Haven't seen this kind of gear in play in a while," he told her. "I forgot how loud it was." He shook his head. "And this is why I never wanted to do the Core World runs most of the big freighters do. Any of the big thirty-million-ton ships doing those runs is being loaded and unloaded by facilities like this."

"I see why they suggested we go aboard the station during the process," Kelly admitted. "But, well...paranoia."

Jeeves's carefully written targeting plan was still active on her screen. If Prime Consortium decided to do something completely unexpected, Kelly could break *Red Falcon* free in short order.

"It's in the job description," her Captain agreed. "It *is* somewhat quieter on the hab ring. Everyone who can has retreated there for some reason."

"Oh, good," Kelly said. "I was hoping I was the only one going insane."

"Not the *only* one, anyway," Rice said with a chuckle. "I'll take over, Kelly. You get to the hab ring and try and sleep. It's not *quiet* there, but it is *quieter* and your sanity might recover a bit."

"Three more hours, that's all," she replied.

"And I'll handle them," he assured her. "Four hours of this cacophony is enough for anyone. Even James is cycling people in four-hour shifts for the maintenance work right now."

Silence washed over them as a spar finished.

"Prime isn't going to try and backstab us, Kelly," Rice concluded. "Not with an entire Martian *fleet* hanging out less than twenty minutes' flight away. Go rest."

CHAPTER 28

FOR ALL of his assurances to his people, David still had to conceal a sigh of relief when *Red Falcon* cleared the exit from Allonsi Station. They were safe in Tau Ceti, but he'd learned never to underestimate a determined enemy.

He didn't *think* they were currently being hunted, but he'd been wrong on that count before.

"*Red Falcon*, we show you clear of the safety margin," the station controller told him. "You are clear to bring up your main engines. It's been a pleasure."

"My crew's aching ears suggest a different description," David suggested with a smile. "Thanks for the help, Allonsi."

"Strangely, I'm *sure* I've heard that complaint before! Clear skies and happy trails, *Red Falcon*."

Still smiling, David brought up *Red Falcon*'s engines and directed the big ship toward the edge of the system. He tagged a channel that linked him to all of his senior officers.

"If anyone has a reason we shouldn't be heading straight to Condor, speak now or hold your peace," he told them. "We're already moving at ten gees, so turning around will become hard pretty quickly."

"I might have left the stove on," Kellers quipped.

"I think I left my boyfriend behind," Leonhart added.

David snorted.

"James, your stove is aboard *Red Falcon*," he pointed out. "Rhianna... isn't your boyfriend in Sol?"

The security chief purred into the radio.

"*One* of my boyfriends is in Sol," she told them. "Don't worry; I wasn't trying to sneak anyone aboard. We should be good to go. I'm liking my shiny new toys."

Those included, from the list David had seen, everything from the assault-shuttle upgrades to several new, super-classified sets of stealth armor. They weren't up to the damage absorption or strength boost of combat exoskeletons, but they were supposed to allow the wearer to hide from both electronic sensors and eyes.

David would believe it once he'd seen it in action.

"Anyone *else* want to be a smartass?" he asked, smiling at the joking. Morale was good. They'd done a damned good thing at Darius and they'd done it *well*, leaving an entire corporate security fleet looking like suckers.

His people deserved to be proud of themselves.

"Nguyen is on duty and ready to jump once we're clear," Soprano replied. "I don't see any reason to stick around, much as I like Tau Ceti."

"Then we're on our way," David said. "Next stop, the Principality of Condor."

It had been a long time since Maria had woken up and not been alone in her bed. It took her a moment to even recognize why there was a warm lump under the blankets with her, and then she turned on her side to smile at the muscular black man asleep next to her.

It turned out that the ship's engineer was a major cinephile, Spanish language not required, and both of them had rather eclectic collections of movies. They'd spent an enjoyable evening just going over the list and making plans as to which movies to watch...and then had got distracted before they had actually watched anything.

James continued to sleep, apparently unaware of her assessing gaze as she looked at him. Maria snuggled closer to him, and he adjusted to let her mold against his heavily muscled chest, seemingly without waking.

There was something different here, and she was a bit confused by it. As she'd told him, James was far from her regular type, but now that she knew he'd been interested, she could think of little gestures and hints he'd been dropping for at least six months.

He hadn't pushed. Hadn't probed. Just quietly sneaked inside her defenses and settled down to wait for her to notice. Now his arms wrapped around her, strong enough to carry her as he'd demonstrated the previous evening...and yet gentle enough that she was far from trapped.

She leaned against his chest, let her breathing sync with his, and continued to smile as she closed her eyes.

"I don't think you have that aligned right," Kelly said into a microphone as she studied the events in the shuttle bay. She leaned against the window of the control room, watching a sensor panel as Kellers's team installed the upgrade kits for Kelzin's shuttles.

"And why do you say that?" one of the junior engineers barked, the tired-looking youth not quite glaring up at the window.

"Because those panels are supposed to absorb radar, and the test micro-pulse I just fired at the shuttle got a signal," she replied levelly. "Looks like we've got a misalignment between panels five and six; they're lined up at the top but out by about three millimeters at the bottom."

The grouchy engineer knelt down next to the shuttle and cursed.

"You got it, XO," he confirmed. He carefully poked at the panel, then shook his head. "Damn it, looks like it got pulled when we installed one of the later panels. We're going to have to yank this entire section and redo it." A sigh echoed over the communicator. "Thanks, LaMonte."

"Better it's caught now than when someone is trying to find Mike to *shoot* at him," she pointed out.

The engineer snorted and gestured his team back to him, and Kelly turned around at a noise to see Mike Kelzin entering the control room.

"I'm looking forward to what those kits will do for my shuttles, but I swear the Marines thought we'd have more gear for the refit," he admitted as he looked over her shoulder. "How are we doing?"

Kelly interrupted the professional conversation to kiss him, then turned her attention back to the screens.

"We have six assault shuttles," she said. "We've got two still up, two stripped waiting for upgrades, this one being worked on, and one complete." She shook her head. "If I were you, I'd leave the two untouched ones untouched. We'll be lucky to have four upgraded before we hit Condor.

"That said, we've got all the gear they'd have on a destroyer. The Marines just figured that they'd have the time and manpower to spare two team-days per shuttle."

"And so do we," he agreed. "We just have a time limit the Marines wouldn't normally have."

"Yeah." Kelly studied the half-reassembled shuttle on the bay floor. "Like I said, I think we'll have four upgraded to the new spec by the time we make Condor, but we won't manage the last two."

"Then we'll leave Bay Three's birds unstripped," he agreed. "We *shouldn't* need to make any assault landings in Condor. Stealth and discretion are the plan, right?"

"Stealth and discretion are *always* the plan," she said. "But when are they ever the reality?"

CHAPTER 29

EVERY STAR system had its own unique nature and complexities, and David found each of them fascinating in their own way. The Principality of Condor was no exception.

The beating heart of the system was the two inhabited planets: Phoenix, barely far enough from Condor to be habitable, and Penguin, barely close enough to Condor to be habitable.

At first brush, Phoenix was a planetwide desert and Penguin was a planetwide snowfield. Neither impression was correct, as both had significant temperate zones and liquid water—and the areas too hot or cold for humans to live comfortably still had their own life cycles.

The single planet orbiting closer to the star than the habitable worlds, Albatross, was a true planetwide desert. A rapidly spinning ball of super-heated rock, David's files suggested Albatross had significant deposits of rare minerals...and that no one had yet judged them worth landing on Albatross to try and extract.

Not when Condor had the Emu and Ostrich Flocks, two massive asteroid belts that came close to being a single belt, dividing the habitable planets from the two gas giants at the edge of the system. Buzzard and Vulture provided hydrogen and other essential gases for industry, and the Flocks provided any mineral raw materials needed.

The Principality was rich and getting richer, held back only by the limited habitability of their planets. Most systems colonized in its round of the diaspora were still Fringe Worlds, but Condor was unquestionably a MidWorld.

A full twelve-ship squadron of export destroyers—Tau Ceti–built ships with jump matrices instead of amplifiers—were split between the two worlds as a pointed reminder of that status. A swarm of smaller home-built corvettes was scattered throughout the system, carrying out the usual High Guard duties of patrol and search and rescue.

The largest concentration of the corvettes was around the facilities at Penguin's L1 point. A zone of stable gravity marked by the interface of Penguin and its oversized moon, Puffin, the L1 facilities were for the storage and transshipment of cargos that would never truly stop in Condor.

Those were the cargos the Prince turned a blind eye to because the fees helped sustain the fleet and military that protected his people. That complex was McMurdo Station, where Mahometus Kovac ran a gunrunning operation heavily linked to *la Cosa Nostra*.

"What's our course, skipper?" LaMonte asked into the silence as everyone went over the same data he'd been consuming.

"Where do you think, XO?" David replied. "McMurdo Station. That's where our cargo stops. That's where our prey is hiding."

He smiled.

"Let's go hunting."

Despite the scale of the area that was apparently labeled as "McMurdo Station," the actual space station that bore the name was relatively small. The space around it was a crowded mess, and David was almost sitting on his hands to stop himself from taking control of the big ship away from LaMonte as she piloted them in.

Most of the cluster of orbitals were zero-gee facilities with limited living space or power, glorified anchor points for stacks of standard cargo containers. A couple of facilities that *looked* like cargo platforms or transshipment facilities showed their true colors to *Falcon*'s sensitive scanners.

Between the corvettes roving the exterior of the Lagrange point and the concealed defensive platforms, McMurdo Station was quite secure. David wouldn't have been surprised to learn that several of the in-system ships floating around also bore concealed weapons installed by *la Cosa Nostra*.

The station that actually bore the name McMurdo was a hub-and-wheel design David had seen a dozen times before. Three rings spun to provide artificial pseudogravity, linked to a two-hundred-meter-long core for ships to dock at.

"You good, Kelly?" he asked quietly as he looked at the ever-shifting artificial reef around McMurdo station.

"Even the smallest gap is a good six kilometers across, skipper," she told him. "I'm fine. We've got a docking slot at McMurdo, so you should be getting ahold of our client. Let's get this cargo sorted, shall we?"

David chuckled at his XO taking him, ever so gently, to task. He'd chosen well when he'd decided to take a risk on Kelly LaMonte. She hadn't, by any stretch of the imagination, been ready to be executive officer.

She'd succeeded at the job regardless.

Turning his attention to his part of the job and leaving her to pilot the ship, he directed *Falcon*'s computers to link in to the station network. Even on a normal ship, that was done through a heavily secured system. On *Falcon*, the external communications network was actually air-gapped from the rest of the ship's computer hardware unless a connection was intentionally made.

If someone tried to poke into *Red Falcon*'s computers, they wouldn't get far.

A few minutes of searching and he linked to the offices of the company they were delivering to.

"This is Caleb Dragoon Storage and Transshipment, Adrian Lionel speaking; how may I help you?" a delicately featured young man answered the video call.

"This is Captain Rice aboard *Red Falcon*," David replied. "We are delivering a cargo for your company from Prime Consortium in Tau Ceti." He listed off the shipment order and Lionel checked their system.

"Of course, Captain Rice," he confirmed. "If you don't mind my saying, the Prime cargos usually come in on Translight Interstellar ships. Do you know why it didn't this time?"

"Translight had an unexpected maintenance casualty and didn't have a ship available," David told him. That said maintenance casualty had consisted of MISS outright bribing Translight to take a ship out of circulation for a slightly early set of repairs was an unnecessary detail.

"Reality intervenes for us all," Lionel confirmed. "I'll connect you to the younger Mr. Dragoon to sort out moving the cargo to our holding facilities. Please hold."

The hold only lasted a few minutes before the screen resolved into a different man, somewhat older than the delicately featured Lionel, wearing a drab black business suit with a bright gold tie.

"Greetings, Captain Rice," he said cheerfully. "I'm Kyle Dragoon, the Manager of Logistics for Caleb Dragoon S&T." He grinned. "Caleb Dragoon is my father, before you ask."

"Always a pleasure, Mr. Dragoon," David replied. "So, I have twenty million tons of some of the most high-tech junk in the galaxy. Where do you want it?"

Dragoon faked a jovial wince.

"It's not *junk*, Captain," he replied. "But there's definitely a lot of it. We'll need to split it amidst several of our facilities, and we only have so much local transport capability. Usually, Translight lends us their shuttle fleet, but..."

"That wasn't included in my contract," David pointed out. "Plus, well, Prime paid us enough under market that I can't really afford to burn the fuel for them, especially if I'm sitting in dock for longer than I expect."

"Well, using your birds *would* get you out of dock faster," Dragoon said, but the spark in his eyes said he knew exactly where the conversation could go. "I'm sure, now that I think of it, that we might be able to provide some sort of fee for the rental of your crews and birds..."

David returned the man's almost-gleeful gaze and got down to the business of negotiating.

Safely docked with McMurdo Station, David pulled Kelzin, Soprano, LaMonte and Leonhart into his office.

"Okay, people, we've got two different tracks going on here, but I see no reason not to cross them over," he told them. "Mike, we're being paid a pretty decent fee for your shuttles to help off-load, so that's going to be occupying you and your people's time for the next few days. That said, that's *days* of you flying back and forth through the heart of this cluster, so I want your sensors on full pickup."

"The suites on the heavy-lift shuttles aren't that great," Kelzin warned. "Better than most civilian small craft, but still...not up to the assault shuttles' standards."

"We're not flying assault shuttles around until we need to," David told him. "But two or three days' worth of data from the transport shuttles' sensor suites adds up to a lot of data. I want them sweeping *everything*. They might not tell us anything we don't already know, but more data won't hurt."

"Can do," the pilot confirmed.

"Kelly." David turned to his XO. "We can't leave here until we've managed to track down Kovac—and we may have to leave in a hurry once we do. Not much you can do about the latter, but I need you to go through the motions of looking for work while making sure we don't actually *get* any."

LaMonte snorted.

"So, jack our prices and look for at least fifteen megatons of cargo, check," she noted. "Can't see anybody out here looking to move that kind of mass."

"I assume Translight probably has a deal with someone for shipments back to the Core," David admitted. "We'll want to be careful that we *don't* find them, at least initially."

His XO nodded.

"I'll make us look productive while doing nothing," she promised.

"Maria, Rhianna." David turned to his Ship's Mage and security officer. "You and I get to be spies. I want Maria to link in with the local MISS office, *quietly*, and get their files on Kovac. Rhianna, do the same with local law enforcement."

"Do you want me to talk to them or hack them?" the Marine intelligence officer said bluntly. "There's risks both ways, but..."

"Hack them," David concluded after a moment's thought. "We're less likely to cross *la Cosa Nostra*'s radar that way, even if it might piss off some potential allies. Discretion is more important than making friends this time around."

"And you, boss?" Soprano asked.

"I'm going to go trawl the underworld and see if I can look like an eager-enough potential gunrunner to cross Kovac's radar," David told them all with a grin. "That corner has to know we carry guns and other illegal cargos for the right price—and that there are things we *won't* carry, too—so making myself visible in certain corners can't hurt."

"The faster we can move on all of this, the better," Leonhart said. "It's been two weeks since we left Darius. Nothing we did there should be a warning to Kovac, but my neck is itching. MISS is throwing a lot of resources at tracking back the cargos from Ardennes, and I can't imagine that's going completely unnoticed."

"Welcome to the shadows," David replied, his grin fading. "We'll find Kovac. Then we'll see what kind of persuasion it takes to get data out of him."

There was a certain *special* kind of bar for the sort of dredging David was currently engaged in. It wasn't dingy or dirty, but it was dimly lit and the music was set at *just* the right volume to effectively replicate the effect of a white-noise generator.

It wasn't in the rundown areas of the station known for crime, but it was right next door to them. The drinks were expensive and quality but plain. The furniture was of much the same style as the drinks, and the crowd was an eclectic mix of shippers, ship crews, businessmen, and criminals pretending to be one of the first three.

David was far from the only ship's officer there, and none of them had come unescorted. Two of the more looming members of Leonhart's security team joined David at the table he claimed as he ordered drinks and bar food.

Like the rest of the officers, he was "here for a quiet drink." No one officially came there looking for business, and he wasn't even sure he'd get a bite tonight. This was about appearing available and letting his reputation precede him.

They were into the second basket of chicken wings when someone unexpectedly dropped down at their table. David looked at the woman who joined them and smiled thinly. She had long blond hair and piercing green eyes, and was dressed like she was out to solicit offers for "paid company"—but he recognized the way she carried herself.

In fact, he realized with a blink, he recognized *her*. Not exactly, her height was wrong, but she fit into a particular bodysculpted and bio-engineered mold he'd encountered before. A very specific one.

"I'm guessing you know a young lady named Turquoise," he pointed out before the woman said a word. "How can I help you?"

The woman chuckled.

"Fascinating, Captain," she replied. "Most men don't get much past the clothing and the staring at my tits. I haven't spoken with Turquoise in years, but yes, I knew her. You can call me Indigo."

David nodded. Turquoise and a number of other young women had been acquired as sex slaves by a crime boss and "upgraded" as his personal assassins and bodyguards. Turquoise had replaced said crime boss when the Blue Star Syndicate had disintegrated by covert if bloody means.

"Well, Indigo"—he inclined his head—"I am Captain David Rice. How can I help you?" he echoed.

"I don't work for my sister anymore, if that's what you're wondering," Indigo told him. "These days, I'm more of an independent information broker here in Condor, and I think I may be potentially able to help you."

David had figured that Indigo didn't work for Turquoise anymore. Turquoise had tried to stab him in the back and had lost her entire pirate fleet doing so. If she was still in control of her little empire, she wasn't going to want to *talk* to David Rice.

"And what help do you think I need?" he asked. "I'm just here for drinks."

Indigo chuckled again.

"Speaking of which, you should buy me one to avoid suspicion," she purred. "It's safer for us both if people think we're negotiating a different kind of transaction."

David echoed her chuckle but waved the bartender over and did so.

"You're here because you're dredging for work of a certain type," Indigo concluded as the bartender drifted away. "You've a big ship, Captain. A fast one, too, if I read the data right. Not many in any business looking for cargo of that scale."

"I've heard of at least one," David said, figuring he may as well test the waters. "Man named Kovac."

"You've done your research, I see," she said. "Not even sure you need little old me." Her throaty purr of a chuckle was sending shivers down his spine, and he *knew* it was a well-practiced act.

"Kovac might be able to fill your hold, Captain, but Kovac doesn't work with strangers," she continued. "I might be able to put you in touch, but it's not easy. He's a recluse at the best of times, and he's been very quiet of late."

"I'll talk to anyone with a cargo worth hauling my ship around, but I suspect he might be the only shadow broker with one," David replied. "And anyone else, well... I can talk to a *regular* broker, can't I, Indigo?"

She smiled.

"I don't take cash up front," she told him. "But I'm not cheap. I'll get you your meeting with Kovac."

"How much?" he asked.

"A million. Bearer credit chits on the Bank of Olympus Mons."

David winced. There was no more reliable payment method—but getting his hands on BOM bearer credit chits in Condor could easily cost him twice the face value.

Of course, David already had that on hand in his MISS discretionary funds, but he didn't want Indigo to know that.

"Five hundred thousand on BOM," he countered. "Or I could do eight on Bank of Condor."

He could get Bank of Condor bearer chits by walking into any branch on the station, though eight hundred thousand would take some fast talking.

"One point five on Condor or eight on BOM," she said. "Not a credit less."

"Six hundred on Olympus Mons," he told her.

"Seven."

"Six thirty."

"Six fifty."

"Done," he agreed. "You get paid when I meet Kovac."

"Agreed," she said. "I'm not guaranteeing a deal, though."

"I know," David allowed. "I'm pretty sure I can manage that on my own."

Or, potentially, kidnap the gunrunner. But Indigo didn't need to know that part.

CHAPTER 30

MARIA WALKED into the plush quiet of the wealth management firm with a strong sense that she was intruding. This was the kind of company where even starship captains were only *potentially* qualified to be clients—though its presence on McMurdo Station suggested that they were the target client for this particular office.

The woman behind the desk had dark brown hair and the kind of agelessly perfect face that spoke to spectacularly expensive bodysculpt. She wore a tailored demure black suit and managed to look down her nose at Maria without shifting position.

"Can I help you, Mage..."

"Soprano," Maria told her. "Ship's Mage Maria Soprano. Whether you can help me, though, depends on whether you have a package waiting for me from Olympus Mons."

The woman was good. She didn't even blink at the recognition pass phrase, though her dismissive body language relaxed slightly.

"We see little traffic from Olympus Mons, but there's always a special package or two; let me check," she said gruffly, completing the recognition sequence.

Maria triggered a confirming transmission from her wrist-comp to the other woman's computer and was rewarded with a quick nod.

"If you don't mind, Mage Soprano, I'll put you in one of our meeting rooms to wait?"

"Of course," Maria allowed. She followed the woman into the office and found herself quickly ushered into a small meeting room designed for maybe four people.

"I'm Kelsey Amber," the woman introduced herself. "Welcome to MISS McMurdo Station, Mage Soprano. How can we assist you?"

"My crew and I need a full background briefing package on the local politics and underworld," Maria told her. "None of us are familiar with the Principality, but duty brings us to strange places."

"Of course," Amber responded. "May I ask what does bring you here, or is that..."

"Classified," the Mage replied with a smile. "What I can tell you is that we're looking for Mahometus Kovac, a gunrunner of some reputation here. Any information you have on him would be valuable."

"Kovac is on our radar," Amber confirmed. "He's been laying low recently, from what we can tell, but we have nothing to suggest he's left the system. Or even McMurdo Station, for that matter."

"That's helpful," Maria said. "How dangerous is this man, Ms. Amber? We need to get information out of him that he isn't going to want to divulge."

"He's..." She sighed. "In and of himself, he's not incredibly dangerous, but he does hire some extremely capable protection. He's not one to pursue vengeance unless there's a profit in it, and he has a solid sense of when to cut his losses. No one in his business is a pussycat, Mage Soprano, and at the end of the day, he's a mercenary."

"Enough money should loosen his tongue."

Maria nodded. They could apply money. MISS's budget wasn't infinite, but they could buy gunrunners out of petty cash without noticing.

"Do you know where he's headquartered?"

"Sadly, no," Amber admitted. "We keep a loose eye on his movements, but he's been surprisingly successful at hiding his home and his offices from our investigation. We've never had a reason to throw full-scale resources at him, though; he's generally fallen into the 'better the devil we know' category."

"Can you make it happen?" Maria asked.

The local sighed.

"Your authentication code says you can make us make it happen," she pointed out. "I'll have to bounce that up the chain and have others redirect resources. Obviously, we'll want to keep your contact with anyone other than me to a minimum, but we can see what we can dig up."

"Good," Maria said. David had his approach. She had this approach. Hopefully, they'd meet somewhere in the middle and squeeze out a gunrunner.

The local MISS files were illuminating, if not exactly cheery. Maria went through the high-level summaries attached to the reports and briefings while she waited for Amber to confirm that her superiors were going to respect the authority Maria's authentication codes gave her.

Covert ops ships like *Red Falcon* needed the cooperation of local authorities, so they were given pretty broad authority to command local resources. The flip side of that, of course, was that said local authorities were supposed to speak up if the requests threatened existing operations or sources—and the ship crews were supposed to listen.

From the file, she could see several areas they might have problems helping with. *La Cosa Nostra*—the current evolution of the Old Earth Mafia—had large chunks of Condor's interstellar shipping tied up hard. They had the resources to cause MISS problems, though they'd generally choose not to pick that fight.

Kovac had to be tied up with *la Cosa Nostra* if he was organizing gunrunning operations out of Condor. Which made the fact that the MISS investigations hadn't found such a link fascinating and was probably part of why MISS hadn't turned over the information they had to local authorities.

The man's operations were intriguing, and his level of information control was impressive. He hadn't been a priority of the MISS, but he'd clearly caught their attention—and by and large, they'd learned nothing.

"Mage Soprano?"

Maria looked up to see Amber standing at the door.

"Yes?"

"We're going to send out our feelers," the local agent told her. "We can't spare everything, but we've a couple of agents who have been the key figures in what investigations we have done into Kovac. They'll focus their efforts on him for the next few days, at least, until we can track him down."

"He's got a fascinating operation," Maria noted. "I don't think I've seen such an odd mix of us knowing both so much and so little about a crime op."

"We're not the people he's hiding from," Amber replied. "He works with *la Cosa Nostra*, but he isn't part of them. He isn't even an associate, which makes him a target anytime a made man wants to try and pull together their own gunrunning operation piggybacking on the existing smuggling runs through here.

"None of them have succeeded yet...and at least two have ended up dead." The artificially perfect MISS operative shrugged. "I don't shed many tears for made men, Mage Soprano, and Kovac has been a useful foil.

"But he's also been an enigma. If he'd been more trouble, that would have been enough on its own to get our attention, but...he wasn't. I'm guessing that's changed?"

Maria chuckled.

"I doubt he's been *more* trouble," she admitted. "But he's definitely got into the wrong trouble."

"We'll find him for you," Amber promised. "I presume you have the resources to go from there?"

Returning to *Red Falcon*, Maria ran into Leonhart on the way. The Marine Forward Combat Intelligence officer looked furious, ready to chew nails and spit bullets. Four of her team were accompanying her, carrying what looked like the results of a decent-sized shopping run for supplies for *Red Falcon*'s security team.

"Chief?" Maria asked softly. "What's up?"

"Not here," Leonhart snapped, glancing around. "Definitely not here. Conners! Keep that damn crate off the ground; let's *not* blow ourselves up, shall we?"

Artificial gravity runes marked a central pathway along most of the corridors in the hub of McMurdo Station. Anything bigger than the single pair of large crates that the security troops were hauling would probably have been more easily transported by sending it drifting along the zero-gravity section several feet away.

Maria kept her peace with a concealed smile. The crate of explosives hadn't come within more than three or four centimeters of the ground, and she doubted that Leonhart had bought explosives crude enough that bouncing them off the floor would be a problem, regardless.

"Can I help with any of that?" she asked instead.

"We've got it," Conners, a fair-haired younger trooper with a broad grin, said cheerfully. "It's all under control boss, ma'am...bosses."

Leonhart rolled her eyes but gestured for her totally-not-Marines-we-swear to lead the way as Maria fell in beside her for the remainder of the walk back to the ship.

"Nice enough station, I suppose," the security chief grumped. "Appreciate the effort to provide at least some gravity here."

At least a third of the stations they visited didn't have any gravity in the sections of the station that were held steady to make docking easier. It was an expensive luxury—an often-useful luxury, but still a luxury.

"The Prince has money and wants to put a good foot forward with the interstellar shippers," Maria replied. "Last I checked, doesn't he own McMurdo Station outright?"

Leonhart snorted.

"No, the *Principality* owns McMurdo Station," the security chief corrected. "The *Prince* 'just' owns the company that manages the docks."

They checked in with the guards at the airlock linking them back to *Red Falcon,* and then Leonhart dismissed her people before leaning against a wall and letting loose a string of profanity in more languages than Maria could count.

"You couldn't get into the law enforcement files, I'd guess?" Maria asked as the stream slowed.

"Oh, we got in, all right," Leonhart replied. "I've seen fucking *ice cream trucks* with more security on their computer systems. We got in. So, it seems, has everyone who has so much as thought of the idea in the last ten years."

The Marine shook her head.

"So, according to the files of the McMurdo Station Police Department, Kovac doesn't even *exist*. Either they're completely incompetent, or their computers are a false front while they do all of their work on paper."

Maria thought back to the MISS files and sighed.

"According to MISS, MSPD is basically bought and paid for by *la Cosa Nostra*," she noted. "Kovac spends a lot of his resources hiding from *la Cosa Nostra*, so keeping the MSPD off his back would be useful to him."

"This doesn't even look like corruption. Just incompetence," Leonhart admitted. "Hell, I'm not sure I even buy incompetence. The MSPD is just..."

"A disaster," Maria concluded. "Competing priorities alongside leadership that's been bought by their major organized crime syndicate. I suspect even the Principality doesn't rely on them for more than the basics if they can avoid it."

"Which might explain why I can't even find an office of the Principality Security Bureau," the Marine admitted. "I'm guessing there's at least one on the station—there's over a hundred and fifty thousand people on McMurdo and the surrounding platforms."

"Not to mention thirty or forty percent of their interstellar trade stops here, and the fees fund a good third of the Principality's budget," Maria agreed. "The PSB has got to be here." She offered a datachip to the Marine.

"And if it is, I'm guessing the MISS files will say where, won't they?"

CHAPTER 31

"WELL, IF IT MAKES anyone feel any better, even the underworld information brokers aren't sure how to get in touch with Kovac," David told his officers after they'd reported in. "You're telling me the cops had *nothing?*"

"I don't mean they had nothing on Kovac. They had nothing on *any-body*," Leonhart replied. "Calling the MSPD glorified mall cops is being charitable."

"And the system security force is disturbingly absent," Soprano added. "They've *got* to be here, but even MISS doesn't know where their offices are located."

"And nobody knows where Kovac works or lives," David concluded. "That's impressive as hell, if damn frustrating." He thought about it for a moment. "Not to mention bloody weird. We did Seule enough of a favor that I'm relatively sure he'd have told us if there was a trick to finding the man."

"From what MISS's files say, you don't find Kovac," his Ship's Mage told him. "He finds you. If you ask enough questions about arms smuggling or him by name in the right quarters, he decides if you're a threat and makes contact."

"So, he should be reaching out to us," David said. He shook his head. "That's not reassuring, really. Him making contact with us doesn't really lend itself to kidnapping and interrogation—and that's assuming he doesn't flag us as a threat."

"What concerns me," LaMonte said quietly, "is the consistent comment from everyone that they haven't heard anything from him recently. That sounds like he's gone to ground, which would be a reasonable response to me if I heard MISS was hunting me."

"If he's realized we're MISS, we may have bigger problems," David replied. "This is a man it's been suggested we might simply be able to buy the details of his confidential clients from. If he knows who we are, he'll sell that, too."

"And that will burn our cover completely," Soprano agreed. "At least as far as those prepared to pay his fee...and there'd be enough."

"I don't think he's made us," David admitted. "I think he's just a paranoid bastard operating in a region that's hostile to independent operators. A hostility we're at risk of running into as well. We present as an independent shipper willing to take on any contract not involving slaves. *La Cosa Nostra* may well come knocking if we look too eager to work."

"There's a bunch of big cargos coming into Condor, but not many that leave on that scale," LaMonte pointed out. "I'm not sure I could find a single cargo our size heading out even if I was actually trying. My guess is that the big lines usually had a broker who preassembles a bunch of smaller cargos into one big lump before they arrive.

"We can do that ourselves given enough time, but we can only justify burning money sitting here for so long before people start to question why we don't just take the biggest job we can find and burn for deep space."

"Agreed," David said. "And to do that kind of job, we need to know where we're going...and until we can pick Kovac's brain, we don't."

"I suggest we pack a cargo for Tau Ceti," Soprano put in, the Mage looking tired. "We can do that pretty slowly, but if it looks like we're at least working on a cargo, we'll attract fewer questions—and if we get a destination from Kovac, we can head via Tau Ceti."

"Our only excuse for talking to Kovac is that we need a big cargo," the Captain replied. "If we fix a destination, we don't have that option. No... Kelly, I want you to start looking for brokers. Take it slow and careful, be paranoid and picky. Interviews, track records, testimonials, the works.

"If this doesn't work out, we'll have them put together a cargo for us, but I want to look available for at least a few more days. Can we make that happen?"

David's review of the files the local MISS office had provided left him with one significant conclusion: he really didn't want to spend a minute longer in McMurdo Station than he needed to. The Principality of Condor was a nice-enough system and he understood the planets to be decent places filled with kind, energetic, and thoughtful people.

McMurdo Station had the same appearance on the surface, but the no-questions-asked nature of the way the Principality allowed the trans-shipment businesses to run had resulted in a *very* different undertone.

There was as much glitz and glamor to McMurdo as any space station had, and the locals had mastered the cleanliness and efficiency only money could afford. Scratch the surface of where that money came from, however, and you started to feel dirty.

Drugs, guns, pirate ships, slaves, untaxed or unregulated goods... Condor wasn't just a major shipping hub in *la Cosa Nostra's* pocket; it was the *center* of *la Cosa Nostra's* interstellar shipping operation. They'd operated out of a dead system once, until one David Rice had semi-accidentally led a Hand there.

Now, apparently, they were operating out of someone else's system where everyone was basically winking at the situation. The station police were owned and the system police simply let the station fester.

A knock on his door dragged him gratefully away from the briefings, and he buzzed it open. Maria Soprano stepped quickly in, grabbing a seat before he could say anything and sighing.

"You look like you just found shit in your coffee cup," his Ship's Mage told him.

"Reading up on *la Cosa Nostra* operations here," he admitted. "I can *see* the logic the MISS is using not to burn this place out, but I sure as hell find it questionable."

"Yeah, I missed the slave through-trade on my first read," she said. "I can't help but feel it was missed from the executive summaries intentionally."

"The right hand likes keeping an eye on the scum and is worried that the left hand might actually, I don't know, try and *free the fucking kidnapped kids?*"

David's coffee cup went flying across the room in a spasming movement, shattering against the metal wall and leaving a smear of cold coffee dregs down the side of his office. The slave trade was what had dragged him into his entire mess with the underworld in the first place. He'd taken a job without asking questions, realized he was shipping slaves, and sold out an entire Blue Star Syndicate facility to the Navy and local cops.

He could justify drugs and guns and tax-evasion smuggling to keep his cover up. Barely. Now MISS wanted him to turn a blind eye to human trafficking, and he wasn't sure he could do it.

"And what can we do about it with one ship, four Mages and forty-odd Marines?" Soprano asked gently. "Because let's be honest, David—if you order it, Leonhart and I will storm McMurdo Station while Jeeves and LaMonte blow anyone who challenges us to hell, but I don't think that's a battle we could win."

"But you'd try anyway, wouldn't you?" he said drily.

"To wipe out a tumor of slavers? In an *instant.*"

David laid his hands flat on the table.

"I *can't*," he whispered. "They didn't give us enough data—and that has to be part of why."

"I'm not entirely impressed with them myself, right now, but I suspect they really do think they can do more good this way," Soprano told him.

"I...don't believe that," David replied. "I can't believe that."

"I happen to agree. And I'm not sure I trust them, either," she said.

"Why not?" he asked. "I mean, this"—he gestured at the data on his screen—"is a nightmare, but it's one they can at least pretend is to serve the Protectorate."

"Because after thirty-six hours, they've given up on finding Kovac," Soprano said grimly. "They apparently haven't turned up the slightest sign of him and have concluded that he must have left the station without them realizing it.

"Which I sadly find far too believable, given that the man would also be evading *la Cosa Nostra*, which seems to be everyone else's focus on this station."

"But that seems a little quick to give up, doesn't it?" David murmured.

"If nothing else, I'd expect them to be able to find where the man *was* on the station before he left, but they have no idea," she said. "Something stinks. I'm not entirely sure it's the local MISS, but they're not helping."

David looked back at his data and smiled grimly.

"Well, if they're not going to be useful, then I feel much better about throwing them to the wolves," he admitted. "Or, more accurately, the Hands."

"David?" His Ship's Mage looked at him questioningly.

"Stealey may be gone, but I still know how to get ahold of Hand Lomond," he reminded her, his smile growing both wider and thinner. "Let's see what the man they call the fucking *Sword of Mars* thinks of this mess."

David had barely stepped into the bar when a long set of fingers ran lovingly up his shoulder and onto his face.

"Good to see you, lover," Indigo purred in his ear. "Good to see you can keep an appointment! Shall we grab a table?"

He hadn't made any appointments to meet the woman that he recalled, though he had stopped in there in the hopes of getting some kind of information from the last chance he figured they had of finding Kovac.

David gestured her to a table and got an eyeful of tonight's outfit as she walked by him to lead the way. It looked more like a net over a loincloth than anything that most worlds would regard as decent.

Indigo was doubling down on the streetwalker act, and her actions toward him were almost certainly intended to set a very specific tone to the rest of the bars' occupants.

She added to that impression by waiting for him to sit and then draping herself into his lap.

"You, Captain Rice, have an interesting choice of potential business partners," she whispered in his ear. "I've made the link to Kovac for people before and it's been a lucrative, if pain-in-the-ass, proposition.

"Now...I wonder if you know what you're getting into."

"Well, I'm not paying for you to shove your chest in my face," David pointed out delicately as Indigo proceeded to do basically that.

She chuckled. Given her position, it was a little distracting even as he was *trying* to stay in control of the situation.

"The men who try to pay for that generally don't like what they do get," she told him. "Look, Kovac has gone dark. I mean *really* dark. I can't find him...and I can find *anyone*."

That was a disturbing-enough statement to get David's attention fully on business at last, and he sighed.

"I need to find him," he said, knowing damn well he was admitting that he was looking for more than just a job from the man. "We agreed to a *lot* of damn money, Indigo."

"I know," she breathed in his ear. "I've got something. More than anyone else would have found. Now I'm going to slap you and storm out. Meet me in an hour at the location I just air-dropped to your wrist-comp. Bring the money."

Before David could say anything either way, she recoiled from him and slapped him across the face.

"That's *it*?" she half-shrieked, half-yelled. "That isn't enough to cover this conversation, let alone what *you* want!"

She was fast. Hell, given what David suspected about her and her relation to Turquoise, the catlike grace she showed as she leapt away from him and stormed out of the bar was her *holding back*.

His own augments were sufficient that he could have caught her, he supposed, but that wasn't the point. The point was to break off their meeting in a way that didn't draw suspicion—and David using his cyber-lung to supercharge his bloodstream with oxygen and then leap off with his cybernetic leg would wreck that.

He let his momentary dazed expression last long enough to help convince the rest of the bar patrons of her act, then slowly rose.

"Ah...bartender?" he said slowly. "Tab, please?"

And then he realized he hadn't even ordered anything before Indigo had arrived.

CHAPTER 32

INDIGO HADN'T said *turn up alone*—and even if she had, David probably would have ignored her. He didn't trust the bodyguard turned information broker further than he could throw her. He brought Soprano and four of Leonhart's Marines.

He and the Marines were armed too. The Macy-Six he wore under his shoulder was an old friend, a six-millimeter caseless pistol built on Mars. The Marines carried its big brother, the Martian Armaments Caseless Close Assault Weapon, Nine Millimeter—the MACCAW-9.

Or the death parrot, when the troops were being irreverent. Which was most of the time.

Soprano wasn't visibly armed, though she'd dressed in a high-collared tight blouse that both concealed her Mage medallion and probably qualified as an area-effect testosterone-poisoning system.

Exposure had rendered David immune to his Ship's Mage's efforts in that direction, at least. Pointed experience had rendered him resistant to people using beauty as a weapon in general. The lawyer turned crime lord who'd chased him across the galaxy had been absolutely gorgeous, after all.

And there were Indigo and her "sisters." The information broker materialized out of the shadows when he reached the time and place she'd indicated. She'd traded the fishnet dress for a military-grade bodysuit more commonly found on recon teams.

Two more women and a man accompanied her. All were dressed in the same bodysuit and carrying the Legatan–built equivalent to David's

MAC-6. Unlike Indigo, her companions had the hoods on the suits up and the face-shields on. They were anonymous...but the women, at least, moved with the same deadly grace as Indigo.

How many hyper-sexualized assassins had Conner Maroon *had?* How bloody stupid did you have to be to think that was going to end well for you?

Indigo and her companions brought the number David knew of to five, though he was sure that Turquoise had more sisters he hadn't seen. He supposed it was *possible* that they'd taken the template and made more like them, but...that struck him as unlikely.

Few people with a brain made their custom-gene-sculpted assassins that top-heavy, after all.

"You have the money?" Indigo asked as she surveyed David and his people.

"Maybe," he said bluntly. "I'm not seeing Kovac around here."

"Fine. Follow me," she snapped, and set off without waiting to see if he responded. David fell in behind her as she led the way deeper into one of McMurdo Station's nicer residential zones. This wasn't a section for the truly rich, but it was the kind of place where a starship's captain might keep a home.

Captains didn't spend *that* much money on houses, since they'd usually want them in three or four systems, so the relatively affordable luxury of a zone like this worked well. It was the haunt of the aspirational upper middle class, the lower upper class, and the rich who didn't want to draw *too* much attention to themselves. The corridors were double-wide and double-high, and small artificial oases of greenery marked the intersections.

Eventually, Indigo stopped at one of the oases and gestured toward a side corridor.

"Six homes in that corridor," she told him. "One belongs to Kovac. He never kept a permanent office, always using rental spaces once or twice and abandoning them. I *had* a drop-code for him, but he never re-sponded, so I tracked this down."

"How come you can find it and no one else can?" David asked.

"Because when I arrived on this station with nothing, I was his paid companion for six months to build up contacts and money," Indigo said bluntly. "This is the only place I can track that hasn't changed ownership since then, and I think it's his actual home."

"That's a lot of supposition for me to go off of," David told her. He was also surprised that she'd be willing to sell out an old client of that much weight and caliber. On the other hand...

"It's all you've got," she replied. "It's all *anyone's* got, which means I have no idea what you're going to find in there. Probably nothing, to be honest, but I said I'd find you Kovac and this is the best I can do."

And she was worried for him but unwilling—or unable—to break into his house herself.

"I'm not paying you the full fee for a house that *might* have Kovac in it," David snapped.

"Fine. Pay me half now, half if you find him," Indigo offered. "Best I can do, Captain."

That was a concerning offer. She definitely seemed to think she'd get that second half, but she wasn't sure.

"All right," he agreed, turning away from her to carefully count out the marked credit chips from the Bank of Olympus Mons. "Three hundred twenty-five thousand," he said, passing her the chips.

She took them and they disappeared into a concealed pouch on the bodysuit.

"The unit at the end, number four. I'm out of here," she told him. "I may not know what Kovac's up to, but I can tell you this: the security systems on that suite are *insane.*"

The locals disappeared with surprising speed, leaving David and his team alone in the space station version of a cul-de-sac. The advantage of neighborhoods like this was that there weren't that many people living there compared to other parts of the station, so they were able to approach the unit without being questioned.

The entrance to Kovac's unit was a single plain door with a number on it. By the standards of the side corridor it was in, the door was positively plebeian. The other units had engraved archways, nameplates, and a dozen other decorations.

Kovac's door had enough engraving and decoration to not look *entirely* out of place, but to David's eye, that was the only reason the decoration existed. This was an apartment that was meant to go entirely unnoticed.

"Check the door," he told the Marines, one of whom promptly produced a scanner from inside her coat and started going over the systems.

"Hermetic seal," she reported. "Reads like an internal airlock on the other side, high-grade cybersecurity." The Marine shook her head. "It may *look* nice and innocent, but I'd guess the entire unit is running on its own life support."

"Can you get in?"

She grinned.

"Of course we can." She glanced down the corridor. "It won't be quick, though. We may catch attention before we're done."

"Do what you have to," David ordered. "We'll keep us safe."

He looked to Soprano.

"Can you hide us?" he asked quietly.

"Yes, but not for long," she said. "Maybe wait until we actually have someone looking for us before we pull that rabbit out of the hat?"

"You know your rabbits better than I do," David said. "You picking up anything in the suite?"

She shrugged.

"It takes a pretty significant thaumic signature for me to pick it up at any distance," she admitted. "I'm not sensing anything, but the place sounds pretty sealed tight."

From the cough from the working Marine electronics expert, Soprano was underestimating it.

"Can you move the conversation further down the hall?" the tech asked plaintively. "This system is slightly *better* than military-grade, so a lack of distractions would be *fantastic*."

David knew better than to argue with experts and gestured for his Mage and the rest of his guard to follow him back towards the main intersection.

"If anyone can get through, it's Binici," one of the other Marines told him quietly as they fell into guard mode at the entrance to the corridor. "Esra didn't just *pass* the FCI's electronics course—she maxed the test. *Nobody* maxes FCI course tests."

"Shh," David ordered, even though he nodded his understanding. They were alone and the Marines were speaking quietly, but the *last* thing *Red Falcon*'s crew needed was for anyone to realize that the security detachment were Marine Forward Combat Intelligence troops.

That would, at a minimum, raise all sorts of questions David didn't want to answer.

David was starting to wonder if he shouldn't take Soprano and the extra Marines and leave Binici alone to work on the door for a few hours, when the Marine waved them back over. She'd opened up a section of the station wall that she was carefully reattaching as they approached.

"Okay, so I now have control of the airlock," she told him. "But, well… that's it. Military-grade encryption and security, and the damn front door is air-gapped from the rest of the house. Any other computers are *completely* cut off from the station."

"Sounds like we found the right place," David said.

"Seems likely, but boss…if the front door is this secure, I'm guessing there's at least one more layer of defenses. And if he isn't expecting anyone to get through the front entrance without either permission or high-level cracking…"

"Said defenses are probably not polite," he agreed. "Maria?"

"We'll deal with it," the ex-Navy Mage said grimly. "Figuring auto-turrets and maybe security bots?"

"That would be my guess," Binici replied. "There's probably a central controller, but…"

"We'll need to disable the systems directly," David concluded. "Are we equipped for that?"

He hadn't been expecting to deal with automated security. His pistol was a perfectly effective weapon against humans in light or no armor, but it wasn't going to deal with automatic turrets and combat robots.

Both of which were *horrendously* illegal for a laundry list of reasons, but the most useful setup for them was a closed killing zone where the system was either on or off and anyone who entered while it was on was expected to die.

That seemed...in character for what he'd heard of Kovac.

"We've got a couple of EMP grenades and, well, Mage Soprano," Binici told him. "It's not an optimal plan, but it should be enough."

"All right," David said grimly. "Then I guess we make it happen. Ready?"

Binici pulled two plain black cylinders from inside her jacket and passed them to the other Marines, several of whom produced identical cylinders themselves.

A quick inventory counted up five EMP grenades across the four Marines, but Binici was going to be hanging back with the kit she'd wired into the door.

"We're ready," she confirmed.

The electronics tech hit her commands and the door slid open. A second door was roughly a meter inside the first, but it proceeded to slide open as well as Binici overrode the airlock's safety protocols—only possible, David suspected, because the exterior was breathable and the hard-wired protocols didn't engage.

Two of the Marines went in instantly, assault carbines at the ready and EMP grenades held against the carbine stock. David had enough time to see that the space past the second airlock door was a gorgeously decorated entryway with wood paneling before the Marines were blocking his view as they retreated.

"Grenades, *now*," one of them snapped as he tossed the EMP bomb he was holding forward and dived out of the doorway, pushing David aside.

At least three EMP grenades went through the doorway to land in the hallway David could no longer see. He heard the CRACK of the grenades detonating and *felt* the pulse wave. His implants were hardened against EMP, and there was a solid wall between him and the carefully designed short-range emitters, but he still felt his cybernetic lung skip a breath.

He coughed against the sudden shortness of breath, but his lung kicked back into gear instantly.

"After me," Soprano barked, the Mage leading the way back into the apartment suite. There was a *hiss-crackle* of lightning, quite distinct from the *crack* of the grenade's emitter.

A few seconds passed. There were the muffled retorts of suppressed gunshots, then silence.

"Clear," Soprano announced. "Let's get everyone in and seal the airlock," she suggested. "The gunfire *shouldn't* attract attention, but..."

David waved for Binici to follow him and stepped through into the entryway.

The plain exterior of the apartment suite gave way to luxury almost immediately after he left the airlock. Wood paneling covered the walls and floor, and what looked to have been several actual oil paintings had adorned the walls.

Despite the obvious presence of money, the entryway had been a six-meter-long and three-meter-wide killing field with a solid-looking door at the other end. The oil paintings had concealed automated turrets, and the paneling had slid aside to reveal squat wheeled robots with guns mounted at about waist height.

All of this had activated when the Marines had first entered, and been exposed when the EMP grenades had gone off. It had all been disabled when Soprano came in and fried the turrets, but the Marines had taken the time to locate and shoot the CPU on each robot nonetheless.

"Door into the rest of the place is locked," Binici reported, then shook her head. "Not even electronic. Expensive mechanical."

"Can you open it?" David asked.

"Not quickly," she replied. "Of course, there's always better options."

She pulled a tube of gray putty from inside her jacket and marked out a square around the lock. Folding up the tube, she snapped the base at a specific notch and shoved it into the putty.

"Clear!"

David had been the last to catch what Binici was doing, and he'd realized it well before she'd activated the detonator built into the base of the tube of explosives. Everyone was at the far side of the room when the small shaped charge detonated and blasted a neat hole out of the door.

A hole that included the lock.

"Go! Go!" Binici barked, and the other three Marines were through the door before she'd even finished speaking, carbines sweeping the space.

"Clear," they announced, and David and Soprano followed their people in.

The main foyer of the house was actually less ostentatious than the killing room they'd come through to get there. The floor was covered in hardwood slats, but the walls had been left as painted metal. On the other hand, the foyer was easily the size of many apartments that David had been in on space stations, which was a type of ostentatious all its own. Panels in the roof and walls provided a carefully calibrated light that didn't strain the eyes.

"Hello, the house," David shouted up the central stairway. Only silence responded and he shook his head as he glanced around the three-story foyer with its balconies and grand stairs. "Are the scanners showing anything?" he asked. "Computers, life signs?"

"Nothing," Binici said quietly. "We probably burned out the control module for the defenses, but the EMP shouldn't have made it past the door. No computers. No people. Not even the usual household machines."

"Check the rooms; Soprano and I will watch the stairs," David decided aloud. The Marines split into pairs and took the doors one at a time.

"Kitchen," one of them announced. "Appliances are all off." The Marine paused. "Fridge has food in it," he continued. "It's all rotten."

"But the lights are on," David murmured. "That seems...odd."

"Depends on how they took the electronics out," Soprano pointed out. "You're the electrical engineer. Could you do something that would burn out appliances and computers and leave lights?"

The starship captain—who had once been an Engineering Chief Petty Officer in the Martian Navy and, as Soprano said, an electrical engineer—studied the lights.

"Those lights are designed to last forever," he concluded slowly. "Low drain, sealed against surges. Most appliances are also sealed against surges, though, but the lights simply don't have the cabling to pull enough power to burn themselves out.

"Appliances and computers *have* to. You could flash a high-energy pulse along the wires. You'd kill *some* of the lights, but you'd definitely kill computers and probably appliances."

Especially since any kitchen appliance in a suite like this would have the hardware and software to link to a wrist-comp.

"But why?" he murmured. The rotten food wasn't a good sign, either. It meant that it had been days, at least, since everything in here had shut down.

So, where was Kovac? If David had been the kind of man to own a mansion-inside-a-space-station apartment like this...

"The office is on the top floor," he said quietly. "With me, Soprano."

Whatever the answer was, he suspected he'd find it in Mahometus Kovac's office.

The smell was the answer. It wasn't strong—the suite had space station–grade air filtration systems and its own life support system, after all—but once they were on the third floor of the suite, he picked up the distinct scent in the air and sighed.

Death and decay were nearly unique. There were other things that smelt like them, he supposed, but they weren't going to be in a luxury suite in the rotational gravity ring of a space station.

The smell was enough for David to find the office and push open the door. Wallscreens covered the walls, gray without power or data feeding to them. A massive desk in the center of the room looked like it held enough computer processing power to run a starship, let alone a trading empire.

Slumped across the desk was Mahometus Kovac, a dark-skinned man with graying hair. There was an ugly exit wound in the back of his skull that matched a smashed hole in one of the wallscreens behind him.

Stepping around Kovac's desk, David confirmed his suspicions. The front of the desk had been ripped open to expose the computer cores, and an unfamiliar black slab of electronics had been hooked into both the computers and the suite's power system.

Someone had wanted to be *very* sure that any hidden backup archives in Kovac's house were destroyed. From the size of the exit wound, they'd even used a hollow-point round to shoot the man, a destructive-enough bullet to make sure any cyberware in his brain was wrecked as well.

"Thorough," he said quietly as he knelt next to the slab of electronics and looked it over carefully, without touching it. "Want to bet the only fingerprints on the surge box are Kovac's?"

"No bet," Soprano told him. "He probably installed it himself, as a safety measure."

"It's possible," David agreed. He rose and looked around the office. "Shot in the head at point-blank range. Suicide?"

"I'm not a forensics expert, but it at least looks like it. All the security measures intact, all of the computers fucked, one perfectly aimed bullet." His Mage shrugged. "I don't buy it, but it *looks* like it."

Looking closer, David confirmed that an old-fashioned semiautomatic pistol was in Kovac's hand, roughly where it might have fallen if he'd shot himself.

"No guards," he pointed out. "Everyone said that Kovac had scary personal security, and they weren't talking about the robots at the front door that only Indigo knew existed. If he killed himself, he might have sent them away."

"He also might have sent them away if he was meeting with someone he didn't want them to know about," Soprano said. "Someone he'd trust enough to let through security and meet in his own home. Someone who'd have the chance to walk into his office and shoot him before he could react."

"So, either a lover, a friend, or a trusted client," David said grimly.

"And fast," his Mage pointed out. "Either fast enough to shoot him before he did anything or good enough to rearrange the entire scene afterwards."

"Hard to fake the bullet wound," David agreed. "No, they walked through the door and shot him in the center of the forehead before he could move. Not many people in the galaxy who could do that."

"Indigo could have."

David winced.

"Yes," he agreed levelly. "So could an Augment."

Both added up, though Indigo's help in getting them there suggested *she* hadn't killed Kovac. A Legatan agent, though...someone who'd been working with Kovac, who Kovac trusted because he'd been instrumental in their plans.

An agent who'd decided that Kovac was a liability with MISS pulling on the strings from Ardennes. Most likely, Kovac hadn't even known the agent was an Augment. The cyborgs were built and trained to kill Mages. An unsuspecting gunrunner wouldn't have stood a chance.

"Let's cover our tracks as best we can and get out of here," David ordered. "However he died, even his records are gone. This whole line of investigation is a damn bust."

CHAPTER 33

IT WAS a subdued group that gathered in the meeting room off of *Red Falcon*'s bridge the next morning. A forensically trained Marine and a grumpy Mage had sufficed to wipe any evidence of their intrusion into Kovac's home except for the wrecked turrets and door.

That would, David was sure, leave whatever investigators ended up going through the poor bastard's home much less likely to accept the neat suicide scenario presented. His people's forced entrance had been at a completely different time from the murder, but he doubted that the McMurdo Station Police were going to get around to checking out the unexpectedly quiet suite anytime soon.

"So, this whole stop was a bust," David repeated to all of his officers. "Kovac is dead, his files wiped, and we're no closer to tracing the supply of guns than we were when we first got to Ardennes."

"We put a lot of fire and blood into finding this man," Leonhart said quietly. "It's...frustrating to find him already dead."

"He's been dead since before we left Darius," Soprano said. "At some point since the revolution on Ardennes, someone decided to clean up loose ends. And this one has been tied off *very* neatly."

"MISS pinged two more leads: one in Amber and one in Sherwood," David reminded his people. "Kovac was the solidest link we had, and I'm worried we're not going to find *anybody* alive, but..."

"We have to keep yanking on the strings," Soprano agreed. "Where do we go, then, boss?"

"Amber has an RTA but Sherwood is closer," he told them. "We may already be too damned late for anybody, but I'm feeling somewhat rushed at the moment. So, Sherwood it is. Can we get a cargo to Sherwood?"

He looked at LaMonte, who shrugged back at him.

"About the only good news is that as soon as I started poking around for brokers, they started materializing out of the woodwork," she told them. "Even with the dance of me being picky and demanding interviews, I was having problems keeping them at bay. I'm not *certain* I can get a cargo for Sherwood, but I think we can."

"Make it happen," David ordered. "I don't think I want to spend an hour longer in this system than I have to."

"What about reporting in?" Soprano asked. "If nothing else, I think I want Mars to know just how much of a blind eye the local MISS office is turning to this."

"There's a fleet base at Taurus," LaMonte pointed out. "They're not right on the route to Sherwood, but if we Navy-jump it, we can detour there and arrive at Sherwood without anyone knowing better. The base doesn't have an RTA, but they'll have couriers."

"And they're only three or four days from the RTA at Kingston," David agreed. "That's a good idea. Maria? Are your people up for it?"

"So long as you don't ask us to teleport cargo down to the surface at the end, sure," she confirmed. "We all trained for that to be the standard. I don't like to push to it unless we need it, but we can do it."

"Then let's make it happen," David repeated. "I want a cargo lined up for Sherwood ASAP, and us in space in forty-eight hours."

He smiled grimly.

"If nothing else, at this point, we're relying on the MSPD's incompetence to avoid getting in trouble over our breaking and entering, and I have a professional problem with relying on police incompetence."

"Hey, skipper, there's a young lady out here who says she has an appointment with you," the airlock guard said over the com, a knowing leer in her voice. "She isn't wearing much, so I'm guessing you want her *right up*?"

David sighed and pulled up the video feed from the lock. It was Indigo, all right. Wearing, in this case, an outfit that looked like a black bikini with rose-color frills.

The woman certainly didn't have much sense of modesty; that was for sure. The Marine at the door, though, had been there when Indigo had led them to Kovac's home. Which meant...

David sighed again, then opened the channel back.

"You know who she is; stop mugging for the audience and escort her up," he instructed.

"Yes, sir. Of course, sir!" the Marine replied crisply. Still mugging for the physical and virtual audience who would, hopefully, see this as the Captain having ordered a woman in for the night.

It was a good thing he never planned on coming back to this system.

By the time the Marine escorted Indigo into his office, he'd extracted the other half of her payment and placed it inside a small folio. He slid it across his desk to the scantily clad woman as the Marine left them alone.

"The rest of your payment," he said quietly.

"You went in. You came out," she replied, staring at the folio. "I'm guessing that you found him. What...what *happened*?"

Her voice choked with what David suspected was honest emotion. Kovac had apparently been more than a client, if not sufficiently close enough of a friend for her to initially worry when he'd gone dark.

"Every recording device, record, file and database in his suite was burnt out," he told her. "We'll never know for sure. It was rigged up to look like suicide."

"'Look like,' huh?" she asked.

"Someone walked into his office and shot him in the dead center of the forehead before he even said hello," he said flatly. "They'd been allowed in past his security, and his guards weren't there. Someone he trusted—and someone *damn* fast. As fast as you or Turquoise...possibly even faster."

"You think I—"

"No," David cut her off. "I know you didn't. But a gene-mod or an Augment did. You did what we agreed, so here's your money. Use it wisely."

"Does 'spend every penny hunting down the bastards who killed Kovac' count as wisely?" she asked.

"Probably not," he admitted. "These are dangerous waters, Ms. Indigo. Even for one such as you."

"I don't give a flying fuck," she snarled. "You're not what you said you were, Captain Rice, but I'm more than I appear too."

"I am exactly what I said I was," he said mildly. "I am the Captain of *Red Falcon*. You are a member of a group of genetically modified women used by a Blue Star Syndicate regional boss as both assassins and a personal harem."

"You're not *just* a merchant captain," she said.

"And I can guess what you are beyond a rogue gene-mod a long way from home," David replied.

His guess was that she was running a semi-criminal intelligence organization keeping an eye on *la Cosa Nostra* for anyone who'd pay, but primarily for Kovac and Turquoise. He wasn't going to say that out loud, though.

She got the unspoken message, too. They were both better off if they didn't try and guess what the other really was.

"Here," he told her as he pulled a datachip out of his desk console and slid it over to her. "Gun and helmet camera recordings from his suite. Sanitized of all of our data, of course, but you might be able to get something useful about what happened from it."

Indigo took it, then looked up at David with dry eyes...that clearly were struggling to stay that way.

"I know most wouldn't believe it about a man like him, but he was a good man," she said. "He got dragged into the muck and made the most of where he was stuck, but he was a good man."

"I never met him," he replied. "And now I never will, so I'll take your word for it. Be careful, Ms. Indigo...but good luck in your hunt."

It took LaMonte less than twelve hours to find a broker not merely willing to meet with David about a cargo to Sherwood but downright eager. They ended up meeting for breakfast at a quiet little restaurant near the docks, where the broker turned out to be a fussy little man with extensive dietary restrictions.

Restrictions, it turned out, that the quiet little restaurant knew by heart to the point where the waitress was chorusing along with him as he listed off the changes to their house special.

"No onions, no tomatoes, extra ketchup and mozzarella, no cheddar," she concluded at the same time as him, winking at him. "We know the list, Benny. We'll get it all taken care of."

"Thank you kindly," Benny King told the girl, then turned his vague smile back on David and LaMonte. "So, Captain Rice, you want a cargo to Sherwood, I hear?"

"We just got confirmation in that a cargo we'd been negotiating for will be waiting for us there shortly," David lied smoothly. "We need to be on our way in about two days, but I *hate* running an empty hold. It's a waste of my money, and there's always *someone* shuffling cargo."

"Especially out of Condor," King agreed. "I don't know what people have told you about the system, Captain, but I need to make one thing very clear: I deal only in completely aboveboard cargos. I know perfectly well what kind of...rubbish gets shipped through my home system. I won't touch it. I hope this isn't a problem?"

"Not in the slightest," David said. "The last thing anyone wants is Martian entanglements, or even just local law enforcement. I just want cargo to haul to Sherwood. What can you do for me?"

King leaned back in his chair as the waitress showed up and filled the mugs with coffee. Despite his particularity on the food, he had no instructions around the drinks and sipped the coffee black.

David took that as a good sign but was pleasantly surprised by the quality of the coffee even so.

"They grow coffee on Phoenix," the broker told David with a smile. "There's a roaster on McMurdo, and Gracie—the owner of this little place—gets her beans fresh each morning. Roasted and ground within twenty-four hours of it hitting your cup. It doesn't get fresher."

It was *very* good coffee, and David took a larger swallow as he waited for King to rally his thoughts.

"I can't guarantee I can fill your ship," he finally noted. "Not with two days. Loading alone would make that almost impossible, and it'll take me most of today to even get anything headed in the direction of your ship. Depending on which of the usual suspects have cargos heading that way... I might be able to get you eight, maybe nine hundred containers."

"That's more than I expected," David admitted with a blink of surprise. That was almost half a cargo for his ship.

"I *might* be able to pull it off," King noted carefully. "I'll get you *something*, I can promise that, but I'm guessing beyond that."

"What kind of cargo are we talking about?" David asked.

The broker gestured at his coffee cup as their breakfasts arrived.

"Lots of things, but a good chunk of what we sell to Sherwood is coffee," he said with a grin. "Now, most of the cargo will be transshipments from Core Worlds, but I can pretty much guarantee you a megaton or so of coffee beans."

"Now, *that*, Mr. King, is a lot of coffee."

"More than even I can drink," he agreed. "I charge a three percent commission of your cargo fee and a fixed fee per shipment to the shipper as well. Straightforward enough from your side. Do we have a deal?"

CHAPTER 34

IT SAID A LOT about the smooth functioning of *Red Falcon*'s crew and the competence of their subordinates that Maria spent the runup to the jump into Taurus using James Kellers's chest as a pillow. Neither of them needed to be on duty for something so "mundane" as magically jumping a full light-year into a Navy-secured no-fly zone.

So, instead, she spent that time dozing on the chief engineer's chest, marveling at the degree to which his muscles felt like steel cords wrapped in silk. As the energy wave of the jump swept over them, he woke up and looked down at her.

"Enjoying the view?" he asked.

She danced her fingers up his chest and grinned.

"Immensely. Sadly, that jump means we're in Taurus, which means we *do* actually need to get to work pretty quickly."

He sighed, which vibrated his skin wonderfully under her hands.

"You're right," he agreed, but made no effort to start moving, just lying there looking at her.

"What?" she asked, suddenly feeling self-conscious.

"You ever wonder what we'll do after this?" he asked. "I mean...I know David. He's not going to be a spy forever."

That thought had honestly never occurred to Maria.

"I've been expecting to die on one of these ops," she admitted. "Long-term planning has never been my strong point."

He chuckled and laced his fingers into her hair. She leaned in to kiss him and then rested her head on his shoulder.

"I...suspect I'm with either David or MISS for life, though," she told him. "I was Navy until I fucked that up, and I'll be MISS until I screw that up."

That was...more honest and whinier than she'd intended, and she felt his hand tighten gently against her.

"You haven't screwed it up yet," he said. "And I can't see you screwing it up, either. The instincts that got you in trouble in the Navy are the instincts MISS wants. Me..."

He shook his head again, brushing his chin against her hair.

"I always thought I'd be David's chief of engineering until he retired," he admitted. "Didn't want a ship of my own, didn't have a plan beyond sticking with him. If he leaves MISS, though...don't know if I will. Might need a reason to stay, though."

Maria took a long few seconds of silent thought to unpack that, then kissed his shoulder.

"Be careful, you lug," she told him. "Or I might think you were saying you'd go wherever I do."

Which was somehow much less terrifying than she would have thought.

"Not anywhere," he responded. "But if you're going somewhere I might think about going, I'll definitely think about going along. If you follow."

"I follow," she said, and kissed him again. "For now, my dear, we need to actually get up. While we didn't jump right into the Navy base, if we followed my calculations, there should be a destroyer showing up to say hello sometime in the next hour.

"We should both be on duty when they arrive."

Maria stepped into the simulacrum chamber, checking the screens as she moved over to the liquid model, and nodded to Xi Wu.

"Nguyen went and fell over," Wu told her. "No active movement from the Navy base. Quiet so far."

Maria shook her head.

"That's not right," she noted. Taurus's smaller gas giant was the base for half a squadron of Royal Martian Navy cruisers. There should have been patrols around the planetary system, and someone should have pinged them by now.

"Station looks live," the younger Mage said. "The refinery is active, but I'm only seeing one cruiser. Aren't there supposed to be more?"

"There should be four, and a dozen destroyers," Maria replied. "Our files are out of date but not that old."

"I'm seeing one cruiser, no destroyers," Wu said. "Seems light for a Navy base."

"It is light," Maria agreed. "I'll buy the cruisers being deployed, but they wouldn't have taken all of the destroyers. Which means..." She sighed and brought up the channel to the bridge.

"Captain, we're being stalked," she told him.

Rice looked at her for several moments, then nodded.

"Of course. If they deployed most of the station's ships somewhere, then the destroyers are stealthing around. I'd rather not go active, Maria," he replied. "But if they're stealthing, a hard radar sweep will show them."

"Plus, Jeeves should know the pattern they'll follow," Maria pointed out. "A civilian ship wouldn't have the scanners to do it, either. Have we transmitted to the base?"

"MISS authenticate codes went out ten minutes ago. They've received them; they just haven't responded."

Maria managed to not, *quite*, visibly roll her eyes. She'd been on the other side of similar exchanges enough to guess what was going on.

"They're playing games," she told him. "They know who we are, but they want to make us sweat because the whole concept of a covert ops warship is enough to make them damn grumpy."

Right now, *Red Falcon* wasn't even flying her civilian transponder. All of her current transmissions identified her as KEX-12. Given the number of ships of her size and design around, it was a mostly pointless gesture, but that was why they were as far from Taurus's inhabited planet as they could get.

"Agreed," Rice said. "Jeeves? If you were ghosting a Militia ship with an egotistical captain back when, where would you have put the destroyer?"

The gunner chuckled.

"That was a little above my grade, skipper," he noted. "But...here or here." Two zones flashed amber on the tactical display feeding to Maria's screens.

"I agree," she said simply.

"Pulse 'em. Read me their damn hull numbers. If they want to be rude, let's return the favor."

The big freighter rotated slightly, almost imperceptibly, to align her main radar arrays with the zones where they guessed the destroyers would be closing. Strict emission controls and a little bit of amplified magic could go a long way to hiding even a starship in space, but it wouldn't stand up to military-grade radar pointed right at it.

To no one's surprise, there was a destroyer in each zone Jeeves had flagged. The high-power radar pulses took just over thirty seconds to get back to *Red Falcon*, but they punched right through the magical cloak over the ships.

"DD-104 and DD-126," Jeeves reported calmly. He apparently had taken Rice entirely literally. "Warbook says *Shining Defender of Liberty* and *Virtues of the Guardian*."

"Send our MISS codes directly to them," Rice ordered.

"Incoming message!" LaMonte interrupted. "From *Shining Defender*."

A video transmission appeared on the main screen, mirrored to Maria's screens in the simulacrum chamber. The woman in the image had skin as dark as her black uniform, almost blending into the sharply creased uniform as she looked at the camera with a wry smile.

"This is Mage-Captain Hanaa Okeke, commanding *Shining Defender of Liberty*," she introduced herself. "My sensor chief reports a brand-new headache, which I have to consider fair play for the game we were playing. Welcome to Taurus, KEX-12. *Defender* and *Virtues* will match velocity with you and escort you in.

"Please behave and try not to give us any more headaches," Okeke continued. "That pulse was fair game, but we're under a degree of alert right now that's making everyone twitchy."

When she'd served in the Navy, Maria had always wondered why they insisted on positioning so many of the major bases around gas giants and well away from the inhabited worlds they were ostensibly there to protect.

The official reasons were all true, of course. That was where the fueling stations were, the cloudscoops that brought up vast quantities of hydrogen, and the heavily secured facilities where Mages transmuted matter into antimatter. The outer system was often easier to access, too, with fewer overlaid gravity wells for the Navy Mages to calculate around.

But it was also true, she realized now, that part of it was just to be out of sight. *Red Falcon* couldn't have just "dropped in" to the Taurus Navy Base if it had been in orbit of Gemini and under a billion-odd watching eyes.

With the base positioned in a quiet corner of the system, they could tuck the big ship into the fueling station and take one of Kelzin's shuttles over to the cruiser *Huntress of Temptations* while LaMonte handled restocking.

Kelzin settled the shuttle down in the cruiser's bay with precision, and the cruiser's safety systems engaged. After a minute or so, it was safe to leave, and Maria followed Captain Rice out onto the cruiser's deck.

There was no formal welcoming party or grand display. They were a covert ops ship, after all, and while there was no hiding "KEX-12" from the sensor crews, only a handful of people needed to know who commanded the ship.

"Captain Rice, welcome aboard *Huntress of Temptations*," an elegantly turned-out man with long red hair and a black uniform greeted them. He had two companions, both with the insignia of Mage-Commanders. "I am Mage-Captain Andrew Verona, *Huntress*'s commanding officer and the current acting station commander for the Taurus Navy Base.

"While I'll freely admit to authorizing the games my captains were playing when you arrived, we are always at MISS's disposal," he continued with a small smile. "How may I assist you, Captain, Ship's Mage?"

Verona had a well-stocked wine cabinet and produced an excellent red wine as they took seats in his office.

"If you don't mind my asking, Mage-Captain, I though the Taurus system had more ships?" Rice asked.

"Hand Ndosi had to borrow a few ships a couple of weeks ago," Verona explained. "Not my place to say what she'd found, but she needed a few cruisers to help get things under control."

"Ah," Rice allowed. "Do you still have couriers on hand after the Hand's arrival?"

Maria wasn't familiar with the name Ndosi, but that wasn't really a surprise. The identities of the Hands of Mage-King weren't secret, but they also saw no reason to broadcast them.

"She only took one of them," the Navy officer said. "I still have two couriers on hand. I suppose that's the main thing you need, Captain?"

"We need to update MISS on our current operations and get a message to Hand Lomond," Rice said grimly. "There are certain...affairs in the Condor System that require a Hand's touch, I believe."

Verona arched a carefully groomed eyebrow but didn't argue.

"I can put FN-2199 at your disposal for whatever message you need to send," he confirmed. "Do we need to send her to an RTA or all the way to Mars?"

Mars was at least a week's flight away, but Maria saw David pause.

"Both would be ideal," she said while her Captain was thinking. "Immediate relay via the RTA of the basic information will enable action, but I think Mars needs our full reports and scan data."

"We can do that," Verona confirmed. "Is there any additional assistance I can provide you? I doubt I need to know your mission, but while I'm short of ships, I can spare a destroyer if needed." He grimaced. "Well,

I can deploy my entire flotilla if *needed,* but that would leave Taurus defenseless."

"The offer is appreciated, Mage-Captain," Rice told him. "But I think KEX-12 is capable of taking care of herself. We, ah, are carrying significantly more antimatter munitions than I think any opponent may expect."

"And a destroyer would attract attention we're trying to avoid," Maria added. "Our job is covert, after all."

"Of course," Verona agreed. "Your XO has already sent over a list of supplies and parts you need, and we're taking the opportunity to top up your fuel from the Mage-King's stocks."

He offered his hand.

"I can't imagine you dropped into a Navy base because your job is being easy and convenient, Captain, Ship's Mage," he said. "Any assistance we can provide, we will. Beyond that, I wish you the best of luck."

"We appreciate it," Maria replied as David shook the Mage-Captain's hand. "As you say, we have a job to do. Answers to find. People to protect."

"And what purpose is His Protectorate if we do not protect people?" Verona said quietly.

CHAPTER 35

KELLY HELD the midnight watch alone as *Red Falcon* drifted through deep space, halfway between Taurus and Sherwood. The ship was quiet, even her massive engines silent as she waited for the Mages to work their spells and carry her farther through space.

Once, they'd thought deep space was inviolate, a safe zone where no one could follow them. They'd been regularly disabused of that notion, sadly. Anyone who knew your route could intercept you with a little luck. Trackers, that rare breed of not-Mages-but-still-magical individuals, could follow a jump with laser precision.

Her job was literally to keep watch and to hit the alert if something jumped into the forgotten chunk of space they occupied. It was a good time to catch up on her reading, which for Kelly ranged from periodicals around management and shipping economics to engineering textbooks to advice books on keeping together polyamorous relationships.

Every time they traveled through a system, her to-be-read pile expanded. She didn't get much time to read.

One of the things she'd started to keep an eye on was the "starting price" of a small jump freighter. She'd attached her star to David Rice and MISS for now, but after two years aboard *Red Falcon*, she was starting to wonder where she went from there.

A *Venice*-class ship like the old *Blue Jay* hauled three million tons of cargo, and the main restriction on its speed was how many Mages you put aboard her. Three-megaton ships like that were the backbone of the Protectorate's economy, but they were also well out of the range she could imagine financing.

Without help from Captain Rice, help she hesitated to ask for, her range didn't even stretch to the kind of small one-megaton ship that either ran with multiple Mages as a fast packet or, well, ran routes nobody else cared about.

Time would change that. Time or, well, help from Captain Rice. Or potentially MISS, if Kelly was willing to tie her future to the intelligence agency. She was, officially, a mid-ranking MISS agent, after all.

The realities of the situation were somewhat more...fluid. *Red Falcon*'s senior crew had been brought aboard as a group. She had an MISS rank and a stack of MISS training, but her membership in the organization was still really via David Rice.

She could change that, Kelly supposed, but that would require her to truly make intelligence and counterintelligence her career.

It would also require leaving *Red Falcon* behind, and that wasn't a decision she could make without talking to Wu and Kelzin. No one had been talking rings or marriage yet, but she certainly wasn't planning on going anywhere without that pair.

Soft footsteps caught her attention, and she looked up to see Captain Rice entering the bridge.

"Captain," she greeted him. "It's a bit late, isn't it?"

As a practical matter, the ship's day operated on "the captain is up," but that also aligned relatively well with the usual Olympus Mons Time used by stations and spaceships, at least aboard *Red Falcon*.

"Couldn't sleep," Rice admitted gruffly. "How's the watch?"

Kelly gestured expansively at the empty screens.

"We are, if my astrography is half as good as I think it is, about seven light-years from the nearest inhabited system and probably about as far from the nearest human," she pointed out. "It's quiet. A time to think and read."

He chuckled and glanced over her shoulder.

"Used-starship listings, huh?" he asked. "Leaving us already?"

"Listings" was an exaggeration. There had been exactly *two* starships for sale in Taurus, and Kelly wouldn't have bought one there anyway.

"Researching," she told him. "Trying to work out where I go from here." She shrugged. "If it was more than research, I'd be talking about it with the others."

"You don't *have* to bring your lovers on your ship with you," Rice observed, "though I'll admit that having them on *different* ships makes things impossible."

He looked sad at that thought, and Kelly wondered just what had wrecked the Captain's half-mythical first marriage.

"I'd rather keep them around," she told her boss. "So, it's a factor."

"Didn't say it shouldn't be, just that it didn't *need* to be," he replied. "If that's your plan, work with it. There's worse people to bring with you than a top-tier pilot and Mage, that's for sure."

"You're not...bothered?" she asked.

Rice chuckled.

"Kelly, like any other student, XOs move on. It was actually a concern for me that it took so long to get Jenna onto her own ship. I never ended up having the resources to buy her one until MISS got involved, and she didn't have the ambition to try and pull together investors herself." He shrugged. "There's nothing wrong with wanting to be XO; some people don't want the responsibility and risk of running a ship they own."

Jenna Campbell now commanded *Peregrine*—as Rice's employee, yes, but Captain of her own ship. There was still a lot less risk in commanding someone else's ship than in owning your own...but Kelly wanted her own.

"I like being XO," she told the Captain. "But...yeah, I want my own ship."

"There's more possibilities than one for that," he pointed out. "You've blown away every MISS training course you've taken. *Red Falcon* is, in many ways, not a particularly covert covert ship. At this point, we could almost certainly get Mars to give you a ship, let you pick your own crew. Who knows what they'd want you to do, but they'd probably be grumpier to see you go than I would be!"

"I'm not sure I want to make this my life," she admitted.

"Neither am I," her Captain said with a chuckle. "Once we're done chasing this chain of guns, though, we'll head back to Tau Ceti to take a breather. I'll back you for whatever play you want to make—if you want to stay on *Red Falcon* a while longer, I'll be glad to keep you. If you want an MISS ship, I'll back you. If you want to buy your own, I'll help you put together a syndicate of investors."

She inhaled sharply.

"That's a hell of an open-ended offer, boss," she told him as she tried to wrap her brain around it. Rice helping her put together a syndicate of investors would inevitably require him to put up a good chunk of the money himself and likely guarantee the rest of the loans.

Kelly would be indebted to him beyond the strict dollar value...but she'd still own her ship and be in charge.

"The last woman I was exec for made me the same one, without the MISS component," he told her. "She helped me put together my first investment syndicate and buy a third-tier *Classical*-class two-megaton ship." Rice shook his head. "*Gods,* was she a hunk of junk, but she held together long enough for me to put together the funds to buy *Blue Jay.*

"Think about it," he instructed.

"What do you think I should do?" Kelly asked.

"I can't tell you that," he replied. "I think you'd make a damn good co-vert ops commander, better than me by a long shot. But I think we could swing you a three- or four-megaton mid-sized freighter pretty easily.

"Think about it," he echoed. "And go rest. I have the watch."

"Thank you, Captain."

Her thanks were for far more than just taking over the rest of her shift.

CHAPTER 36

"WELCOME BACK TO SHERWOOD, everyone," David said with forced cheer as the jump flare faded. "Everyone has fond memories, I hope?"

He forced a bitter-sounding chuckle as he said that.

The last time he'd visited Sherwood, the youngest child of the McLaughlin had died teleporting David and *Blue Jay* safely away from a pirate attack to safety there. He'd delivered Kenneth McLaughlin's body to his father...and been banned from the system.

The consequences of that had been messy, but the end result had been that he'd picked up Mage Damien Montgomery as his replacement Ship's Mage. The consequences of *that* recruitment had in many ways been messier and farther-reaching.

On the other hand, without Damien Montgomery, David Rice would be dead. He was okay with the trade.

"Well, not much has changed," LaMonte noted. "Still has the one big stick with rings on it for an orbital, though... Yeah, those are new."

David's XO flagged a new set of stations orbiting above Sherwood Prime. Like Prime itself, they were an idiosyncratic local design...but like Prime, he recognized their purpose.

"Shipyards? That's...a hell of an investment."

"And there's the return," Jeeves told him. "Looks like three ships, three-quarters-scale cruisers."

"Three yards, finished with ships under construction in them," LaMonte reported. "Three more under construction; their second tranche of ships will probably all start at the same time."

"What are those things?" David asked, studying the ships. They were big bastards for what were obviously Militia warships, six million tons apiece and with a sweeping organic design quite contrary to the usual Martian structure.

"At a guess? Pirate-killers," Jeeves said. "If you're worried your local pirates are going to get their hands on destroyers or even just a flotilla of jump-corvettes, well, you want something that can eat that for lunch without getting hurt in the process."

"Anything in our files on them?" David said.

"Just a note that Sherwood was founding a new anti-piracy force, the Sherwood Interstellar Patrol," LaMonte told him. "I guess they were taking it a lot more seriously than MISS thought they were."

"Those aren't civilian-designed floating wrecks like Stellarite's ships, either," Jeeves pointed out. "Just from what I can see, they've got anti-matter drives and modern sensors. Probably the missiles and beams to back them up, too. I wouldn't bet on them versus, say, an equal tonnage of Navy ships, but they look like competently built ships."

"And competently commanded ones," David murmured, watching as the closest of the three ships adjusted her vector. The big new ship wasn't on an intercept course for *Red Falcon*—she was leaving that to a sublight corvette that was much closer to them—but she was in position to back up the corvette.

In fact...David checked the numbers. If the Patrol ship was carrying the Phoenix VIIs the Protectorate authorized for System Militia use, they would be able to land missile hits on *Falcon* before *Falcon* could hit the corvette with lasers.

It was a *very* well-arranged interception pattern that made the best use of their limited resources.

"Send our bona fides in-system and request an approach pattern and docking port with Prime," David ordered. "We have cargo to deliver, and then, well, we need to find this Mehrab Gorman."

Sherwood Prime had its downsides and upsides, in David's opinion. Its biggest downside, of course, was being the poor bastard trying to dock with one of the rings close to the center of the "stick." With twelve spinning ring sections providing artificial gravity, docking with any of them was a pain. Docking with the central ones, with spinning sections on both sides, was a nightmare.

Fortunately, a ship of *Red Falcon*'s size had to dock at the end, where there was only the zero-gravity core. Unlike many stations, Sherwood Prime had no artificial gravity runes to make ship access easier, which was another downside.

Prime's big upside was that it concentrated all of the transshipping, cargo loading, ship repairs, and orbital residential space into a single massive platform. Putting a quarter of a million people in one space station allowed for significant economies of scale, but most systems didn't have the foresight or cash to build an orbital as large as Sherwood had as their first space station.

Leonhart escorted him to the ship boarding tube, the Marine looking curious.

"First time to Sherwood?" he asked.

"Yup," she confirmed. "I've seen some big stations, but this one is pushing it for the MidWorlds."

"Sherwood has a lot of things the Core Worlds want, even if most of it is luxury goods," he pointed out. "They do a good job of using that money, and the system cops are good."

"Think they'll have files on Gorman?" Leonhart asked.

"If anyone does," he confirmed. "Do what you need to, Chief. If that's hack their files, that's probably preferable, but we might have more luck flashing badges here. SSS are *good*."

Hacking McMurdo Station's police databases had been one thing. Hacking Sherwood System Security...yeah. David wasn't taking bets on his Marines succeeding.

"We're better off playing nice, are we?" Leonhart asked.

"It's your call, Rhianna," David told her. "Whatever it takes."

She sighed.

"I know that tone," she replied. "We'll sneak in and show some badges. If they're as good as you think, there's got to be at least one quiet office no one is watching."

"All right. I need some escorts to go meet our cargo broker," he said. "I'll leave making friends with the local cops to you."

Leonhart laughed.

"I'll send Binici with you," she told him. "If I'm not hacking their systems, I don't need her for this."

The disadvantage of the kind of brokered cargo that David had brought to Sherwood was that there was no single point of contact. He had eight point four million tons of cargo—eight hundred and forty-three ten-thousand-ton containers—and just over six hundred deliveries.

The biggest cargo was a hundred and twenty containers of coffee beans. At the other end of the scale, ten containers held no less than one hundred and seventy separate cargos. Back when he'd been barely making ends meet on *Blue Jay*, he and Jenna had handled all of the individual cargos themselves.

"Barely making ends meet" meant something very different for a starship captain than most, but it had been tight enough that a one percent brokerage fee could cut their reserve in half. Now, though, *Red Falcon* delivered cargos in a quarter of the time *Blue Jay* had. She charged the same amount per ton-light-year and only cost twice as much to run.

Plus, even half-empty, she was delivering three times as much cargo as his old ship. He not only could hire a broker to handle this end of the deal, he *had* to.

Leaving the office of the man he'd engaged to take care of that project, the last thing he expected was a quartet of grim-faced Sherwood System Security officers staring down his bodyguards. They weren't heavily armed...but they were the law here unless he chose to blow his cover.

"Captain David Rice?" one of them said sharply.

"That would be me," he confirmed carefully.

"We'll need you to come with us," the officer told him.

"What is this about?" David asked. "Am I being arrested? For what?"

"Whether or not you are being arrested is to be established at a later point," the officer said formally. "You *are* being detained for violation of a directed executive order from the Governor, which requires you to be brought before an appropriate authority."

"Captain?" Binici asked slowly. "What did you do?"

David swallowed. He hadn't actually expected the order to still hold.

"I came back to Sherwood," he admitted. "The McLaughlin told me to never come back again after his son died on my old ship."

"And that order was entered in the formal records," the SSS officer confirmed. "So, I repeat. You are being detained. Are you going to make a fuss?"

"May my escort accompany me?" he asked.

"For now," the officer told him. "You may also contact your ship to let them know what's happening. Further communication once you reach the station will be at the discretion of higher authority than I."

The worst that the McLaughlin could do for something like this was kick him out of the system, which would be *hell* for their cargo-delivery contracts but not insurmountable...for their official business.

There was no way he could find Mehrab Gorman if the Governor kicked him out. His MISS codes could probably avoid that, but that was going to be more trouble than he wanted.

"I'll let my XO and Ship's Mage know immediately," he told the officer, but sighed. "I see no other choice; I will of course comply."

The Security officers were polite enough and he managed to at least dodge a cell. He was separated from Binici and her team and put inside what was probably a visitor's office. Office or no, it still had a lock and he heard it click shut behind him.

The console at the desk was designed to interface with a wrist-comp, and his didn't have the codes. Depending on what software they'd used, he might have an MISS override that would get him in, but that would give away more than it would help.

He settled into the chair and considered the situation. He hadn't forgotten that he'd been ordered to never come back, but most of the time, that kind of order was more bluster than anything else. He should have known better to expect bluster from the McLaughlin.

Miles James McLaughlin was the patriarch of his clan and had been elected Mage-Governor of Sherwood eight times now. He didn't bluff. He didn't bluster. When he issued orders and commands, he *meant* them.

David suspected that the SSS officers, at least, expected that David would be released pretty quickly. It was a four-year-old order now, and even Governor McLaughlin didn't hold grudges that long. By locking him up, they were making a point and trying to scare him.

They were probably doing him a favor. If the Governor found out he was there without there being *some* kind of consequence, it might have ended up biting him in the ass.

His morose thoughts were interrupted by the door unlocking and someone stepping in. The stranger was a petite redheaded woman in an unfamiliar dark blue uniform with insignia of a single gold circle. If she was using RMN patterns, this was a full Captain...and then he recognized her.

"Grace McLaughlin," he greeted her. Once an interviewee for a Ship's Mage job on his second ship. Once before that, the lover of the Ship's Mage who'd become a Hand. Now...a starship captain?

"*Captain* Grace McLaughlin," she corrected him, her voice sharp. "You, Captain Rice, have managed to cause me a large degree of trouble just by showing up. Fortunately for you, my grandfather is quite fond of the coffee you brought, so that may help your case."

Her sharp tone wasn't quite what he'd expected from a woman he'd thought had positive opinions of him. On the other hand, she was now a Captain in the new Sherwood Interstellar Patrol. Who knew what that meant?

As he was thinking that, she stepped into a corner of the room and pressed on a panel he hadn't realized was there.

"All right," she continued, her tone calmer. "All recorders are off, Captain." She indelicately hopped onto the desk, using its height to level their eyes. Like Damien Montgomery, she was *much* shorter than David.

"And why would that be?" he asked carefully.

"Because I need your MISS papers," she told him. "*Now*, Captain."

David nodded and tapped a series of commands on his wrist-comp. A file decrypted and bounced to her computer via a secure short-range transmitter.

She glanced over it and grumbled.

"This would be enough to get my grandfather off your back," she told him. "You weren't going to be in *that* much trouble, not once I spoke to him. Even he knows he overreacted to your role in Kenneth's death."

"It was a terrible situation all around," he replied. "How did you know I was MISS?"

"Your chief of security, Leonhart, I think her name was?" McLaughlin replied. "She made contact with SSS and they bounced her to me. I command *Robin Hood*, the first of our frigates, but I also run our shore establishment."

She shrugged.

"We'll need to actually promote someone past Captain to take command of the Patrol shortly. Last I heard, my name was one of two on the list of possibilities. Nepotism, in my opinion, but I'll do the job if they give it to me."

"So, you would be who we'd need to talk to," David concluded.

"I also, regardless of promotions, do have the authority to get you out of this room," she told him. "But it seemed like a good time for us to have a nice private chat that no one was going to question too much. You're in Sherwood under an MISS warrant, hunting somebody. Gorman, I believe the name was? Why?"

"That's classified," he replied.

"Yes, and I need to know," McLaughlin told him levelly. "You may trust my discretion, Captain. More importantly, you have no choice but to trust my discretion. SSS will give you everything if I tell them to...and *nothing* if I tell them not to. Are we clear?"

David nodded. Whatever she might think, he figured that second name on the list for the Patrol's overall commander was probably there for form's sake as much as anything else. The young woman sitting on the desk in his glorified cell had risen to her challenges and was still rising.

"Mehrab Gorman crossed our radar as a potential middleman for the supply of arms to the rebellion on Ardennes," he told her. "I won't... I *can't* tell you who we think the source was, though I imagine you can guess.

"But we need to track the chain further back—and at least one middleman we did track down is dead."

McLaughlin exhaled and nodded thoughtfully.

"Part of the reason the SSS passed your security chief on to me is that Gorman is ours," she told him. "Not everything that the Patrol wanted or needed was officially available to us, so we made a deal: we 'lost' our files on Gorman and he made sure we got our hands on the gear we needed."

"I don't need to bring him in," David noted. "I need him to answer some questions, questions he may not want to answer, but I don't need to arrest him."

"You'll have to find him first," McLaughlin said. "He's a collared crook, Captain Rice, so we keep a pretty close eye on him...and he went missing a week ago."

"*Fuck.*"

David could do the math on that. That was more recently than when Kovac had died, but it lined up with the same methodology. It even lined up with someone taking a ship directly to Sherwood from Condor and moving on the second man.

"That was my thought, yes," McLaughlin agreed. "We know he left the station; he has a house on one of the equatorial beaches, and we don't insist he stay in touch more often than once every day or two. He never made it to the house. Somewhere between his shuttle touching down at Sherwood City and him getting home, he disappeared."

"No sign of the man at all?" David asked. "I'm guessing you're looking for him."

"We're looking," she confirmed. "SSS has operatives combing the roads, but...no sign so far."

David sighed.

"Can we help?"

"Unless you have better people than a system security force's forensics teams, not really," she pointed out.

"We have sanction you don't," he replied. "Collared crook or not, you need a warrant to rip open his house, don't you?"

Grace McLaughlin paused, then sighed.

"Fair enough. We know he didn't make it to his home, so we haven't pushed any of those rules. But you're counterintelligence, aren't you?"

"And I have a general warrant for Gorman," David told her. "I can kick his door down and tear his house to pieces. If there's any sign of him or of the data we need, my people can find it."

"Your people, yes. Not you," McLaughlin insisted. "I can funnel a portion of your security team down to the surface, probably your Mage, too, but it's hard to justify sticking a Captain we just detained and tried to scare the crap out of on one of our shuttles as an 'honored guest.'"

David chuckled.

"Soprano and Leonhart are the better choice, anyway," he admitted. "My skills have a different focus."

CHAPTER 37

THE SYSTEM SECURITY shuttle skimmed over the ocean at breakneck speed as Maria checked her body armor. It had been a while since she'd geared up herself, and she mostly relied on her magic to protect her.

Today, though, the body armor and its face-concealing helmet were critical to the plan. The SSS crew knew that their passengers were agents of the Martian Interstellar Security Service. They didn't know who their passengers were, and that was for the best for everyone.

The shuttle was a Tau Ceti–built stealthed troop transport designed for exactly this role. An actual assault shuttle or atmospheric interceptor would dance rings around it, but it could sneak up on any civilian encampment and catch most civilian atmospheric craft and spacecraft.

They were going fast enough to leave a wake despite being at least fifty meters above the water, but slowed as they approached their destination. Checking the cameras feeding to her armor's helmet, Maria recognized the target: a luxurious beachside villa mixing the architectural influences of the last few millennia or so with a master's touch.

It wasn't huge as villas and mansions went, but it was a five-level building that descended down the beach and blended into its surroundings like it had always been there. A small tributary that ran into the ocean there had been incorporated into the structure, a transparent atrium above it forming the central line of the house.

"I see being a boxed crook pays well," she murmured.

"From the files the Patrol gave us, he had the house *before* they caught him," Leonhart pointed out. "Considering Kovac's place? Being a broker for criminal gunrunning pays *way* better than I expected."

"Plotting a career change?" Maria asked as the shuttle swept toward the landing pad behind and above the house.

"Given that every one of these brokers whose houses we've broken into has been *dead*, I don't think so," the Marine replied. "Ground in twenty. Lock and load!"

They weren't expecting trouble, and the body armor the Marines and Maria were wearing were relatively standard gear, neither stealth armor nor combat exoskeletons. Most of what Maria's people were carrying was sensors—but they all also packed MACCAW-9s.

They inspected those weapons as the shuttle grounded, clearing safeties and checking magazines. The door swung open and the Marines were out first, with Maria and Leonhart right behind them.

"Keep the bird warm," Maria told the crew. "I don't expect to have to leave here in a hurry, but, to be honest, I'm not sure *what* to expect."

The house looked nice enough, but so had Kovac's apartment. And Kovac's apartment had contained an automated death trap and a corpse.

The door leading from the landing pad to the house was unlocked. That was...not what Maria had been expecting. The house was sufficiently isolated to allow most people to rely on seclusion for security, but criminals tended to be more paranoid.

"Is anyone in there?" she shouted. "We have a warrant and are entering the house!"

There was no response, and Maria shrugged and shoved the door open to move in. The layout of the house, she quickly realized, was probably a significant part of the security. The combination of glass walls and mirrors made rooms look smaller or larger than they were, probably concealing entire sections of the building if you didn't already know the layout.

Their door led into a decorative entryway that resembled nothing so much as a hall of mirrors, extending off into infinity. Gorman, it seemed, had a very distinct style.

Whoever had put it together for him had been very, *very* good.

"Do you smell that?" Leonhart asked softly and Maria looked over at her.

"No. What?"

"Death," the Marine replied. "Let's move."

Maria still had no idea what Leonhart was smelling, but she followed the Marine down the stairs to the middle floor—and into the leftovers of a clearly unexpected fight.

Nobody lived in the house while Gorman was gone, but clearly somebody visited to clean and upkeep the place—and feed the dogs. Four large black animals were crumpled in heaps around the main atrium, along with a young man they'd clearly been attempting to protect.

"Check them," Maria ordered grimly. The atrium would have been gorgeous normally, with a burbling brook and living trees surrounding an expensive set of comfortable-looking living room furniture. The dead animals and youth ruined the ambience.

A Marine stepped over the youth, kneeling over the body with a scanner for half a minute before reaching down to gently close the staring eyes.

"Shot in the head," the Marine reported. "Not at close range, no flash burns." He shook his head. "Perfect shot, from over there." He gestured. The only stairway in that direction was at least four or five meters away.

"Augment," Leonhart concluded sadly, looking over the dogs herself. "The dogs smelled a stranger, tried to get the caretaker out of the room. He didn't realize there was a threat, tried to get them under control, and attracted attention. Intruder walked in and shot them all."

"Given everything else, I would have expected them to clean up," Maria noted.

"Probably panicked, figuring someone would come to check in on the missing person." Leonhart stood up. "How long, Naheed?"

"Five days," the Marine replied. "There probably is a missing-person report out, but no one has gone far enough to start kicking down the doors of his clients. I doubt Gorman was the only person the kid was taking care of pets for."

"*Fuck.*" Maria glared around the room. "Scan the place for computers—and appliances. I have a bad damn feeling about this."

The scans confirmed what she was expecting. She hadn't noticed it before, as the house was built to use as much natural light as possible, but all of the electronics were down. Someone had cut external power and then overloaded the internal circuit, much as had been done in Kovac's apartment.

It was clean, effective, and professional, but combined with the bodies and *Red Falcon*'s encounters in Condor, it set a pattern. Someone, almost certainly a covert Augment agent from Legatus, had been tying up loose ends.

Maria doubted they were going to find the contact in Amber alive, either. Someone had been *very* thorough, and while they could try to trace back the murderer, she didn't expect them to have much luck.

It was easy to assume Legatans, too, but they had no proof. The never-ending story of MISS's shadow conflict. They believed they knew who the enemy was...but they didn't even have proof *they* would trust, let alone that they could take to the government.

"Rhianna, when the Patrol said he never arrived home, did they track him or did he not check in?" Maria asked as she looked up and down the atrium "spine" of the house.

"He didn't check in," Leonhart replied. "He was apparently checking in every twelve hours or so and had a remotely activatable tracker on his wrist-comp. He *may* have dumped the comp and disappeared on his own, but...they couldn't find the comp at all."

Which didn't rule out Gorman making a run for it, Maria supposed, but it fit with the pattern they were seeing.

"Let's check his office," she ordered. "And sweep the damn house. This place was built to hide secret rooms. I'm guessing there's at least something in here he didn't want anyone to find."

The main office was a gleaming room of chrome and wallscreens and lies. It was *too* sterile, too clean. Nothing about the room even suggested that it has been personalized, and Maria looked around it with faint distaste.

"This *might* be where he met people," she allowed. "But it wasn't where he worked. How's that mapping going?"

"From what I'm seeing, I'm guessing about a quarter of the house is hidden," Leonhart replied. "Plus, I would bet the damn *Falcon* herself that there's an entire floor under the house that isn't accessed by any visible means.

"Finding all of this house's secrets could take a while."

"Well, can we at least confirm there's no computers in there?" Maria asked. "That would render finding them, well, useless."

"I don't know," Leonhart admitted. "It wouldn't take much shielding to make it impossible to tell if you had computer equipment hidden in the secret rooms, and almost none if you buried the underground section well enough."

Maria studied the room around her contemplatively.

"How far does our warrant stretch?" she asked.

"Um. We could basically dismantle the building brick by brick," Leonhart told her. "Why?"

"Because that's basically what I'm planning. Hold one."

She was done being patient. Magic flared around her hand, lighting up the two runes on her right palm—the rune that interfaced with the simulacrum to jump a starship and the projector rune that made it significantly easier to use her magic as a weapon. She gathered heat and force for a moment as she studied the room.

Then she obliterated a meter-wide hole in all four walls with a gesture. The Marine standing guard outside the office looked through the hole at her with some distress, but she flashed the woman a thumbs-up.

Two of the walls led into the rooms she expected. One linked to the atrium, one to the master bedroom. The bedroom at least looked like it was actually used...and it *also* shared a wall with the space the fourth hole revealed.

Tucked away and concealed by mirrors on all sides was a room that was completely contrary to the luxurious décor of the rest of the house. The walls were plain steel, made of panels that would probably slide aside at a verbal command if the house computers were working.

A large wooden desk took up the center of the room, its exterior paneling dismantled to allow someone to get at the computer cores within. There was no body in this office, but it otherwise resembled where they'd found Kovac—someone had found the central computer nexus and linked in an EMP bomb to be very sure they'd got all of Gorman's files.

"Well, someone was very thorough," Maria said grimly. "Start knocking down walls, Leonhart. I want to know every secret Gorman left here. I don't know if we'll find any answers...but we've run out of other places to look."

Maria spent most of the search half-expecting to find Gorman's body, but wherever the smuggler had died or been kidnapped to, he hadn't been left for dead in his own home.

He also hadn't, despite what they'd expected, been using his home as a staging depot. There was an underground level, exactly as Leonhart had expected, but it looked more like a museum than a storage facility.

Here, it appeared, was where the gunrunner had stored the more esoteric and strange finds he'd acquired over his career. There was a pair of blasters—one-shot compressed-plasma guns that made great portable anti-tank weapons. There were over twenty combat exosuits going back almost two hundred years of the evolution of the technology.

Swords, guns, armor—the room was a treasure trove of the strange, the fascinating, and the lethal.

And then, at the very back, Maria found Gorman's last secret, the one that even the Patrol would probably have broken their promise of clemency over. They almost missed it as they ran their flashlights through the dark room, thinking that it was just another exosuit...and then Maria realized it was halfway across the room and refocused her light.

"What in all bloody hells is *that*?" she barked as she studied the mechanical troll occupying the entire far wall. At least five meters tall, the war machine had four legs and six "arms"—two with hands and four with an assortment of weaponry.

Leonhart swallowed audibly as her own light shone on it.

"That should *not* exist," she said flatly. "It's a United Nations ODD—Orbital Drop Dreadnought. They were ASI-driven war machines that they built to drop into 'strategic target zones' on Mars during the Eugenics Wars."

Maria swallowed.

Artificial Sequential Intelligences were self-learning, heuristic algorithms. They weren't smart—they got called "artificial stupids" a lot—but if well coded, they could do a lot of things. She still wouldn't have trusted a modern one, even written by Kelly LaMonte, whose skills she trusted, to distinguish between civilian and combatant.

"They weren't intended to distinguish targets," the Marine said, in response to Maria's unspoken thought. "They were intended to wreck everything around them until they ran out of ammunition, then pick up enemy weapons and *continue* wrecking things until someone destroyed them.

"They were a violation of a billion treaties then and a violation of those treaties *plus* the Charter now. All of them were supposed to be destroyed."

"And Gorman has one." Maria studied it. "It's dead, right? Everything else in here is dead."

There were other combat droids in there, but they were all obviously disabled. Most didn't even have their weapons. The ODD did.

"My files say it had an internal fission pile," Leonhart said distractedly, the Marine clearly looking up more data even as she approached the war machine. "I'm not picking up any rads, so it has to be decommissioned, but what the hell was he *think*—"

A searchlight on the dreadnought's torso lit up, highlighting the Marine in the middle of the collection as she froze.

"You are not Mehrab Gorman," a calmly feminine voice said. "Identify."

"Who are you?" Leonhart snapped.

"You are not Mehrab Gorman," the machine repeated. "Identify."

"Marine Forward Combat Intelligence," the Marine replied. "Stand down!"

An upper arm rotated, leveling what looked like a gatling gun of terrifying scale on Leonhart.

"Where is Mehrab Gorman?" it demanded.

"We don't know," Maria told it, stepping up next to Leonhart and studying the machine. It didn't have a power core and it didn't look like the weapon was loaded...but she raised a defensive shield between them and the war machine anyway. "All evidence suggests he is dead."

The robot was silent.

"No signal from command protocols," it confirmed. "House power and systems are dead. Evidence aligns. Who killed Mehrab Gorman?"

"One of his clients," Maria said, wondering just what chain of commands they were working their way down. Were they headed toward a command sequence where the terrifying machine helped them...or one where it turned out to still have enough power to activate the laser on its other arm.

Or even just its hands. The thing could rip them to pieces, armor or no armor.

"Security protocol 9B activated," the robot chanted. "Report situation to Sherwood Interstellar Patrol. They are advised to investigate Paladin 6B aboard *Robin Hood*."

It paused.

"Power levels insufficient for further action."

With that, the searchlight died, and Maria breathed a long sigh of relief.

"Did...did Gorman program a fucking *war robot* to help people find his killers if he got murdered?" she asked aloud.

Everyone else in the room was too shocked to try and answer.

CHAPTER 38

THE ADVANTAGE of working with professionals who knew who you actually were was the ability to set up secure and covert channels. *Red Falcon*'s communications systems now had a link into a hard cable, hidden amidst the resupply hookups, that tied her into the Patrol's encrypted communications network.

Even within that network, David's communications with Grace McLaughlin were double-encrypted and running through the equivalent of a virtual private network inside the larger network. No one should have been able to even tell that they were talking, let alone what they were saying.

Which was good, because the Sherwood Captain looked perturbed as she relayed Gorman's message.

"He had an ODD?" she asked. "How the *hell* did he sneak an ODD onto *my bloody planet*?"

"That's a question for SSS," David pointed out. "I'm more concerned about his message. Does 'Paladin 6B aboard *Robin Hood*' mean something to you?"

McLaughlin shook her head.

"Sorry, still wrapping my head around the illegal warbot. No sign of Gorman himself otherwise, though?"

"Nothing," David confirmed. "Maria says there was a dog-sitter there who was killed along with the dogs. We passed on what we knew to the SSS; hopefully, they'll coordinate with local authorities to make sure the family is informed."

"And, of course, no cameras, no records, nothing. Just some asshole who walked onto my planet, murdered one of my assets, and then killed an innocent for good measure." McLaughlin looked pissed. "Aren't you supposed to stop this happening, Mr. MISS?"

"That would actually be the guys with one less 'S' in the initials," he replied. The similarity between the initialisms for the Martian Investigative Service, the interstellar cops, and the Martian Interstellar Security Service, the interstellar *spies*, was not unintentional.

"But yes, the Protectorate should have stopped this. Now we're trying to make sure it doesn't happen again. And you didn't answer my question," he pointed out.

"Right, sorry." She sighed. "Technically, I think this falls under self-incrimination. You're not familiar with the name? I thought you served in the Navy?"

"Not in the last couple of decades."

"Ah. Would 'Redshield 6B' make more sense to you?" McLaughlin asked.

"Redshield was a brand-new program when I left," he admitted. "All-in-one ECM computer and emitter slaved to central control. Made for a more redundant and efficient unit for the price of some volume."

"Redshield was replaced by Redeye, which was replaced, about two years ago, by Paladin," she told him.

"Then 6B would be one of your sternward dorsal emitter units," David concluded. "How would he have left something there?"

"Militias are supposed to only have access to the Redeye system," McLaughlin admitted. "Paladin is supposed to be restricted to the Martian Navy. They were one of the major systems that Gorman sourced for us. Hence *self-incrimination*."

She sighed.

"*Robin Hood* is my command. I'll have my engineering team rip Paladin 6B apart and see what our gunrunner friend left us."

McLaughlin called David back six hours later, managing to look tired, angry, and excited at the same time. She was back aboard *Robin Hood* now, pacing her office in front of a small pile of electronic parts on her desk.

"So, Gorman decided that the Patrol made a *great* place to hide his insurance policy," she told him, gesturing to the parts behind her. "An additional memory module and encrypted channel receiver were installed inside Paladin 6B. Nothing significant, just enough to receive irregular burst transmissions from him as he worked with us."

"He was keeping backup records?" David asked.

"More blackmail files," she said. "Enough to nail a few people to the wall if they fell into the hands of the right authorities, though there's also enough in here to void *our* deal with him and send him back to jail.

"He never stopped working for others as well, smuggling guns and weapons for everyone who'd pay," McLaughlin concluded. "We'll transmit you a copy of the data, but there are a number of people in here we'll be having sharp words with ourselves."

"Send one over to MIS as well," David told her. "We're following a specific line, and they'll be better equipped to handle those kinds of investigations."

"Fair enough," McLaughlin said with a sharp nod. "I'm glad we were able to help in the end, Captain Rice. We don't know which of Gorman's contacts turned on him...but his insurance policy turns them *all* in."

David smiled coldly.

"Shucks. Looks like MIS is going to roll up the local arms-smuggling rings, doesn't it?"

She laughed.

"So it does. I hope you find what you need in here, Captain. The Patrol is always ready to help the Protectorate's people."

By morning, Binici and LaMonte had gone through the entire database in Gorman's insurance policy. David's XO didn't look like she'd *slept,*

but she certainly looked victorious as she gestured the rest of the senior officers to sit.

"Gorman is probably dead," she admitted, "but he gave us the next link in the chain. We managed to cross-reference his files with the information MISS forwarded us on the Freedom Wing's deliveries, and identified three shipments.

"All were arranged and paid for by the same person."

"A Legatan?" David asked hopefully.

"No." She shook her head. "The name doesn't show up in any of our records. Coral Drummond. Gorman's contacts with them were via dead drops and couriers, but..."

"You're about to wow us, aren't you?" he asked. "Lay it out, XO."

"Gorman didn't know where Drummond was. They were someone he worked with remotely, coordinating cargo ships to meet in distant locations. Few of the cargos the two of them worked together on ever came anywhere near Sherwood.

"For that to work, the couriers and dead drops had to be delivered to Sherwood and back to Drummond for their contracts and plans and payments to take place. One delivery wouldn't be enough for us to identify where Drummond was. Even three might be a problem."

LaMonte grinned.

"Gorman was *very* thorough in his insurance policy. He gave us the dates and times of *forty-six* interactions with Drummond, and we matched them all up with ships in Sherwood at the time. Three systems stood out: Antonius, Míngliàng, and Java. There were ships from or headed to each of those systems during each of Gorman's contacts with Drummond.

"A little bit of research tells me that Antonius is an uninhabited system that Sherwood shares exploitation of with Míngliàng. There's almost *always* ships headed to one or both of those systems.

"Java, on the other hand, is an UnArcana MidWorld some twenty light-years away," LaMonte concluded. "Not a world that gets involved in politics, not a world that has a lot of shipping. They export some raw minerals and some rare gemstones and have developed some pretty impressive crystal-manufacturing industries but are still a bit of a one-trick pony as their economy goes."

"On the other hand, they're the main source of laser optics for Legatus, last I checked," Leonhart noted.

"For Mars, too," Soprano said. "The Navy sources them from a few places, but Java is probably in the top three."

"So," David concluded. "An UnArcana world with no major shipping to or from Sherwood has always had a ship here when our last known link in the chain made contact with this Drummond. I think that's the best we're going to get."

He shook his head.

"And now it's time to see how good the Patrol and our local broker are," he continued with a smile. "Because someone is going to have to come up with a reason for *us* to go to said quiet UnArcana World."

CHAPTER 39

THE ANSWER turned out to be laser optics. The Sherwood Interstellar Patrol was about to begin production of a new set of six warships, each of which had twenty main battle lasers and a hundred RFLAM turrets, for a total of over a thousand individual lasers per ship.

Each of those lasers required carefully calibrated crystals for their optics and spares. The Patrol had been putting together an order to acquire them from several potential sources, and Java had been leading the way anyway.

"So, we send you with the order on contract to pick up the optics," Grace McLaughlin told him after they'd gone over the details. "We pay you to act as a courier one way—obviously, you see what secondary cargo you can pick up here, but there probably isn't much—and to haul several million tons of carefully calibrated crystals back."

"That will definitely work," David agreed. "Will they have that much on hand?"

"We don't know," she admitted. "Probably not, but the worst-case scenario is that we look excessively eager to get those optics—which we are. So, it doesn't cost us anything we wouldn't be spending in the first place, and we do a favor for the Protectorate."

David snorted.

Few System Militia units were going to turn down the chance to do that. Especially not local militia fleets where MISS now knew they had ECM systems that were supposed to be restricted to the Navy.

"And in exchange, MISS and MIS turn a blind eye to that collection of Paladins, huh?" he asked.

"That would be optimal for us, yes," she agreed cheerfully. "Favor for a favor, Captain."

"I can make that happen," David admitted. It wasn't really worth the Protectorate's time to push back on a System Militia going through black-market channels to get more advanced systems than they were supposed to.

"I appreciate the help nonetheless," he told her. "You've been incredibly helpful—and we've been damn lucky."

"And Gorman was damn paranoid," McLaughlin said. "For the record, we have opened up his vault and called in specialists from Sol to deal with the ODD. I know the power plant *appears* to be missing, but I don't care to take risks with a robot that can go rogue and level cities."

"Cities are probably safe," David replied. "It was designed to wreck military bases, I believe."

She shivered.

"I'll be happier once it's dismantled and not on my home planet," she said. "We'll have the contract for your review soon enough—twenty-four hours or so. You'll see it in the morning.

"Good luck, Captain Rice."

"Thank you. My experience suggests we'll need it!"

"So, this Drummond isn't in our files at all?" David asked as his people gathered for a war planning session.

"Nothing," LaMonte told him. "I checked and triple-checked. They may be in our files under a different name, Gods alone know how many names some of these people work under, but there's no Coral Drummond.

"We do have files on Java, primarily because it's a major supplier to the Navy," she noted. "One of the only major suppliers that's an UnArcana World, actually. I guess they figure Mages' money spends the same."

"What do the files tell us about arms smuggling or the underworld in general?" David asked.

"Arms smuggling isn't apparently a thing in Java," LaMonte admitted. "Now, optics being produced without record and smuggled out to be turned into illegal lasers of all stripes? Gods, yes. But actual guns, spacecraft, weapons? Nothing."

"So, who is doing the smuggling? Are we looking at another Blue Star fragment?" Soprano said.

"*La Cosa Nostra*," the XO replied. "Most of those laser crystals and gems that get smuggled off-world? They go to Condor." She grimaced. "The people putting together the files aren't sure, but they think Java may be one of the systems the made men prowl for vulnerable people looking for a new start."

David grimaced.

"Trafficking victims," he said.

"Exactly."

For all of humanity's advances, slavery of one type or another simply refused to die. It was mostly about sex and power now, though he'd heard about facilities using carefully supervised slaves for technical manufacturing.

The most common victim of slavers in the Protectorate, unfortunately, was someone in their late teens who wanted to be somewhere— *anywhere*—other than home. They were promised work and new lives, boarded planes and shuttles...and found themselves in very different situations.

Sometimes, they were lucky and ended up passing through the hands of someone like David Rice who broke them free. But for every shipment of fifty thousand cryo-frozen kids that was intercepted, three made it through.

Working for MISS had given him far too much detailed information on the fate of the millions trapped in slavery and human trafficking in the Protectorate. The Navy, the Hands, and the rest of the Protectorate infrastructure burned it out wherever they could find it, but it continued to exist.

That was why the blind eye the MISS office had turned in Condor had infuriated him so badly.

"So, we're heading to a *la Cosa Nostra* source world," he said. "We can expect made men and associate thugs, and it's not unlikely that Drummond is *la Cosa Nostra* themself."

"What do we do?" Leonhart asked.

"We go in, we get the data we can from the local Martian offices, and we hack the fuck out of local law enforcement," he replied. "We pull together all the data we can on Drummond, and then we try to find the bugger.

"If they're working for Legatus, I'm prepared to authorize—what did you call it, Rhianna? 'Involuntary asset extraction'?" He shook his head. "I want the links, people. Let's trace this all the way home. All the way back to the sons of bitches who want to tear apart human civilization."

CHAPTER 40

KELLY LAY sprawled across the bed in the quarters she shared with Mike and Xi, luxuriating in both the expensive mattress and the general afterglow while listening to Mike putter around in the kitchen, making supper.

It was the first evening the three lovers were scheduled to have off together since *Red Falcon* had left Sherwood, and Kelly was enjoying being lazy. Mike was determined to make some wonderful dinner for the three of them, and Xi had picked the movie they were planning on watching together, but Kelly's plan was to spend the evening avoiding decisions.

She made enough decisions on a day-to-day basis that just letting her lovers make some for her was the most relaxing thing she could do.

"Hey, Kelly, can you come out and taste test this for me?" Mike called from the kitchen.

With a sigh, she dragged herself from the bed's warm embrace and threw on a flimsy robe. She doubted it left anything to Mike's imagination, and the only reason that was a problem was that he *was* cooking.

His momentarily stunned happy look as she came into the kitchen made it entirely worth it. For all that he'd been living with the two women for over a year now, Mike Kelzin had a way of looking at Kelly that warmed her down to her toes. That look, that sheer awe at how lucky he was, was enough for her to keep him.

Plus, he had other talents too, and she purred at him as she plastered herself against his side to taste the spoonful of soup he offered her.

"Mmm. That's good. What *is* it?"

"Something the Sherwood folks call Scotch broth," he told her. "Lamb, barley, carrots. It's our starter, with a ground mutton pie for the entrée."

She chuckled.

"You spoil us."

"Hey, to be clear, I *bought* the pie before we left," Mike confessed. "I can make soup from scratch. Pie is *way* beyond me."

"You should have asked me," Xi interjected as the door slid shut behind the petite Asian Mage. "Meat pie is out of my experience, but I make a *mean* fruit tart."

Xi slipped through into the kitchen, still in her shipsuit, and stole kisses from both of the pair hovering over the soup. She had her own moment of pleased appreciation of Kelly's robe, sending another warm tingle down to the XO's toes.

"The soup is ready, if you two want to grab a seat," Mike told them. "I hate to even suggest it, love, but that robe probably won't protect you from hot soup!"

Kelly laughed.

"All right, all right, I'll change," she promised. That took only a minute, and she rejoined the other pair as Mike served up the soup. Xi had changed as well, both of them ending up in matching light shorts and tops perfect for the ship's carefully moderate temperature.

The Mage seemed nervous but focused on the soup. Kelly didn't see any reason to prod her lover and did the same.

After the savory broth had vanished, Xi waved a hand at Mike before he could do more than gather up the bowls.

"Hang on a moment, love," she instructed. Obediently, the fair-haired pilot retook his seat and turned a patiently adoring gaze on her.

Kelly chuckled. The way Mike looked at Xi *also* warmed her heart. She was very, very lucky.

Xi, on the other hand, looked nervous, and Kelly's humor began to fade as her heart started to race. What was up?

"Sorry, just steeling my nerve," Xi told them. "I spent a lot of time thinking about us over the last few weeks, as we get tied up again and again in explosions and gun smuggling, and I decided there was something I needed to do.

"Then, well, details took a while," she said with a smile.

Xi removed a mid-sized flat box of Sherwood oak from her pocket and laid it on the table. Kelly stared at it, wondering just what the Mage had found for several seconds, until Xi popped it open with a gesture and a whiff of magic.

The inside of the box was lined with velvet and contained three matching rings of braided metal in three different sizes, and Kelly inhaled sharply.

"Three metals," Xi said quietly. "Copper for Kelly, our engineer and electronics whiz. Titanium for Mike, our pilot and fighter. Gold for me, the Mage and the girliest." She grinned as she said that.

"They all match. They should fit. So...um." She swallowed, the grin shifting.

"Will you marry me?" she asked. "And, well, each other? All of us? Together?"

Kelly took the mid-sized ring from the box with gently shocked hands, turning it in the light with awe and then closing one eye to look through the ring at Xi Wu. The other woman was looking at her with wide, nervous eyes, and Kelly winked through the ring.

"Yes," she told her lover. "Yes, I'll marry you. And him." She gestured to Mike, who was still sitting and staring at the rings in shock. "Assuming he finds his voice sometime this week."

Mike coughed and shook himself.

"I am...so unbelievably lucky," he breathed. "Yes, I'll marry you both. Gods, how crazy do you think I *am*?"

They ambushed Captain Rice the next morning, as he was settling into his command chair with a cup of coffee and reviewing the inevitably blank bridge screens while they were in the middle of deep space.

"XO," he greeted Kelly, then looked at her companions. "First Pilot. Mage." He shook his head. "Or perhaps, from the looks of it, I should be greeting Kelly, Mike, and Xi?"

Kelly was relatively sure none of them could wipe the silly grins off their faces. That, combined with the three of them showing up as one and the fact that ship captains retained their ancient legal rights, almost certainly told him what they wanted.

"Xi decided to finally jump the gun on Mike and me," she told her boss, then held out her hand with the ring. "She asked us to marry her and we both said yes. We were wondering—well, hoping, really—that you'd be willing to perform the ceremony for us."

He smiled at the three of them.

"With absolute pleasure," he agreed instantly. "Should we be planning on going somewhere soon to get your families involved?"

That had been part of the discussions that had kept the three of them up late the last night.

"We talked about it," Mike said when Kelly didn't reply immediately. "My family is ship's crew, so we're pretty scattered. Xi's is back on Mars."

"And, frankly, won't be happy with my marrying non-Mages, so wouldn't show up anyway," Xi Wu added.

"This ship, this crew—they're our family," Kelly told the Captain. "They're all we'd want."

"We have a couple of days left before we reach Java," he said after a moment's thought. "If you want to jump on it right now, we can arrange things for tomorrow? Give yourselves time to find clothes and the rest of the ship time to put together food and some decorations."

He grinned.

"You won't get much in terms of gifts with the lack of warning, but I figure that's not the point."

"Not in the slightest," Kelly agreed. "I just want to make sure this pair doesn't get away!"

CHAPTER 41

PULLING TOGETHER a wedding on a day or so of notice would have been a nightmare anywhere in the galaxy. On a starship, though, there was only so much that *could* be done, so it came together with surprising ease.

Maria took over the organizing as soon as Rice told her what was happening. The Captain had other things on his mind, and it certainly wasn't right for LaMonte to organize her own wedding!

She'd found food, got James Kellers to fabricate linens—it wasn't the *usual* use of the fabric shop aboard the ship, but it was certainly possible—and pulled Nguyen and Barrow into a three-person magical sweep of the mess hall.

They'd also made sure that Xi had the last thirty-six hours of the trip off. They couldn't give the trio much in terms of a honeymoon, but if the other three Mages were willing to take on Navy six-hour rotations instead of merchant-shipping eight-hour rotations, they could give her a day off.

It all came together with speed and grace, and Maria found herself in the front row of the mess hall, watching David Rice wait for three of the ship's senior officers to walk up the aisle of hastily magically cleaned floor.

There was no one to give any of them away, and the questions of precedence were always dangerous ones, but Maria had had a moment of inspiration.

As the sound system started to play an old classical piano tune, James Kellers walked into the room with Rhianna Leonhart at his side. Both of them were in full merchant navy uniform, a formal outfit rarely seen outside of exactly this kind of affair.

The pair made it three-quarters of the way down the aisle, then turned to face each other and stepped back to clear a space between them. A second pair, this time fully dress-uniformed Marines, followed them. Another set of Marines took up the last marker, the three pairs forming a formal guard.

The piano music picked up the pace, and the three spouses-to-be walked into the room arm in arm. Any appearance of the two young women locking arms behind Mike Kelzin to drag him to the altar was entirely coincidental, Maria hoped—and the shocked silly grin on his face suggested she was right.

They'd pulled together another merchant officer's white dress uniform for Kelzin, and both girls had gone for floor-length red gowns that offset the stark white of their husband-to-be perfectly.

The guards fell in behind them, two by two, as they stepped up to the front, where Rice waited for them with a massive grin on his face.

"Welcome, everyone," he told the gathered crew. "This is a rare honor and privilege for me, though I doubt it's a day any of us are surprised to see. Today, we are gathered to see these three bound together in a formal recognition of their marriage and union, before the assembled eyes of us, their shipmates, and the laws and many varied Gods of humankind..."

Maria wasn't the type to cry at weddings, but the whole affair certainly left her feeling more than a little bit sappy. Everyone had spent the last couple of years watching the three young officers dance through the complicated dance of their relationship, and it was good to see them decide to stick together.

Their current career didn't leave them with much certainty for the future, but at least those three now had each other. Even if, after several abortive attempts to dance with all three of them, they'd started switching up partners for each dance as the music continued to play.

"All right, James," Maria told the chief engineer. "Let's get out there."

He didn't even grumble as she dragged him out onto the dance floor. They hadn't been concerned about keeping their new relationship secret, but they'd exercised a degree of discretion. Dancing at the younger officers' wedding with her head on his shoulder was significantly less discreet than that.

No one seemed particularly surprised, though.

"Guess we were less quiet than we thought," he murmured in her ear as he held her close.

"It's a small ship and we're all basically family," she replied. "No one knows what happens next. Every system we walk into could be a trap. Everyone needs to find what happiness they can."

She wasn't entirely sure what the content rumble of agreement from James could be described as, but it sent warm shivers down her spine.

"Wedding's not giving you ideas, is it?" he asked.

"Ha!" she laughed. "Bit soon for ideas for you and me, isn't it? We can let things be for a while yet."

"Oh, good," he told her. "I can make a lot of things with what I've got on this ship, but a ring worthy of you isn't one of them."

That sent another warm shiver down her spine, and she leaned a bit more heavily against him.

"Be careful, you big lug," she said warmly into his ear. "I might start to actually *like* you if you keep being that much of a sap."

"Oh, I'll get over it as soon as you need me to fix a starship or something minor like that," he replied brightly. "I'm sure we'll make things work."

It was lightly said and yet carried such conviction and confidence that it actually struck Maria dumb for a moment. He was right. Neither of them was young. They'd been through their batterings and bruisings, and they had a better idea of what they were getting into.

They really could make this work. He was joking about a ring...but it was in that moment that Maria knew that if he decided to offer her one, she would take it.

And probably turn it into a wedding about as fast as LaMonte had. Like the XO with her pilot and Mage, she wanted to make sure this one didn't get away.

Whatever happened next.

CHAPTER 42

KELLY LAMONTE couldn't help humming happily to herself as *Red Falcon* flashed into the Java System. There wasn't *that* much difference between being with Mike and Xi and being married to them...and yet it was enough to keep a solid core of warmth in her stomach and chest.

Warmth summed up the Java System, too. Java itself was on the hot end of stars likely to produce habitable worlds, a large F-class sun that had burned most of its interior worlds to cinders. Espresso was the fifth planet out and still uncomfortably warm for humans.

It was comfortably warm to its energetic ocean and jungle life, however. Much of the value in the system came from the pharmaceuticals harvested from those jungles. The rest came from the gems and crystals formed in the superheated magma fields of those four half-molten lava balls orbiting inside Espresso.

There was more sublight traffic than in most MidWorlds, but Kelly picked out only a handful of other starships. Two more freighters and one obnoxiously golden private jump-yacht.

"Well, welcome to UnArcana space," Rice said from behind her. "If this is the last time I bring a crew of Mages into one of these systems, I'll breathe a sigh of relief when we leave."

"You'll do that anyway," Kelly replied as she continued to collate data. "Jeeves, can you double-check contact sixty-two?"

The tactical officer whistled quietly.

"Well. I know we've met the Golden Bears and their 'monitors,' but as a student of naval history, let me tell you: *that* thing is much closer to what the original ships were intended for!"

The contact in question was big. She was big for a starship, let alone a sublight ship, and her orbit and energy signatures suggested she didn't have a simulacrum chamber. Massing four million tons and six hundred meters long, it looked like she packed a *lot* of lasers and missile launchers.

"There's another one," Kelly pointed out. "And another?"

"I make it four in total," Jeeves replied. "Transponder are identifying them as 'guardships' of the Java Self-Defense Force." He paused. "Looking closer, it looks like they've got spinning hab rings on their 'bottom' sides. I'm guessing their combat tactics include some strict instructions on 'this end towards enemy?'"

"It is an UnArcana World," Rice said. "They don't have Mages, so no gravity runes. Ring stations and spinning hab sections for everyone."

"We're also seeing a bunch of gunships," Kelly reported. "Either Legatan-built or Legatan-designed. Who do they think is going to attack here?"

"Mars," her Captain said grimly. "I.e., us."

"Wonderful." She shook her head. "Sending in the request for a docking port and approach vector."

They didn't have much of a cargo, but they had some and they had the contract for the pickup for the Patrol. They'd see what they could find out.

"I've got incoming on the screens," Jeeves announced. "Clever buggers—pair of gunships on ballistic orbits that just lit off their drives."

"Hail them," Rice ordered. "We're not here to start a fight."

"Channel open," Kelly replied.

"JSDF ships, this is Captain Rice aboard *Red Falcon*," he introduced himself. "We are here under contract from the government of the Sherwood System and are carrying approximately one point two megatons of cargo for delivery.

"I'm attaching our IDs and paperwork. Please advise if you need anything else from us."

They waited.

"They're coming in fast," Jeeves reported. "Still burning our way at four gees. Without gravity runes, they can only do that for so long." He swallowed. "We're being pinged with targeting radar, sir."

"Charge the guns," Rice ordered. "No targeting radar of our own. We're being tested, I think."

Seconds turned to minutes as the gunships flung themselves across the void of space. Kelly studied them. *Falcon* could obliterate them in a heartbeat, but not before they fired. Two dozen antimatter missiles was a threat they could overcome...probably.

On the other hand, everyone would prefer that *Red Falcon* not get into a fight with the local authorities. She just didn't know what the buggers were playing at.

"They're breaking off," Jeeves suddenly reported. "Timing is about right for them to have relayed your transmission in-system and got a response from authorities in Espresso orbit."

Rice sighed.

"We *did* message the orbitals, right?"

"Of course," Kelly confirmed. "They just decided to poke us first." She checked her systems as a light flashed.

"Incoming message."

"Play it," Rice ordered in a tired voice.

"*Red Falcon*, this is Commander Deuce of the JSDF," the audio-only transmission informed him. "We have scanned your ship and you are carrying a lot of guns for a merchant vessel. Per our authority under the charter, we are ordering you to adjust your course for zero velocity relative to Espresso at a minimum of two million kilometers distance.

"Contact with the planet and cargo delivery may be carried out by cargo shuttles and small craft, but you are not to approach the planet closer than two million kilometers. Disobedience to these orders will be met with lethal force."

The transmission ended, and Kelly looked back at her boss with concern.

"Adjust our course to comply, XO," he ordered. "And send your new husband my apologies. His people are about to have one of the shittiest weeks of their careers."

Two million kilometers was a blatantly arbitrary line in space. Kelly knew it. Her boss knew it. Even the locals had to know it. From the orbit they settled into, two million kilometers "behind" Espresso, they could obliterate every space station in orbit with their lasers or even fire missiles into the atmosphere.

Of course, neither the targeting computers nor the missiles themselves would cooperate with being fired into atmosphere. The failsafes could be disabled, but Kelly suspected there were layers of mechanical and software failsafes she didn't even know about to prevent their space-to-space missiles being used as bombardment weapons.

"Even at five gravities, which is going to *suck* aboard the shuttles, let's be clear, that's a three-and-a-half-hour flight each way," Kelzin noted on the channel. "Do we take the cargo straight in or do we go over and clarify delivery and everything first?"

"Pull one of the personnel shuttles," Kelly told her husband. "Run... the Captain and Leonhart over first. Let Rice sort out the details while we load our cargo into the heavy shuttles."

"That's a good plan," Rice said as he stepped up behind her. "I'll take a few of the security troops as well; we'll stay on the station while everything gets sorted out. Unless they have the crystals to hand already, we're going to be sitting like this for a few days at least."

"Hopefully, they'll eventually let us dock," she replied. "Seven hours' flight there and back is going to put a huge crimp in anything we're trying to do."

"That's life," he admitted. "We'll make sure to take Binici across. I don't suppose you can crack open the system security files from here?"

"With a fourteen-second round trip for radio coms?" she replied. "Not a chance, unfortunately. Binici is almost as good a cracker as I am, though, and she's probably better at that kind of tactical work."

"We need to find Drummond." Rice shook his head. "Things could get very, *very* messy if we need to kidnap them, though. Think we can manage to sneak someone off-station without them being noticed for three and a half hours?"

"Wouldn't need to," Kelly replied. "Get everybody aboard and run for the limit at five gees. *Red Falcon* can pull double that with the gravity runes; we can match course and velocity and scoop the shuttle up.

"They don't have anything with gravity runes, so *Falcon* can outrun anything they've got."

"We can't outfight them, though," Rice reminded her.

"So, try and be sneaky," she told her boss. "If I'm keeping the lights on, then that part's on you. Take Soprano?"

"If they're being this grouchy, we're not taking a Mage in," he said sadly. "No, it's me and the Marines. We'll get it done. Mike—you're with me. Make sure your people are ready to handle the cargo, but I want my best pilot at the stick of what's probably going to end up as my getaway vehicle."

"If we get that indiscreet in an UnArcana system, we have problems," Kelly warned him.

"I know. But given a choice between saving our cover and getting proof of Legatan treason, well...there are other ships and other spies," he told her. "And the Mage-King *needs* that proof.

"So, we do what we have to."

CHAPTER 43

IT WAS a long, *long* flight. Normally, five-gravity stints were reserved for the stages of takeoff and landing closest to the ground, where they were needed. The shuttles in *Red Falcon*'s boat bays were perfectly capable of five gravities of acceleration for extended periods.

It was the passengers who were less enthused with the idea.

By the time Kelzin tucked the personnel shuttle into a docking port on the largest of Espresso's orbital ring stations, David was even more grateful than normal for his cybernetic lung. Leonhart and the Marines looked battered, even with their experience with hard flights. His lung had allowed him to adapt to the acceleration better than he'd expected.

"Get her fueled up and ready to go on the drop of a credit," David told the pilot, who groaned. "I don't expect to be leaving for a few days, but I want to be ready to leave if something comes up."

"We'll be here," Kelzin replied. "I'm staying on the bird, just in case." He grimaced. "Feeling a touch paranoid, but it seems called for. I'm having flashbacks to Chrysanthemum."

David shared the grimace. Chrysanthemum was another UnArcana World, one where a bounty hunter had convinced the local government to try and arrest David and his people. It hadn't ended well...for anyone.

He was reasonably sure, for example, that Chrysanthemum had been the first time Mike Kelzin had killed anyone. That it hadn't been the last was *also* David's fault, which he couldn't help but feel guilty about.

"Leonhart, can we spare some people to stay with him?" David asked the security chief.

She was already gesturing to her people.

"We'll want to grab a hotel nearby, then we can cycle a shift," Leonhart told them. "The shuttle can sleep four, but my people are only so good at guarding while asleep."

"It's an orbital. There should be *something* near the shuttle docks," the Captain replied. "Especially if they make a habit of making people leave their ships behind.

"I think they may reserve that for ships that can threaten their home guard," Kelzin said. "I'll hold down the fort, but I won't object to a couple of burly souls with guns."

"Don't worry; Jiang will be a *great* babysitter," Leonhart promised.

With rooms booked for their stay, David rented a meeting room in the dockside hotel and got to work. They didn't have a lot of cargo, but making sure it all was delivered was still his job.

Of course, while *he* was doing that with two security troops guarding the room, Binici and Leonhart were out wandering the streets, "shopping." They'd scope out the nearest law enforcement stations and see what they figured was most accessible for their data theft.

He, meanwhile, did some quick research on brokers and called up the one that the Patrol had given him to contact. They'd apparently had some exchanges with him to get quotes for their crystal shipment, though David's arrival would be the first evidence the broker had of his success.

"Good afternoon, Captain Rice," the broker, an older gentleman named Vishal Antuma, greeted him the instant the channel connected. David hadn't even introduced himself yet, and his surprised expression must have been obvious.

"There are only so many ships that come through Java, Captain," Antuma told him. "The vast majority of my day-to-day work is organizing in-system shipments, but I keep an eye out for jump-ships. Since yours is the only new one and my in-system contacts don't call me from hotels, it could only have been you."

David snorted.

"And you are apparently correct," he allowed. "Would you care to guess what I need?"

"You have a set of individual cargos, only a small portion of your capacity," Antuma said. "Therefore, you don't need much help disposing of them, though it would make your life easier. But, nonetheless, you are looking for someone to source material as much as you are looking for someone to help conclude your cargo deliveries."

"All right, now you're making me nervous," David told the other man with a grin. "I do need your help sorting out our deliveries, mostly because my ship was forbidden from getting close enough to directly off-load onto the stations. The JSDF is apparently concerned about armed merchant ships."

"If you build an organization to protect against a threat that is imaginary, it is inevitable that organization will imagine new threats at every turn," the local said frankly. "The JSDF sees enemies in every mirror to justify their existence. If you return, they will be better the second time. For now..." He sighed. "That is a delay I doubt any of your contracts were expecting. If you give me the list, I'll pour some oil on troubled waters and arrange deliveries."

"That would be helpful," David confirmed. "We have the shuttlecraft to deliver our cargo, but it will take a couple of days with the flight time included. What will this cost me?"

"There will be a fee for arranging the docking, but otherwise, consider it included in our real business," Antuma told him. "What kind of cargo brings a twenty-million-ton megafreighter to Java, Captain Rice? Especially nearly empty. Someone paid dearly to get you here, and I wonder what they expected you to bring back."

"You don't know?" David asked.

Antuma chuckled.

"I guess much, but in this case, I hesitate to leap to conclusions," he noted. "So, why don't you let me know who sent you, Captain Rice, and what you and they hope for me to acquire?"

"Sherwood," David told him. "I understand that you submitted a proposal to the Patrol for the round of laser optics they'd require for their new frigates. They tasked me to act as both courier for the contract and pickup driver for the cargo."

"Ah," the broker allowed. "Yes, I was looking forward to hearing back from Sherwood." He smiled thinly. "You do understand, Captain, that one does not merely snap fingers and produce millions of tons of specifically attuned and aligned crystal optics? To acquire Sherwood's order, depending on its details, could take weeks to months."

"I wasn't going to turn down their money," David told Antuma. "So, here I am. They're paying me to stick around for two weeks, and I'm *hoping* to actually be able to dock before that's up, but I have no idea how long it will take you to put together that cargo."

The broker chuckled.

"Send me their order, Captain Rice," he instructed. "And your list of cargos. I will see what can be made to happen."

By the time David had finished sorting out things with Antuma and spoken to the recipients of several of the larger cargos himself, Leonhart and Binici had returned. He gestured the two of them wordlessly to a seat as he checked the area jammer he was running on the table.

"The advantage of using a space like this for confidential business is that no one really begrudges you jamming potential bugs," he noted. "So, we can have *our* discussions in security without worrying about them.

"What are we looking at?"

"There are three precinct stations in the docks district, but I don't think any of them are going to have what we want," Leonhart admitted. "They're beat-cop rest points, not real police stations. From what Binici says, we need a detective's office."

"We need an investigation department," the younger Marine hacker confirmed. "Their organized-crime team would be best, but any of their senior teams would have a channel to their central databanks I could use."

"And those offices aren't the beat stations in the docks," David agreed. "Would they even be up here? I'm not sure we can swing getting you down to the surface, with how the JSDF is treating us so far."

"There is *always* an organized-crime office on the orbitals," Binici replied, which made sense to him.

How much trouble had *he* got into with crime bosses and mobs on space stations? Of course the cops were up here.

"But those offices are kept quiet and usually separate from the local police," she continued. "Our best shot is the System Security headquarters."

David sighed. He'd been hoping that wouldn't be the answer. Unless there was a military presence on the station, there was rarely anywhere more heavily secured than the headquarters of the system security force.

"All right," he agreed. "Let's track it down and then go make some trouble for the greater good."

It wasn't quite as bad as David had been afraid of. Often, the local headquarters of system security aboard a space station was a heavily locked-down section of the station, buried away from the main thoroughfares behind multiple levels of security.

Java's Systemwide Investigative Bureau was less paranoid than that, apparently. The JSIB office wasn't open to the public, but its entrance was right next to the main-station police office, which was. Of course, getting into the Bureau office to hack their systems was an entirely different problem.

He and his team stood in the busy "street" in front of the two offices, people streaming from an administrative section of the station through to the restaurant area on the other side of the police offices.

"How close do you need to get?" he murmured to Binici.

"Inside," she told him. "Past the front desk security, for at least a couple of minutes. I can do everything remotely after that, but I *need* to get a tap into their internal network."

Short of flashing their MISS IDs, in which case he'd simply ask the JSIB detectives for what he needed, David didn't see any way they were going to get the hacker past the security on the office.

"Any ideas?" he asked. "I don't suppose we have a local office we can lean on?"

"There's an official one on the surface. Nothing up here that anyone admits to," Leonhart told him.

Their conversation was silent for a moment as a couple wandered close enough to them to potentially overhear.

"What about going under or above and trying to cut in from there?" David suggested.

"Won't work if they're remotely competent," Leonhart objected. "I'll admit, I was counting on a publicly accessible neighbor, at least."

"We might be looking at asking officially," David warned them. "And that's risky for us here."

"Binici, do you need to plant the tap?" the security chief asked. "Or is it something anyone can do?"

"It needs to be within about a meter of a main network hub," the junior Marine replied. "I can pick those out by sight...not many can."

"What are you thinking, Chief?" David asked.

"JSIB works with the Martian Marine Corps sometimes," she replied. "There's a Marine company providing security for the Mage Testers hidden away up here—and I'm more comfortable pulling weight for a favor with the Marines than with the locals."

He nodded. Every child in the Protectorate, by law, had to be tested for the Mage Gift. Testers weren't popular on the UnArcana Worlds, since they were the only Mages that those worlds were required to permanently host. So, they hid away on space stations and had RMMC security.

And those Marines probably had connections with the local cops.

"Make contact," he told Leonhart. "Let's see what we can do."

CHAPTER 44

DAVID SHOULD have known better than to expect anything less than the highest and best efforts from Marines. *Especially* bored Marines on guard duty in moderately hostile territory.

Binici and Leonhart disappeared into the Protectorate embassy and left him to his negotiations and cargo offloading for a full day. He was starting to worry when the two women reappeared, looking like the proverbial canary-swallowing cats.

"We got our tap," Binici told him once the jammer was back online.

"Do I want to know how?" he asked drily. His authority and sanction with MISS covered a long list of sins, and yet he still wasn't sure he wanted to know what the Marines had done.

"Probably not," Leonhart admitted. "Nobody's dead, I promise."

That was a very low bar to clear, even for intelligence operations.

"What do we have?" he asked.

"I don't know yet," Binici replied distractedly, pulling a rolling case out from the stack of supplies sitting in one corner of the meeting room David was using. The case turned out to contain a miniature version of a shipside desktop console, vastly more powerful than the wrist-comps everyone wore.

"What we have so far is *access*," she continued. "And it's fragile access, too. We need to be careful what questions we ask—the larger the data pull we're looking for, the more likely we are to get cut off. On the other hand, no matter how small the data pulls are, we're probably only going to get so many access requests before we get cut off."

She shrugged as she unfolded the console and booted it up.

"It's a balancing act," Binici noted as she pulled out a pair of virtual gloves and linked into the system. "And it boils down to the very simple query: just what *are* we looking for?"

David considered. It was an important question.

"*La Cosa Nostra's* gunrunning operation," he told her. "Coral Drummond won't be working here under that name; I want to know who they think is running guns for the mob. Once we have that, I want to know who they think is brokering long-distance deals for them, too. Names. Locations.

"We don't just need to know what they think is going on. We need to know *where* and *who* is doing it."

"They may not know that," Binici warned.

"They almost certainly can't *prove* it, but I guarantee you they have a damned good idea."

At some point, the hotel was probably going to come complain to David about the fact that he was jamming the recording devices that were "only there for your safety, sir." The fact that the jammer he was using was almost ubiquitous among businesspeople meant that it would take them a while to raise any stink about its use in the private meeting room, though.

That gave them time. Time for Binici to set up her hacking console and use the tap that the Marines had left in the Java System Investigative Bureau's offices to break into their main database. David didn't pretend to entirely follow what people like Binici and LaMonte did to computers, so he took the Marine's word that it would take a while.

Once she was in, she saw that the wall next to Binici had begun to resemble the red-string-connected diagrams of bad cop shows. She projected a second screen onto that wall and was moving data around on it with her virtual gloves as she pulled bits and pieces out of the local database.

Then, suddenly, in mid–data pull, she stopped and sighed.

"There we go," she told him. "JSIB detected the hack. They let us keep the last query going long enough for them to locate the tap." The Marine shook her head. "They were clever about it, too. It looks like they managed to short-circuit the self-destruct and take the tap intact."

David turned a level gaze on his subordinate, who seemed far too blasé about that fact.

"Isn't that bad?" he asked pointedly. "What if they trace the gear back to its source?"

"I intentionally used a tap with a glitchy self-destruct," Binici said with a brilliantly white-toothed grin. "It was built in Legatus, and if they track it back, it belonged to a 'commercial market analysis' firm known for dabbling in corporate espionage. It doesn't lead anywhere useful."

Binici, it seemed, was another of the snarky and ridiculously competent women MISS seemed to keep finding for him.

"What did we find?" he asked. "Should we get Leonhart back in here?"

"Probably," the Marine confirmed. "Gives me a minute to marshal my thoughts and data, in any case."

With a chuckle, David left her to it and stepped out of the meeting room into the hotel corridor. The two security troopers outside tentatively returned his smile as he nodded to them.

"Ping Leonhart for me," he instructed. "It looks like it's briefing time."

"All right, Binici, what have we got?" David asked after Leonhart had shut the door behind them and regained their privacy.

"Less than I was hoping," the hacker admitted. "The good news is that it looks like *la Cosa Nostra* presence here is smaller than we expected. MISS files really don't say much beyond that there is one, but the locals keep a closer eye on it."

"How small are we talking?" Leonhart said.

"Not small enough to make this *easy*," Binici replied. "But we're looking at maybe fifty made men and ten times that in associates. That limits our potential targets, especially since we're relatively sure our 'Coral' is from *la Cosa Nostra*."

"I thought they were running multiple operations here," David said. There'd been the notes on kidnapping as well.

"They *were*," she confirmed. "Until about a year ago, when JSIB finally managed to pull together enough evidence to come down like a ton of bricks on the human-trafficking side. Looks like about half or more of the made men in the system got caught up in the sweep, and one of the major dons was 'killed resisting arrest.'"

"My heart bleeds for them," he said drily. "So, they're left with gunrunning and crystal theft?"

"Most of what's left seems to be focused on acquiring and smuggling gems and laser optics," she confirmed. "JSIB seems to have that on a far lower tier. What I find interesting, though, is that according to their files, *la Cosa Nostra* doesn't *have* a gunrunning operation here in Java. The system actually has quite strict gun control and doesn't manufacture heavy weaponry at all. All shipments of weapons, aircraft, armored vehicles, et cetera are strictly controlled and only under government control."

"So, the weapons didn't come from here. That doesn't help us much," David noted.

"No. All I ended up with in the end was a list of the thirty or so made men on the station," Binici warned him. "Which is, thankfully, more helpful than you might think."

"Well, I'm considering authorizing Leonhart to carry out a mass kidnapping and interrogation that can't help but draw attention, so 'more helpful' is good," he told her. If JSIB's files couldn't get them to Coral Drummond, this whole endeavor was starting to look more and more like a waste.

"It turns out that the local dock records are significantly easier to acquire than JSIB's files," Binici told them, using her data gloves to toss a list of ship names and dates on the screen. "As an UnArcana world,

Espresso obviously doesn't have an RTA, so if our 'Coral' is organizing interstellar shipments, they're sending messages by ship.

"We know when the courier drops and messages were heading this way from Sherwood for Gorman's orders, so I cross-referenced those arrivals with ships that left within seventy-two hours."

A number of names turned green on the screen and others disappeared.

"I then looked for people and companies that showed up more than others and cross-referenced those with the list of made men."

Some of the names stayed green. The rest disappeared, and new data appeared around them: contracting companies, ownership, more names...

"Three different companies," Binici concluded. "All majority-owned by the same shell...a shell that shows up in JSIB files as being managed by one Gianna Antoni. JSIB has her flagged as a made woman of *la Cosa Nostra*, but they have no idea what she does for them."

"Brokerage of interstellar smuggling would be hard for the locals to identify, wouldn't it?" David murmured. "Well done, Binici. Well done.

"Do we have a location?"

"I know what trading firm she works out of," the junior Marine said. "Looks like it's a combined office and apartment, so I'd guess she lives there, too.

"Well, then." David turned to Leonhart. "You brought those stealth suits, I assume?"

"We did," she confirmed. "I even had one sized for you. Shall we go hunting?"

"You read my mind, Rhianna."

CHAPTER 45

THE STEALTH SUITS were sneaky but not unobtrusive. They helped the wearer blend into walls with a layer of active chameleon camouflage and absorbed radar and so forth, but the armored full-body suit didn't blend into crowds well.

Fortunately, they packed easily into duffle bags, and David and his Marines made it through the station to the mixed-use area their target worked and lived in without incident. Changing into the suits in the quieter section of the station, they rapidly transformed into anonymous blurs against the walls.

Even the blurs faded as the Marines moved out. They had a far better idea of how to move in the gear than David did, though even his un-trained movements were nearly invisible against an unchanging back-ground.

Micropulse transmitters and a well-designed heads-up display kept David aware of where the other members of his team were, despite their cloaks of invisibility. Rhianna Leonhart led the way, the Forward Combat Intelligence Marine the best qualified with the gear and for the mission.

"Security is active," she noted softly. "Binici?"

The electronics expert moved up, at least according to David's HUD, and a panel on the wall moved away. As the background began to move, the Marine became more visible, but there was no one around to see right then.

"Active, expensive, and crap," Binici concluded after a few seconds. "Someone definitely paid a lot of money for this. Shame the installer didn't bother to set up a system for the software updates."

There was a *click* and the side door to the office unlocked.

"Let's go," Leonhart ordered.

Two Marines stepped through the door, then David and Leonhart, then the last two Marines. David didn't miss that he was being surrounded and guarded, but that was also part of his people's job.

The area they'd entered was a cubicle farm, a style of office that had never quite gone away over the last half a millennium or so. It was quiet and empty, and David scanned the room for exits.

"Do we have a floor plan?" he asked.

"Oh, we have one," Leonhart confirmed. "It says this is a corridor with side offices. Someone renovated and didn't tell the station staff."

"Where do we go, then?" he asked.

"There should be an apartment attached to the office over there," Binici told them, using her suit to drop a waypoint on everyone's HUDs. "It's late enough that no one should be working, but Antoni does live here; she might be home."

"Let's move," Leonhart ordered, suiting actions to words and leading the way toward the waypoint.

The office portion of the unit had been opened up significantly from the layout they had, with all but one set of individual offices cleared away to create a large open-plan office. The entrance to the apartment shown on the floor plan was completely missing.

There was, in fact, no sign that the apartment the station schematics showed being attached to the office was there at all. Just smooth walls where the doors should be.

"Scan for entrances?" David suggested. "They're either still there and hidden or moved around to somewhere else."

"I'm guessing hidden," Leonhart agreed. "Binici?"

The electronics tech gestured for one of the other Marines to join her as she pulled a roll of small sensors on a tape strip from inside her gear. Unrolling it along the wall, they taped it at chest height to cover the entire section where the apartment should have connected, and then Binici hooked it into her suit's computer.

"All right, what secrets are you hiding?" she murmured. "And...there you are."

She highlighted the door on the team's HUDs. It wasn't where it had originally been. When they'd concealed the access to the apartment, they'd moved the door about two meters over to make it harder to find.

Its main security had clearly been its invisibility. It took Binici under ten seconds to pop the concealed entrance open. It swung wide, revealing a complete lack of light on the other side.

"Conroy, Victor," Leonhart said quietly, using names in lieu of orders.

They went through the door in the same order as they'd entered the apartment, with David and Leonhart in the middle as they swept the apartment entrance.

All of the lights were out and a chill ran down David's spine. There'd been no sign of trouble in the front office, but this was starting to seem eerily familiar.

"Lights?" he asked softly.

"IR lights, people," Leonhart ordered in response. The suit's optics were able to pick up the invisible light, and the room "lit up" in gray and white.

The entryway looked like it was tastefully decorated with a small quantity of artwork that the infrared lights weren't enough to show clearly. There was no one there, and the Marines moved forward.

"Apartment seems to mostly match the station blueprints," Binici said quietly. "Office should be over there."

A new waypoint appeared and David set off for it immediately. The IR lights showed him what he needed to see as he stepped around the furniture and reached the indicated door. There was no sign of life anywhere in the apartment, and he was grimly certain what he'd see when he pushed the office door open.

If he hadn't been wearing the suit mask, he'd probably have smelt the problem before he stepped in. The woman in the office had done more than the other victims David had found. She was sprawled backward across her desk with a heavy pistol still in her hand.

With a sigh, he stepped up to the desk to examine the body, popping the face mask and pulling out a regular flashlight to take a closer look.

"I wondered," a voice suddenly echoed in the darkness. "The timing for *Red Falcon*'s arrival was suspicious, with everything that had been going on, but command was *so sure* that you were a usable contact, that your war with the Legacy had been personal."

David's flashlight turned toward the speaker and he found himself looking up at a heavyset stranger who smiled down at him.

"But if you're here, Captain Rice, then we were wrong and *you* are MISS," he continued as he produced a pistol from nowhere.

Bullets smashed into the door behind David as he dove for cover behind the desk. Taking the mask off earlier wouldn't have helped. It would have taken a few hours for the smell of death to permeate the space.

And Gianna Antoni's killer was still there.

Cover only helped so much, and fire seared David's scalp as a bullet tore through his hair, shredding the hood of the stealth suit. More gunfire answered as his own people responded by charging in and producing guns.

He wasn't sure where the second hostile came from, the stranger wearing a stealth suit of similar design to theirs. The hostile appeared from the wall and produced a gun of their own, opening fire into David's Marines.

Leonhart was in the lead, and she went down hard as bullets slammed into her. Her own fire went wide and David forced himself to lean over the cover with his own gun.

He shot at the newcomer, who seemed to have dismissed the Martian captain as out of the fight. David's bullets hit home and the stranger recoiled—before returning fire, seemingly uninjured.

David's focus had been on the wrong target. As his fire hammered the second hostile into the wall, the original agent vaulted the desk to land next to him. An impossibly fast foot swept his legs out from under him, and an open palm flashed toward his face.

Falling on the ground freed David to use his cybernetic leg to its full potential. His hip had been reinforced to allow him to use its strength, but there was only so much he could do while standing without preparation.

From the ground, he kicked his attacker. The stranger's gun went flying and his arm *should* have broken.

It didn't. Both of the men they were facing were Augments. That wasn't really a surprise, but it was a problem. David fired the last rounds in his gun at the attacker, who simply ignored the six-millimeter rounds as they hit his chest and charged again.

Just the velocity of the rounds should have had some effect, but the Augment powered through, grabbing David's hand and pinning him as he smashed his open palm successfully into David's face this time.

David had enough time to be confused before the electrodes embedded in the Augment's palm sparked out and jammed into his face. Electricity blasted through him and pain wracked his body.

He went black for what was probably only a few seconds, but the gunfire had stopped when he was aware of things again. He started to move—and the Augment's taser-augmented palm struck him again.

It was a lower charge this time, just enough to send his muscles into useless spasms as manacles clipped around his wrists.

"You and I are going to have a long chat, Captain Rice," his captor said softly. "And, well, I suspect it's going to be a problem for your ship when the local police arrive to find that your people stormed a trade brokerage and murdered a respected citizen."

David couldn't speak through the electricity still rippling across his body. He was yanked to his feet by the inhumanly strong Augment and stared around the room. Stealth-suited bodies were hard to make out, but he could see where Leonhart had fallen.

He was dragged out past the body of another Marine and saw the other Augment already beginning to set the stage for the deception they'd use his people's bodies to solidify. He didn't know what tools the presumably LMID agents had, but he suspected that the scene would definitely match the scenario his captor had described.

His people would be blamed for Antoni's death...and the locals were already being hostile.

CHAPTER 46

DAVID'S CAPTOR WAS a professional. There was a fine art to hustling a manacled prisoner through public spaces without drawing unwanted attention, and the Augment had apparently mastered it. David had expected to be able to raise some havoc and try to escape, even if the wooziness from his head injury might have impeded him.

Instead, he rapidly found himself locked into the side room of a small rental apartment. Both the side room and the living room he'd been dragged through had that spartan look only places with no long-term residents could have.

He took a moment to be glad they'd ditched their wrist-comps at a public locker when they changed into the stealth suits. The combat gear had specialized computers—ones that intentionally lacked any real long-term storage.

His wrist-comp wouldn't be easily cracked, but its contents would reveal more of MISS's secrets than he was comfortable with. Most of those secrets were in his own brain, but software didn't die if you interrogated it too hard.

Given that his untreated head wound was still oozing blood when he touched it, David wasn't sure how well he'd survive under the interrogation his captor clearly planned. He wasn't utterly convinced that he would die before he revealed anything, but he certainly wasn't intending to give up.

He wasn't sure how long he'd been left manacled and sitting on the bed before the stranger came back in, a smirk on his face as he tossed David a warm, wet cloth that he barely managed to catch.

"Clean yourself up; you can't answer my questions if you're concussed," he barked.

David looked down at the cloth, sighed, and dropped it on the floor. He stared back at his captor wordlessly and the Augment chuckled.

"Your heart rate is elevated but your blood pressure is fine," he told David. "You don't show any signs of a concussion and the blood loss is slowing. You'll live to answer my questions—and you'll find the next few days much less unpleasant if you do."

Of *course* the Augment had enough sensors for him to be able to assess David's health at a glance.

"I know who you are," the cyborg continued. "Captain David Rice, captain of *Red Falcon*, once of *Blue Jay*. You've made both friends and enemies over the years, and, well, some of those friends are going to be very sad to learn which side you've chosen."

He shook his head.

"But my intel says someone has been chasing the loose ends I've been tying up. Should have realized the time lag in the reports I was getting meant they were catching up—but then, lo and behold, you show up. So disappointing, Captain."

David said nothing. The more the stranger decided to monologue, the more likely he was to learn something useful. Sadly, that seemed to be the end of it as the Augment studied him.

"So, I now know you're MISS," he concluded. "At least some of your people were either MISS or Marines...I'm guessing Marines; they may have died easy, but they were good, for all that. Who else is on your big, shiny ship, Captain?"

There was no point in answering his questions. The best-case scenario, David suspected, was that answering the questions would get David hauled back to Legatus and stuck in a relatively comfortable cell.

The more-likely scenario was that he got shot in the head.

His silence earned him a thin smile.

"Let me show you something," the stranger said, pulling up his own wrist-comp and activating the holographic screen.

It was running a news report, with footage of the office they'd been in barely an hour before. Dark green tarps were draped over the four bodies visible in the room as an announcer reeled off what they "knew."

"Police have identified the attackers as crew members of a ship visiting the Java System and believe that the Captain, one David Rice, was involved in the murder and escaped," she reeled off. An image of David appeared on the screen.

"David Rice is to be considered armed and dangerous, and all sightings should be reported to the JSIB tip line immediately."

The image turned off.

"Java has the death penalty for murder, you know," the Augment told him. "My friend set up some nice damning evidence. Open and shut, especially if your shuttle or ship crew resist. I figure they'll shoot you well before your friends back home can try and intervene.

"So, you see, David, your only way off this station is to cooperate with me."

David's captor, who still hadn't given him a name or even the remotest identifier, left after that. Presumably his intent was to let David stew, but the MISS agent instead started trying to assess the situation for ways out.

The manacles were the biggest problem. The door looked sturdy enough, but he'd learned once before that he could break open just about anything with his cybernetic leg and a little bit of time. Of course, he'd need to somehow be sure that his captor wasn't there.

Time was another problem. If an "advise the police on sight" video was already being distributed of him, then Kelzin was almost certainly already being harassed and the odds were that threats were being sent to *Red Falcon* as well.

He was still wearing the stealth suit, which was an asset. Even if he was missing the hood and face mask now, the suit itself was armored and had the chameleon weave and computers. He could use that to get pretty far across the station without being spotted.

But it all boiled down to finding some way out of the steel manacles the Augment had slapped on him. He wasn't a Mage and his cybernetics were limited. If he tried to use his leg to snap the manacles—theoretically possible, barely—he'd also probably break his wrists.

He managed to get to his feet, pacing out the tiny room he was in and studying its features. No windows—not in a space station! One door. One bed. One dresser that quickly proved to be empty when David awkwardly checked the drawers.

He was poking at the dresser when the door opened again and he heard his captor chuckle.

"What, did you think I'd leave a gun or the key in there?" the Augment asked. "No such luck, Captain Rice.

"Luckily for you, however, my orders have been updated," he continued. "My superiors want you alive, without damage from interrogation. So, we don't get to go to phase two and we *do* go find ourselves a starship."

"Where are we going?" David asked, as calmly as he could.

His captor laughed.

"Please, David. I'm not going to tell you that. Once you're there and we can be sure you won't escape, maybe someone will tell you enough to try and recruit you, but for now, well." He grinned.

"For now, it seems we both get to keep our secr—"

There was no warning. One moment, the Augment was grinning at David and telling him everything had gone wrong.

The next, his *head* exploded as gunfire echoed in the enclosed space and a burst of at least five bullets tore through the Augment's skull. From the fact that the bullets hit the wall across the room and *kept going*, someone was using armor-piercing rounds.

Someone it still took David a moment to even *see*, until Binici pushed her face mask up and entered the room he was locked in.

"You okay, Skipper?" she demanded, the MACCAW-9 in her hands more visible than the rest of her.

"A little bloodied up, but yes. Leonhart?" he asked.

"Rhianna didn't make it. Neither did Victor or Conroy," she admitted. "Kavanagh made it back to the shuttle and picked up heavier guns while I tracked our new friend."

Even with the stealth suit, he saw her shiver.

"We had to leave Rhianna and the others behind," she whispered. "And...did you see the news?"

"He showed it to me. We need to go." David hated leaving people behind, but while some of his people were Marines, they were *all* spies. And like it or not, the Java System was now hostile territory.

"Kelzin is warming up the shuttle and Kavanagh is running overwatch outside," Binici confirmed, her voice brimming with forced confidence, then paused.

"The locals are almost certainly going to try and stop us," she admitted.

"Then I hope you packed stunguns," David told her. "Because fucked-up as this situation is, I do *not* want to add dead cops to the disaster."

"They're with Kavanagh," she said instantly. "I wasn't going to count on them working on the Augment."

CHAPTER 47

WITH ANOTHER AUGMENT on the loose and the cops looking for them, speed was now the key more than anything else. There was another Marine with Kavanagh, wearing a long civilian coat over regular body armor. They'd only had so many stealth suits, and they'd brought even fewer aboard the shuttle.

"Stungun," David ordered grimly. The Marines handed him the weapon wordlessly and he checked its readouts. It had a full magazine of the computerized SmartDarts that were all but guaranteed not to kill a human.

"What's our people's status?" he asked.

"Everyone who wasn't at the shuttle should have made it there by now," Binici told him. "Local security hadn't moved on it when we left, but given what's hitting the news, they're almost certainly heading in that direction.

"Then we better get there first," David said. "The best resolution to this is that we get the hell off this space station without even arguing with local police. Under no circumstances do we get ourselves in a firefight."

He shook his head.

"This may be an UnArcana World and the local cops may be taking their marching orders from LMID, but they're still cops and they're still going after people they think are murderers. We are *not* stacking their bodies in the streets, understood?"

"Hence stunguns," Binici confirmed. "I've mapped out what I *think* should be a back route back to the shuttle, but it adds almost ten minutes. Or we can head straight there...we'll be there in fifteen, but we're almost guaranteed to run into cops."

David stared blankly at the nonlethal weapon in his hand. Unless the local cops were completely incompetent, they'd already been moving on Kelzin's shuttle when the request to report his movements showed up on the news.

Fifteen minutes or twenty-five, the cops were going to be there when they got there. Ten minutes, though, might make the difference between the cops posturing and attempting to negotiate...and riot squads storming the shuttle bay in gear that would ignore SmartDarts.

"We can't spare the time," he said slowly. "We're going to need to go straight there and take the risk. We don't stop, we don't answer questions, we try not to draw attention to ourselves...but we do *not* stop."

"Boss, you're a floating head," Binici pointed out. "Attention is going to be hard not to draw."

"Did you retrieve our gear?" David asked. "I'll grab a coat like his."

Covering the body armor with a coat would at least allow him to turn off the chameleon without looking like he was wandering down the corridors in battle armor.

More than a coat would take too long. They needed to get off this space station.

David rapidly concluded that he shouldn't have even bothered with the coat. The four of them were moving forward at the brisk, determined pace every soldier in the galaxy learned sooner or later, and the crowds started scattering out of their way.

Something in their demeanor or their faces warned the people around them that trouble wasn't going to be tolerated.

That, or most of them had seen the news broadcast, he supposed. An "armed and dangerous" official status did tend to open up a pathway, after all.

Either way, someone called the cops. Security aboard a space station didn't have much more access to vehicles or other mobility enhancers than anyone else, so there were no sirens and minimal shouting.

David and his people had just rounded a corner at the edge of the shuttle docking area when they found their way barred by a dozen determined-looking men and women in light body armor. They were carrying the same stunguns he and his people were wielding and had set up a barricade across the corridor.

It was good work for short notice, he reflected as he paused in the crosshairs of a dozen weapons.

"Captain David Rice, you are under arrest," the lead officer declared. "Throw down your weapons and submi—"

For a horrible moment, David thought that Binici had completely ignored his instructions not to kill the police and thrown a grenade. Then the flashbang went off and he wasn't thinking much of anything. Without the shielding and ear protection built into the suit hood he was no longer wearing, he was even less protected from the light and noise than the cops were.

By the time he blinked the spots away from his eyes and regained some awareness, he realized he'd been flung against one wall by the Marines—and the cops were collapsed backward from their barricade.

"Some warning?" he said bitterly to Kavanagh as the Marine helped him up.

"There wasn't time," Binici replied as she rejoined them. "They'll live. SmartDarts and Nix solutions."

"Nix" solutions were neutralization compounds, carefully calibrated knockout gases. Less capable of adjusting their efficacy to their target than SmartDarts, they still shouldn't have seriously injured anyone healthy enough to be a serving police officer.

David hoped.

"Come on," Binici continued. "The shuttle is still five minutes away, and if there were cops to blockade us..."

"There's cops at the shuttle," David concluded, shaking aside his distaste for injuring cops just doing their jobs. "We'll deal with that when we get there."

"Then let's get there."

Stunguns fired their rounds at a far lower velocity than regular firearms—otherwise, the SmartDarts would be just as lethal as regular bullets—which resulted in a very distinct soft coughing sound when they were fired.

That sound was echoing repeatedly down the corridors as David and his Marines rushed toward the shuttle. With everything going to hell, he considered stopping to assess the situation for only about five seconds... and then decided to fall back on the age-old standby of Navy officers and soldiers all over.

He charged to the sound of the guns.

His three Marines followed him and they burst out into the open bay connecting to the shuttle airlocks. While the Java police were lacking the heavy armor of their true riot squads, they had brought up riot shields and mobile barricades that were allowing them to cross the bay despite the hail of fire Mike Kelzin and the Marines with him were laying down.

It was as genteel as a firefight could get, with both sides sticking to the nonlethal SmartDarts, trying to avoid fatalities despite entirely contradictory objectives. David knew Kelzin wouldn't hold back for long, especially as the cops' shields prevented the SmartDarts striking home.

Unfortunately for the locals, David and his people were on the wrong side of the mobile barricades, and they opened fire into the rear of the police assault. Stunguns weren't particularly rapid-firing weapons—but they were fast enough.

Half of the cops went down in convulsing heaps before they even realized someone was behind them, and the rest found themselves caught between a rock and a hard place. Kavanagh took a SmartDart and went down, David took a partial shock from a near-miss...and then it was over.

David levered the still-twitching Marine up onto his shoulder and hauled him across the bay as the defending Marines spread out to cover them. SmartDarts didn't take someone out for very long, seconds to minutes at most.

If any of the cops regained enough control to be able to act before David made it onto the shuttle, they decided discretion was the better part of valor.

"Kelzin, please tell me we're moving," David barked as the Marines closed the airlock behind him. "The locals are going to be *very* grumpy."

"Yeah, they locked us down an hour ago," the pilot replied. "Refused to unhook the umbilicals; even turned out to have big, heavy clamps to hold us in place."

David winced.

"Please tell me you dealt with those," he said.

"Not *yet*," Kelzin told him, grinning as his Captain entered the cockpit. The pilot was running some kind of code sequence on his panels, adjusting it every few seconds, and then...David felt the clamps give way.

"On the other hand, Kelly left us some prepared code for just this kind of incident," the pilot continued. "Clamps are free and the umbilicals are their problem. Sit down and strap in."

David barely made it into the chair before Kelzin hit the throttle, opening up the shuttle's main engines and tearing them away from the station. It was a violation of about sixty safety protocols and most likely welded several of the shuttle airlocks shut behind them, even as Kelzin was clearly making sure he didn't hit any surface with enough heat to burn through and, say, crisp a bunch of stunned cops.

Somehow, David didn't care much about infrastructure damage.

"Take us out after *Falcon*," he ordered. "No turnover; just burn for the outer system. Kelly will be able to catch us."

The shuttle could pull five, maybe six gravities without injuring its passengers. *Red Falcon*, with gravity runes throughout the ship, could pull ten. She could catch them and jump out.

The problem was going to be if someone intercepted them along the way.

"Yeah, they are *not* happy with us," Kelzin quipped, and David shook his head.

Four corvettes were now vectoring toward their shuttle. None of them were particularly close, but they all had the angle advantage on the course they had to take to meet with *Red Falcon.*

"Anyone launching missiles yet?" the Captain asked. Five gravities of acceleration were enough to push him back into his seat hard, but the controls were designed for that.

The shuttle had a few toys it wasn't supposed to, but he doubted they were enough to stand off the salvos of four warships, even sublight pocket warships.

"Not yet," the pilot replied. "On the other hand, they're not hailing us, either. I suppose they might not be guessing that *Falcon* has ten gravities of acceleration, in which case we would need to slow down to match velocities with her."

"Or they're just planning on saving ammunition and shooting us with lasers," David said grimly. "How confident are you feeling, Mike?"

"I don't plan on dying in this shithole system less than a week after I got married," Kelzin replied. "Those corvettes might be able to kill us, but they sure as hell aren't going to *catch* me."

"I don't suppose we have a plan for that?"

Kelzin chuckled.

"I'm going with 'don't get hit,'" he admitted. "I'm open to other suggestions. You've got the dirty-tricks panel, boss."

David nodded and started running through the tools available to him. They were about what he figured. They didn't have anything resembling an active defense, just jammers and decoys that were pointless to launch until their pursuers had fired.

"Any word from *Falcon?*" he asked.

"Kelly confirmed our course," the pilot replied. "Still a bit before they need to start accelerating. It's going to be a near-run thing, boss."

"It always is," David said, engaging presets throughout the system. He'd probably have a lot of warning of incoming fire, but it didn't hurt to be ready to deal with whatever they threw at him.

"And there it goes," Kelzin suddenly said, flagging icons on the screen. "One missile from the closest corvette. Fusion drive, four thousand gravities. That's a hell of a missile, but it's got to be a warning shot."

"Let's not take that as a given," the Captain replied. "This is just a civilian shuttle, so far as they know. That missile out-accelerates us almost a thousand to one."

"You can deal with it, right?"

"Probably," David confirmed as the shuttle's passive sensors sucked in all of the data they could. "I'm not even sure how many launchers those corvettes have, though. We can deal with one, maybe two, missiles at a time.

"I'm guessing four corvettes can fire off more than...what the *fuck*?!"

Red Falcon was moving. Her antimatter engines were flaring to life at full power, flinging her toward the shuttle at a combined fifteen gravities—and new icons sparked on the screens as her launchers engaged. Antimatter-drive signatures flared brightly enough to be seen across the star system.

"I make it six missiles," Kelzin replied, his voice distracted. "They're not sticking to a single salvo...what are they *doing*?"

"Warning shots," David concluded as the vectors traced themselves in on the screen. "They're warning the locals off."

Two of the missiles came screaming in at the weapon the locals had fired at Kelzin's shuttles. The Phoenix antimatter-drive missiles weren't designed to be counter-missiles, but they were almost three times as maneuverable. The fusion-drive missile died easily.

The other four missiles flashed toward the local corvettes. The tiny ships hadn't been prepared to be fired upon, and their ECM and jammers were offline. Their RFLAM turrets came on late and slow, though David judged that they'd *probably* intercept the incoming fire.

They didn't get a chance. At a hundred thousand kilometers of distance, each antimatter missile detonated.

Red Falcon's message was very clear: *do not fuck with our Captain.*

For a few seconds, David wasn't sure if the locals were going to call his people's bluff. It would have been a bad idea—*Falcon* could definitely obliterate the corvettes and probably take on the guardships as well.

Then the corvettes broke off. They could still range on the shuttle, but accelerating away from it was the clearest sign they could give.

Message sent, received, and acknowledged—and all without a single radio transmission.

CHAPTER 48

KELLY KNEW perfectly well that she wasn't the best pilot aboard the ship—that honor went to her husband—but she was one of the handful qualified to fly *Red Falcon* herself. She'd barely scraped a pity pass on the hands-on flying component of her merchant officer's exam the other year.

That had been then and this was now. She'd been aware of her shortcomings and worked on them, hard, with David Rice's expert guidance.

Now she maneuvered the multi-megaton freighter through space with the skill of a seasoned veteran, matching velocity and acceleration with the fleeing shuttle perfectly and then nudging them together. Scooping up the shuttle without either vehicle even reducing acceleration was a complicated task, a carefully calculated swoop.

She nailed it perfectly and Kelzin handled his part just as well. The shuttle bay swooped around the fleeing shuttle, and Kelzin shut off his engines in almost the exact same moment.

Kelly exhaled a long sigh as she double- and triple-checked the cameras from the shuttle bay. The small craft seemed to hang for a moment, and then her husband gently brought it in to touch down on the floor.

"Mage Soprano, we've got the Captain," she said into the link to the simulacrum chamber. "I make it thirty-five minutes to space clear enough to jump. You?"

"Much the same," the Ship's Mage agreed. "Any problems on the screens?"

Kelly studied the sensor feeds. Four of the Java Self Defense Force's big guardships were now moving toward *Red Falcon*, but their courses were quite specific.

"We're being herded out-system, but the locals don't want to actually get in a fight," she concluded aloud. "They're in our missile range, but I don't think we even need warning shots. Everyone knows what's going on."

She was half-expecting a lecture from Captain Rice when he made it to the bridge. Using antimatter missiles to intimidate the locals risked their cover. On the other hand, the locals might well have thought it was a bluff—it was possible, after all, that they'd acquired a small number of the missiles and were using them to test the locals' nerve.

If the JSDF had thought she was bluffing, they had decided not to call it...which was good for everyone. Kelly LaMonte didn't *want* to kill the local security people.

But if it was a choice between that and getting her own people out, well, she'd deal with her conscience later.

"Jumping now," Soprano's voice echoed onto the bridge, moments before David Rice strode in.

"Captain!" Kelly rose from the command chair and saluted crisply.

"XO. Well done," he told her as he stepped up to the chair, looking more than a little shell-shocked. "We're in deeper shit than we hoped, but we pulled everyone out we could."

Kelly winced.

"'We could,' boss?" she echoed back to him. "We didn't get much of an update."

"Rhianna, Victor, and Conroy didn't make it," he said quietly. "The Augments that captured me killed them. Our lead is dead, and...we have no proof the Augments were LMID. Everything we've done was a waste of our goddamn time."

He turned to the channel to the simulacrum chamber.

"Maria, keep us jumping," he ordered. "How many random jumps can you put us through?"

"Four," Soprano replied with a dry "we all know you know the answer to this question" tone. "Then we're stuck wherever we end up for six hours."

"Do it," Rice ordered before turning back to Kelly. "Our cover is fucked," he said bluntly. "We may not be able to prove that the two Augments who were cleaning up the loose ends from Ardennes were LMID, but they definitely were reporting home. Whoever is behind this, whether it's Legatus or some third party we don't know about with almost-identical resources, knows who we are now."

"What do we do?" Kelly asked.

"We get clear of Java."

Another twisting distortion rippled through the ship as the Mages teleported her again.

"Then we go home," the Captain finished after coughing against the discomfort. "Back to Tau Ceti to report in. In terms of digging into this shadow war, *Red Falcon* just became less of an asset, so we'll see what our superiors think."

Kelly nodded.

"Is Mike okay?" she asked softly as another jump rippled through the ship.

"Everyone's fine," Rice told her. "Everyone who lived, anyway." He shook his head. "I don't think the locals will be able to ID our lost Marines. On the one hand, that means they won't try and hold the Augments' murders against Mars...but on the other, it means we won't be able to get their bodies home to their families."

"Damn." Kelly wasn't even sure how to respond. The Captain seemed to blame himself, but it felt like the enemy had been one step ahead of them the whole way. "Isn't...Gods, isn't the fact that Augments kidnapped you and seem to be working for whoever's arming the rebels proof enough?"

"Legatus isn't the only system that produces military cyborgs," Rice replied. "And even if we could prove that our attackers were Legatan cyborgs, that doesn't mean they were an officially sanctioned operation or were even Legatan citizens anymore."

He shook his head.

"It goes on the mountain of circumstantial evidence that leads MISS to be deathly certain who our enemy is…but it isn't the ironclad proof we were after. We needed Antoni for that, if she was the one working directly with them."

"So… what do we do?" she asked again, as the fourth and final—for now—jump tore through the ship, leaving *Red Falcon* most of four light-years away from Java in a completely random set of directions.

"Like I said, we go home," Rice repeated. "Our work here is done. Others may be able to follow up on what we discovered, but I think this whole mess is a dead end."

He smiled sadly.

"As for right now, I have the con. You go check in on your spouses. Mike may be fine, but he did get shot at and that isn't really part of his job description."

"He's fine," Kelly told her boss. "But *I* need to see that."

"I know," Rice agreed. "Go!"

Kelly considered where everyone would be and headed toward the simulacrum chamber instead of their quarters. She guessed correctly and found both of her spouses about halfway back to the hab ring. Xi Wu was, as usual, utterly shattered from the jump.

Mike was supporting their wife, but he didn't look entirely present himself. Kelly shook her head and then wrapped both of them in her arms.

"You both look like shit," she told them conversationally. "Neither of you is going anywhere except to bed."

"Is that a promise or a demand?" Mike asked, but his voice was tired. "Sorry, long day."

"Yeah, we generally prefer that nobody gets shot at," Xi said, her own voice drained. "Especially not our husband."

Kelly took over from Mike, draping Xi's arm around her own shoulder as she pulled both of them forward.

"We'll be fine," she told them. "We're a long way from anywhere now, and no one can follow us through four random jumps. We didn't even file a course before we ran, so they have *no* idea where we are."

"If there's one thing I've learned on this ship, it's never say never," Mike said grimly. "Bed sounds good. I might even be tired enough to keep my hands to myself."

"Drat," Xi complained, but there was no energy behind it. Kelly was by far the most awake of the trio.

"You two," she told them with a smile. "I love you both. Don't overdo it."

She'd watched enough shuttles blowing apart with friends aboard and Mages burning out their brains overusing magic for one lifetime. Friends were bad enough.

"We'll be safe," she reiterated. "And if someone pulls off a miracle and finds us anyway, I'll *keep* us safe. No matter what."

"I know," Xi murmured, leaning her head against Kelly's shoulder. "We both know, my love. I'll make sure he sleeps."

They reached the door to their quarters, and Mike took their Mage lover from Kelly again.

"And I'll make sure *she* sleeps while you keep watch over us," he told her. "We're going to be okay, all of us. It's just been a long day."

Her spouses entered their quarters, and Kelly was about to follow when her wrist-comp buzzed gently. She glanced after her lovers, then softly closed the door before checking the device.

Somehow, she was *damn* sure her day had just grown a lot longer.

CHAPTER 49

"ONCE, JUST *once*, I'd like to face an enemy who plays by the *normal fucking rules.*"

Jeeves's curse echoed across *Red Falcon's* bridge as the jump flare began to dissipate into the background of deep space.

"We're playing with the best," David replied grimly, regretfully sending an alert to Kelly's wrist-comp. "So, they don't necessarily play by the rules of the rest. What have we got?"

"Breaking it down," Jeeves replied, the tactical officer running through his data. He sighed. "Well, at least I know *how* they found us."

"Beyond a Tracker?" David asked.

An icon on the screen flashed red.

"That's the same ostentatious gold jump-yacht that was at Java. Tracker has to be aboard her, and she had friends waiting in hiding to come meet her. Big friends." Jeeves sighed. "*Familiar* friends."

The new icons began to propagate and David recognized the iconography.

"Monitors," he concluded. "The Bears?"

"And apparently, the good Admiral Commanding replaced his losses from the last time he tangled with us," Jeeves agreed. "I've got *eight* of his seven-hundred-thousand-ton pocket destroyers closing on us. Fucked if I know where they came from, though."

"They were waiting in hiding somewhere near the system, and they sent a second ship to retrieve them," David concluded. "They have to have at least four Mages per ship, maybe even five to make it here with sequential jumps."

Their Tracker was also better than the ones who'd been chasing him before. Those had needed an hour or two to resolve a jump direction. This one had apparently pulled it off fast enough that he'd barely been out here for an hour.

Which meant he was five hours from being able to jump.

"How far are they from missile range?" he asked quietly.

"We're both effectively at rest," Jeeves replied. "Our new Phoenix VIIIs outrange the VIs they had last time, but the less flight time we give them to dial in our birds, the better."

The monitors' engines lit up at twelve gravities, lunging toward *Red Falcon* in a maneuver that left no doubt to their intentions.

"They're just over thirty-five light-seconds away and burning at full accel," the gunner concluded. "Forty-five minutes to range if they're carrying Phoenix VIs."

"Enough time for everyone to be ready for what's coming," David agreed. "Not enough time for us to jump away. This is going to suck, Jeeves."

"I know." The gunner shook his head. "There's no way he'll fall for our old tricks, either."

Last time, the Bears had been using standard Phoenix VIs with militia-grade sensors and targeting software. They'd collided with the MISS databases aboard *Red Falcon* and been shredded.

The Bears had come off much worse that time, though, and had agreed to sell out their Legacy employers in exchange for money and their lives. They'd been supposed to keep their noses clean, too.

"Let's get a com channel," David ordered. "I doubt chatting is going to get us anywhere useful, but Aristos made promises he doesn't look like he's keeping. Let's see what he has to say for himself."

David turned on his recorders and faced them with a calm smile.

"Golden Bears. I'm guessing from the sheer number of you that Jason Aristos is here, and I seem to recall some degree of him promising to behave himself.

"Your presence here suggests that you're doing something *very* different, and I feel I must remind the Admiral Commanding that I still hold more than enough evidence to destroy his mercenary license.

"I don't think any of us want a fight here, so I suggest we keep the range open and leave each other be."

He waited. There was over a minute of time lapse in the communications loop right now, but he had time to play with. The mercenaries were already in his range, but they wouldn't be in their range of him for at least forty minutes still.

The response arrived in several minutes and it began as David expected. The video was focused on Aristos, a tall, thickly built man with tanned skin and pitch-black hair that hung to his shoulders, lounging in a command chair and smirking.

"Captain David Rice, I really did plan on keeping my nose clean," he said brightly. "I hate to seek out trouble I'm not being paid for after all. But, well, I lucked into a contract that really didn't need me to do more than hang out and be backup for a couple of guys doing a hard job."

His smirk left David in very little doubt as to which two guys he was talking about. The Golden Bears had been backing up the Augments killing their way through David's loose ends since the beginning. They'd even been at Darius...and he wondered now if that had been a coincidence after all.

If the Bears' passengers had been hunting Seule, following the chain all the way back from Ardennes, then they had been seeking the same man for the same reason.

"When you showed up at Darius, I wondered," Aristos noted. "But Bear was sure you were his ally, not his foe. Given that Bear is now *dead*, it seems he was wrong. On the other hand, that error works to my advantage."

There was an edge to the Admiral Commanding's smirk now. Bear, at a guess, was the Augment David's people had left dead in a rental apartment in Java.

"You killed a lot of my people and shattered our reputation. Our new contract let us rebuild, but I do not forget my dead, Captain Rice...but I couldn't afford to fight you. Not then.

"Now, happily, my *new* employer wants you dead and they've put quite a large sum of money on that idea," Aristos concluded. "There's no games, no bets, no compromises this time, Captain Rice. I know how many Mages you have. You can't jump, you can't run...and I have twice as many ships this time.

"I'm going to kill you, David Rice. And there is nothing you can do about it."

David swallowed hard as the message ended, and checked the scanners. The approaching fleet was still well over thirty minutes from range, and he traded gazes with Jeeves as LaMonte finally rejoined them.

"I was listening on my wrist-comp," she said softly. "What do we do?"

"He's right. We can't run," David told them. "We can turn, keep the range open, and hammer him with missiles. That's all I can think of."

"That buys us over an hour," LaMonte pointed out. "It's not nothing—we can empty our magazines of the Phoenix VIIIs and reload in that time."

"Get on nav," David ordered, his fingers dancing across his console. "Jeeves? Let's send the bastard the only response he's going to pay any attention to. Did we identify which ship was his?"

"No. Transmission was bounced from all nine."

"All right." David considered the screen for several long seconds, then tapped the second ship from the front. "Designate them Bandits One through Nine based on distance for the monitors. The yacht is nine. We may try and take her intact; we'll see how this goes.

"Otherwise, target Bandit Two and open fire. Maximum rate of fire, maximum velocity. Let's kill the—"

"Incoming fire!" LaMonte barked as she dropped into her console. "That son of a bitch—I'm reading twelve thousand gravities."

David winced. Those weren't Phoenix VIs. They were Phoenix VIIs, and that extra acceleration meant that the range he'd been hoping to maintain was already gone.

"See what games you can play, Kelly," he ordered. "Hold back *nothing*. Our enemies already know we're MISS. Let's show the damn Admiral Commanding just what that means."

As he spoke, *Red Falcon* shivered as her own launchers spoke again. The incoming missiles were inbound at twelve thousand gravities. His own missiles were five hundred gravities faster and would hit first.

"We can't run, not and keep the RFLAMs lined up," he continued. Almost all of his ship's weapons faced forward. For a long-range missile duel where he was outside his enemy's range, that didn't matter. If he was facing incoming fire, however, he needed his defenses pointed toward the enemy.

"I'll use the hull thrusters to push us back, keep the range a bit more open," he said aloud. "We can only pull about three gravities with those, so this is going to hurt."

"We have at least four hours until any of the Mages can jump," LaMonte murmured.

"I know," he confirmed. "So, let's kill these sons of bitches to keep everyone safe, shall we?"

Red Falcon's missiles had launched a few seconds later than the Bears' weapons, but they accelerated *much* faster and arrived first. They also came crashing in at a much higher velocity, had more powerful electronic warfare systems, and were running custom code written by James Kellers and Kelly LaMonte.

They were probably only a bit deadlier than their sisters in the Navy's arsenals. The specialist MISS code the two engineers had access to was only mildly superior than that available to the Navy.

Compared to the older missiles the Bears had they were probably at least twice as dangerous—and they needed every edge as ten missiles charged into the teeth of a hundred and twenty RFLAM turrets.

The enemy's defensive lasers were drawn in on David's displays as innocent orange lines. The time delay meant that everything he saw was already thirty seconds old by the time it reached him. The lasers were old. The explosions were old.

None of their first salvo made it through, but antimatter missiles also had the side effect of lashing the entire area they detonated in with devastating waves of radiation. The hash made it harder to target the ships behind it—but it also made it harder for those ships to hit the incoming missiles.

Follow-up salvos of antimatter missiles grew more dangerous in a way no other weapon in David's experience matched.

The salvo incoming on *Red Falcon* was terrifying. The sixty-four missiles might be a generation behind the modern weapons the Navy had given David and his people, but *Red Falcon* only carried twenty-five antimissile turrets.

Under normal circumstances, he'd expect to stop twenty incoming missiles. Today, he had to stop over sixty, and he wasn't sure his people could do it. He remained silent, his hands gripping the sides of his chair with white fingers, as Jeeves and LaMonte set to work.

Decoy drones fired into space, a half-dozen shuttle-sized electronic emitters blasting clear of the freighter's shuttle bays. They'd never used that system before—only the Navy was supposed to have systems new enough to be truly effective—but today it was needed.

LaMonte was using the decoys like an artist, dancing electronic emissions from decoy to decoy and back through *Red Falcon*, confusing the missiles as to just where their prey actually was. The confused missiles were easy prey to the RFLAMs, but there were so many of them.

David blinked as even thicker lines were drawn on his displays, Jeeves bringing the freighter's ten battle lasers online. The five-gigawatt beams weren't designed for the antimissile role, but any missile they hit was instantly blown to vapor.

A handful of missiles made it through everything only to fling themselves on LaMonte's decoys, sharp bursts of white antimatter flame wiping two of the emitter platforms from existence.

Two more came directly at *Red Falcon*, and for a handful of seconds, David thought he was going to die.

Then the fist of an angry god slammed into his chest as his ship *spun* in space, her engines going to maximum emergency thrust for a few fractions of a second.

Her engines and structure couldn't take fifteen gravities for long... but she took it for long enough to force both missiles to miss by over half a kilometer, their inertia carrying them off into the deep.

"One down," LaMonte said grimly. "Eight more salvos incoming."

David inhaled sharply as he studied the screen. Another salvo launched from the monitors even as he watched, bringing the total Aristos had fired to ten, six hundred and forty missiles.

A single Phoenix VII was worth millions on the black market. Whatever Aristos's "new employers"—presumably LMID—had offered him to kill David, it was more than David could match.

And if Aristos was willing to spend money and missiles like this, David wasn't sure he could keep his people alive.

"Ideas, people?" David asked softly as their last six decoys shot out of the shuttle bays. "This isn't an exchange we can keep up for four hours."

"I'm trying to hack them," LaMonte admitted. "They're using a non-standard encryption on the command channels, but they do have them open."

"You can't do that, run the decoys, *and* fly the ship," David pointed out. "I'll take over nav. Pass the decoys to your second and link Kellers in. If the two of you can't do it, nobody can."

"I could take some long-range shots at them with the lasers, but our odds of doing anything useful are piddling," Jeeves suggested. "Plus, well, if they return the favor, they'll do a lot more if they do hit."

David grimaced, watching their own second salvo slam into the brick wall of the Golden Bears' defenses. The radiation hash from the first salvo wasn't enough to even the odds. They were throwing far too few missiles to have any chance of punching through the mercenaries' defenses.

"What happens if we charge them?" he asked. "We have more beams still. The odds of landing a hit are in our favor even if their guns are bigger."

The monitors were built around guns from old cruisers. Their ten-gigawatt beams would rip *Falcon* in half.

"Two hours to range, boss," Jeeves pointed out. "We won't live that long."

The Bears' second salvo was passing through the radiation hash now, and their RFLAMs were lighting up the incoming missiles. With ten decoys out, the junior engineer running the electronic warfare didn't need to be as good as LaMonte to do as much.

Which was good, since the engineer *wasn't* as good. He still managed to draw off most of the missiles through the radiation hash, sending them careening off onto courses that would never threaten *Falcon*.

Others ran headlong into RFLAM fire as Jeeves's people targeted the ones that remained a threat. David twisted his ship through another series of emergency acceleration maneuvers, ignoring the grunts of half-complaint around him as he danced around the missiles.

It...wasn't enough. Two missiles detonated within a kilometer of *Red Falcon*. Even nuclear warheads wouldn't have been enough to cause damage, but these were *antimatter* weapons. Gigaton-range explosions sent waves of shock and radiation into the big freighter and she lurched.

And then kept going. Sensors and ECM emitters were fried and the big ship was reeling, but she still responded to David's commands and danced away from the radiation cloud.

"Report," he barked.

"Sensors are fucked. ECM is fucked. We're still here, but we're half-blind and our little jingle dance isn't working so well anymore," Kellers told him grimly. "We're going...shit, we got it!"

"James?"

"We broke their encryption," LaMonte told him. "Hang on and buy me time!"

David took his XO at her word, diving the ship at ninety degrees to their previous course and forcing major course corrections on the part of the incoming missiles. It wouldn't buy them much, merely seconds really, but...

The closest wave of missiles simply detonated. Then the next, and the next.

One moment, hundreds of missiles were bearing down on *Red Falcon*. The next, the space between *Falcon* and the Golden Bears was a massive wasteland of debris and radiation as David's people cheered.

"Bloody amateurs," LaMonte finally noted. "They bought a super-secure encryption and used it...but they only bought *one*."

"I don't think they were counting on us having MISS's decryption algorithms and supercomputers," David said drily. "Well done."

Their own missile salvoes continued to crash down on the mercenaries, and as David turned back to study them, the MISS ship finally got lucky. A single missile made its way through the radiation hash and the defenses and hammered into Bandit Two.

The monitors' designers had built them to avoid being hit, sacrificing armor for acceleration and defensive turrets as well as overwhelming firepower. Even if they hadn't, only the Martian Navy built ships that could stand up to antimatter missiles.

The front third of the monitor disappeared and the rest spun out of control, the pocket destroyer falling out of formation as the other ships continued their charge at David.

"They're not firing," he said quietly.

"They're disabling the receivers on their missiles," LaMonte told him instantly. "If they don't have a sequence of encryptions to run through, then that's their next step. They'll lose efficiency...but we won't be able to do that again."

"So." David studied the screens. "*Next* set of ideas?"

CHAPTER 50

"I CAN'T even leave you lot alone long enough to take a decent nap, can I?" Maria Soprano grouched as the channel from the simulacrum chamber reopened. "How deep a pile are we in, Skipper?"

"Deep," David confirmed. "There are seven of the Bears' monitors out there, and my last math says you're still a few hours from being able to jump."

His Mage closed her eyes in a way he'd learned long ago meant she was assessing her internal reserves, then sighed and shook her head.

"Three hours, maybe two if I push, or maybe five if I do too much to defend the ship," she admitted.

"Do what you can," David told her. "But we may have this in hand."

Soprano arched one elegantly maintained eyebrow at him.

"Really?"

"No," he admitted. "But I'm not asking anyone to die for me today, either."

"They're spreading out, clearing their defensive lines of fire and getting clear sight around the radiation fog," Jeeves reported. "I don't think we're going to get another lucky hit, boss."

"Feel free to fling some lasers their way," David told the other man. "I'm running out of ideas."

He was still running as best he could, but without turning the ship around and taking most of his defensive laser turrets out of action, he could only move so fast. The Bears were gaining on him at nine gravities.

New lines drew into his screen as the big battle lasers spoke. Even at thirty-plus light-seconds, there was no way for the Bears to anticipate the beams. On the other hand, there was also a full minute between when the light Jeeves was using to target them originated and when the lasers arrived.

To David's surprise, they actually *hit* the ship they targeted, all ten beams bracketing a single monitor. At this range, they didn't do much damage. The monitor lurched sideways and started leaking vaporized metal and atmosphere, but she kept coming.

"And there they go again," Jeeves noted grimly. The mercenaries returned the favor, thankfully with less luck as their lasers flashed through the space around *Falcon*, but they also opened fire once more.

"Aristos has a lot of those damned missiles," David replied. "How's our stockpile?"

"Two more salvos, then we need to reload the magazines," the gunner replied. "We have enough missiles to do so, twice, in that container we have tucked in under the hab ring, but... it'll take time."

David nodded grimly as the first of those two salvos shot out.

"Or we can do what we did with those fusion missiles way back," he said as inspiration and memory struck. His gunner stared at him blankly, but he turned to LaMonte.

"Kelly, we dumped an entire cargo container of fusion missiles at those pirates way back. They got away by jumping—and I don't think these guys can jump any more than we can. Can we do that with the Phoenixes?"

"Neither the missiles nor the container is designed for it," she said slowly. "But...if we eject the container into space and slice it apart with the lasers, we shouldn't lose more than ten percent.

"The rest won't have our updates and we can't control that many missiles—but we can feed them telemetry."

"Our telemetry sucks right now," Jeeves pointed out.

"Then we're not losing much by hamstringing our missiles," LaMonte replied. "Launching the container into space is manual; I'll take care of it."

David considered telling her to send someone else for a moment, but she really was one of the best qualified for every part of this.

"Go," he instructed. "And the rest of you..." He turned to look at the rest of the bridge. "Let's keep everyone alive, shall we?"

The first salvo arrived several minutes after LaMonte had headed back into the ship, missiles sweeping down on the big freighter like suicidal vultures.

Red Falcon herself had ceased firing. They were out of missiles in their ready magazines now except for a small number of Rapier fusion-drive missiles—weapons that didn't have the range for this fight.

The siren song of the drones danced across space around *Falcon*, luring missiles off-course and leaving them vulnerable to missing or laser fire. Their onboard ECM emitters were trashed and the usual jamming was missing, though, which gave the missiles a new edge.

Their lack of updates after launch weakened them. Many would have missed on their own, and the decoys made it worse. The first salvo came apart, shattered under the defensive fire.

Others followed, but they had no advantages over the first salvo. David knew the odds weren't in his people's favor, but they could hope.

Then...

"We got one!" Jeeves crowed. "Bandit One, the one we tagged with the laser. Didn't zig fast enough, bitch!"

David checked the scanners and confirmed his gunner's cheers. The damaged monitor had taken a single missile amidships, almost exactly where the laser had hit. With the middle third of the ship missing, two chunks of it spun off into deep space.

Twenty-five percent of their enemies were gone. It had taken every missile in their onboard magazines, over four hundred weapons, and their enemy was *still* firing at them. Hundreds more antimatter missiles were in space, yet...

"Wait, did they stop firing?" David asked.

"Checking," Jeeves replied. Several seconds passed. "Yes, sir. They have ceased fire. Looks like they finally ran out of damn Phoenixes."

Even with the lost ships, Aristos had fired over eleven hundred Phoenix VIIs in the last hour. The range had fallen to "merely" nine point three million kilometers.

"Can we hold off the missiles?" he asked his gunner.

"Maybe?" Jeeves replied. "Let's not forget they almost certainly have almost as many Rapiers *and* those big lasers."

"We can jump before those lasers get into useful range," David replied. "Let's worry about the damn Phoenixes."

Another salvo collided with *Falcon*'s defenses as they spoke, antimatter explosions and distracted missiles flickering across the sky.

The ship shook as the last missiles died just barely far enough away to count as a miss, radiation still washing over the ship as David shuddered.

"Jeeves?"

"We're down a decoy and some more sensors," the gunner reported. "This...isn't going great, boss."

"Captain, it's LaMonte," the XO's voice suddenly echoed onto the bridge. "We've programmed the missiles and are ejecting the container into space. Jeeves should have the control link on his console...and the firing pattern he needs to open the box up as efficiently as possible."

"Jeeves?" David repeated, turning to look at the gaunt gunner.

"Got it. Waiting for the container...there it is."

Seconds ticked by and David swallowed his impatience as his people worked, then Jeeves pressed a single command on his console.

A dozen of the RFLAM turrets lit up simultaneously, slicing into the container spinning through space at minimum power. The cuts were almost delicate, compared to the usual devastating energy transfer of even the defensive weapons.

For a few more seconds, that was everything...and then five *hundred* missiles lit up their drives.

"Now, *that's* a sight," David breathed.

"Not really," Jeeves complained. "There were *eight* hundred missiles in that box. Checking the links, seeing if I can get any more on—"

A Rapid-Fire Laser Anti Missile turret like *Red Falcon*'s defensive systems used a five-hundred-megawatt laser. That wasn't enough to vaporize most missiles completely, but it was enough to deflect them or ignite their fuel storage to finish the job.

The missile that came screaming in out of the night had been hit and flagged as destroyed by Jeeves's computers. Instead of being vaporized, the beam had detached and destroyed the warhead. The explosion had registered as destroying the weapon, leaving the computers confused when the engines came back online a few moments later and entered terminal acquisition.

Red Falcon's forward dome was the only truly armored part of her hull. Even the engine pod at the rear of the long "mushroom stem" of the ship's spine was only lightly armored, but the missile came in off-angle and late and missed the dome.

It tore through the engine pods like an avenging angel. Multiple antimatter chambers shattered, their safety measures engaging to vent their contents into space. Engines broke apart, pressure chambers overloading and detonating.

The entire ship was *flung* out of position, hurtling away from her original course even as her drives failed and her primary power cores ejected into space. A halo of antimatter explosions lit her up, bathing her in radiation and burning away many of her remaining sensors and emitters.

With the magical gravity runes throughout the ship, it had been years since David had felt enough force in the ship's bridge to need his safety restraints, and he'd lost the habit. That mistake caught up to him now as his ship jumped underneath him and he was flung from his chair.

He managed to avoid hitting his head and struggled back upright, dazed by the impact.

"Jeeves?" he snapped. "Are you okay?"

All he could hear on his bridge for a moment was his own heavy breathing, and then his gunner exhaled a heavy sigh.

"I think everyone is fine but you, Skipper," the ex-convict replied. "You would have torn a strip off anyone *else* who forgot their restraints."

"What happened?" David demanded as he stumbled back to his chair. The room was dimly lit with emergency lighting, but at least the magical gravity didn't need power to stay operational.

"We got hit," Jeeves said flatly. "I don't have enough sensor resolution left to tell what happened to the rest of their missiles, but the fact that we're still breathing suggests that the hell that just enveloped us took care of most of them."

"Get me Engineering," David barked. "We'll need more than emergency..."

The lights came up as he was speaking, and he turned in his chair to see Kelly LaMonte standing by the often-neglected engineering panel at the back of the bridge. His XO was pale, and her arm was twisted at an angle that told him everything he needed to know.

"The dome has its own power," she said in a somewhat faint voice. "It can't fuel the main engines, but it can power the guns and the secondary thruster suite."

The secondary thruster suite. The one for if they blew half of the damn ship off.

"Do we have engines?" he asked.

"I can't tell," she admitted. "Data links to Engineering are gone." She blinked. "I'm...not in great shape, but I think I can get us sensors back."

"How?" Jeeves demanded.

"Your thermals are gone, but your radar receivers are fine. You just don't have transmitters," she snapped. "The decoy drones do, even if that's not what they're designed for. Give me a couple of minutes and I'll give you eyes."

David nodded for her to go ahead, even as he looked at her broken arm in concern.

"Help her," he ordered Jeeves. "Keep her to using one hand."

His XO snorted. It was a pained, forced sound, but it was there.

"I'm a lot more worried about us dying than making my arm worse," she admitted. "Right now, we can't even tell what our missiles are doing!"

David watched her for a few seconds, then turned back to internal coms. As LaMonte had said, the links to Engineering were down...but he could reach the simulacrum chamber.

"Soprano, report," he said grimly as he reopened the channel.

"I'm fine," she snapped. "What the hell happened? I don't have any sensor feeds down here."

"Engineering took a hit and the antimatter cores got ejected," he said shortly. "We've lost coms. I need you to get down there and see if anyone is still alive."

"It's...that bad?" she asked.

Until she hesitated, he'd forgotten that she and James Kellers had been becoming an item. He'd have kicked himself, but they didn't have time.

"I don't know," he admitted. "But I need you to get everyone who's still alive into your Sanctum and let me know."

"David?"

"Just do it," he snapped. "We don't have *time*."

He doubted their salvo of abandoned missiles were going to finish the job, which meant he needed a ship that could fight. There was only one way he could get that...but he wasn't going to abandon any of his crew who were still alive!

CHAPTER 51

MARIA DIDN'T make it very far along the spine of the ship before she started to run into problems. Twisted metal barred her way, and the careful structure of the gravity runes was fraying. Instead of the usual one gravity of pull, they were flickering between nothing and two gees.

The debris was easily dealt with. Just because she was too weak to jump didn't mean she couldn't do things that would be impossible for a mundane. She blasted a hole through the wreckage, hammering the warped hull and conduits into place to form a new, smaller, corridor toward Engineering.

Then, with a sigh, she severed the rune constructs creating gravity in the area. She held herself to the deck with a spell of her own, but the damaged runes would be dangerous for anyone else. With that done, she kicked off, releasing her gravity spell to launch herself down the hole she'd made.

Twice more she found her way blocked by debris, and by the third time she'd reopened a passageway down the ship, she was starting to feel the strain. Fortunately, that seemed to be the last, and the blast doors sealing off Engineering itself still had status lights blinking away.

Those status lights were...unpromising. The air on the other side was breathable. Barely. Pressure was low and the toxic content was rising. From the way the pressure was dropping, there was at least one microbreach and the systems were struggling to compensate.

Despite what the automated systems thought, Maria was grimly certain that there were living crew on the other side. That meant she had to get through the blast door—and as Ship's Mage and First Officer, she had the override codes to tell the security system to sit down and shut up.

Air blasted past her and she barely managed to keep herself in place hanging onto the edge of the door. Once the initial equalization was complete, she pulled herself into Engineering and inhaled sharply.

The massive space that had served as a center point for the engine pods was a nightmare. Fires were visibly burning and debris was scattered everywhere. She could *see* the gravity runes flickering in random patterns across the decks.

Fortunately, she could also see crew members and cross to them quickly.

"Report," she ordered, interrupting the engineers' shock.

"We've lost all the engines," the very junior officer in charge of the team managed to gasp out. "Antimatter containment failed; radiation levels in here are dangerous, ma'am. We're trying to stabilize the fusion cores but we don't have enough control to shut down the feed. They're heading for overload."

Maria winced.

"How long if you leave the cores?" she asked bluntly.

"Two, maybe three minutes," the senior technician next to the officer replied. "These need someone babying them."

"No, they need to be blasted into space," Maria corrected him. "Get everyone moving back to the Mage's Sanctum. Stop there; I don't think we want to be in the spine at all."

"Ma'am, if we leave the reactor—"

"It will explode," Maria finished for the engineering officer. "And at this point, it isn't going to matter. Who else is left down here?"

"We have wounded but we can't spare the hands to move them," the senior tech replied instantly. "If we're all going, we can take them, I think."

"No one gets left behind," Maria ordered. "Where's James?"

"He's one of the wounded," the officer told her grimly. "He manually ejected the antimatter cores and got hit with the backlash. We *think* he'll live, but...none of us are doctors."

Neither was Maria. All she could do was make sure everybody got out alive to make it to the medical bay.

"Help me get them moving," she ordered. "There's no gravity along most of the spine between here and the simulacrum. We don't have much time."

The tech snorted.

"If we stop babying this reactor, that's going to be very, very true," he pointed out.

"Then you're the last one out after the wounded are moved," Maria replied. "But we are *all* getting out of here. Right now."

Maria ended up carrying most of the wounded herself, her magic lifting up and moving a dozen unconscious, hopefully alive, forms on her own. One of those forms was James Kellers, his muscular form probably the limpest of the lot and his face covered with a spray of fast-hardening bandage.

She was very specifically not taking the time to check him over more closely. It did not look like her lover was in good shape—but he was alive. She was going to make damn sure he stayed that way.

It was easy to tell once they got back into the portion of the spine that was more intact that the rest. Even before they hit the working gravity runes, they could see flashing lights and hear an automated announcement.

"Emergency conversion process initiated," the calm recorded voice told them. "Please evacuate all areas with red lights. These areas are not safe. Blue light areas are safe. Orange light areas are not safe but will be once the conversion is complete.

"Repeat, emergency conversion process initiated."

It kept cycling to the point where Maria could have recited it back to the recording—but the red flashing lights lining the spinal corridor she was leading and hauling people through were far from calming.

"David, I need more time," she snapped into her wrist-comp.

"I know; I'm watching you," the Captain replied. "Everything behind the simulacrum chamber is going to get blasted into space. *Hurry up.*"

That was not the response Maria had been hoping for, and she glanced behind her. She was still thirty meters, at least, short of the armored pod containing the Mage's Sanctum and the simulacrum pod. Some of the engineers were as much as fifty more meters behind her.

Even carrying the wounded was starting to strain her, but they were out of time. She closed her eyes, feeling for the runes beneath her feet. She couldn't see them and often couldn't even feel them, but right now she *needed* to.

Her power reached out, to the end of the corridor, and then hammered into the floor with a line of fire that severed the gravity runes.

"What the—"

The running evacuees from Engineering found themselves lifting off in mid-step, but Maria was already acting. Her magic swept backward now, catching the entire collection of engineers, techs, and wounded and carrying them forward through zero gravity.

She picked herself up with them, hurtling them all along the corridor at a frankly dangerous pace, collecting everyone as she came.

Then they crashed through into the corridor outside the simulacrum chamber and collapsed back down to the floor. Maria was grimly certain she'd probably *caused* a slew of new injuries, but she wasn't done yet.

Blinking away liquid from her eyes, careful not to try and tell what it was, she forced herself back to her feet and slammed the emergency lock. A heavy steel shutter slammed shut behind them, and she took a moment to be sure that the space she'd got everyone into was lit up in blue.

Then she grabbed her wrist-comp.

"We're clear," she told David.

Then she passed out.

CHAPTER 52

BROKEN ARM OR NOT, Kelly LaMonte remained one of the best programmers and engineers David had ever seen. It took her just over two minutes to get *Red Falcon* some semblance of eyes back, and just as Soprano was starting to haul the wounded out of Engineering, David and the bridge crew knew just how bad the situation was.

Their massed salvo of missiles had done their job and done it well. Of the six remaining functional monitors, three were simply *gone*, a fourth was as badly damaged as the first two, and the remaining two ships had taken at least near-misses.

Unfortunately, that wasn't enough. Two of Aristos's monitors remained combat-capable, and they were now accelerating toward *Red Falcon* at their maximum thrust.

"They think we're crippled," Jeeves said quietly.

"They're not wrong," David replied. "Unless we dump the engine pod, we're fucked. Even if we *do*, we have no missiles left and the conversion hurts our acceleration."

"I'm not seeing much choice, boss," his gunner replied.

"Agreed." David tapped a command that started a warning sequence running through the ship. He was only vaguely aware of just what the "emergency conversion process" entailed, only that it would ditch his cargo, if he was carrying one, and eject the engine pod.

"We still have lasers?" he asked.

"Capacitors are pretty badly drained," Jeeves replied. "The forward power cores *can* charge them, but, um…"

"Lay it out," David ordered.

"We never kept them fully fueled," his gunner reminded him. "That much hydrogen was a fire hazard. We can break down the water in the cap supply to *make* hydrogen…but not quickly. Give us a day and we'll have the forward cores fully fueled and able to charge the lasers."

"And until then, what's in the capacitors is what we've got," David concluded. "What can you give me?"

"All ten guns at half power or four of them at full with two at half," Jeeves said. "Either will take me time to switch out, but we've only got four guns I'd trust at full power if you give me a choice."

"Start switching for as many full-power shots as we can get," David said with a sigh. The monitors were closing the range, but unless they decided to start launching missiles, he had some time. Not a lot. Not with *Red Falcon* unable to maneuver.

The monitors' big lasers could easily wreck his ship at seven or eight million kilometers. The real range limitation was the dodging…and *Red Falcon* couldn't dodge.

"David, I need more time," Maria told him over her wrist-comp.

He looked at the inner sensors. She was most of the way to the simulacrum chamber and the armored pod around it that would be fine. But… they only had minutes at best until the mercenaries were in range to finish them off, and he needed engines.

He wasn't willing to sacrifice his people. Not unless he had to—but if they didn't make it, he'd have to.

"I know; I'm watching you," he told her, even as his heart tore in half. "Everything behind the simulacrum chamber is going to get blasted into space. *Hurry up.*"

Then her magic flared, carrying the wounded forward in response to his demand, and he inhaled sharply. He *knew* how much jumping took out of a Mage, and Maria couldn't have that much left.

The health-warning transmission from her wrist-comp a moment later told him all he needed to. She was alive, but she'd pushed herself well past what was reasonable. Without proper care, she could easily die.

From the sounds of it, that was true of many of the people she'd pulled out of Engineering.

"Everyone is clear of the red and orange zones," Jeeves reported. "What do we do?"

Red Falcon was spinning in space, unable to bear on anything or anyone until she had engines again. Her velocity vector was solid enough, that the Bears would be able to hit them cleanly.

"Hang on," David ordered, and punched a command he never thought he'd use.

From the outside, it must have looked like the ship was exploding. First, explosive charges placed around the spine at the simulacrum chamber's pod detonated, severing the entire rear half of the spine, engine pod and all, from the ship.

The force flung the five-hundred-meter-long chunk of starship away from *Red Falcon* barely in time. It was only a few kilometers distant from the freighter when the fusion cores finally overloaded despite the programs the engineers had left running. The rest of the *Red Falcon*'s transformation process was hidden under the brilliant light of a tiny new sun as the fusion reactions overcame their containment.

As the sun lit up the back of the ship, the front half of the spine was disintegrated as smaller charges blasted the exterior hull and cargo spars away. A few seconds passed as thousands of tons of cargo control and storage technology cleared the area, and then the umbilicals and conduits connecting the simulacrum pod to the forward dome and hab ring began to coil up.

Normally, the heavily armored cables and pipes were far from flexible, but the designers had accounted for that. Sections of piping folded in on themselves, new links forming as entire hundred-meter pieces of supply umbilicals were ejected into space.

The entire process took a little under twelve seconds, and when it was done, the simulacrum chamber and its armored pod slammed into the rear of the forward section with bone-crushing force. Inside, the magical model of the ship would already be adjusting, changing to show *Red Falcon*'s new shape.

Finally, the last connections popped into place and a new set of green indicators lit up on David's screen.

Something like a third of *Red Falcon*'s unfueled mass was now scattered around her in pieces, and she would never carry cargo again. The freighter was, in a very real sense, dead.

What was left was a two-million-ton pocket warship, and David took live control of his ship once again as his enemies opened fire in panicked fear.

The secondary engines buried in the forward pod weren't as powerful as the main thrusters he'd lost, but they also didn't need to push twenty million tons of cargo and three million tons of starship plus fuel.

Falcon went from zero to eight gravities at the touch of a button, the newly shrunken ship responding to David's hand with an eagerness he'd never felt from her when she was a freighter.

"Lasers and Rapiers," he said quietly to Jeeves. "Hit them with *everything*."

Ten-gigawatt laser beams flashed through space where *Red Falcon* had been a moment before, their sudden acceleration sparing them from the mercenaries' fire—and then Jeeves returned the fire.

The light from *Red Falcon*'s newly activated engines hadn't reached the enemy when Jeeves fired. They had seconds to evade, seconds they clearly lost to a very human moment of shock.

The range was too long for the freighter's battle lasers to be effective on their own, but the lead monitor took six lasers to her forward armor. Even dispersed by distance, it was enough to rip the ship open like a rotten banana.

Missiles poured in afterward as Jeeves emptied the magazines. They only had a hundred Rapier fusion missiles left aboard, but it would be enough. It *had* to be enough.

The monitor's laser flared again and again, but she didn't launch missiles. Apparently, Aristos hadn't brought the lower-tier missiles with him this time. With only a single beam, David managed to dance around the long-range fire until it was too late for anyone.

Rapiers didn't carry warheads. They didn't need them. Arriving at just over ten percent of lightspeed, the six missiles from the first salvo that made it through were all it took. Hammering into the monitor like the fists of the Gods, they shattered the mercenary ship.

The rest of the missiles continued on for several more seconds until Jeeves hit a command to detonate them. Their engines overloaded and the remaining missiles blew apart.

Silence reigned.

"Now what?" the gunner finally asked.

"We flag this location for MISS to send search-and-rescue out to," David told him. "We check in on our Mages and our wounded...and then we get the hell home to Tau Ceti before anyone *else* finds us."

The Golden Bears' jump-yacht was still around somewhere, but he doubted she could rescue the survivors from the ship. *Falcon* certainly didn't have the capacity anymore, but he owed it to fellow spacers to make sure that people who *could* help knew they were here.

Even if they'd tried to kill him.

CHAPTER 53

"I'M PRETTY sure we told you that you could only do that once."

Commodore Rasputin Burns, the main dockmaster for the Tau Ceti shipyards, had been the man to deliver *Red Falcon* to David. The sharp-featured and dark-haired man hadn't changed much since the last time they'd met, though he looked tired as he studied the hologram of the newly abbreviated *Red Falcon* floating over his desk.

"Honestly, I was surprised it worked once," David admitted. Both men stood in the Commodore's office in the shipyards' main command center.

"*Worked* is a strong word," Burns agreed. "You're alive, though. That's important. *Falcon*, on the other hand..."

The yardmaster sighed and tapped a command. Red lines appeared on the hologram, lacing their way through the entire hull.

"We knew we wouldn't be able to use her as a freighter, but our survey came out even worse than I was afraid of," he said. "She isn't flyable, Captain. She's done. She gave you everything she had and she kept you alive, but at the only price she could pay."

David nodded stonily. *Red Falcon* had served him well, but in the end, he supposed she was only a ship. It still felt inglorious.

"She gave us her all," he agreed. In the end, only twenty-seven of the big ship's four hundred crew had died in the fight. Others, like James Kellers, were still in critical care, but most of David's people had come home.

"I don't know if we're giving you a new ship," Burns admitted. "That's between you and MISS. I can tell you that we can't fix *Red Falcon*. Not even a little bit. I recommend she be evacuated—in an orderly fashion but evacuated nonetheless.

"Then we'll take her to the Navy scrapyards. She deserves better," he said sadly, "but at least she's going to go into new warships and not just general scrap."

"She deserves better," David agreed. There wasn't much else to say. His ship was a wreck. He could buy a new one now, but that left all kinds of questions as to what happened next. He still had *Peregrine*, too, he supposed.

"Much of what you did in command of her is classified," Burns told him. "Given that you were supposed to be a regular shipper for most of that time, I find that fascinating...but I also understand that you did well by her. She fell protecting her crew and the Protectorate.

"Not much more for a warship to ask, is there?"

To call the strange freighter a warship was perhaps the greatest courtesy and honor the two men in that office could give.

The infirmary room was dimly lit as Maria stepped in after silence answered her gentle knock. Given James's injuries, the dimness was probably unnecessary, but she understood. Her own burnout had thankfully been relatively easily treated. More had been required than just wiping the blood off her face, but she'd recovered by the time they got back to Tau Ceti.

James...James was the worst-wounded member of *Red Falcon*'s crew still alive.

"I can still hear, you know," he noted aloud in the dim light. "And I apparently know your breathing, Maria, even if you don't introduce yourself after knocking."

"That's fair," she told him, and crossed to his bedside. His entire head was wrapped in bandages, concealing the injuries she knew were underneath it.

Even without the bandages and the dim lighting he wouldn't have been able to see her. James had lost both of his eyes in *Red Falcon*'s Engineering.

He reached out, hesitantly, for her. She met him halfway, sliding her hand into his and squeezing gently.

"You big lug," she said softly. "How are you holding up?"

"From what they tell me, you may want to reassess your plans," he said quietly. "I'm on the list for cybernetic eyes; they just want the rest of the injuries to heal up a bit more first. A week or two, at most."

"Then what's the problem?" Maria asked. "You'll see. What more do we need?"

James chuckled softly, then coughed.

"They can't do much about the scarring, Maria," he told her. "I'm... I'm going to be hideous, is my understanding."

"I don't *fucking care*," she snapped. "Do you hear me on that, James Kellers? I. Do. Not. Care."

"I don't want you to stay with me out of pity," he replied, his hand starting to slide away.

She grabbed his hand before he could move it away, and pressed it to her lips.

"No," she whispered. "Never. You run, I'll chase you. You quit, I'll support you. You stay with MISS or follow David or go buy your own damned ship, I'll back you. It was never your *face*."

"Ah. *Fue que hablé español*," he noted with a somewhat forced chuckle.

"If you want to think that," Maria replied. "I'm with you, James. Scars or no scars. Cyber-eyes or regrown. Whatever it takes, I'm with you to the end of the line."

His grip on her hand was tight now, both of them clinging together as if the world would try to tear them apart.

"Be careful, you lug," he said softly, throwing her own words back at her. "Or I might think you were saying you'd go wherever I do."

"I am," Maria Soprano said fiercely. "That is *exactly* what I'm saying."

MISS had been kind enough to put an entire lodging facility at the disposal of David and his crew while they sorted out just what they were going to do with him. One of his conversations suggested that they might end up shipped down to one of the resorts on the surface if their limbo lasted much longer.

What none of his conversations *had* explained was why they were in limbo. He hadn't decided what he was going to do yet, but at least part of that was that MISS hadn't made any suggestions on their side. He was starting to look through ship-builder websites and assess his resources.

He couldn't build a ship like *Red Falcon*, but he could pay to have a decently equipped—and armed—six- or eight-megaton ship built. If MISS didn't get their act together, he could put in that order.

David was wavering back and forth over a message to one of the civilian shipbuilders, asking for a meeting to put together a proposal, when the door buzzer to his rented office went off.

"Come in," he instructed.

The last person he expected to walk through the door was the tall, graying, and heavily built man who did. Even without the golden hand resting on his chest, there was no question that Hand Hans Lomond owned any room he happened to enter.

The Hand grabbed a spare chair and grinned at David as he took a seat, waiting for the Captain to get his thoughts sorted.

"Didn't expect to see a Hand here, Lord Lomond," he admitted.

"We try to keep our movements at least *somewhat* quiet," Lomond replied. "In my case, I just got back from Condor. Interesting mess you found there, Captain. The team I left behind is going to be busy for weeks. Possibly months. The good Prince is going to be *much* poorer once we're through with him."

"And the mob?" David asked.

"Oh, we're already done with *them*," the Hand purred. "A lot of MISS people suddenly found themselves short a job, too. I'd have stayed longer, but the Mage-King called and a Hand answers."

"What brings you here, then?" If the Mage-King had called one of his Hands in, they had more important places to be than David's office.

"You," Lomond said simply. "You deserve to know what you achieved, even if it's all going to be dark and secret forever."

"We achieved nothing," David said bitterly. "No new evidence. No proof. Just a lot of dead people and my own ship wrecked."

"That's what it looks like, huh?" the Hand replied. "That's probably a good thing in the end. Do you want to know what you *did* achieve?"

He stared at Lomond in silence, then made a "go ahead" gesture.

"You have to understand, Captain Rice, that the Protectorate is only granted a certain amount of money from the colonies under the Charter," Lomond reminded him. "Technically, the Mage-King only commands the resources of the Sol System and a tiny stipend from each world.

"Funds beyond that have been negotiated with each system on a term basis, including those that fund the Royal Martian Navy. We can't embark on a mass expansion of the Navy without all of the systems knowing.

"Including Legatus."

David winced. He hadn't thought through that component of the Protectorate's funding. He hadn't even really known it, not in detail.

"That's why we needed proof," he said. "Proof we didn't get."

"You didn't get proof, no," Lomond agreed. "Not proof we could drag into the Council of the Protectorate and throw at Legatus's feet. Not proof that would enable us to take fleets and armies to Legatus and take down their government.

"But you got *enough*, Captain Rice. An Augment assassin murdered their way across half the galaxy to cover up the Legatan arms supplied to Ardennes? That's hard to brush away as a coincidence, even if it remains circumstantial. We can't meet a legal standard of proof...but thanks to you, we *can* convince people."

"Of what?" David asked.

"Project Weyland," Lomond said simply. "Tau Ceti and five other Core Worlds are now directly underwriting a top secret expansion of the Royal Martian Navy. The money is coming entirely outside normal channels, so Legatus will never know it's happening.

"Thanks to you, Captain Rice, when Legatus moves, we will be *ready*."

"Doesn't seem like enough," David admitted with a sigh. "Not for the amount of blood that got shed."

"It is enough," the Hand told him. "You made a difference and we're not done with you yet, not unless you want us to be."

He gestured at the ship drawings on the wall screen.

"If you want to buy or build a civilian ship and go back to being a merchant, we won't stop you. Hell, we'll pay for the damn ship; we owe you that," Lomond said. "But we can use you. Hell, I'm planning on poaching young Officer LaMonte regardless."

"That woman will make a superb covert operator," David told him.

"We agree. My next stop is to offer her a ship. Right now, however, I'm offering you one."

"What kind of ship?" David asked. "My cover's blown. Legatus knows who I work for."

"So? Legatus is hardly our only enemy. In passing, Captain Rice, you allowed us to neutralize a major *la Cosa Nostra* transshipment center. *In passing*. You moved through the system and found our enemy.

"We want to give you a new ship. Less ostentatious than *Red Falcon*, but still a high-tier merchant ship. We'll arm her with concealed weaponry and stick you with a new platoon of Marines. You'll do what you did for us before, with a slight edge of staying away from Legatus."

"And if I'm done?" David said softly.

"We'll buy you a new ship anyway," Lomond replied. "Pay you a pension, if you just want to retire on Amber. We can use you, Captain. We can always use agents like you, but Mars wants volunteers, not conscripts."

David considered it for a moment. His own luck suggested that he'd end up right in the middle of the fight against the Protectorate's underworld no matter what he did.

"All right," he said slowly. "I guess I can stick myself back in uniform one more time."

Lomond chuckled.

"You're like me, Captain. You don't have it in you to walk away. Neither do any of the young men and women you've trained. I haven't met Montgomery yet, but I've spoken with my master about him. Officer LaMonte seems cut from the same cloth.

"You forge us agents of skill and integrity. Mars will always need men and women like you—and like your protégés."

"You give me too much credit."

"No. I don't think so."

Kelly stepped into the meeting room she'd been asked to attend with trepidation. Mysterious meeting invites were generally one of the more dangerous parts of being a spy, though she figured anyone who could get a meeting room in an MISS lodging and send her the invite through the MISS system was probably on her side.

Mike and Xi were both due in the same room in ten minutes, which left her both concerned and curious.

The heavily built older man sitting at the table wasn't familiar to her, but she knew the golden hand he wore on a long chain around his neck.

"My Lord Hand," she greeted him, suddenly unsure if she should bow or what. Her awkwardness must have shown, as he laughed and gestured her to a chair.

"I am Hand Hans Lomond," he introduced himself. "Please, Officer LaMonte, sit."

She sat and he gestured, conjuring a hologram of a ship above the table.

Kelly studied it with a practiced eye. There were enough details given to work out scale, at least. The ship was roughly the same size as the Golden Bears' monitors, a hundred and fifty meter-long egg shape roughly thirty meters across.

Other than a vague hull resemblance, it was nothing like the monitors. She could pick out hatches for concealed weapons and shuttle bays, but the ship was *trying* to look like a half-megaton fast packet courier.

"What's this?" she asked carefully.

"*Rhapsody in Purple*," Lomond told her. "MISS covert operations ship KEX-26. She's a commando insertion ship, a jump-ship that can pass for a fast courier but really isn't designed to pretend to be anybody so much as to be invisible."

"Invisibility in space is impossible," Kelly objected.

"Magic can change that, but in the main, yes. *Rhapsody in Purple* and her sisters have a slew of new tech to help, but her main stealth is appearing to be something else at a distance. Her job will be to provide a level of black striking capability to the Protectorate that we've never truly had or needed before."

Kelly blinked and continued studying the ship.

"She sounds classified as hell. Why are you showing her to me?" she asked.

"There are three *Rhapsodies* under construction," Lomond told her. "*Rhapsody in Purple* will be the first to commission, in just over two months. We want you to command her."

"Me?" Kelly half-squeaked. "I'm an XO, not...a..."

"Not a covert operations commander?" the Hand asked. "You've demonstrated the skills for the job and, well, frankly...no one else is qualified to command a *Rhapsody* either. We need to start somewhere, and you're a better fit for the job than Captain Rice...*Captain* LaMonte."

"I need...to think about this," she admitted. She was tempted—*Gods, was she tempted*—but she couldn't do anything without...

Without asking Xi and Mike.

"That's why you have Xi and Mike coming as well, isn't it?" she asked accusingly.

"Of course," Lomond agreed cheerfully. "You'll need a Ship's Mage and some damn good pilots for the job we want you to do. I wouldn't dream of taking you away from your spouses—and the three of you will make amazing agents of Mars."

ABOUT THE AUTHOR

GLYNN STEWART is the author of Starship's Mage, a bestselling science fiction and fantasy series where faster-than-light travel is possible–but only because of magic. His other works include science fiction series Duchy of Terra, Castle Federation and Vigilante, as well as the urban fantasy series ONSET and Changeling Blood.

Writing managed to liberate Glynn from a bleak future as an accountant. With his personality and hope for a high-tech future intact, he lives in Kitchener, Ontario with his partner, their cats, and an unstoppable writing habit.

OTHER BOOKS
BY GLYNN STEWART

For release announcements join the
mailing list or visit **GlynnStewart.com**

STARSHIP'S MAGE
Starship's Mage
Hand of Mars
Voice of Mars
Alien Arcana
Judgment of Mars
UnArcana Stars
Sword of Mars
Mountain of Mars
The Service of Mars
A Darker Magic
Mage-Commander (upcoming)

Starship's Mage: Red Falcon
Interstellar Mage
Mage-Provocateur
Agents of Mars

Pulsar Race: A Starship's Mage Universe Novella

DUCHY OF TERRA
The Terran Privateer
Duchess of Terra
Terra and Imperium
Darkness Beyond
Shield of Terra
Imperium Defiant
Relics of Eternity
Shadows of the Fall
Eyes of Tomorrow

SCATTERED STARS
Scattered Stars: Conviction
Conviction
Deception
Equilibrium
Fortitude (upcoming)

PEACEKEEPERS OF SOL
Raven's Peace
The Peacekeeper Initiative
Raven's Course
Drifter's Folly (upcoming)

EXILE
Exile
Refuge
Crusade
Ashen Stars: An Exile Novella

CASTLE FEDERATION
Space Carrier Avalon
Stellar Fox
Battle Group Avalon
Q-Ship Chameleon
Rimward Stars
Operation Medusa
A Question of Faith: A Castle Federation Novella

SCIENCE FICTION STAND ALONE NOVELLA
Excalibur Lost

VIGILANTE
(WITH TERRY MIXON)
Heart of Vengeance
Oath of Vengeance

**Bound By Stars: A Vigilante Series
(With Terry Mixon)**
Bound By Law
Bound by Honor
Bound by Blood

TEER AND KARD
Wardtown
Blood Ward

CHANGELING BLOOD
Changeling's Fealty
Hunter's Oath
Noble's Honor
Fae, Flames & Fedoras: A Changeling Blood Novella

ONSET
ONSET: To Serve and Protect
ONSET: My Enemy's Enemy
ONSET: Blood of the Innocent
ONSET: Stay of Execution
Murder by Magic: An ONSET Novella

FANTASY STAND ALONE NOVELS
Children of Prophecy
City in the Sky

Made in the USA
Columbia, SC
21 October 2022

69827967R00221